EVERGREEN

MATTHEW S. COX

DIVISION ZERO PRESS

Evergreen

A novel

© 2018 Matthew S. Cox

ISBN (eBook): 978-1-949174-92-2

ISBN (Print): 978-1-949174-93-9

CONTENTS

BAD PEOPLE

Brittle nerves frayed with every shadow that leapt out from the darkest recesses of Harper's dreams. For hours, she ran down an endless series of ruined streets, hiding from monsters of her imagination until the terrifying loneliness faded to the reality of rancid garbage on every breath.

She grumbled to herself, irritated at being up early. Ever since alarm clocks started controlling her life, she always woke an annoyingly short time before the buzzer went off: not enough time to go back to sleep, but much too early to get out of bed right away. The horrible stink in the air needled at her half-awake consciousness. Her usual complaint about why they had to start school so damn early died before it reached her lips. It hadn't been a nightmare. She wouldn't be going to school today.

Or ever again.

Her alarm clock would also never emit another sound. It sat dead in her bedroom, somewhere behind them in a house she couldn't go back to. Careful to remain silent, she sat up amid the crinkling of plastic, opening her eyes to a bleary vision of a slender black-haired girl huddled asleep against the corner of a cinder block wall, snuggled in a nest of trash bags. Her younger sister Madison had passed out clutching her iPhone to her chest, still expecting to get a text or call from their parents or one of her friends.

Harper hadn't the heart to tell her the truth.

A ten-year-old's hope shouldn't be shattered so cruelly, especially not after she'd watched their parents die. Harper frowned at her sister's pink flip-flops. The only reason she even had them is because they'd been forgotten in the front yard, an easy grab while fleeing the only home they'd ever known. Madison had been wearing the same denim shorts and white T-shirt for days, not enough to fight off the early November chill. Dad's bloody handprint stained the left shoulder, half concealed by her sister's long hair. The girl used her rolled-up denim jacket as a pillow.

Harper raked both hands through her wild red hair, still shaking from the dream creatures chasing her

They'd holed up in the corner of a parking lot behind a building marked Family Medical Center at the end of a strip mall of fast food places. A cinder block 'bunker' for trash dumpsters offered a reasonable degree of safety even though it stank like hell. The sour smell of months-old garbage beat getting shot—or worse.

Harper long ago gave up sleeping with a teddy bear, but she had a new security blanket to cling to: Dad's Mossberg shotgun, which had spent the night resting across her lap. The sight of it frightened her and wracked her with guilt. If she hadn't hesitated, maybe at least her father would still be alive. One of the crazy thugs who'd attacked them had been only a few feet away from her after barging in their front door. But, she couldn't do it... couldn't pull the trigger on another human being. As soon as he'd realized she pointed a shotgun at him, he tried to blow her head off. Dad whirled around and shot him a second before he killed her, but the distraction proved fatal. Another man coming in the kitchen patio door shot him.

She'd grabbed her sister and ran like hell.

For about two months, her family tried to remain at home after the world fell apart. But the gang found them eventually. It seemed as though all the decent people fled Lakewood, leaving only the criminals or those who simply went crazy in response to surviving a nuclear strike behind. She shuddered, remembering what her parents warned her about, what those men would do to her—and even Madison—if they were captured. She hated thinking about her little sister screaming as some grown man assaulted her; however, Harper forced herself to keep that mental image in her head to overpower her squeamishness about killing. Dad already died because of her. She couldn't allow anyone to hurt Madison.

At thirteen, Harper had won her first trophy for a shooting competition, using the same shotgun... she'd won a few more in the years since, but hitting clay pigeons or paper targets had been easy and fun. Shooting people? That made her want to throw up.

Harper clutched the Mossberg's pistol grip and closed her eyes. *Next time, I won't hesitate.*

She absentmindedly picked at her fat denim purse full of extra shells, Band-Aids, and a couple plastic bottles of water. To make room, she'd dumped out the useless stuff: her keys, cosmetics, phone, mp3 player… and all the other random junk she'd been carrying for three years, ever since Mom gave her the bag for her fourteenth birthday. It had only been two months since the world went insane, but it felt like forever ago.

"At least I don't have to stress out over the SATs anymore."

She forced herself upright, stretched, then peeked out the plastic doors of the 'trash pen' at a narrow parking lot containing a few abandoned cars, not one of them as helpful as a rock. Flakes of ash still fluttered down from the sky like snow, only a pale sooty grey instead of white. Random chunks of debris, concrete from buildings, traffic lights, bits of signs, littered everywhere. She wondered how much of it had been miles away before the detonations.

Dad dragged everyone out of bed to the basement with mere minutes to spare before the closest one had gone off.

So far, every building they'd seen had been scorched on the south face, some with eerie person-shaped negative silhouettes where a body had lessened the burn on the wall. Many cars had partially melted. Some trees and telephone poles had fallen over wherever they lacked the cover of nearby buildings. Few windows remained intact anywhere in Lakewood. Some shards of glass had even stuck into the walls of her home like knives. The lingering smell of 'burnt' had become so pervasive, she only noticed it due to having spent the night breathing the fetid horror of rotting fast food.

Word said Colorado Springs had suffered a direct hit, and the EMP reached as far north as Greeley, possibly well past it. Every bit of electronic tech here in Lakewood had become about as useful as a lawyer. Not like anyone cared about courts or laws anymore, least of all the gang that took over her old neighborhood.

Seeing no one, she crept out of the 'bunker' onto a tiny lot of sparse grass behind three large recycling containers, dropped her jeans to relieve herself, and squatted. She clung to the shotgun and kept her eyes on the gap between bins. Once finished, she hurried back into the trash enclosure and grasped her sister's shoulder, giving her a light shake.

"I don't wanna go to school," muttered Madison. "I don't feel good."

Harper stood there a moment, watching the girl breathe. "Come on, Termite." Again, she nudged her. "We have to keep going."

Madison opened her eyes, then curled up in a ball, peering over the top of her dead iPhone. Harper averted her gaze from the red handprint on her sister's otherwise white T-shirt. She couldn't exactly toss it and make the girl run around topless, but that didn't mean she had to look at the morbid reminder of Dad's death.

"We gotta keep going to Evergreen," said Harper. "It's morning."

After a yawn, Madison glanced down at her phone and pushed the button. Nothing happened. A few minutes passed. When she spoke again, her voice had a far off quality that matched her stare. "Dance class is at five. We can't go to Evergreen. Mom said she'd take me to Starbucks after."

Harper squatted in front of her, eyes watering from the trash. "It stinks here. Let's get some air."

"I guess." Madison continued staring off into space, occasionally flexing her toes. "It smells bad."

"Yeah." Harper grasped her sister's wrist and pulled her upright. "Get your jacket on."

Madison picked it up and wriggled into it with little enthusiasm. She looked a bit silly wearing a jacket longer than her shorts, but it had been near the door on the way out. Going home again to grab any of their things would be too dangerous. They'd barely escaped the gang a few days ago. Being chased away from home—plus the thought that her parents' bodies would still be there—got her crying and clinging to Madison. The girl didn't appear to mind playing the role of stuffed animal.

She couldn't let Madison see her cry or understand how much of a chicken she'd been. Even before everything went to hell, she'd been afraid of leaving home for college. Weeks before the war, she'd argued with Dad about that. He had been pushing her to apply to a big name school out of state, thinking her transcript might get her in the door with at least a partial scholarship. She kinda enjoyed school and pulled decent grades, but wanted to stay at home and go someplace close.

I'm a living oxymoron... a shy ginger.

"You forgot your books. You're gonna fail the SAT test," said Madison in a toneless voice while fussing at her phone.

"The T in SAT means test."

"Brainy," muttered Madison.

Harper gave her a squeeze and released the embrace. "Come on. We should keep going."

"I wanna go home." Madison kept pushing the phone's main button.

Yeah. Me too. Harper took her sister's hand and led her out of the trash 'bunker.' "We can't right now. It's too dangerous."

"I gotta pee."

"There's grass behind those bins. Go there."

Madison finally looked away from the blank screen, scrunching up her face. "Not outside! I need a bathroom."

It doesn't matter anymore. Nothing does... except for surviving. "It's fine. You won't get in trouble."

"Don't look," said Madison.

Harper pulled the Mossberg off her shoulder and held it sideways, her back turned, standing guard while her sister scurried behind the bins. In a few minutes, the soft *pop-pop-pop* of flip-flops approached behind her. Harper again took her sister's hand and walked the length of the narrow parking lot to the street. An inch-thick layer of ashy 'snow' covered the road, the sidewalk, ruined cars, and everything else in sight. Scattered footprints made the hairs on the back of her neck stand on end. Here and there, some fires continued burning, hazing the air with smoke that shrank visibility to merely a couple blocks in any direction.

"You wanna play Xbox tonight?" asked Madison.

"Maybe. We'll see."

Their game system, like every electronic device in the city, had died. They'd lived for two months on candles and whatever canned food Dad found in neighbors' empty houses. Fearing another strike, most people had fled the big city, though she had no idea where any of them had gone. One group tried to convince Dad to head to Evergreen since they heard it survived relatively intact and good people had collected there, but he hadn't wanted to venture out so soon after the detonation.

"Mom was gonna get me a new game after the recital."

The monotone voice coming out of her little sister raked like a claw over her heart. Madison also inherited the 'shy' gene, but not to the same degree as Harper—hence why Mom often treated her to stuff like Starbucks as an encouragement to dance class or other activities she might've avoided doing otherwise. More stressful things like recitals sometimes required a bribe of a new video game. Up until a few weeks ago, she'd been full of life, even bubbly. More than for what they did to the world, Harper hated the people who started the war because they'd killed her kid sister *inside.*

"Can we go to Subway?" asked Madison. "I'm hungry."

Harper rooted around her purse and pulled out an energy bar. One bit of good luck they'd had so far, finding a convenience store that still had some food in it. Someone else had beat them to it, cleaning it out of almost everything except the granola bars and rotting sandwiches or salads.

"I'm sick of these. I want a veggie-burger." Still, Madison took the bar and peeled the wrapper open.

They continued to the end of the block and went up a small ash-covered hill into another parking lot in front of a liquor store and the New Peking Chinese restaurant. Harper crossed over to the restaurant, shards of glass crunching under her sneakers near the door. Madison gingerly stepped among the remains of the windows, following her inside.

The first fridge she opened nearly knocked her out from the stink of rotting chicken, seafood, and beef. Harper gagged and slammed the door. *Ugh. Why did I even open that? Nothing in Lakewood has had any power for like two months.*

"Hey Siri, call Mom," said Madison.

Harper checked cabinets, but found only cans of sauces or seasonings. "Figures the place makes everything fresh. It's all gone bad."

"Hey Siri, Call Eva." Madison shook her phone. "Call Becca."

Ugh. Harper peered over her shoulder at her kid sister. *Is she pretending or does she really not know that thing is dead?* She shut the cabinet doors and stood out of her squat. "'Mon, Termite. There's nothing here."

She ducked back out the broken door and went left, heading for the road. The street signs had melted, leaving her clueless about where she was. Too much haze blocked off the sky for her to find the sun, though intermittent gunshots in one direction gave a clue regarding which way *not* to go. Harper again turned left, following the road toward an apartment complex. She paused a few seconds, gawking at a partially molten steel beam stuck in the ground like a giant arrow.

"This isn't home," said Madison.

"I know. We can't go home. Bad people are there."

"Bad people are everywhere."

Harper squeezed the shotgun. "Yeah."

"Why are there so many bad people now?" Madison tried to catch an ash flake on her tongue, but missed.

"Don't eat that. It's poison."

Madison looked up at her with a 'so what?' expression.

"There aren't any more bad people now than there used to be. But, all the cops are gone, so the bad people just do whatever they want."

"Oh," said Madison, head down.

She walked along a gradually curving road between facing rows of two-story apartments, dark beige walls visible in patches under the dusting of ash. Awnings protected lots of cars, almost every space full. The attack had happened early, before sunrise. In the shade of the buildings and awnings, the cars appeared intact, but she knew none of them would work. A few had small burn marks from where wiring had caught fire in response to the EMP wave. Maybe if she found a car from like 1970 or so, it wouldn't be dead.

The abandoned apartments offered a potential treasure trove of cool stuff, though all the video games or computers would be useless. Another I-beam jutted out of a roof, stabbed into the building on the left like an enormous spear. She pondered the idea of trying to stay here, moving from apartment to apartment, but didn't trust being alone with Madison anywhere near Lakewood. The gang would eventually find them.

Harper had to sleep at some point.

They searched a few apartments, collecting some canned goods, a can opener, and a backpack to carry the stuff with. None of the places they checked had any child-sized clothing, though Harper did swipe a denim jacket for herself. The whole time she rummaged, Madison continued staring at the iPhone. Every few minutes, she'd tell Siri to call Mom, Dad, or one of her friends.

After a hurried meal of canned ravioli, she slung the backpack on so she could keep holding the shotgun, and resumed walking.

"What day is it?" asked Madison. "Is school open yet?"

"No, it's still closed."

Madison shook the iPhone. "Harp, my phone won't turn on. Can you fix it? My friends might try to call."

She really believes it'll work. Harper looked down, biting her lip at her sister's bare feet in flip-flops. *I need to find her some real shoes... and pants or something. It's too cold.* She eyed more apartments on the right, but fear of the gang pushed her onward. *I should be worried that Maddie isn't complaining about being cold. Better she shivers than those bastards get us.*

"You cold, Termite? Want my sweatshirt, too?"

"No." Madison clutched the iPhone to her chest. "I think I need to charge it."

The apartment road ended at the next cross street. Ahead, a stone wall dotted with small decorative cubes jutted out from a big hill, too high to see over. She veered to the right, following a sidewalk up to a dirt trail, then cut left past some trees. A momentary thinning of the haze in the air offered a hint of the sun's location, so she put her back to it, hopefully going west.

"Home's the other way." Madison stopped where the dirt path met sidewalk. "I wanna go home."

Harper took a knee in the soft ash, eye to eye with her sister. "I'm not going to let the bad people hurt you. Do you understand that?"

Madison nodded.

"If we go back there, the bad people will find us." She balanced the shotgun in one hand and squeezed Madison's arm. "Mom and Dad would want us to stay safe. And right now, staying safe means going to Evergreen because there's good people there."

Madison stared down at her ash-covered feet.

They stood for a moment without speaking, the eerie silence of a city without a single working vehicle broken by distant shouts and a gunshot or two.

"Mom's gonna take me to dance class." Madison kicked at the ground.

Again, the image of Dad firing his AR-15 at the man pulling a gun on her replayed in her mind. Another guy slipped in the patio door at that second, shooting him in the back. Mom lay slumped over the kitchen sink, already gone, a giant knife sticking out of her.

None of this seemed real anymore. Not this ash-covered street, not spending two months living out of her basement, not ash falling from the sky like snow, not her parents dying in front of her, not her kid sister retreating into this robotic shell.

"Come on." Harper took Madison by the hand and dragged her onward.

At any second, one of those crazy bastards might put her right back in that same situation she'd found herself in days ago, and she no longer had a father to save her ass. If—no *when*—it happened again, she'd have to kill someone...

Or die.

2

SURVIVING

Harper hurried along under the raining ash and haze, heading as west as she could manage without being able to see the sun— or even the mountains.

They rushed past more apartments, crossed swaths of dirt where grass had burned away, and navigated the char-blackened remains of trees. Madison remained quiet, except for the occasional cough or attempt to make Siri call her friends or parents.

Hours after waking, they reached a residential neighborhood full of houses, a pleasant sort of suburban area full of two-car garages like something out of a sitcom. One surviving street sign read S. Youngfield Circle. The houses here all looked huge, way bigger than the one she'd grown up in. In response to a twinge of hunger, she approached the nearest house on the corner. The street-facing side had scorched almost entirely black and bore numerous holes from flying debris. It occurred to her at that moment she could use the burns to navigate. The warhead, according to what she overheard her father talking about, had detonated in Colorado Springs to the south. So, any wall that looked melted or blackened had to face south.

Whoever had lived here had fled, leaving the door open.

"Let's check inside. I'm a little hungry."

Madison shrugged.

Harper headed straight to the kitchen. She ignored the fridge and raided the cabinets, grabbing a few cans of Progresso soup. Neither the electric stove nor the microwave worked. Even the wall clock had stopped at 5:53. She stared at the mechanical hands, thinking back to Dad dragging her half-awake ass out of bed. That he barked at her to move while physically hauling her down to the basement had terrified her. The man had barely raised his voice to her in the past seventeen years. Even without words passing between them, for him to practically carry her said something had gone *very* wrong.

She'd been so dumbfounded she hadn't even managed to ask what was going on before the roar came.

Harper blinked, once again finding herself staring at the plain white hands of a dead wall clock, stopped the moment the EMP wave hit.

Scuffing, gritty footsteps approached her from behind. "TV won't turn on."

She rested the shotgun on the counter, then glanced at Madison, who still wore a completely neutral expression. One of the drawers contained a manual can opener. Out of laziness, she used it instead of the one in her backpack. "A lot of things are broken."

"Is that why you're using the grandma can opener?"

"Yep."

Harper took two bowls from a cabinet and dumped a can of soup into each one, chicken for her, vegetable for Madison. She carried them to the table, went back for the shotgun, and sat, laying the weapon on the table to her right. It felt so strange to be sitting in someone else's kitchen, with a loaded Mossberg in arms' reach like some other normal bit of table setting. Madison trudged over and took the chair beside her, still clutching her iPhone to her chest.

Her sister stared at the bowl for a minute or so before frowning. "The soup is cold."

Harper ate a spoonful. "I know. The stove doesn't work."

"Microwave it."

"The microwave is broken, too."

Madison swung her feet back and forth. One of her flip-flops fell off. "Mom's gonna yell at us if we eat it right out of the can."

"We're not eating it out of the can. That's a bowl."

"Duh. I meant it isn't cooked. I want hot soup. I'm cold."

"We'll look upstairs after we eat. This is a huge house. They might've had a kid. Maybe there's some clothes your size."

Madison tucked the iPhone into her jacket pocket. She spent a moment making faces at the soup but eventually started eating. After three spoonfuls, she glanced over. "Is there soda?"

"Ugh. If I open that fridge, we won't be able to eat anymore."

"Why?"

"Everything in there will be spoiled and stink."

Harper got up and approached the sink. *Is the water going to be radioactive?* She held a glass under the faucet and turned it on. The flow seemed weaker than it should be, but clear water did come out. She held the glass up to stare at it, thinking about one of her science teachers mentioning water acted as a radiation blocker, which is why they used it in nuclear reactors. That water *did* become radioactive, but only after prolonged exposure to a strong source of radiation. A distant missile exploding probably wouldn't have irradiated the water too much to drink.

We're probably both going to get cancer in ten years anyway... if we even survive that long.

She carried two glasses of water back to the table. Madison picked hers up in both hands and chugged most of it in one go. They ate fast and quiet, scraping as much of the soup out of the bowls as they could.

Once they finished, Harper set the dirty bowls in the sink and proceeded to search the house. As expected, nothing electronic worked. Some things, like the television or computer monitors looked obviously blown out and burned. Whoever lived here before had owned a nice stereo, but the rack components had caught fire—fortunately, it went out on its own and didn't take the house with it. Or maybe the people had still been here when it caught fire.

Or they're still here in the basement like we were.

Harper clutched the shotgun tighter.

In a pantry cabinet, she found a huge bag of assorted candies marked with a Post-It note that read: 'do not touch until Halloween.' Harper closed her eyes and tried to swallow the lump in her throat. *Who buys Halloween candy in September?* Madison had been looking forward to trick-or-treating as Wonder Woman... but October 31st had come and gone without anyone even noticing a week or so ago. The temperature probably hovered at 'not quite fifty,' too cold for Madison to be running around in shorts and flip-flops. Too cold for them to be sleeping outside. She needed shelter, blankets, something.

But, not here. Not this close to Lakewood.

She took the giant plastic bag of candy and mushed it into her backpack. Sugar equaled energy. Plus, it's not like anyone would ever make more. At least, not for a long damn time if ever. Dad's radio had lasted long enough that morning—about twelve minutes—for a news guy to mention nuclear detonations all over major cities like Washington DC, New York, Los Angeles... she didn't think much of the First World remained. Manufacturing candy seemed pretty low on the list of priorities given the state of everything, which made it precious.

Having no interest in anything else downstairs, Harper hurried up to the second floor, her sister following in no great hurry. Two immaculate guest bedrooms suggested the former residents didn't have kids, or at least any kids they had grew up and left. She grabbed a comforter from one bed and wrapped Madison in it like a cloak.

In the master bedroom, she discovered a gun safe in the closet—but couldn't open it. However, she found three boxes of shotgun shells on a shelf next to it as well as boxes of pistol and rifle bullets. She dumped the shells loose into her enormous purse to save space, but left the other bullets alone. No sense carrying heavy ammo she couldn't use.

A male voice murmured something downstairs.

Harper froze.

Madison looked up from the dead iPhone screen with a worried expression.

When the voice muttered again, Harper crept to the bedroom door.

"Yeah, this is the one," whispered a man from downstairs. "Saw a girl go in here."

"Still here?" asked a different man.

"Yup. Didn't see her leave."

Crap! Harper spun in place, searching for a hiding spot. Under the bed didn't work, neither did the closets. She swallowed hard, clutching the shotgun, not trusting that she wouldn't hesitate again. *I'm only seventeen! I shouldn't be shooting people.*

She raised the shotgun, aiming down the hall toward the top of the stairs. *Shooting them is going to be loud. It could attract more. The second guy might shoot back. I shouldn't fire as soon as I see the first man. Maybe I should back up and jump out to surprise them?* She thought about the competition course she used to run with the pop up targets. Springing out into the hall and rapidly shooting two pie-plate sized targets— someone's heads—would be easy. Except for them being *people.* Harper started to turn back to look at the room, but froze when she spotted a two-by-two foot slatted cover at the end of the hall, the intake for the house's central air. The passage appeared big enough for them to crawl into.

Perfect!

Harper rushed over and pulled the vent cover open, exposing plain ductwork. Madison ran out of the comforter and crawled in, taking the backpack so Harper could both fit and keep the shotgun ready. She snugged the cover back in place barely ten seconds before a man in a black T-shirt emerged from the top of the stairs. A scrap of blue cloth around his neck like a redneck version of an ascot identified him as one of *them*. She didn't know if they considered themselves a gang, an army, or if they had any sort of name for themselves. Dad called them a gang, and well, they acted like one. Only, instead of selling drugs or robbing places, they took over.

As slow and quiet as she could make herself be, Harper scooted back from the opening, keeping the Mossberg aimed. If he noticed them in the air intake, she'd have to fire. The shotgun trembled in response to her shaking hands.

The man eased himself off the stairs and approached the first door on the left, sneaking along in an effort to surprise the girl he believed to be there. Upon reaching the room, he leaned on the doorjamb to peer in. The instant his head went out of sight, she edged farther back, pushing Madison deeper.

Whew. He didn't see me.

A tiny finger jabbed her hard in the side, but Madison didn't say anything.

Harper risked a peek back over her shoulder.

Her little sister pointed at a drop where the intake duct took a ninety-degree bend straight down... probably all the way to the basement. Another inch or two and Madison would fall thirty feet. The flimsy screen at the end of the curve where the duct became a vertical drop wouldn't absorb the weight of a child.

Eep! Harper edged forward to make more room. Madison tucked up behind her. Caught between a deadly fall and two men who'd no doubt do unspeakable things to both of them, Harper trembled, screaming in her mind for her father.

The man crossed the hall to the next guest room as a second, darker-skinned man in a winter coat came up the steps. He had an AK47, but held it sideways in a casual posture like he didn't plan on using it any time soon. Harper stopped breathing.

Both men came closer, within five feet of the vent cover.

A tiny *snap* came from behind.

Harper jumped, almost pulling the trigger.

They didn't notice the noise and continued into the master bedroom.

She swallowed all the saliva in her mouth, trying not to shake hard enough the shotgun rattled and gave her away. It seemed so surreal that three months ago she could've run into those men anywhere and probably carried on a normal conversation. Would they have been thinking about kidnapping her then, too? Did nuclear war make them stop caring about common decency or had they been creeps the whole time?

"Shit, Ed. Ain't no one in here."

"Was," said the other man. "What's this blanket doing on the floor?"

"You're seeing shit. And that's a comforter, not a blanket."

"Aww, suck my dick. Who the hell cares what the shit we call blankets? And I'm not seeing things. That girl had long red hair. Nice ass. Little on the young side but old enough."

Madison held the iPhone over Harper's shoulder, pointing at the mute switch, which she'd activated.

"Screw it, Ed. If you did see someone, she's gone. Might as well at least grab what we can from the kitchen."

The dark-skinned guy walked out of the master bedroom, shaking his head.

Ed, armed only with a handgun on his belt, ran after him, wallet chain swaying at his side. "Ajay, wait. There's a girl in here somewhere."

"Did you look under the bed. Closets?" Ajay stopped and spun around.

Harper held as still as she could. If Ajay saw her through the slats, she'd have no choice but to shoot him.

Ed grumbled and went back into the master bedroom. The clatter of closet doors followed.

"I'll check the other ones." Ajay tromped into the nearer guest room.

Crap. Please go away. Please don't see us. Harper struggled to swallow with a dry throat. Again, she pictured faceless men grabbing Madison and assaulting her while she screamed and begged them not to. She imagined the men being cruel and forcing her to watch them hurting her sister to build up disgust and anger, enough she might be able to shoot them if she had to.

A creak came from the Mossberg's pistol grip.

I will not hesitate. I can't hesitate. They will not touch her.

The men moved to the second guest room, yanking open closet doors and kicking stuff about.

"Dammit," said Ajay. "If there *was* a girl in here, she got past us and is long gone."

"Swear I didn't see anyone leave."

"Hell with it. Let's grab what we can and keep going."

The men rumbled down the stairs.

Holy shit! Harper couldn't bring herself to let go of the shotgun, but lowered the barrel tip to rest on the floor. She sat there listening to random banging and rummaging from downstairs, until at long last, the two men exited the house.

Harper finally pried her left hand off the shotgun, squeezed her sister's leg where it stretched past her, and whispered, "We should wait a little while before we move, in case they come back."

They sat in silence for a few minutes.

Madison leaned closer, her lips at Harper's ear. "I gotta pee."

3

PAPA TACO

Hearing the word 'pee' made Harper have to go, too.

She peered down at the shotgun, the weapon she could have used to save her father's life. Well, technically save her own life. If she'd shot the guy coming after her, Dad wouldn't have needed to spin around and take his attention off the patio door. He'd still be alive. They'd still be at home—or more likely hurrying to Evergreen with him. Nothing Harper could've possibly done would have changed what happened to Mom.

Her hands started shaking at the memory of her father, mortally shot, returning fire rapidly out the patio door while screaming at her to run. She had no idea if he hit anyone, but he bought her enough time to grab Madison and get out. Dad used his last breath to tell her to run and she'd done exactly that—after he collapsed to the floor.

She picked at the texture on the pistol grip, then teased her finger at the trigger. One tiny piece of metal could have made the difference, if she hadn't been such a chicken.

Who am I kidding? I can't kill anyone. I almost had a breakdown that time I shoplifted on a dare.

"They're gone," whispered Madison. "Can we go to the bathroom now?"

"Okay." She crawled out of the vent—mostly to get her sister away from a likely fatal fall.

Madison followed, pushing the backpack of canned food ahead of her.

After a brief stop at the upstairs bathroom, Harper picked up the comforter again and rolled it into a log. If her sister tried to wear it like a cloak, it would drag on the ground and pick up all sorts of glass shards, ash, and other nastiness. Of course, the two of them already looked like they stood ten feet away from a grain silo explosion, covered head to toe in pale grey ash. At least she could save the comforter for sleeping warm. She grabbed some curtain string from one of the guest rooms and tied it into a bedroll, then hung it on the backpack.

The master bedroom had 'old people clothes,' none of which would fit Madison well, though a sweater made for an improvised dress that would keep her warm—or at least warm*er* than shorts. Once outside, Harper used the burned sides of houses as a compass and traveled as 'west' as she could guess.

Her need to get the hell away from this place and the 'blue' gang kept her from wanting to explore any more houses. If Evergreen still had a population of decent people, someone there would surely help out providing better clothes for Madison.

Fear and need fought each other for some time as she navigated a network of suburban streets and once-expensive houses. If not for the coating of ash everywhere, burned walls, the constant smell of wood smoke and melted plastic mixed with a faint hint of overdone meat in the air, these could've been abandoned for no particular reason. Most remained intact, though a handful sported holes from rather large hunks of formerly airborne debris. Colorado Springs sat like ninety or so miles south. The thought that some of this junk might have flown from that far away brought a shiver.

I gotta get her some better stuff to wear.

She bit her lip, almost ready to risk the delay of searching houses for kid-sized clothing, but couldn't build up the nerve to risk another brush with creeps. A few minutes of walking later, a commercial area emerged from the haze ahead. The road she'd been following led toward a small Mexican restaurant.

"We're lost, aren't we?" asked Madison. "We'll never find our way back home."

That's not home anymore. She forced herself not to cry over her parents, or admit that she, too, wanted desperately to return to the place she grew up. But... doing that would bring them right into the heart of the gang's territory. Even if they managed to avoid being kidnapped, going to their old house would also mean confronting her parents' bodies. Somehow, she doubted those creeps would've bothered burying them.

"We're gonna get in trouble."

Harper patted her on the shoulder. "No, we won't. We're not in trouble. Dad wants us to go to Evergreen so we can be safe. There's too many bad people where we used to live. We can't go back there."

Madison blinked, her expression devoid of emotion.

They crossed the street and paused at the door of Papa Taco.

"It's going to be dark soon. We spent a long time hiding in that vent. This place might have something we can eat so we don't have to use up the supplies we've got."

"Why are we carrying cans if we're not going to eat what's inside them?"

Harper ruffled her sister's hair. "Because, Termite. If we find food here, we'll have those cans when there isn't anything else to eat."

"Oh. Duh." Madison looked at her iPhone. "They didn't call yet."

Emitting an inaudible sigh, Harper raised the shotgun and ducked under the push bar on the aluminum frame door, sneakers crunching over billions of tiny glass pieces on the floor.

"Snow," said Madison.

"It's glass. Like special glass that breaks into little bits instead of big shards."

"Oh."

"You still shouldn't step on it without real shoes."

Madison scuffed her flip-flops across the tiles, plowing the debris aside, and followed Harper to the register counter. She climbed up to sit and played with the computers.

"C'mon. Don't stray off." Harper stood by the kitchen entrance, waiting.

"There's no games on these." Madison frowned at them.

Harper pushed the door open with the end of the shotgun and stepped into the kitchen. The burned smell from outside intensified in the enclosed space. Three windows afforded a measure of light, but between the late hour and hazy gloom, the hulking forms of industrial refrigerators loomed like waiting monsters.

"It's scary in here," whispered Madison. "Turn on the lights."

"I can't." Harper approached a door that led to a pantry. Shelves full of dry goods and cans offered more promise than refrigerators.

Madison refused to go into the even more frightening pantry, and wandered around looking at the stoves and restaurant machines. She flipped a few buttons and switches, but nothing reacted to her.

"Who broke everything?" called Madison.

Harper grabbed a big can of refried beans plus a pack of burrito shells that didn't feel *too* stale, and retreated from the pantry. "Politicians did."

"I don't like them."

After sitting cross-legged on a rubber mat the cooks used to stand on, Harper fished the can opener out of her pack. She scooped the brown bean paste into tortilla shells, making two bean burritos while Madison continued exploring.

"C'mon, Termite. Time to eat."

Madison traipsed over and sat nearby. She accepted the offering of food without protest and stuffed her face. Harper found the tortilla a bit staler than she would've eaten normally, but nuclear war had lowered her standards quite a bit. Thoughts of how often she'd complained about food not being fresh or flavorful enough drifted across her mind. Her little sister shivered, making Harper feel even colder. No building in Lakewood had functioning heat ever since the blast, at least not without a fireplace. That smoke had likely been what brought the 'blue gang' to their door.

Watching Madison shivering while trying to eat punched her in the stomach with guilt. *We really should find better clothes.* The day of the attack, Madison had put on those jean shorts because they were clean. All her long pants, she'd worn for days already and the washing machine no longer worked. They'd expected to spend yet another day hiding in the basement under blankets. Shorts shouldn't have mattered.

Harper unrolled the comforter, pulled Madison close, and bundled up with her. The girl looked at her with the same neutral expression that had been on her face ever since they had to flee the house. After a few seconds of asking 'we're gonna die, aren't we?' with a stare, Madison huddled close to her.

We're kinda close to the mall. Bet those idiots looted it already, but I doubt they'd take kid clothes. She tossed the last of her burrito in her mouth and scooped more refried beans onto another tortilla. Going to the mall offered a much higher chance of finding clothes for Madison instead of randomly breaking into houses hoping the former owners had kids. Of course, the mall also seemed like it would be a magnet for those creeps. However, she knew the layout of the Colorado Mills Mall, including the back hallways behind stores. If she *had* to willingly go into a dangerous situation, better to do it on familiar ground. She couldn't allow Madison to run around in November wearing a T-shirt, shorts, a light jacket, and flip-flops. *It's either houses or the mall... and I like the odds more at the mall.*

She folded up the burrito. "You want another one?"

Madison nodded, so Harper handed it over and made another.

After finishing her second burrito, Madison crawled out of the comforter and started doing leg stretches.

"C'mon, Termite. It's too cold in here. Get back in the blanket."

On one foot, her other leg straight up, Madison pivoted toward her. "I have dance class tomorrow. Gotta practice. Is Mom gonna drive me?"

Harper flinched at the memory of her mother screaming. She'd shot a man trying to come in the window over the kitchen sink, but not well enough to kill him. He stabbed her before she finished him off—but her mother had collapsed dead right after. "I... I'm sure she wants to."

"Okay." Madison crawled out of the comforter and started doing stretches and a few dance moves.

With the sun nearly down, the air took on a biting chill, even inside the abandoned restaurant. Harper looked around, figuring they had only a few minutes of light left. Though it didn't seem likely the gang would go exploring in total darkness, she also didn't want to chance being found while sleeping. While her little sister worked her way through a warmup routine, Harper grabbed an empty Corona bottle from a bin and relocated their possessions to a large storage closet. She set up a hasty bed of empty trash bags between two metal shelves laden with cleaning supplies.

"C'mon, Termite. It's going to be dark any second."

Madison scurried over. Harper shut the closet door and balanced the empty bottle on the knob. If anyone opened it, the crash of it breaking would probably wake her.

"It's dark. I can't see anything," said Madison, somewhere behind her.

"I know."

Working by feel, she crawled to the 'bed' and rested the shotgun on the floor to her right. Madison found her way over and cuddled up beside her in the comforter, the soft puffs of her warm breath at Harper's neck.

"Heh. We just ate burritos, now we are a burrito."

Madison didn't laugh, or even sigh.

Ugh. She stared into the darkness, unable to see the ceiling or the row of mops leaning against the wall behind her. Never in her life did she imagine sleeping in a restaurant closet or an alley like a homeless person. Watching those men murder her parents in the kitchen ruined her memory of the place she'd called home for her entire life. It would never feel safe again. But, beyond the end of civilization and narrowly escaping being kidnapped, her little sister's silence worried her the most.

Her mind teased her with scenes from the past, mostly Madison smiling, laughing, or arguing with her. At that moment, she'd have been happy for even that kind of outburst. Any emotion, even bratty anger, would've been an improvement over the android-like nothingness that had taken over for the past three days.

Harper tried to tickle Madison's side.

The girl didn't squirm, protest, or even whisper 'stop,' merely clung a little tighter.

Since Madison couldn't see her, Harper closed her eyes and surrendered to silent tears.

4

HIDDEN

Constant fidgeting woke Harper.

Madison squirmed, but remained quiet. A thin line of daylight under the door chipped away at the complete darkness of the supply closet, allowing her to make out the vague forms of metal shelving on either side. It remained too dim for her to see the bottle or the doorknob. Eager to get the hell out of Lakewood, she forced herself to wake up and fought her old habit of rolling over for another fifteen minutes of sleep.

"Hey, Termite. Morning." Harper squeezed her a little tighter, then sat up.

"I have to pee."

"Yeah. I do, too. Ready to get up?"

"Okay."

Harper begrudgingly extricated herself from the comforter, grasped the shotgun, and crept to the door. The bottle remained as she'd left it, so she set it on the floor before grabbing the knob. Near blinding daylight made her squint when she peered out at the kitchen. Much to her relief, everything looked the same as she expected. The giant can of refried beans had sat out open all night, but given the temperature, it may as well have been in a fridge.

She bundled the comforter, tied it back into a bedroll, and escorted Madison to the bathroom, grateful for a dose of normal instead of going in an alley. None of the toilets had water in them, and the flush didn't work… but she didn't care as they'd likely never come back to this place. It would only be a matter of time before the 'blue gang' or someone else came here to raid the pantry. Any place that looked like it might have food would be a first target.

Though, perhaps not restaurants. It had been roughly two months since the war—if the events of about forty-five minutes could truly be called a war—so any fresh food in freezers or fridges would be spoiled by now. Grocery stores made better targets due to the vast reserves of canned or dry goods.

Despite having to go bad, Harper sat on the toilet with her head in her hands, staring down into her jeans, gathered between her feet. The shotgun dangled from the coat hook on the inside of the stall door. Her mind swam with too many worries and fears.

Amid the soft snap of flip-flops, Madison walked to stand right outside the stall.

We can't stay here.

Focused on that thought, Harper forced her bladder empty, cleaned up, and stood. She decided to collect all the toilet paper from the six stalls afterward, carrying it in a bundle back to the kitchen. There, she put it in take-out plastic bags before making them breakfast—more burritos.

She stared at her sister while they ate. The girl poked at the dead iPhone, resting on the floor mat beside her. Madison had stopped shivering, and didn't seem to mind the chilly weather, though looking at her bare legs made Harper feel colder. She sometimes had gone outside in November, even December wearing flip-flops, but she'd at least had long pants or leggings on.

I gotta get her some pants and real shoes while we still can.

"We're going to stop by the mall."

"Okay. Can we get Subway?"

Harper grimaced inside. "I don't think they're open."

"That stinks. What are we shopping for?"

"You need something warmer to wear." Harper poked her in the foot.

Madison shrugged. "I have stuff at home, but it's dirty. Mom didn't do laundry."

"She was busy trying to make sure we had enough food."

"Siri, call Mom," said Madison.

The iPhone sat there like a brick.

Harper thought of trying to distract her by talking about something she liked, but everything she came up with from dance class to movies to video games made *her* too homesick to speak. It felt too much like lying to talk about any of those things, since none of them would ever exist again... well, at least not in their lifetime. While the blast didn't harm Blu-ray discs or DVDs, it fried anything capable of playing them—not to mention the power grid. She'd never much thought about how pervasive the use of electricity had been until it went away.

A ripple of distant gunshots startled them both, though Madison didn't make a noise.

"C'mon," whispered Harper. "Finish eating and let's get out of here."

After inhaling the rest of her burrito, Harper grabbed another pack of tortillas and a second giant can of refried beans. She stuffed them into the backpack, handed Madison the plastic bag of toilet paper to carry, and grabbed the shotgun.

She went out via a door that led from the kitchen to the parking lot and headed northwest in the direction of the Colorado Mills Mall.

Madison followed close behind, head down, staring at the iPhone.

Shouts and random gunshots continued, though they came from far enough behind her that she almost allowed herself to hope they'd left the 'blue gang' behind. Still, she didn't believe for an instant that those people would stay put in one area around her old neighborhood. The group of people who tried to convince Dad to leave home and go with them to Evergreen had been convinced a large number of survivors gathered there.

Dammit, Dad. Why didn't you agree to go with them? You and Mom would both still be alive if we'd left.

A clatter made her jump and point the shotgun at a row of large plastic trashcans. Two raccoons paused their rummaging to stare at her.

"Ugh." She slouched.

Her father had been worried about radiation from fallout and wanted to wait at least five weeks before leaving the house just to be safe. Harper knew only what she'd seen in a few movies about nuclear war, and had expected the entire world would become a radioactive deathtrap. According to Dad, the fallout decayed at an exponential rate, falling off to almost nothing after about eight weeks—except for places where the detonation occurred at ground level.

He thought we might *get sick and die from fallout, but he died to bastards.*

Two tears fell on the Mossberg. Dad had given it to her so she could help defend their home... and she'd failed. A man pulled a gun on her and she simply stared at him like a terrified child, not a seventeen-year-old with a little sister to protect.

She replayed that moment over and over in her mind as she walked among abandoned houses. The ash snow kept falling, though slower. She looked out at the smoky haze, wondering if it would ever go away. Based on the smell in the air, some places still had to be burning. The farther south one went in Lakewood, the more burned everything looked. Her former home had been lucky, tucked away in an L-shaped street with two other, larger, houses shadowing it from the nuclear glow.

Of course, other houses didn't stop a giant chunk of concrete from punching a hole in her bedroom ceiling. Fortunately, the whole family had been in the basement when that happened.

Harper went to take a right at the corner, but stopped short at the sight of a dead body sprawled on the sidewalk. He appeared Asian, later thirties, and had evidently been beaten to death with pipes or bats.

She started to cry out in disgust, but stifled the urge and backed up into Madison.

"What?" her sister looked up from the blank iPhone.

"We can't go this way." Harper put an arm around her sister, keeping the girl's face against her chest while scurrying by the corpse.

Madison didn't protest, or even ask why.

Her little sister *always* asked 'why,' and the absence of protest worried Harper.

The soft *pop-pop-pop* of flip-flops provided a constant background accompaniment to distant gunshots, screams of pain, or shouts of aggression. Madison occasionally whispered to Siri, asking her to call Mom, Dad, or one of her friends.

She took the next right turn onto a residential street, all the houses, lawns, and cars coated in a dusting of grey ash like a morbid snow globe. Except for the smoke making it difficult to see much past about thirty feet, the scene before her resembled a Colorado Christmas card. Most of the driveways here appeared empty, which likely meant the vehicles that belonged to them sat abandoned on highways somewhere. No one had enough warning to evacuate before the bombardment, so she figured these people had gone to work early.

Out on the road when the blast came. They're probably all dead.

Sudden rapid footsteps echoed out of the fog ahead.

Harper grabbed Madison by the hand and rushed to the right, entering a front yard with waist-high hedges. She hunkered down behind the shrub wall, a white-knuckled grip on the shotgun, and peered past the tiny leaves at the road beyond.

"Stop!" shouted a man.

Two men and a woman, all adult but younger than her parents, emerged from the haze at a full run. A loud *bang* broke the stillness. Madison twitched.

"I said, stop!" yelled the same man. "Next one won't be a warning shot."

The three slowed to a halt and raised their hands.

Another figure crept up behind them, rifle trained on the three. The smoke thinned as he approached, revealing a green camouflage military uniform. Another apparent soldier followed, also with a combat rifle aimed at the three civilians.

Harper kept quiet, watching as the soldiers ordered the people flat on the ground, tied their hands with plastic binders, and proceeded to search them. None of them wore a necklace of blue fabric, so she didn't think they belonged to the gang that killed her parents... but why would soldiers arrest them? Why would anyone 'arrest' anyone anymore?

She tightened and relaxed her grip on the shotgun. While she didn't consider herself a 'gun expert' like her father, she'd played enough video games to understand that military combat rifles had a much longer range than a shotgun. Not that she had the least bit of intention to get into a gunfight with them, but if she had to, she'd need to be much closer to have any chance at all of survival. While it might be possible that the country hadn't been *totally* destroyed and some fragments of real military remained, she worried these two maybe just found some uniforms and weapons. They had as much chance of being legit soldiers as they did of being thugs from a different gang. Even if they had been real soldiers, with the country destroyed, they might've gone crazy, too.

Those three people might have done something bad and been chased, or simply run in a panic from two men with rifles. If those men *were* actual soldiers, they'd probably protect a pair of young girls. Of course, if they only dressed up like soldiers... they could do anything to her or Madison.

After nuclear war, the difference between arrest and kidnapping didn't amount to much.

Harper decided not to risk it and stay hidden.

"Why are we hiding?" whispered Madison.

"I don't trust them. Maybe the government's doing bad stuff, or they're not real soldiers."

Madison muted the iPhone. "Are we going to the mall?"

"Past it, to the mountains, but yeah. Gonna stop there."

"I need new clothes. I've been wearing the same stuff for days. It's itchy."

Harper scooted away from the bush after the soldiers dragged their prisoners off into the fog. "'Mon."

She crept along between two houses, cutting across a backyard to the street she'd skipped. The dead guy should be far enough back that Madison wouldn't see him. A few minutes after reaching the sidewalk, it occurred to her that the constant patter of flip-flops behind her had ceased.

About to panic, Harper whirled around. Madison hovered mere inches behind her, unharmed, clutching her iPhone and flip flops to her chest. Too wound up to speak, Harper looked down at the girl's bare feet and legs, covered in grey ash. Both of them had been out in it so long their hair, clothes, every inch of them had a coating of pale grey.

"Put your shoes back on. Your toes will freeze."

"They're too loud. Bad people will hear them and find us."

"Not so loud it's worth getting hurt."

Madison dropped the foam shoes and stepped into them. "I want a bath."

"There's no hot water."

"I don't care. I'm itchy everywhere."

Harper trudged on. Wanting a bath seemed like the most random, ridiculous thing in the world given their present situation. But, all that ash came from a nuclear explosion. It might be—probably was—radioactive. Getting rid of it sounded like a good idea.

"Okay... I'll think about it."

5

NOT QUITE NORMAL

Harper marched across a long strip of dirt, her sneakers crunching over the burnt remains of grass.

She skirted a street on the right, too packed with dead cars to walk on. All had been abandoned with their doors open, a handful burned down to their frames. Seeing them there made her think about all the money people had spent on them. How many millions of dollars sat useless on roads across what remained of the country? Driving around had been such a normal thing to do. She struggled to process the idea of never again being in a functioning vehicle. If the nukes had knocked out all the cars in the world, it would've definitely killed the factories that made them, too.

Though, perhaps some places—like third-world countries—hadn't been as affected by the war. Why would any superpower waste one of their nukes on a place like that? What about Australia? If someone shot a nuke all the way down there, it would've only been out of spite or cruelty. Central America and large parts of Africa probably hadn't changed much. Those places had become the new First World, assuming the war hadn't thrown so much dust into the air that the whole planet died from nuclear winter.

Maybe since no one is driving anymore it'll balance out. No more carbon monoxide emissions.

The field ended at a big highway. Despite the condition of everything, she paused at the edge and looked both ways before continuing. Madison's flip-flops pattered over the paving. Ash obscured any sense of lane markings, though she figured they'd crossed roughly twelve lanes. Though the area looked totally different than what she remembered, it had to be Route 6.

She climbed a dirt hill on the other side and trekked across a large field. So much ash had fallen there, the landscape resembled the surface of the moon. They passed a few cindered trees, one of which still smoldered. The chemical-plastic stink in the air lessened, giving way to a mostly wood smoke aroma which she found pleasant by comparison.

The field came to an end at a small bit of residential area directly across from the Colorado Mills Mall. She paused at the corner and wiped ash from a street sign that indicated the corner of Gardenia Street and West Seventh Ave.

"No one's called yet. Do you think they're mad at us for getting lost?" asked Madison.

"They're not mad at us, Termite. They're…" Harper bit her lip before saying 'dead.' Of course, she *knew* their parents had died, but had no clue what happened to her sister's friends. "Busy."

She gazed down while plodding along, mesmerized at the way the ash billowed around her shoes. Both she and her sister had turned grey from an overall dusting. *Ugh. How radioactive is this crap? Maybe we should take a quick bath or something.*

Harper randomly chose the second house on the right, a white single-story duplex with a two-car garage in the middle. She headed to the farther door, closer to the mall, since someone left it open.

"Hello?" called Harper—but not too loud—while leaning in behind her shotgun. "Is anyone here?"

She counted to ten before stepping inside. Ash had blown into the living room via the open door, but the rest of the house didn't show much sign of damage. She went from room to room, checking for sleeping occupants, intending to leave as fast and quiet as possible if she disturbed anyone. The place was empty, so she headed into the bathroom.

Madison stepped out of her flip flops, set down the toilet paper bag, then removed her jacket and bloody T-shirt. Ash had somehow gotten under it, covering her pale skin in grey blotches.

"I'm gonna check the house while you clean up, okay?"

"Please stay." Madison spun to look up at her, a faint trace of fear in her eyes. "I don't want to be alone."

"Are you sure? You yelled at me not to look when you peed."

"That's different." Madison shoved her shorts down, noticeably paler where they had covered her. Darker grime coated her arms and legs. "I'm more scared of being alone."

Harper pulled the bathroom door shut. "Okay. Remember, there's no hot water. There might not even be water at all."

Madison leaned into the tub, flicked the stopper, and turned only the hot water faucet on. Water came out in no great hurry. She tested it every few seconds with her fingers, but gave up after a short while and cranked the cold water spigot open as well, increasing the pressure.

Eventually, enough water had collected in the tub that she cut the faucets and gingerly stepped in. She gasped, but didn't scream or make much noise at all as she lowered herself to sit. Her teeth chattered in seconds, but she picked up a bar of soap and proceeded to wash herself.

"Oh, hell with it," muttered Harper.

She set her backpack, shotgun, and purse down, stripped, and approached the tub. Madison scooted forward to make room. It took every ounce of willpower Harper had not to shriek when she put a foot in the water. It reminded her of summer camp one year where the river they used for swimming had been so cold it should've been ice.

As she did back then, she repeated here: getting it over with as fast as possible. She dropped in, gasping. Once the paralysis wore off, she washed herself with a focus entirely on speed since no way in hell could she ever relax in a cold bath. It also didn't strike her as too healthy to sit in cold water in an unheated house.

They helped themselves to the former resident's shampoo. Harper dumped some in her hand and worked it into her thick, red hair. Other than having her kid sister sitting in front of her, taking a bath in an actual bathroom again made her feel strange, a peek at normality that didn't seem believable. If she closed her eyes, she could pretend she'd dreamed it all, and didn't have a loaded shotgun on the floor in arms reach. She could pretend she might not have to kill someone just to stay alive. If she thought really hard, she might even be able to imagine she had to still worry about getting into a college good enough to please her parents but close enough to let her stay at home.

"Are we gonna get in trouble for stealing someone's bathroom?" asked Madison in a whispery voice that echoed.

"No." Harper almost chuckled. "The people who lived here are gone. This isn't anyone's house now."

"Sorry," whispered Madison.

"What for?"

"Being scared. It's kinda weird taking a bath at the same time, but…"

"It's okay. Bad people are out there and will hurt us. I don't have the luxury of being embarrassed anymore. Besides, you're my sister. We used to share baths before when you were like two."

"We did?" asked Madison in a dead tone.

"Yeah. Guess you don't remember, but you were really small. I was your age then. You know I pretended I was your mother giving my baby a bath."

Madison stopped moving. She sat still for a few seconds, then leaned back against her.

Harper couldn't say a word past the lump in her throat. She wrapped her arms around Madison and kissed the top of her head. *I'm all she's got left.* Tears started, and she squeezed her kid sister tight.

The girl remained eerily stoic, responding to Harper sniffling at the back of her head by grasping the arms encircling her chest. They sat in total silence for a few minutes, except for the faint sloshing of water from their shivering.

Once the emotional storm subsided, Harper released the hug and ruffled her sister's soaked hair.

"C'mon. We need to dry off before we get hypothermia."

They rushed the rest of a bath and got out of the tub. Madison went straight to the toilet. Though she didn't demand Harper not watch, she turned her back anyway. The water had become nearly black, leaving a nasty ring on the tub once it drained. It didn't seem a worthwhile use of time to rinse it since they'd never come back here, so Harper grabbed towels and dried herself off as fast as she could. Madison sat on the toilet, still dripping, staring at the iPhone in her hands. Harper offered her a towel. It took her a moment to notice. With a soft sigh at the phone, her sister got up and took the towel. Harper blushed but also used the toilet.

Madison dried herself off, then stared down, prodding her jacket with a toe. "If we have fallout on our clothes, are we gonna get sick? Should we do laundry?"

Harper stood and flushed. "Do you want to wear wet clothes or spend all day in this house naked until they dry?"

Madison shook her head. "No and no. We can like wear these towels, or the comforter."

"No way. It's not safe enough here to sit here that long."

"Maybe there's stuff here we can wear instead?"

She briefly pondered going to check the bedroom instead of putting her filthy jeans and T-shirt back on. *I'm not ransacking a house bare-assed.* "We're right across the street from the mall. We can get new stuff in our size there. I don't wanna wait as long as it would take our things to dry, and it's way too cold to go outside wearing damp clothing. We have to get to Evergreen. The bad people are right behind us."

"Is that where Mom and Dad went?"

Harper stared at her sister, worried that her ribs had become so noticeable. *We're not eating enough.* "They wanted to go there, yeah."

Madison nodded and got dressed.

Screams from behind drew Harper's attention. She swiveled around to face the toilet, peering over it out a tiny window. A pack of men wearing the blue cloth scraps chased a lone man across a field behind the house, waving bats, axes, and pipes over their heads.

Oh... shit. We have to get the hell out of here!

Harper ducked down below the window level and scrambled back into her clothes. While she pulled the backpack on, Madison added a couple more rolls of toilet paper from the cabinet under the sink to her plastic bag, as well as soap bars and some toothpaste.

"Ready?"

Madison pulled the iPhone out and stared at it. "What if Mom is trying to call me? She knows I have dance class later. I gotta charge it."

"She'll understand. The power's out."

"For how long?"

"It's gonna be a while before they fix it." Harper put on a plastic smile. *Yeah. A while. Like decades if ever.*

"C'mon. Let's go before those idiots find us here."

Madison went wide-eyed, stuffed the iPhone in her jacket pocket, and picked up the plastic bag of toiletries.

Though she'd searched the house before, Harper crept into the hall outside like a cop making entry to an unknown crime scene. She did her best *Resident Evil* sweep, feeling a bit like the video game character exploring a dangerous ruin.

Maybe if I think of them like monsters in a game, I can shoot. She closed her eyes for a few seconds. Whether or not Madison had intended it, that moment she leaned against her in the bathtub had been as good as her begging Harper to protect her like a mother.

She never took karate lessons, didn't even do sports. Harper couldn't fight at all.

But she had a shotgun.

If only she had the nerve to use it.

6

COLORADO MILLS

U pon exiting the house, Harper headed to the right and trudged into the hazy miasma the world had become.

Ash blew diagonally from the left, the wind stirring up small cyclones of grey here and there. She followed Gardenia Street to a T-intersection and crossed the passing road to a short dirt hill where a waist-high iron fence blocked the way. From that vantage point, she could barely make out the enormous shape of the mall building up ahead. Harper glanced back at the way they'd walked. *Huh, wow. That had to be cool, living close enough to walk to the mall.*

After boosting Madison over the fence, she slung the shotgun on her shoulder via its carrying strap and jumped down the five or so feet to the ground beyond. Another drop, like ten feet—too far to jump—separated her from the parking lot. Grass here had survived, shielded from the nuclear flash by a shallow wall and a series of terraces. Harper went right, following a downhill grade until she reached a spot where the jump down didn't look scary. Small pine trees remained mostly green, though the ash coating looked eerily like dirty snow.

They crossed the ring road surrounding the mall, entering a giant parking lot that held only two cars: an older green Ford pickup truck with a bunch of Army bumper stickers, and a white SUV with the word 'security' on the door in black lettering and amber emergency lights. The pickup had a toolbox in the back with handprints in the ash dust, but whoever fussed with it must've given up as the lid remained closed.

She headed straight for the mall, going past the Sports Authority doors to a main mall entrance at the end of a small courtyard. Four large signs labeled 'Colorado Mills Entry 5' depicted various images of outdoor activities, biking, swimming, maybe mountain climbing. One sign had stopped halfway rotated to the next image, its slats pivoted open, stuck between two different scenes. She remembered the courtyard having red paver stones, though ash had turned everything grey.

Voices came from behind along with the clatter of aluminum. It sounded as though a group of people walked out of Sports Authority. Without a sound, she grabbed Madison's wrist and pulled her to the right, hiding in a small grove of pine trees by some benches. Her little sister crouched low, but didn't appear worried.

Harper took a knee, raising the shotgun in the direction of the voices. Six men walked past the corner into view. Two, she recognized from school, both a year ahead of her, already graduated. Jeff and Louis had been part of the 'bad' crowd: drugs, drinking, even getting in trouble with the law. She figured they would've only become worse with the collapse of order. Alarmingly, they both wore scraps of blue fabric around their necks. The others looked older, the eldest well into his thirties. All carried weapons ranging from new baseball bats to handguns.

"Yo, check this out," shouted a woman who hadn't walked past the corner yet. The men stopped, looked back, then sauntered once more out of sight behind the corner.

Harper leapt to her feet and rushed at a sprint for the mall entrance, pulling her sister along by the arm. Madison's flip-flops clapped on the concrete deck a few times before the pat of bare feet took over.

"Harp!" said Madison.

"Carry them," whisper-shouted Harper. She skidded to a stop, let go of her sister's wrist, and swiveled to point the shotgun at the corner in case anyone came running to check out the noise they made.

Madison scurried back a few steps to collect her flops, then ran for the door.

Harper dashed after her to the entrance, ducking inside before any of the gang members came walking past the wall again. At least, Harper *hoped* so. She hadn't looked back to see. No shouts or gunshots happened outside, so she assumed they'd gotten away.

A vast expanse of dimly lit abandoned stores stretched out before her. Heavy, humid air thick with a stink like a locker room, only stronger, filled her senses. Distant dripping echoed, making the place feel even emptier.

"Eww," said Madison, deadpan. "The floor is slimy."

Harper ignored the squish of her sneakers on the tiles. Condensation covered most of the store windows, turning them into opaque panels like frozen smoke. It occurred to her the mall didn't feel all that cold, as if somehow the heating system still limped along. *The mall's got generators, but wouldn't they have fried in the EMP?*

"Are we going shopping?"

"Kinda." Harper looked around, focusing after a few seconds on a skylight overhead. Water gathered in droplets, falling every few seconds to a silent landing on the floor a few paces forward of where she stood. "We're not gonna stay here long. I wanna get some clothes for you."

Madison pulled her phone out from her jacket pocket and fiddled with it. The blank, black screen still didn't respond.

We're going to be okay. Harper clutched the shotgun, trying to hold it in a posture that seemed right. Playing *Call of Duty* had been pretty cool. *Living* it, not so much. She advanced down the concourse, shifting to aim at any shadow that moved. Madison dallied a moment to put her flip-flops back on before catching up.

Dad's voice drifted out from Harper's memory, a discussion they'd had over his decision not to try heading for Evergreen right away. According to the group of people who told them about the sanctuary in the mountains, a lot of people had taken refuge up there and started rebuilding it into a proper town. Of course, they wouldn't have electrical power, cars, or anything like that. Total *Little House on the Prairie* stuff... but it sounded a whole lot better than whatever would happen to them if the blue gang got them.

That could go wrong in any number of ways from being forced to help thugs murder and loot to being raped, or maybe even killed and eaten. Cannibalism did seem a bit farfetched for people who had once lived in normal society. Stuff like that probably wouldn't happen for at least a few generations if at all. However, Harper had been groped, whistled at, pawed, and touched so often *before* the breakdown of law, she had no doubt what would happen to her now that police had stopped existing. A man who thought nothing of squeezing her ass as a form of hello would now probably rip her clothes straight off.

Dad thought the lack of organized society brought out the worst in everyone, as if the only thing holding humanity back from tearing each other apart had been the law and expectation that the majority of people in a civilized society would condemn aberrant behavior. Mom hadn't been so nihilistic. She'd clung to believing every person had some amount of good inside them—right up until the man trying to drag her out the window stabbed her.

Harper flinched at the memory of her mother crumpling to the ground in their kitchen. At least Madison hadn't witnessed it. She'd been hiding under the dining room table. Dad shot it out with a bunch of punks on the deck while Harper stood paralyzed with dread. She had been supposed to guard the front door, but wound up staring at a man forcing his way in, unable to pull the trigger. The way the gang punk smiled at her made her skin crawl. The *hunger* in his eyes freaked her out so much she couldn't move. As soon as he'd noticed the Mossberg in her hands, he went for a gun, but she couldn't bring herself to kill a man.

Dad's AR-15 and the Beretta Mom had been using likely served the gang now. The mere thought that weapons her father owned might hurt her or Madison increased her need to get so far away from Lakewood that couldn't happen. He had been so diligent in keeping the weapons locked up, not wanting them to hurt anyone, especially his daughters. Again, the expression on his face when the bullet tore into him from behind overwhelmed her thoughts.

"There's a Starbucks," said Madison, dragging Harper out of her daymare. "I know I missed dance class, but can we get something?"

"It's not open." Harper kept on walking, trying to ignore all her memories of this mall. The abandoned brokenness of everything looked *so* wrong, made worse by the near-total silence. As often as she used to come here, every storefront triggered one recollection or another—but seeing it like *this* waved reality in her face. It mocked her dead parents, missing friends, and the life she would no longer have.

"That's stupid. It's the morning."

"Look for a place with clothes your size."

"I wanna cake pop."

"They're probably stale and hard as rocks now."

"Aww, Harp. Please?"

She sighed, weighing the potential danger of remaining near Lakewood with some little thing to make her sister feel better. "Okay."

They crossed the hall to the Starbucks and raided it. Madison grabbed two pink cake pops from the display case. They did seem stale, but she ate them anyway. Harper nibbled on some equally past-their-prime cookies, savoring the chocolate. Of course, none of the coffee machinery worked. The place reminded her too much of taking her sister to dance class, too much of Mom. She collected the rest of the cookies into a bag, and pulled her sister out into the mall again, unable to tolerate the painful reminder of her old life.

Madison followed for a while in silence before asking, "Why are we hiding?"

"Those people are dangerous. They'll hurt us."

"Like they hurt Mom and Dad?"

Harper's throat closed off with a lump she couldn't speak past. She gazed down at the floor. The soft snapping of her sister's flip-flops seemed deafening.

"Harp?"

She cleared her throat, trying to compose herself. "No, worse."

"What's worse than being dead?" asked Madison, no life at all in her voice.

"Don't worry about it," said Harper. Her mind again filled with horrible images of her little sister fighting a faceless gang thug carrying her off to do unspeakable things. "I won't let it happen."

At the junction where the concourse widened to an atrium, Harper paused and crouched behind a large planter box of greenery, aiming the shotgun out at the dead mall. She *should* be sitting on the nearby bench sipping coffee with her friends, *not* running around with a gun. Or, at this hour, sitting in school. She'd have turned eighteen two weeks before graduation. Of course, graduation would never happen now… and if she didn't hold it together, turning eighteen wouldn't either.

Harper sighed at the Halloween decorations arranged all over the area where two mall concourses met. The attack happened early in September, yet they'd already hung witches, ghosts, pumpkins, and bats everywhere. Despite the décor, crappy Christmas music haunted her memories. Every year on November first, the mall put on the same track for the holidays, music that would never play here again.

Almost every store she looked at brought her back in time to visiting it with her friends. What was Andrea doing at the moment? Or Christina? Or Renee? That girl had always been jumpy, getting nightmares even from lame movies. Veronica loved going to karate, so she could probably take care of herself. Darci, a big fan of weed, probably still hadn't realized there'd been a war.

Of course, some or all of her friends could be dead.

Harper had fled her home while the men who'd killed her parents barged in the kitchen patio door. Perhaps the hazy smoke had kept them hidden. She hadn't thought about checking Christina's house, only three away from hers, until she'd run herself to the point of collapse. Christina liked the coffee place on the corner of the court here, mostly because it wasn't a chain. She had a thing against the 'corporate takeover' of America. Every time they'd gone to the mall together, they'd stop in.

The smell of 'wet' grew stronger in the next concourse. Shops on both sides offered mostly jewelry, electronics, and such. Nothing in that Apple store would be useful ever again. The place looked like it burned, no doubt the electromagnetic pulse had caused all the demonstration computers and tablets to explode in flames.

A short distance ahead, an escalator offered a way downstairs. Harper paused to look back, wary of being followed. Being inside felt weird because she could see more than thirty feet. Though the smell of burn persisted, the smoke remained outside. Nothing moved or made noise, except for unseen dripping.

"My phone won't turn on," said Madison. "The battery's dead."

"Got the charger?"

"Yeah."

Harper crossed her fingers. *White lies.* "We'll have to find a plug. Maybe there'll be one in Evergreen you can use."

"Not here?" Madison squatted beside her, half her pale face concealed by a wall of straight, black hair.

"All the stuff here broke, remember?" asked Harper. "I don't see anything dangerous. Come on."

She approached the escalator. At the top, she paused with an annoyed sigh. The ground floor had flooded several feet deep. Harper spent a moment debating if she'd rather deal with water or hope the gang thugs decided to go somewhere else.

They're probably going to come inside.

"Damn."

"Why is there a swimming pool inside the mall?" asked Madison.

"I dunno." Harper sat at the top of the escalator. "Pipe probably broke or something."

She pulled her sneakers and socks off, stuffing them in her giant purse. Wet jean legs would be bad given the chilly weather, but soggy sneakers— ugh. Still, the last thing she wanted would be to have the gang find her exploring a mall in her underpants. That would be like waving meat at a starving dog.

Barefoot, she crept down the escalator, shotgun poised to deal with anyone who looked dangerous. Since they likely had bad guys entering the mall behind them, Harper figured she had no choice but to keep going forward, even if that meant a confrontation with whoever might be down there.

At the bottom, she stepped into cold water a little deeper than her knees. Plastic cups, trash, and a handful of volleyballs floated by. Without skylights, the lower floor sat in darkness except for where the corridors met at atriums open all the way to the ceiling. Each hallway leading off held plenty of shadows.

"It's cold," said Madison as she entered the water, which almost touched the hem of her shorts. "I left my swimsuit at home."

Harper looked over at her kid sister, who clutched her flip-flops to her iPhone, holding it protectively away from getting wet. "We're not swimming, Termite."

She sloshed onward with Madison grabbing at her arm. As much as she wanted to offer the comfort of holding hands, she didn't want to let go of the shotgun. If she needed it, every second would matter. Eventually, Madison settled on clutching her belt.

Most of the stores on the lower floor looked as though riots had stormed through already. Much of the inventory had been looted and an alarming amount of blood spatter painted the walls in places. A few hunting arrows even stuck out of the wall by a store full of skinny mannequins.

They headed into the shop, 'D-zign,' but it sold trendy dresses in sizes that only slim teenagers or Korean fashion models could fit into. Harper rolled her eyes at some of the price tags, and considered taking stuff purely out of spite… but none of the sheer dresses would be practical for living rough.

Harper had spent enough time in the mall over the past few years to know her way around, and remembered a kids' clothing store near one of the entrances on the north side. She usually avoided that door due to the legion of smokers who always hung out there—not so much an issue anymore. A short walk down another concourse brought them to a food court.

"Where is everyone?" asked Madison. "Are they all in school now?"

"Umm. A war happened. They're too busy to shop."

"Oh." Madison approached a small place with Japanese writing. "Ooh! Sushi!"

Harper cringed. "Nothing in there is going to be safe to eat. You'll throw up as soon as you open the fridge."

"Aww." Madison backed away. "I thought you liked sushi."

"I do... or did. I don't want to eat it after it's gone bad." She crept forward at a speed that didn't make too much splashing. Without music or a crowd, every tiny noise echoed over the entire mall.

"Siri," whispered Madison, "I know you probably don't have enough power to turn on the screen, but please send Mom or Dad a text and tell them we're okay."

Harper blinked away tears. If she looked into one more store, it would trigger a memory that would leave her curled up on the floor, bawling. She stared straight across the food court, her thoughts stuck in a nowhere land between a past beyond reach and a future reduced to ashy snow.

Metal slammed into metal with a great *crash*.

Barely managing to stifle a cry of surprise, Harper spun to the left, pointing the shotgun at an Auntie Anne's shop.

Madison leapt into her, clinging, but didn't make a sound.

No one appeared obviously in sight, though a shadow moved behind the register counter. Shivering from the icy water lapping at her legs, Harper stood her ground, waiting, watching—and listening. Madison peered around her.

Seven breaths later, a shirtless, shoeless boy with a spherical mop of black hair climbed up to perch like a miniature Tarzan atop the counter in the pretzel shop. He appeared to be about Madison's age, skinny, and possibly Chinese. As soon as he spotted Harper—specifically the shotgun she had pointed in his direction—he let off a yowl of alarm and jumped from the counter into the water.

"Hey!" shouted Harper. "Wait!"

The boy didn't bother trying to run. He dove under the surface and swam to the left so fast his shorts almost came off. She trudged after him as he raced away from the Auntie Anne's, heading deeper into a dark concourse.

"Kid, stop!" yelled Harper. "I'm not gonna hurt you."

Madison struggled to keep up behind her. "I don't think he wants to be friends."

7

PLUS TWO

Harper ran after the boy as best she could in knee-deep water. He slowed momentarily to pull his shorts up, then swam hard for a corner some fifty feet from the pretzel shop, easily outpacing her and disappearing around the bend about ten seconds before she reached the intersection. Harper rushed after him, rounding the corner straight into the tip of an enormous silver handgun pressed to her forehead.

A tiny whine escaped her nostrils. It took her a second to collect herself enough to realize a man held the gun. It took her a moment more to remember how to breathe. She stared past the handgun at the face of a man a little past forty, with a short, scruffy brown beard and shaggy hair. Somewhere between muscular and mildly overweight, he filled out the uniform of a mall security officer with little room to spare.

"That's a hell of a cannon for a girl your size."

After six seconds of having a pistol touching her, she recognized him.

"Officer Cliff?" squeaked Harper.

The glower on his face relaxed. "Oh… I remember you—and your attitude."

"Please don't shoot me," said Harper in a mostly calm voice. "Umm, there's been a war. There's no such thing as shoplifting anymore. Besides, I don't think there's even anything left to steal."

The boy peered out from behind Cliff, eyeing her warily.

"What were you doin' chasin' the kid?"

Sloshing behind and left reminded her of Madison, but she dared not look away from a man holding a gun to her face. "I wasn't going to hurt him. Kids shouldn't be alone."

Cliff patted the boy on the head with his free hand. "People haven't exactly been nice to him."

"Why?" asked Harper, chancing a peek left at Madison, who crept into a Hot Topic on the other side of the hallway.

"As you so astutely pointed out, we had a war. Numbnuts out there assume he's Korean and 'his people' nuked us, or started the whole shitstorm."

"My great-grandparents are from China," said the boy, barely over a whisper. "I'm not a Korean."

Harper sighed at the kid. "People are stupid. You're an American like everyone else here. I swear I wasn't going to hurt you." She looked up at Cliff. "I just saw him alone and figured he was too little to be on his own."

Cliff lowered his gun. "All right. You're still a kid, too. S'pose you may as well stick around if you want. At least until the supplies run out."

"I'm seventeen. I'm—"

"Still a kid." Cliff smiled.

"Hi. I'm Jonathan," said the boy. "You kinda scared me with the gun."

"Sorry. Just heard a noise in there, and saw some bad guys outside." Harper glanced to the left, watching her sister rummage the store. "Surprised there aren't more people here. It's like abandoned."

"Yeah. Most everyone hauled ass away from big cities once the fireballs stopped. We got real damn lucky nothing landed on our heads."

"Heard one hit Colorado Springs." Harper relaxed enough to stop watching Cliff, and instead kept tabs on Madison exploring the variety store. "Any idea who nuked us?"

"Nah. I was in here on night shift when the shit hit the fan. Only ran outside for a little while to grab some gear. Could'a been Russia, China, Korea... hard to say. One nuke goes off, the computers take over and blow everyone to shit. All the targets are loaded into the computers already. Hell, could've even been hackers that fired the first shot and everyone else just responded."

"I'm trying to get out of Lakewood," said Harper. "My dad..." She choked up, remembering him scream *Harper! Shoot!* while she stood there frozen. "Uhh"—her voice quivered—"my, umm, dad, talked to a guy who told us about a settlement or something up in Evergreen. It's supposed to be safe. My… umm… parents both died."

"Sorry," said the boy. "Mine are dead too. People thought they started the war."

Her heart sank. "People suck."

"Ain't that the truth," muttered Cliff. As if forgetting he still had a gun out, he glanced at it, then stuffed it in a hip holster.

"We're not safe here. The gang's getting bigger, and scarier. It's just me and my kid sister."

Cliff waved his hand around by his throat. "You talkin' about those jackasses with the blue scarves?"

She nodded.

"Yeah… I can see why you'd wanna get the hell away from them." Cliff winced. "Those boys would, umm, yeah."

The former mall guard hadn't meant anything inappropriate, but he'd called attention to her looks all the same. Dad always joked that he bought the shotgun because he had a pretty, blue-eyed, redhead daughter. She didn't need the reminder of why letting the gang find her would be a *bad* idea. Of course, Dad liked guns. He would've bought the Mossberg anyway. Madison didn't mind guns. Neither did Harper really. She'd grown up with them, learned to shoot young, won some trophies even, but she *hated* the very idea of hunting. Madison had gone vegetarian three years ago. Even she thought going to the range for target shooting had been fun, though she never wanted to shoot an animal—or a person.

"You want a hand getting to Evergreen?" asked Cliff. "S'pose me and Jon could help make sure you two make it there in one piece."

Harper narrowed her eyes. "What are you gonna ask for in return?"

"Nothin', kid." Cliff shook his head. "You're a kid and I'm a trained professional. That's just how stuff is supposed to work."

Something clattered to the floor in the Hot Topic, but Madison didn't yell in alarm, so Harper resisted the urge to dash over there.

"Trained professional?" She raised one eyebrow. "You're a mall cop."

Cliff laughed. "Wasn't always. I *thought* this job would come with fewer bullets flying my way. Mostly, that was true. Though, past couple days, seems I was wrong. 'Course, they're flying everywhere these days."

"Since when do mall cops have guns?"

He grinned. "Not supposed to carry on duty, but I keep one in my truck."

She looked down at her feet, well under water. It would be nice not having to do *all* the protecting. "Okay. That would be really cool of you to help us get to Evergreen."

"Not a bad cannon you've got there. What's that a 930?"

"Umm. Yeah, I think so."

Cliff leaned closer, eyeing the shotgun. "Yeah. Semi-auto, right? That's gotta be a 930."

She shrugged. "Guess so. Umm… Be right back."

Harper sloshed across the hall into the Hot Topic. Thousands of little plastic baubles floated like a layer of pond scum, clinging to a glass counter, various toys, collectables, and other kitsch in various states of drowned. A few electronic items had scorch marks from the EMP, as did the cash register and the walls behind flat panel TVs.

Madison knelt atop the counter, clutching an armload of cheap jewelry, everything from skulls to pixies she'd rummaged from a bin beside the register. "Can we get these?" She held up a pair of plastic unicorn earrings. "I left my allowance at home."

"Yeah, it's fine. There's no more money. Just take them."

For the first time in two weeks, Madison's face finally showed a hint of emotion: worry. "But, Harp!" She lowered her voice to a whisper. "He's a mall cop. I can't like steal right in front of him. I'll get in *so* much trouble."

"It's fine." Harper grabbed a purple-and-black backpack from a shelf and transferred her sister's haul of cheap jewelry into it before handing it over. "Take whatever you want, but you have to carry it."

After a long, worried stare, Madison accepted the backpack. She hopped down and added a couple more things, including a few adult-sized T-shirts. After collecting the plastic bag of toilet paper, toothpaste, and soap, she followed Harper out of the store, wading over to where Cliff and Jon waited.

Cliff led them back upstairs to a TGI Fridays at the corner of a large four-way atrium. He stooped to unlock a rolling security gate. Two large front windows stood on either side of it, packed with tables in makeshift barricades. A few cracks and pieces of missing glass frightened and reassured her in equal measure. People had tried to break in, but couldn't.

Harper twisted to scan their surroundings, unnerved by this place being so damn quiet. Two dark concourses led off along the length of the mall in opposing directions with a pair of smaller hallways heading for the sides. Dead escalators, half-assembled Halloween decorations, and a vast mess created by looters stretched as far as she could see into every passage. Any one of the shadows where the skylights couldn't reach might hold dangerous people—not the holiday shopping rush that should be going on in November.

At the rattle of the security gate going up, Harper pulled her gaze off the ruined mall, sighed, and ducked into the restaurant. Once everyone made it inside, he closed it again. Jon hurried down an aisle of booth seats, grabbing the last one so he didn't slip and fall while rounding the corner. She followed him to a section they'd made something of a home out of where hanging sheets served as walls, creating bedrooms of cots and sleeping bags. Madison, iPhone clutched to her chest, padded along behind her.

Cliff walked up to stand beside Harper, gesturing at everything. "Figure we'll leave first thing in the morning so we have the most daylight, plus some time to pack provisions. Might as well get comfortable. I'll whip up some food."

The boy stepped behind a sheet 'wall.' A second later, his soaking wet shorts hit the floor.

Madison strolled over and sat in a padded booth seat, swinging her feet back and forth as though they'd simply gone out for lunch and nothing at all terrible had happened to the world.

Jonathan emerged from behind the sheet wall, having changed into a dry Nike T-shirt and cargo shorts, with a blanket draped from his shoulders. He still didn't have any shoes, but seemed much less skittish than he'd been earlier. He flashed a weak smile while going by on the way to the booth where Madison sat, and climbed up into the opposite bench before offering her another blanket.

Harper stood there staring at her wet jean legs and bare feet for a little while before taking a seat on the end of the bench next to her sister, resting the shotgun across her lap. A moment later, she second-guessed herself and checked the safety. *I can't believe this is real.* Two months ago, her biggest fear had been Renee and Christina dragging her to a Taylor Swift concert. Not that she had anything against the music, but crowds bugged her. Harper hated being out among *so many* people.

I am the anti-redhead. Introvert Prime.

"Hey," said Jonathan. "It's cool to have another kid around. What's your name?"

For the most part, the girl ignored him as he kept trying to start a conversation, but after about five minutes, she finally said, "I'm Madison. My phone needs a charge. I'm worried about my friends."

"I miss my friends, too," said Jonathan. "Glad I found Mr. Barton."

"I've gotta go to dance class at five." Her kid sister spoke in that same, toneless, far-away voice that stabbed Harper like an ice dagger. "Mom's gonna pick me up. I can't call her 'cause my stupid phone won't turn on. I don't even know what time it is."

"Oh, that's cool." Jonathan again tried to hand her the second blanket. "I took dance, too. It was kinda weird being the only boy there, but I liked it."

Madison looked up from the dead screen. "You didn't go to Taekwondo?"

Jonathan rolled his eyes. "Why, 'cause I'm Chinese?"

"No. Because you're a *boy*. My dance class didn't have any boys. We had one for a couple days, but his father came in and got mad, made him go home." She resumed staring at the blank iPhone. An awkward silence hung between them for a moment. "I think it's pretty cool you took dance."

"Yeah, I got teased for it, but I don't care. I liked it."

Madison almost smiled. She set the iPhone down on the table long enough to grab the blanket and wrap herself in it.

Harper exhaled with relief. She watched the restaurant entrance while the kids talked about their dance classes, comparing how the teachers differed. Her mind filled in the ghosts of shoppers wandering back and forth. Cliff returned after a while carrying a tray and handed everyone a plate with a burger and fries. Madison stared at the plate with a horrified expression, but sniffed, then calmed. She picked up the burger and sniffed at it again. Satisfied, she nibbled at it.

"How'd you cook this?" asked Harper. "There's no power anywhere in Lakewood. We've been eating out of cans."

"That's true." He scooted in to sit beside Jonathan. "Mall generators had been working up until a day or three ago when the flood finally killed them. But there's still wood."

"Veggie burger," said Madison, a note of approval in her voice.

"Meat's gone bad by now." Jonathan shook his head. "This stuff lasts forever."

"It's all chemicals," said Harper.

"Tasty, delicious, still-edible chemicals." Cliff winked, and took a big bite. "The fries might be a little stale, but it's cold enough outside to be a fridge."

Harper dug in. The veggie-patty gave off a definite twang of wood smoke and the fries had obviously been heated in a pan. However, compared to the cold canned food she'd been surviving on the past few days, it amounted to a feast.

"Well, cars are pretty much toast after the EMP blast." Cliff finished chewing a bite and shook his head. "Figures. Just paid off my damn truck, too. We're gonna have to hoof it to Evergreen."

Harper nodded.

"Dad just got a new Expedition," said Madison, her unfocused stare boring into her burger like a seer gazing at the depths of a crystal ball. "It's nice. We can all fit in it and it still smells new. It's got a sun roof. Do you think Mom will drive it to take me to dance, or will she use her old car?"

Cliff shot a glance over the table at Harper. His eyes seemed to say 'that poor kid ain't handling it well.'

Jonathan mouthed 'wow' without giving it voice.

Harper looked down. "I need to get Maddie some better clothes. Is there anything left in any of the stores here?"

"Probably. Most of the people who stuck around aren't interested in kid-sized clothes." Cliff scratched at his beard. "We can check on that before we head out. Yeah, she's gonna need somethin' better than flip flops. And you need shoes."

"I have shoes. They're in my bag. Didn't want them to get wet."

"Wet shoes suck," said Jonathan.

"That they do." Cliff grinned and took a big bite of fake burger.

After they finished eating, Harper helped Cliff sort canned goods in the restaurant pantry. They put food in the 'take' pile and stuff like cranberry sauce or gravy aside. She knelt in the kitchen pushing corn and baked beans into piles, wondering how they'd ever manage to carry so much stuff.

Madison approached, holding her iPhone and its charger. "None of the plugs are working. Can we go home?"

Overcome by grief, Harper sank to her knees and wrapped her little sister in a hug.

"I miss Mom and Dad," whispered Madison. "What if they're trying to call us? It's too dark now. It's after five. Mom didn't come to take me to dance class. Are they gonna kick me out for missing too many?"

The dam broke. Harper burst into tears and clutched Madison tight, rocking her back and forth.

"I dunno, Termite. I dunno."

8

AFTER THE BLAST

H arper snapped awake, stretched out on a booth seat bench. Madison had curled up on top of her for the night, but she'd disappeared. An inch from panic, Harper grabbed the Mossberg and leapt out of the booth, ready to scream.

Flickering light to the left drew her attention. Her little sister sat on the floor a short distance away in a circle with Cliff and Jonathan around a single lit candle. The kids listened to him telling stories about the stupid things a clumsy friend of his did when he'd been deployed in Iraq. Madison almost even smiled, wide-eyed and intent.

The lump lodged itself once again in Harper's throat. Watching the two of them reminded her of Dad, reminded her of how Dad died because she chickened out and couldn't shoot a man trying to hurt her. If Dad hadn't turned to save her, he would've been able to shoot the other guy coming in the patio door.

A toxic mood came over her, making her want to lash out at Madison for forgetting their father so fast. That man wasn't their father. How dare she smile at him and let him pretend to be someone he would never be. Her lip curled in guilt disguised as jealousy, and she narrowed her eyes at the impostor.

The last time she'd seen Cliff, she'd been fourteen and spent two hours handcuffed by one arm to a metal chair in some back room here at the mall. It didn't matter that she *had* shoplifted and probably deserved to be arrested. However, Cliff had called her parents instead of the cops... something about not wanting to ruin her future over a crappy pair of overpriced pants. The store manager agreed not to press charges since her mom paid for it. Being grounded for a month beat having a juvenile record.

Okay, so he's not a dick. Harper sighed out her nose, letting her anger evaporate. *I messed up once and got Dad killed. Maddie seems to like this guy. I shouldn't mess up again.* She wept in silence, mourning her parents. With a deep breath, she pushed her sadness back down into a little box. *I can cry later. Right now, I gotta get her outta this place.*

She didn't feel much like trying to sleep, nor did she want to interfere with 'story time.' Her present mood would only ruin it for the kids. She trudged down the aisle to the restaurant entrance and stood by the table barricade, staring out into the mall atrium. A little moonlight made it past the haze outside, enough that she could perceive the railing overlooking the opening to the ground floor and a hint of a store or two across the way. Nothing moved or made any sound.

The shotgun hung in her grip, heavy as a ball and chain.

Her thoughts drifted to her former home, her bedroom full of clothes, posters, and stuff. She pictured the little figurines her mother had gotten her for Christmas a few years ago. They'd probably still be sitting on her dresser around a couple small trophies she got from soccer like eight years ago. Not that she'd been that good a player, but her team won. The concrete chunk that smashed a hole in her ceiling didn't hit the dresser, but it took out her TV and Xbox.

She leaned against the tables, trying not to cry as her head filled with memories of sitting at home playing video games, talking with her friends on the phone, dreading homework... how she'd been so anxious about her driver's test to get a full license she couldn't sleep. It all seemed so stupid now. No government existed to care about licenses anymore, nor did any cars still work. A mere two months ago, everything had been so different. Starbucks running out of 'skinny' mocha syrup had been a tragedy.

All the stuff in her room, she'd run away from it without a second thought. Some of it had memories attached to it, little gifts from her friends, photos, stuff Madison had made for her like that paper flower. Those things—and clothes—she missed, but not for the items themselves as much as the sense of normality they brought.

Harper closed her eyes, apologizing to the universe for ever complaining about having to go to school, or study, or work, or do any of the annoying things she used to hate so much. *Please let me wake up from this nightmare. I swear I'll never bitch about anything ever again.*

The murmur of Cliff's voice in the background didn't go away.

She opened her eyes to the same ruined mall, the same shotgun in her hands. It had really happened. Idiots had blown the world back to the Stone Age. Worry about getting into a good college gave way to worry about living to see tomorrow. Not wanting to wear something because her friends would make fun of it had become not wanting to freeze.

I'm not dreaming.

She really had hidden in the basement with her parents and sister, terrified at all the horrible noises going on outside. The low, building roar of the distant explosion would forever be burned into her memory, the same way the silhouettes of some people had been burned into buildings. A brilliant flash invaded the basement windows as her family huddled low to the ground. A moment later, the glass shattered amid fierce winds and a distant growling rumble. The rain of pelting debris came next, persisting for what felt like hours.

We should've stayed in the basement.

About a week after the blast, Dad decided everyone could go back upstairs and live in the house like normal people instead of 'basement trolls.' If they hadn't done that, her parents would still be alive. The gang might not have even targeted their house. She still didn't know if they searched every house looking for canned goods or if they wanted to grab people. If they'd been hunting for resources, they would have invaded the house anyway, but at least being in the basement would've made it easier for defense: one point of entry. Harper wouldn't have been put in a situation to choose between killing someone or just standing there and being shot.

It struck her that she tried to blame Dad for his own death by moving them out of the basement. Guilt brought more tears, though she kept them quiet, pretending to be standing 'guard duty' at the door instead of sulking off alone. Her father died because she couldn't kill a bad guy.

Footsteps scuffed up behind her. She tensed her grip on the shotgun and glanced back. Upon seeing Cliff, she exhaled and resumed staring out at the dark mall.

"Hey," said Cliff, barely over a whisper. "I'd ask 'you okay' but that seems like a pretty stupid question."

"Yeah."

"Anything you wanna talk about?"

She picked at the shotgun grip. "Why did this happen?"

"Oh… someone with no brain, too small a heart, and too big a mouth got too close to *the button.*" Cliff took a step closer to the security gate, hands on his hips, and sighed. "Never did understand the point of nukes. Only an insane person would ever consider actually using a weapon like that. Most politicians want to *rule* the world, not end it."

"Yeah. Total movie villain stuff. 'If I can't have the world, no one will.' This is just so stupid. I should be in school, getting ready for life. Not sleeping in dumpsters or alleys. We should be home with our parents…" She paused before her voice broke up.

He glanced over at her, his expression somewhere between sympathy and pity. Harper sensed an offer of a hug if needed, but she couldn't betray the father she failed so epically. Before the temptation to cling to him like the frightened child she felt like grew too strong to resist, she looked down.

"Are we going to get sick from radiation?"

"Where were you when it went off?"

"In our basement. Dad dragged me out of bed at stupid-o'clock in the morning. I wasn't even awake enough to ask what was going on. Mom always got up super early, so she saw the news talking about nuclear war and woke him up. We had nowhere else to go, so we just went into the basement."

Cliff nodded. "That's probably the best thing you could've done. Fallout radiation breaks down pretty rapidly. We're all soaking up way more than we would have normally, but Springs is reasonably far away. How long before you two went outside?"

"We left the house a couple days ago." Harper teased her finger up and down the trigger guard. If not for her chickening out, she might've still been there.

"Unless we go *toward* a strike, we should be reasonably safe. You were underground for the worst of it. Probably ought to get some contractor's masks at least until we're out of the haze. That smoke all over the place could still have some radioactive particles in it."

She took her left hand off the shotgun to grab her throat. "Really?"

"Ehh. Sorry. Didn't mean to scare you like that. It's possible. Don't have a Geiger counter on me, so…" He patted her shoulder. "You should get some sleep."

Harper gave him a 'yeah right' look. "Should and can aren't the same thing right now."

"At least try. I'll keep an eye on the door."

"'Kay."

She trudged back down the aisle to the 'bedroom' area. Madison lay in one of the sleeping bags on a cot, her shirt, shorts, flops, and underpants on the floor next to her. White fabric at her shoulder said a man's plain T-shirt served as a nightgown. Jonathan occupied another sleeping bag on a cot across the room, only his head sticking out. His shirt and pants also sat on the floor beside the bed.

Harper didn't trust things enough to strip down to her underwear for sleep. Already barefoot, she crawled fully dressed into the only remaining cot. It probably belonged to Cliff as the one Madison had taken didn't look used. Still, having him watching the door offered a rare sense of security she hadn't felt since she'd left home. Because he'd called her parents instead of the cops three years ago, she trusted him.

A shotgun made for a less comfortable bed buddy than one of her plush animals, but it offered real security.

If she could ever bring herself to use it.

9

SCAVENGERS

T he fragrance of potatoes nagged at Harper until she opened her eyes.

She peered out at the room defined by sheets, most still bearing creases from their packaging. Cliff had likely taken them from a nearby store. Jonathan emerged from his sleeping bag in his briefs, stretched, then pulled on his shorts and T-shirt. Drawn by the smell of food, the boy wandered off to the 'door,' a gap between sheets, and disappeared.

Harper sat up and yawned.

Madison entered from the same gap, having already changed back into her bloody-hand-print shirt and tiny denim shorts. She hadn't bothered putting her flops on. "Bathroom's busted."

"Huh?"

"No water." Madison sat on the edge of her cot and stared at her iPhone.

Harper pulled on her socks and sneakers, stood, and walked out, pausing to pat Madison on the head. "Be right back."

"'Kay."

She headed to the ladies' room. None of the sinks worked and all the toilets had gone dry. Still, for what she had to do, a drain worked fine. Once finished, she hurried back into the seating area. Cliff had the kids at a table, picking from a giant bowl of French fries. He'd found a jar of nacho cheese sauce and a bottle of dried bacon bits, which they liberally dumped over the potatoes. Madison guarded her fries with her hands to defend it against the evil meat product.

Without a word, Harper joined them for the strange breakfast.

While eating, she kept thinking about home with an increasing sense of indignation at losing all her precious stuff, not to mention clothes. Irreplaceable keepsakes like gifts from her parents or sister, things that reminded her of her friends, and so on had been taken away by that stupid gang. For all she knew, everyone she went to school with had died already. Only a handful lived close enough to visit without driving, and she hadn't seen even one of them since the strike.

Cliff collected the dishes after the meal and carried them to the kitchen. Taken by sudden inspiration, Harper got up and followed him past a pair of flapping plastic doors. He went over to a counter by a giant steel sink and wiped off the bowls and plates with a rag. She almost asked if he was going to wash them, but remembered the water didn't work here.

"Umm," said Harper.

Cliff looked up. "Oh, hey."

For an instant as they made eye contact, Harper became acutely aware that she'd left the shotgun on the cot. If this guy wanted to do anything to her, she'd have no way at all to stop him. Her unexplained fear abated as rapidly as it had manifested. Nothing about Cliff's demeanor suggested he possessed the least bit of inclination to hurt her. Sure, he once kept her chained to a chair for two hours, but she *had* stolen something. And he could've been a total prick and called the police, but didn't.

"Hey. Umm… I was thinking about trying to go back to my house and get some of our stuff. Clothes mostly, but I kinda wanna grab some stuff to remember my parents by. It's too scary to go alone with the gang all over the place. Think you'd go with me?"

"Planning to bring your little sister and Jonathan along with us straight into their territory?"

Harper bit her lip. "Uhh. No."

"So you're going to leave them here alone and hope they're okay when we get back?"

"Ugh." She hung her head, staring down past her long, red hair at the floor. "You're right. It's too dangerous. We barely got away from them once. Going back there would be stupid. All that stuff there will only make me sad anyway. All the pictures I had of my friends and parents are either online or on my phone. Probably don't even exist anymore. Even if the devices worked, does EMP erase hard disks?"

Cliff kept working the rag around the big bowl. "Not sure on hard drives, but anything in the phone is toast. Flash memory would be burned out. Hey, stuff is nice, but it's not everything. Electromagnetic pulses can't take away your memories."

"Getting old and going senile can, but we probably won't get old."

"That defeatist attitude isn't going to help anyone." He grinned while scraping cheese sauce off a plate into the sink.

She shrugged. "I don't think it's defeatist. There's no more medical technology. We're probably not going get old enough to go senile. Didn't people in medieval times used to drop dead at like fifty or so?"

"Yeah, I guess. But they also didn't eat all those preservatives and chemicals to get cancer. But, you two could both use more clothes. Don't have to go all the way back to your house for that. Should be plenty of stuff right here in the mall."

"Cool." She pointed at him. "Why are you cleaning dishes if we're gonna be leaving?"

Cliff looked at the plate in his hands and laughed. "Force of habit I guess. Might as well head down the hall now and get you two some stuff."

"Okay."

He tossed the rag aside and headed out to a cabinet near the 'bedroom' that looked like a computer station where the wait staff had put in orders and run payments. He'd gotten rid of the monitor and used the area for his gun kit. While he put on a green belt with a holster and pouches, Harper headed to retrieve the shotgun from the cot.

Jonathan and Madison worked on dance stretches nearby. She grimaced away from the boy standing on one leg with his other leg tight to his chest, pointing straight up. The mere sight of it made her muscles ache. The only time she'd ever done anything even close to a split involved an icy sidewalk, bruises, and walking funny for a few days.

She collected the shotgun and searched for something smaller than her massive denim purse to carry some extra shells in. Nothing jumped out at her, so she slung her purse over her left shoulder as usual and walked back out of the cloth-walled bedroom.

"C'mon guys. We're going scavenging."

"Okay." Jonathan nodded.

The relatively normal expression on Madison's face retreated back to the emotionless stare she'd had ever since the second or third week after the bombs. She sat on the cot and resumed staring at the iPhone.

"I don't wanna. Can I wait here?"

Harper sat beside her, an arm around her shoulders. "I can't leave you alone. I gotta protect you."

The blank look Madison gave her could've said 'like you protected Dad?' Or, simple disassociation from reality. "What if someone tries to call me?"

"Cell phones are portable. They can still call you if we're down the hall a bit." Jonathan took a step toward Cliff, waving for Madison to follow. "Come on. It'll be fun."

Harper opened her mouth to say 'please,' but closed it. Back in the bathtub, her little sister seemed to want a mother more than an older sibling. Maybe she should try talking like Mom. "Maddie, come on. We have to do this. I know you're not really interested, but it's important."

Head down, Madison stood and stepped into her flip-flops.

Cliff opened the security gate to let everyone out of the Friday's, then closed it before heading off toward the long concourse on the left.

Harper tapped Jonathan on the shoulder upon noticing he still went barefoot. "You don't have shoes? Are the stores all empty?"

"They're inside." He pointed at the restaurant. "We're not leaving the mall, right? If we hit a flooded spot, I don't want them to get wet."

"Oh... okay."

Madison's flip-flops snapped and popped as they made their way down the hallway past abandoned stores and vendor carts full of random junk. Keychains or mugs with peoples' names on them didn't seem at all useful anymore. She could bash open all the cash registers and take more money than she'd ever seen in one place before... but it would probably be useless. Would anyone even care about paper bills anymore? Most people used debit or credit cards anyway. Everyone's money had been nothing more than bits inside a computer somewhere. All of that had evaporated in an instant.

Cliff stopped at a place a little beyond the halfway mark and unlocked the security gate. Child-sized mannequins stood in the windows modeling clothes. Harper pulled Madison inside and wandered the display shelves. After a minute or so, her kid sister put the iPhone back in her jacket pocket and began looking around like they'd merely gone shopping on any ordinary day.

Jonathan checked out some cartoon-character shirts in his size. He tried a few on before noticing a rack of underpants. He ran over, rummaged a few packets, and changed into them right there in the open.

Madison gawked at him, blushing. She tugged at Harper's arm and whispered, "I need new underwear too. I've been wearing these too long."

Cliff appeared with two giant shopping bags, into which he tossed various shirts and pants. Harper walked with her sister over to the girls' section. Upon finding a shelf of underwear, she grabbed a few packets in Madison's size, ripped one open, and handed her a clean pair. The girl took them, but continued standing there.

Harper grabbed a pair of jeans she thought would fit her as well as a clean shirt, pink socks, and a pair of sneakers. She tried to hand the haul over, but her little sister didn't move to take any of it, seeming not to care.

"Come on, Termite. This stuff is yours now."

Madison shrugged, continuing to ignore the clothes while staring at her iPhone. "Mom hasn't called."

Harper swallowed the lump of guilt that formed in her throat. "Okay… I'll pack it. You can put it on later. It'll be too cold for flops and shorts soon."

"It's too cold for flip flops *now*," said Cliff.

Jonathan, in a new *Wolverine* T-shirt and jeans, ran over. "It is kinda cold. You won't be able to dance if your toes freeze off."

"You're not wearing shoes at all." She playfully stepped on his toes.

"We're inside, and there's water all over downstairs. I didn't want them to get wet. It's still too cold."

"I'm not cold."

Harper sighed at the floor. "Please? It'll make me feel better if you look warm. I don't want you getting sick."

Madison continued staring into the iPhone for another moment, but eventually looked up with a resigned sigh. She tucked the phone away in her jacket, accepted the bundle, and headed off to a changing room. At the entrance to the dressing area, she looked back at Harper with a 'why are you just standing there' sort of expression.

"Okay…" Harper trotted over, worry gnawing on her gut.

The last time they'd been shopping, her sister didn't want Mom anywhere even near the dressing area while she changed. Then again, the odds of random bad guys showing up and trying to kidnap her had been quite a bit lower then. Madison held the booth door open for her, so she squeezed in with her. The space made for tight quarters with a shotgun in hand.

Madison undressed, frowning at herself in the tall mirror. "I'm gonna get in trouble for being too skinny. Mom thinks I'm not eating."

"You're fine," said Harper.

"Miss Clare's gonna yell at me for not eating. She thinks everyone in class who's thin is bulimic or something." Madison pulled on the clean underpants, then jeans. She sat on the floor to pull the socks and sneakers on, then stood.

Harper pulled a T-shirt over her sister's head. "Forgot something."

Madison shifted her weight, testing the sneakers.

"Do they fit?"

"They're okay. Mom would never get these. They're way too expensive. We're gonna get in so much trouble for stealing all this stuff."

Harper leaned the shotgun on the wall so she could hug her sister in both arms. "No we won't. We're not in any trouble."

"You don't have to lie." Madison stood there tolerating the hug. "We're in big trouble… and not the getting grounded kind."

Harper couldn't think of anything to say, nor could she have gotten any words out if she had some in mind.

"You need new stuff, too. Your clothes smell like trash."

"Yeah…" Harper managed a weak chuckle. "We slept on garbage a few times. Happens."

Madison made a face as she picked up her dirty shirt and shorts.

They headed back out to the store. Cliff and Jonathan had stuffed one of the shopping bags full.

At the sight of it, Harper laughed for real.

Both of them looked at her.

"What?" asked Cliff.

"It's just ironic that you kinda arrested me for shoplifting one pair of pants. Now you're helping us raid a whole store."

He laughed. "Yeah, I guess that is funny."

Madison put her clothes and flops into the other shopping bag. She sat on the floor beside it trying to make her iPhone work while Harper ran around gathering more stuff for her to wear, grabbing anything in the girl's size, plus a couple of larger items she could grow into.

"That should about do it." Cliff nudged the overstuffed shopping bags with his shoe. "We should probably take this whole store, but we're going to have to carry it all."

"Yeah." Harper reached for the bag of 'Maddie clothes.'

Jonathan beat her to it. "I'll carry it. You got shotgun."

"Heh." She smiled on the outside, but cringed mentally. Dad trusted her with a gun, but that had been a big mistake. She should've been hiding under the table with Madison.

Harper acted tough, but dreaded she'd freeze again the next time someone wanted to hurt her.

10

NEXT TIME

L ooting done, they headed out and crossed the hall to another place that had clothes in Harper's size.

There, she filled another shopping bag. Unlike the kids, she didn't have to worry too much about growing out of things. It didn't seem terribly likely she'd get fat given that food had become more a question of 'will there be any' instead of what to eat. Had she been there only with the kids, she'd have changed by the display rack, but with Cliff there, she couldn't bring herself to. Harper collected new jeans and a shirt, along with clean underwear. Madison refused to leave her side and followed her into the changing room. After bathing together, a quick change didn't bother her at all. Wearing stuff that still smelled new made her feel a little better. She gathered her dirty stuff—no sense wasting clothing—and went back out to the store, spending a few minutes collecting extra clothes in her size, which she stuffed into a bag.

On the way out of the changing room, she spotted a rack of long-sleeved sweaters. She pulled one on and collected three more to take with. It felt like such a waste to leave so much stuff behind, but no way could she carry the store's entire inventory up into the mountains. Harper contented herself with their modest haul. Wearing the same few items over and over again beat having only one outfit. Also, once they got to safety in Evergreen, she could think about washing clothes.

"Hey, Cliff?" asked Harper as they left the store.

"Hmm?"

"How did people wash clothes before laundry machines? Or did they?"

He laughed. "By hand, then hang them up on a line to dry."

"Oh."

"Shit," muttered Cliff.

She pulled her gaze off the floor, looked at him, and followed his stare to a group of men emerging from a cookie shop, all wearing various types of blue fabric scraps as necklaces.

One guy swung a compound crossbow off his shoulder and aimed it toward Cliff. "Hey old man. Hand over the girls and maybe you get to walk away."

"Dude," whispered a guy next to him, armed with a metal bat. "Sick. The one's way too little."

"She won't be little forever, dumbass," said Crossbow Man. "Gotta catch 'em all."

"Down!" yelled Cliff.

The barked command punched Harper straight in her childhood, and she obeyed without thinking. Whether or not he'd meant it for her or only the smaller kids, she ducked behind a vendor cart full of cheap earrings, grabbing Madison close. Jonathan scrambled over and she clamped onto him, too.

Cliff drew his pistol, diving to the right. A strange *thwoonk* preceded a distant *crack*. Wherever the crossbow shot went, it hadn't hit anyone. Two quick gunshots came from Cliff's direction. A man screamed in pain. Multiple other men shouted war cries.

Harper cringed each time the pistol fired. Sneakers squeaked on tile, and the grunting of men fighting accompanied deep meaty *thuds* and groans.

A guy in cargo shorts and a Marlboro T-shirt zipped around the earring cart and smiled down at her. "Hey, Red. Relax, baby. We'll take good care of you."

She raised the shotgun at him.

"Aww, don't be like that."

They stared at each other for a few long seconds, the grunts and thumps of Cliff fighting still going on behind her.

Marlboro grinned. He grasped the front of the shotgun and pushed it aside.

"Harper," said Jonathan. "What are you doing? Shoot him."

"Screw off, kid." Marlboro pulled a knife from his belt and pointed it at Jonathan. "Get outta here while you still have a tongue."

Madison whimpered.

"Aww, it's okay, girlie." Marlboro smiled. "You ain't gotta do anything 'til you grow up."

Dad's death replayed in her mind over the span of a half second. Harper lunged to her feet. She tried to aim the shotgun at him, but he controlled the end, keeping it pointed into a video game store.

Jonathan looked about ready to attack the guy, but hesitated, staring at the knife.

Another man came around the cash register side of the earring cart and grabbed Madison from behind.

Harper screamed in anger and lunged forward, ramming her knee into Marlboro's crotch. He let out a gasping *oof* and doubled over. The instant he lost his grip on the shotgun, she mashed the butt end into his face, knocking him over backward with blood streaming out of his mouth. She spun, putting the barrel of the gun inches from the other guy's nose.

"Let go of her."

The guy dropped Madison and took a step back, hands in the air. Despite her calm expression, Madison dashed over and clamped onto Harper with a fierce hug. The man who'd grabbed her backed up another step. They stared at each other for three seconds. Evidently convinced she wouldn't shoot, he bolted off.

Harper's eyes welled with tears. "I'm sorr—"

"Look out!" shouted Jonathan.

Marlboro jumped on her from behind, knife at her throat, other hand around her waist. "Bitch. You're gonna bleed for that. Drop the goddamned cannon."

She tightened her grip on the shotgun. *He wants to rape me. He's not gonna kill me.*

A gunshot went off nearby, along with Marlboro twitching. The strength left his arms and his knife fell from her throat, clattering to the ground beside the body. She shifted her gaze to the left at Cliff, six feet away, his handgun still up.

He didn't appear seriously hurt, though had a bloody lip. "You okay?"

"Y-yeah." Harper looked down, overcome with shame.

"Hey..." Cliff hurried over and put a hand on her shoulder. "It's okay.

You're still a kid yourself. I'd be more worried if you could shoot people like it was nothing."

"They almost got Maddie."

"They didn't." Cliff grasped her head in both hands, forcing her to make eye contact. "You're okay. Your sister's okay. Jon's okay. C'mon. We're getting out of here. Evergreen's safe, right? No idiots there with blue sashes."

Harper managed to nod. "Sorry, Termite. I'm sorry."

"Dad doesn't like hurting people either. He only did it to protect us." Madison stared into her eyes for a long moment that left Harper unsure if she'd meant Dad or Cliff by that statement.

Her mind swam with nausea and guilt. Again, she had hesitated. This time, it might not have meant someone she loved would die, but being locked up in some nightmare harem situation with her little sister sounded worse than death. The nausea came partly from that, but also at the thought Cliff had shot Marlboro in the head while he held her from behind. That bullet had come within inches of *her* head, too.

Jonathan gathered up the shopping bags he'd been carrying. Cliff took the crossbow and a nylon case with more bolts. They returned to the TGI Friday's in silence, fortunately without any more contact from the 'blue gang.' Madison headed to a wall outlet near the kitchen door, plugged in her phone charger, and sat with the device in her lap, staring at it while waiting for it to get enough power to turn on.

Harper sighed. *Does she really think it's going to work?*

Cliff took the shopping bags and transferred their contents to one giant duffel, carefully folding each piece to maximize how much he could cram into it. "Gonna go grab a couple of other things real quick. Are you okay to stay here and keep an eye on the kids?"

He knows I messed up again. Is this some kinda test or did he really not realize I'm a chickenshit? "Uhh, sure."

"Good. I won't be long. Gonna lock the front gate after I leave."

She blinked at him.

"You're not trapped. Back door goes to the employee hallway, but it can only be opened from inside. I'd rather get started on a long walk earlier in the day. Figure we'll head out first light tomorrow."

"Okay." Harper sat on the floor next to Madison, setting the shotgun down to her right.

She kept quiet, too ashamed of herself to even apologize. Her brain threw her into a waking nightmare that spanned every scenario between the gang treating her like a battered wife in a relatively normal house to her and Maddie winding up chained in a basement like slaves.

The rattle of the security gate closing pulled her back from the precipice of sobbing uncontrollably. Cliff's blurry figure headed off into the mall. She wiped at her teary eyes and picked the shotgun up.

Madison kept staring at the dead iPhone, outwardly calm.

After a few minutes of puttering around inside the 'bedroom,' Jonathan wandered over and sat on Harper's right. "Nice shot."

"What? I didn't... I couldn't..."

He grinned and mimed bashing someone in the head with a rifle. "Naw. You whacked him in the face."

"She protected us," said Madison, matter-of-factly. "I think the man who grabbed me crapped his pants when she pointed the gun at him."

Jonathan laughed. "Yeah. Never saw anyone run that fast before."

No. No. No. I didn't protect you guys, I messed up. If Cliff didn't shoot him... She started to cry again. At least he hadn't been killed for saving her like Dad.

Madison hugged the iPhone to her chest. "Mom's trying to call us. Come on. Work."

Jonathan leaned against Harper, a big, trusting smile on his face.

Stop looking at me like that. I'm gonna mess up and get you killed. She squeezed the shotgun. *I can't mess up again. I won't let anyone hurt you guys.* Harper let a slow breath out of her nose. Killing a man trying to hurt them couldn't possibly be as bad as listening to Madison scream in pain. How old would they let her get before they...

Harper shuddered at the thought, then stared at the Mossberg in her hands. Next time she hesitated, Cliff might not be able to help. If she chickened out again, horrible, evil things would happen to Madison. Jonathan would have it easy. They'd only kill him.

She couldn't allow there to be a 'next time.'

11

EXODUS

Harper spent the time waiting for Cliff to return thinking about playing *Fortnite*, *Call of Duty*, and any number of a dozen other games where shooting people had been no big deal. Of course, it had all been pixels, not real people. Dad had taken her to the shooting range all the time. She'd been around guns for years, even winning competitions. She never had a problem with guns or paper targets. Even her vegetarian tree-hugging little sister found target practice fun. Hunting, not so much. Fortunately, their father hadn't been a big proponent of hunting to begin with and the first time Madison had a freak-out at the thought of shooting a deer, he'd given it up.

Cliff returned not quite an hour later with a huge hiker's backpack and some other supplies he'd likely raided from the Sports Authority, mostly camping stuff. He'd also brought winter coats for everyone. Jonathan broke out an Uno set, and they whiled away the remainder of the daylight with that. Cliff went to sleep two hours before anyone else, right after dinner, after telling Harper to put the kids to bed and wake him up as close as she could guess to two hours after sunset.

She felt like she'd gotten away with a horrible crime by his trusting her to 'stand watch' while he slept. Again, she questioned if he knew how badly she'd wimped out. Though, if anyone tried to break into the restaurant, she wouldn't have to kill them. If that shotgun went off once, even if she missed on purpose, it would wake everyone up.

Jonathan wore only his briefs to bed. Madison didn't react much to that other than blushing. She retreated to the bathroom to change again into the big white T-shirt, and crawled into the same sleeping bag she'd used the previous night.

Harper wandered the restaurant, the only one awake, trying to picture it normal and open for business. It couldn't be *that* late yet. The place would've still been open at this hour if not for a nuclear strike. She leaned against a column and daydreamed about people eating. More than the quiet emptiness, standing there with a loaded shotgun and not the least bit of worry that a cop would show up to arrest her felt unreal. It didn't seem probable that the gang would roam the mall looking for girls at night, since no one could see a damn thing. Still, she kept away from the front gate to avoid being seen.

After waking Cliff at the appointed time, Harper decided to accept a little comfort, and changed into one of his T-shirts before sharing the cot with Madison. Even asleep, her sister noticed her presence and snuggled. Harper held her like a living doll. Overcome with guilt, she cried herself to sleep.

For breakfast, they ate pre-wrapped brownies, likely a smaller component of some 10,000 calorie 'diabetes-on-a-plate' dessert the restaurant had once served. Still, the things would probably last twenty years. The toilets remained dry and nonfunctional, likely due to all the water being loose downstairs. Still, using them beat going outside.

Cliff distributed their supplies for the trip. He took the huge backpack and the duffel bag full of everyone's clothes. Harper carried her backpack of canned food as well as her giant purse. Madison had the toiletry bag plus her little backpack of things she liked from Hot Topic. Jonathan wore a child-sized hiker's backpack with some provisions, extra shoes, and some of the camping supplies. Cliff handed out white facemasks like something house painters might wear.

Surprisingly, Madison didn't protest, even if the mask wound up being big on her.

"Ain't much, but it'll help a bit with all the dust in the air," said Cliff.

Upon exiting the restaurant, he shut and locked the security gate.

"Umm?" Harper raised an eyebrow.

"Just in case we need a place to come back to."

She cringed. Never had it even occurred to her that Evergreen could be a lie. It made sense to at least take the precaution of locking the gate. She nodded, grateful he hadn't aired his doubts aloud and worried the kids.

They made their way around to the escalator. Everyone except Cliff removed their shoes. Then again, he had some kind of Army boots on that looked like they could handle getting wet much better than sneakers. Harper rolled her jean legs up. Jonathan removed his jeans entirely, content to deal with the flooded downstairs in his briefs. Madison peeled her socks off but made no effort to protect her jeans from water.

"Maddie…" Harper put a hand on her shoulder. "Might not be a bad idea to keep your clothes as dry as possible. It's cold out."

Her sister looked at Jonathan, shrugged, and took her pants off. "I feel stupid being outside in my underpants with a winter coat on."

"Stupid is better than pneumonia." Harper frowned at her pitiful attempt to roll her jean legs up, and also pulled them off. "I hate floods."

"So do most people." Cliff led the way down the stairs, sloshing into the not-quite-knee-deep water.

"Any idea where all this water came from?" asked Harper. The instant her foot touched the freezing liquid, she squealed.

"Main gave out in the boiler room. The water tower down the road emptied into the mall," said Cliff.

He avoided the front entrance, opting instead to take a maintenance hallway in back that led to a loading ramp for trucks. Trash bags, mops, and other debris floated by in the flooded passage. The air stank of rotting garbage strong enough that Madison gagged a few times. Harper decided to hold her breath as much as she could. They waded across the storage room and climbed up out of the water to the inside of the loading dock by a row of large roll-top doors.

Harper fished a towel out of her giant purse and handed it to Madison.

"If you ever run out of ammo for that Mossberg, you can use that bag as a club," said Cliff.

Harper smirked, but couldn't resist a slight chuckle.

Once everyone had dried off and gotten dressed, they exited the mall in a single file line with Cliff in the lead, Jonathan behind him, then Madison, Harper bringing up the rear. Spending two days inside the mall made the smoky haze outside feel thicker and more claustrophobic. The suggestion of wearing facemasks sounded a bit lame at first, but with it on, the air tasted less like burning. She coughed a few times at the mere thought she'd been breathing this stuff.

They crossed the parking lot to the edge of the mall property and kept heading west. Cliff had snagged a compass when he'd gone off on his solo scavenger hunt, so Harper didn't pay too much attention to the surroundings, grateful to be able to let someone else deal with figuring out which way to go. Having to do that *plus* keep an eye out for danger had been nerve wracking.

Everywhere she looked, for the thirty or so feet the fog let her see, she found broken windows, scorched buildings, and half-melted cars. Harper thought back to hiding in the basement of her home with her parents and Madison for several days after the blast. No official warning ever came from the government; not until detonations started happening along the East Coast did media outlets have a clue the proverbial shit had hit the fan.

She'd been convinced a nuclear wave would tear the house away above them, but after a few days passed, she accepted it wouldn't happen. Harper tried to make a deal with the universe in her head, willing to give anything to go back in time to when she'd been cowering in her basement, shaking whenever a terrifying rumble came from distant explosions. The loudest one had to have been the hit on Colorado Springs, since tornado force winds ripped by overhead soon after. The instant the power went out, the world became a scary dream. When the gang first showed up a month or so later, the scary dream had become a terrible reality. If she could go back to that point, she wouldn't hesitate. Dad would still be alive. Better, she'd protest going upstairs.

But time travel only existed in movies. She shook the shotgun to chase away a light coating of ash. Cliff headed out of the parking lot, up onto Route 70. Ash flakes, or maybe actual snow, stirred in the wind. The haze cut off vision after about forty feet, making the city she'd grown up in feel like an alien environment. Every lamp post they passed tilted to one side, no doubt a result of the blast wave.

They walked in silence, save for the rattle of cans in her backpack. Harper gazed around at smashed cars, bent traffic signs, patches of dried blood here and there, and even a few bodies strewn about. She couldn't keep both hands on her shotgun *and* make sure Madison didn't look at any of the gore, so she hoped her kid sister remained preoccupied with her iPhone. Like everything else electronic, it had blown out the first day. She wondered if Madison truly believed the battery had gone dead, or if she refused to accept reality. Dad's horrible joke about the EMP wave frying the banks made her tear up again.

Well, the house is paid off!

Shouts came from the left. Harper swiveled in that direction, aiming at a pack of men rushing toward them from a Hyundai dealership. They whooped, hollered, and pointed at the highway.

Harper's tears retreated back into her eyes. Her heart raced.

"C'mere, Red," shouted one. "That one's mine! I call dibs!"

"The hell you say, Spider," roared another, before laughing.

"Get 'em!" yelled another. "You all come wif us an don' fight none, we promise not ta hurt 'cha."

Madison looked up from the dead screen, her face noticeably paler than usual—which said a lot. "I think he's lying."

"Down," said Cliff. He grabbed Jonathan by a fistful of jacket and dragged him to the right, taking cover behind parked cars in a lot across the street from the Hyundai place.

In Harper's mind, a pack of thugs grabbed Madison and carried her screaming into a dark place. *No!* She dashed left, toward the middle of the highway and took cover behind an abandoned police car. Bullets whizzed by from the distant thugs, though they seemed to be firing at Cliff—not a girl they wanted to grab. The hazy scene in front of her looked like something out of a zombie survival video game. Imaginary screams in Madison's voice haunted the back of her mind. She rose up on her knees, lifting the shotgun and firing over the hood at the pack of men closer to her. The Mossberg hammered her shoulder, but she held her balance.

Madison, who'd followed her, fell to her knees and screamed at the *boom.*

Three of the thugs hit the ground; the one in the middle didn't move again, but the two on either side of him writhed about, wailing in pain, covered in blood trails from stray pellets. Harper dropped down and scooted to the left as the other guys in that group all opened up on her with handguns. *Clanks* and *cracks* surrounded her from the barrage striking the car. A spray of red plastic fragments fell around her when a bullet hit the emergency lights. Hunkered against the rear wheel, she glanced over at Cliff, in the other parking lot about twenty feet away from her. He popped up, fired his hand cannon twice, and ducked a split second before return fire riddled the small orange SUV in front of him.

Jonathan curled up in a ball next to Cliff, both hands over his head.

Madison, sitting on the road beside Harper, kept poking the button of her iPhone, making angry faces at it for not turning on.

"What are you doing?" rasped Harper. "Get down!"

"I'm trying to call 911," whispered Madison. "And I *am* down. I can't get any more down without digging a hole."

"You goddamned bitch!" shrieked a man, sounding frighteningly close. "I'm gonna—"

Harper sprang up, aiming over the trunk. She locked eyes with a twentysomething guy in a black leather jacket. His face warped with rage, he ran toward her as if intending to jump clear over the car. Imagining this guy tearing Madison out of her clothes destroyed hesitation. Harper squeezed the trigger. The Mossberg bucked into the tender spot it made on her shoulder; most of the man's face disintegrated in a spray of red schlock and flying teeth. The body twisted into a fatal pirouette, collapsing mere feet away from the car.

Another gang punk lay dead atop a rifle in the middle of the intersection, bleeding from the chest, Cliff's first target. The others, all armed with a mixture of handguns, bats, and axes, had scattered to cover behind cars. One idiot tried to hide behind a decorative boulder at the edge of the Hyundai lot. Harper didn't bother firing a shotgun at a guy thirty feet away, but within a second of her noticing him, a spritz of blood flew from his head along with a *bang* from Cliff's direction.

The remaining three guys focused on Harper threw a few more bullets her way, but nothing came closer than gouging the roof of the police cruiser. She fired twice; her second shot blew out the windshield of a blue car and sent the man hiding behind it running.

Guess Dad was right. Shotguns scare people away.

Madison let out a scream.

Harper whirled, aiming at a scrawny man with a shaved head who had come out of nowhere behind them and grabbed Madison. She tried to point the gun at his head, but couldn't bring herself to pull the trigger for fear of hitting her sister. The man grinned evilly at Harper while shielding his chest with the thrashing child. Madison screamed and flailed, pounding and kicking at him, but he largely ignored her, still holding a handgun to the side of her head. At the touch of metal to her temple, Madison went still.

"Drop the cannon," said the guy.

"Not happening." Harper kept the shotgun pointed at his face. "I drop this, we're both as good as dead. How stupid do you think I am? Put her down *now.*"

He hiked Madison higher, using her head to protect his face. "Go on, girlie. Shoot us both. You ain't got the nerve. Scatter shot gonna kill your precious little kiddie, too."

Madison squirmed, both hands clutching the arm at her chest.

Jonathan darted out from cover and sprinted across the street. A bullet or two pinged off the ground behind him. He charged in and leapt onto the man's back, hitting the guy hard enough to make him stumble into a spin. Madison fought like a shrieking wildcat the instant the gun broke contact with her skin, wriggling loose from his grip and dropping to all fours. The guy grabbed Jonathan by the jacket, hauling him off his back and around in front of him. He bit the man's wrist, drawing blood, clamping down with his teeth until the man lost his grip on the handgun, which clattered to the pavement.

Cliff fired a few times rapidly, but he had his hands full from the rest of the gang peppering his cover with a steady hail of bullets.

"Jonathan, get down!" yelled Harper, angling for a clear shot.

The thug wrestled with the boy, trying to cling to the only reason he hadn't eaten a face full of buckshot. Harper considered lunging in and walloping him with the butt, but didn't want to risk having him grab the weapon and yank it away from her. He looked stronger than her by a good margin.

Growling, Jonathan tried to kick him in the balls, but the guy saw it coming and twisted away, redirecting the hit to his hip. He backpedaled, seeming content to run off with Jonathan instead of Madison.

Bang.

A spurt of blood sprayed from the man's side. He let off a wheeze and collapsed to one knee. The instant Jonathan wormed free of his grip, Harper blasted him near point blank. Buckshot slapped into his chest, flinging him into the pavement atop a spatter of crimson.

Stunned, Harper glanced over at the source of the single shot.

Madison stood in a wide stance, both hands clutching the thug's dropped Glock. A wisp of smoke curled up from the barrel. She shifted her gaze to Harper. "Ow. This thing hurt my hand. And it's too loud, not like Dad's."

Cliff lunged to his feet and fired another shot. A groaning "Oof" replied from the distant haze along with the *thump* of a body hitting the ground. "Kid, you okay?"

Madison stared at the gun, continuing to hold it in both hands, aimed forward. "What do I do with this? I can't find the safety. I don't wanna shoot myself."

"Get down!" Harper whirled to cover the street, but the only guys with blue sashes in sight lay dead where they'd fallen. The rest had run off either scared or wounded.

Cliff jogged over and took the gun from Madison. She smiled, happy to be rid of it.

"We gotta move. More will have heard that." Cliff tucked the Glock in a side pocket of his backpack.

"Yeah." Harper hefted her shotgun in one hand and grabbed Madison by the wrist.

Barely ten steps later, a man leapt out from behind a truck and charged at Harper with a hatchet. Cliff rushed sideways, intercepting the guy. Before Harper could even blink, Cliff had flipped him over onto the ash-covered ground and broken his arm. He yanked a knife from the thug's belt and jammed it into his back with two precise thrusts that killed the man in seconds.

Harper gawked. "Holy shit... are you like a Navy SEAL or something?"

Cliff stood, waving them to keep going. "Nah. Army."

She trotted along after him, dragging Madison, who struggled to keep up. "Seriously? Army? Which part?"

Cliff checked over the AR-15 he'd grabbed from one of the dead men. "My last tour was with the Seventy-Fifth Ranger Battalion."

"Oh." Harper nodded out of reflex. That sounded pretty impressive, whatever it meant. "Cool. Kinda overkill for mall security, isn't it?"

"Hah." He laughed. "Like I said, I saw enough crap to last a lifetime over there. Wanted something quiet."

"Sorry for shoplifting," said Harper. "Thanks for letting me just go home."

"It's okay, kid. Geez, you were scared shitless. You didn't seem like the kinda kid who got off on stealing. I couldn't do it to ya." He chuckled. "Now those little punks with the bad attitudes, they needed the object lesson."

Warmth spread over Harper's cheeks. Yeah, maybe she had been terrified. Probably why she never shoplifted again—or spoke to Denise after that. The girl dared her to steal as a 'coolness test.'

A faint thump came from behind, but Harper ignored it.

"Harp! My phone!" yelled Madison. "I dropped it."

"It's dead," said Cliff. "Junk."

Madison burst into tears, wailing, "But Mom is gonna call me! An' I don't wanna miss it if Becca, Melissa, or Eva text me!"

Harper kept going, grimacing at the heart-rending sobs coming from her little sister. The phone *was* junk. It would never work again. Even if it somehow came back to life, the whole cellular network had been fried.

"Harp! Please!" Madison set her heels, her sneakers plowing trenches in the ash layer. "My phone."

It was pointless, but… it did make her feel better. Harper slowed to a stop. "Okay. Hurry up."

Cliff spun, raising the rifle to cover the rear as Madison sprinted back for the gleaming patch of black glass embedded in the moonlike fluff. Harper ran after her, refusing to let her sister get more than an arm's length away.

A handful of people in blue sashes, likely attracted to the gunfire from earlier, came running out of the smoke on the left. One charged straight at what he must've thought an easy grab of a child, and about shit himself when Harper shoved Madison aside and raised the Mossberg. The other two fired down the street toward Cliff.

Harper squeezed the trigger. Madison clamped her hands over her ears and fell on top of her phone, cringing from the deafening *boom*. The guy who'd come running at her lurched to a halt as his chest erupted in a ripple of red spots. Harper fired again, reducing his face to a ruin of flesh. In her blurry awareness of the world behind him, the other two thugs collapsed dead on the steps of the building they'd come from.

She glanced back at Cliff who must've taken them out with the rifle.

Harper grabbed for Madison's arm. The girl swiped her phone from the road, still sobbing, and darted away from her toward Cliff. Harper raced after her.

"I'm sorry!" wailed Madison. She flew into a hug, wrapping her arms around Cliff and bawling, her face buried against his chest.

Harper slowed to a nervous jog when she noticed the blood running down his arm.

"Just a through-and-through," said Cliff. "Keep going."

She looked down.

"It's fine." Cliff patted Harper's shoulder and muttered, "Kid needs it."

Madison let go of Cliff and pounce-hugged Harper, sniffling.

"C'mon, Termite. We gotta get out of here before more bad guys show up."

"'Kay." Madison took Harper's hand.

They walked for hours, following the highway, mercifully free of contact with any more hostile idiots. One guy at the edge of visibility in the haze waved at them, but made no move to approach or flee. For much of their journey, they passed by lines of abandoned cars left in place when the EMP washed over everything. By early evening, they walked along where scrub brush dotted the ground on both sides of the pavement, and the air had become noticeably less hazy.

Cliff guided them to a spot where they could rest and shrugged off his backpack. While Jonathan and Madison wandered off in different directions to pee, he dug a small box out of the backpack and handed it to Harper. Next, he unpacked a glass bottle of clear liquid.

She looked down at it. "Sewing kit?"

"Yeah. There's tweezers in there too." Cliff pulled his sleeve up, exposing a bullet wound on his bicep. "Gonna need you to dig the slug out and sew the sucker closed. Toss a splash of this in the hole after the slug's gone."

"What is it?"

"Everclear."

"Booze?"

He nodded. "Almost pure alcohol."

She squirmed. "You want me to like sew *you*?"

Cliff leaned closer, giving her a flat look. "Cellular plans are getting expensive these days."

"Sorry." Harper bit her lip. "I know it's broken, but I couldn't make her—"

"Yeah, I get it. No harm, no foul. Just do the thing."

Jonathan, evidently aware of what went on with the needle-and-thread, occupied Madison a safe distance away so she wouldn't see the amateur surgery. The two of them practiced a few dance moves, which appeared to pull Madison out of her shell at least for a little while.

Cringing every step of the way, Harper knelt beside Cliff and picked at the wound with the tweezers until she unearthed a deformed pistol slug. Though he grimaced plenty and turned bright red, the man barely made a sound the whole time, even as she splashed Everclear into the hole and stitched it up.

Watching him withstand pain like that got her hands shaking. "You're like the terminator of mall security."

He forced a chuckle. "Is that my cue to say something cheesy like '*I'll be back*'?"

"I don't wanna go back there." Harper squinted into the wind, staring over her shoulder in the direction of the foggy mess that used to be Lakewood. "It's not my home anymore. There's nothing there but bad memories." She let out a long breath. "So, umm. Now what?"

"Now..." Cliff snagged the bottle of Everclear. Much to Harper's surprise, he capped it rather than drank. "We head on up to Evergreen and hope what you heard was right. If not, maybe we keep going until we find some place better than that mall. Too damn many of those shitheads out there, and it's only going to get worse."

She nodded, then leaned in to rest her head on his un-shot shoulder. "If Evergreen's what I'm hoping it is, are you gonna stay with us?"

"Hmm." He patted her back. "Yeah. Maybe I can do that. You don't seem like the 'alone type.'"

Harper smiled, watching her sister and Jonathan dancing about and grinning at each other. The two of them looked well on their way to being close. Madison had always been slow to make friends, hence only having three—but she made *close* friends. Despite him being the only other kid her age around, she warmed to him abnormally fast. *Guess I'm not the only one who's changed.* She took a couple shells from her purse and stuffed them into the Mossberg. "I used to be so shy and timid."

"Used to?" asked Cliff. "Got over it?"

She pulled back the side handle to chamber a shell, then stuffed one more into it. "Yeah. Stupid nuclear war."

Cliff laughed. "Ready to get going?"

"Yeah. You?"

He rolled his left arm around at the shoulder. "Hurts like hell, but I'll deal with it."

"Cool. I guess we should keep walking. Evergreen or bust."

Cliff groaned as he stood and pulled the backpack on. "Never say that. The 'or bust' part. Don't taunt luck."

"Sorry." She waved for the kids to come back over. "After you."

Cliff led the way down the road. Harper followed a step behind and a little to the right, scanning their surroundings for any sign of danger. She couldn't figure out exactly at what point she had gone from being afraid to leave home for college to roaming a highway with a loaded shotgun. The world had plunged into utter chaos, but she'd do whatever it took to protect her little sister.

Her lips curled in a furtive smile at Cliff and Jonathan.

She even wanted to protect the new family she'd found. Harper teased her finger at the trigger guard. She'd killed someone. Several someones. While she took no joy in it, that she didn't feel crushing guilt over it worried her. Maybe it would hit her some night soon and she'd wake up in tears. For the moment, shooting those thugs had no more impact than killing enemies in a video game.

"Can we stop at Starbucks?" asked Madison, her voice somewhat muffled under the face mask.

"I'll think about it," said Cliff. "All that sugar's bad for your health."

The kids laughed.

As did Harper.

12

INTERSTATE 70

C liff advanced at a cautious pace, opting for quiet. The roughly two-inch-deep ash layer padded their footsteps, but it also made it possible for anyone to sneak up on them.

They walked for barely an hour before Madison asked for a bathroom break. She didn't like it when Cliff stopped right on the road and said, "Okay." She liked it even less when Harper pointed out the lack of a toilet anywhere nearby. Reluctantly, she wandered a few steps off the road. Everyone turned their back.

"So, we're gonna take Route 70 until it splits to 74, which'll go right into Evergreen." Cliff pointed ahead.

"How far is it?" Harper looked around at the hint of a residential neighborhood south of the highway. They hadn't gotten too far away from the mall yet, but the haze killed any sense of familiarity the area might've had.

"On foot? Probably somewhere between six to eight hours depending on pace. No reason to bust our asses though." Cliff bounced his backpack up a little higher. "You almost done, kiddo?"

"I can't start. It's too cold. Don't look!"

"Think about a waterfall," said Jonathan. "All that water pouring over a cliff and falling down."

"Aww, dammit," muttered Cliff. "Gimme a sec."

He walked over to the opposite side of the road from Madison. Jonathan laughed, but shrugged and went over to stand next to him. Harper sighed—deliberately not thinking about waterfalls. She figured it would be pretty difficult to get lost. Following a highway composed of two three-lane roads separated by a dirt median had to be one of the simpler things she'd ever done. Of course, the hard part came in not being shot or kidnapped.

She contemplated history before the modern sense of morality developed. The society she'd grown accustomed to didn't exactly treat women and girls well, but it had been *way* better than ancient times or even some foreign countries. Without the courts and police, only the shotgun in her hands stood between her and whatever men wanted to do to her. Of course, she didn't expect *every* man to be like that—Cliff certainly wouldn't treat her like an object—but it would only take *one* bad guy. And Lakewood sure seemed to have a ton of them. Had they all lost their minds after the blast? What could've driven reasonably normal people to becoming a roving gang like that?

She clenched her jaw, hoping with all the energy she could project into the universe that Evergreen would be safe.

I've been through a horrible experience. The whole world can't be full of crazy people trying to have sex with everything that moves.

Once bathroom breaks finished, they continued walking. She glanced left at the hints of houses in the haze, at the top of a hill covered in ashy grass. A woman's scream drew her attention further back. Harper stopped and squinted into the fog. Cliff, evidently having heard the woman as well, also stopped.

Madison and Jonathan scurried off to the side, taking cover by a small box truck abandoned in the middle of the highway.

A woman emerged from the haze at a full run. Something about the way she moved seemed strange... until she drew closer and it became clear her arms were tied behind her back—and she had nothing on from the waist down. Three men with blue sashes came running after her, one carrying a baseball bat, the other two apparently unarmed.

The woman veered to the right, sprinting straight at her. "Help!" she shouted. "Please!"

Harper raised the shotgun, aiming at the guy with the bat. "Stop!"

All three thugs skidded to a halt, staring at her. Bat Man looked ready to wet his pants. The guy on the right leered at Harper while the other man narrowed his eyes in anger. The woman ran up to her, bare feet kicking up an ash cloud. She doubled over, gasping for breath, wheezing and crying.

"Get out of here and don't let me see you again," shouted Harper.

The three men stared at her for a few seconds in uneasy silence.

A gun went off to her right, nearly startling her into pulling the trigger. Squinty's head rocked back, a spurt of blood flying as he collapsed. The other two men ran off, screaming and zig-zagging around. Harper glanced over at Cliff. He lowered his arm and replaced his gun in its holster.

I could've shot them if they came after us. She flinched at the mental image of that one man's face exploding when she'd shot him. *I'd do it, again and again, to keep Maddie safe.*

Harper turned toward the woman. She looked thin, early twenties with long brown hair and light brown skin. Her grungy T-shirt gave off a 'worn for a couple weeks' vibe. Given the lack of dirt on her lower body, she'd only been recently deprived of pants. Thick plastic cable ties secured her wrists behind her back, so tight her hands had turned red. Seeing this woman reminded her of the 'soldiers' arresting people, but she didn't look like the same woman who'd been taken away by the men in camo.

"That lady doesn't have any pants." Madison crept over.

"Thank you!" The woman squirmed, cringed, and turned her back. "Hey, could you please cut me loose?"

"Why'd you shoot that guy?" Harper looked at Cliff. "They were probably going to run."

"One, they were gonna do... stuff to this woman. Two, she needs clothes and he was the closest in size."

Harper blinked. "You killed a guy for his clothes?"

Cliff smiled. "Not entirely. He was about to pull a gun. Just got lucky on the size thing."

Her mouth hung open.

"I know you didn't notice. That's why I shot him." Cliff walked over to the dead guy and rolled him onto his chest, revealing a handgun tucked in the waist of his pants. "Lotta guys hide weapons back here. In a situation like that standoff, always watch their hands, not their eyes."

The boy approached, blushing but unable to stop looking at the woman. "Hi. I'm Jon."

"Summer."

"It's winter." Madison shot her a confused look.

"Her name is Summer. I'm Harper. So, umm, what's your story?" Despite the woman's present state of clear helplessness, she didn't fully trust her.

"Why don't you have pants?" asked Madison. "It's too cold for flip flops, so you should have pants on."

"Uhh, I lost them." Summer looked off to the side.

"How do you lose your pants?" Madison scrunched up her nose.

"I'll explain later." Harper nudged her sister toward Jonathan. "You two go sit by that truck and stay down for a bit, okay?"

Madison leaned against Harper, stare fixed on the woman. "Why are you tied up? Did you get arrested?"

Summer went scarlet in the face, shivering. "No. I was kidnapped."

Cliff removed the dead man's sneakers, socks, and pants—leaving the underwear on him.

"The bad people wanted to do bad things to her," said Harper.

"They started doing bad things to me, but I got away."

"Oh. Are you cold?" asked Madison.

"F-freezing." Summer looked at Harper as if searching her. "You got a knife or something? Will you please cut me loose?"

Madison pulled her iPhone out. "I'll call 911."

"I don't have a knife and I don't think you want me to use this"— Harper hefted the shotgun—"on zip ties."

"I've been stuck like this for hours," said Summer. "Running all over trying to hide, but they kept finding me somehow."

Jonathan pointed at the ash on the road. "Footprints."

Cliff hurried over, handed the pants/socks/sneakers bundle to Jonathan, and pulled a knife from a sheath on his belt. "I gotcha."

He gingerly sawed at the plastic binding Summer's wrists, trying not to draw blood. While he worked, Jonathan held the pants so she could step into them. He pulled them up, buttoned them, and even did the zipper.

Eventually, the plastic gave way. Cliff grasped her left arm, slipped the knife under the remaining cable tie, and sliced it off.

"Oh, holy shit..." Summer waved her arms around. "Major pins and needles."

"The cops aren't answering," said Madison in a solemn tone.

"Cliff Barton." He offered a hand.

"Summer Vasquez." She shook hands, then hugged him. "You guys are awesome. Thank you *so* much. I barely got away from those bastards." She let go of him, hugged Harper, then sat on the road to put on the socks and sneakers, which looked a bit big on her. When she stood, Cliff gave her his winter coat. He took two sweaters out of the duffel to keep warm, then once again hoisted the large backpack on.

"Welcome to come with us if you want," said Cliff.

"Yeah… okay. That's cool. Where are you guys going?"

"Evergreen," said Jonathan. "Supposed to be people there."

Summer nodded. "Anywhere away from those lunatics is good with me."

Cliff resumed walking.

"So… how's a guy wind up with three kids?" asked Summer a few minutes later.

"You're not much older than me." Harper smirked.

"Thanks, but I'm older than I look. Twenty-two. You're what, seventeen or eighteen? Maybe sixteen?"

"Seventeen," grumbled Harper.

"Nothing wrong with being that age. I wish I could go back now that I know what's gonna happen. Wouldn't have wasted four years in college." Summer pulled her shirt up over her mouth and coughed. "Or I wouldn't have majored in business with a marketing minor."

"That'll come in handy," said Harper with a roll of the eyes. She sighed mentally at her parents taking her on various college tours. They must've wandered the campus of every college or university within an hour-and-a-half ride from home. Strange tidbits of randomness jumped out in her memory like a water fountain that squeaked at one place, a statue in a courtyard somewhere else or a funny glue-like smell in the dorms at the farthest campus. Driving almost two hours each way would've made commuting painful enough that she considered rooming at the school *if* she'd gone there. But she wanted to stay closer to home.

Summer laughed. "Yeah, seriously. I should've studied something useful like civil engineering. Took me months to even find a job after graduating. Everyone and their mother goes for business. Only got hired last May."

"Rough break." Cliff chuckled.

"Not really." Summer flapped her arms. "I'm still alive. We got nuked and all I lost was my job, that's pretty tame. Well, okay… my job, my apartment, car, I've got no idea where my friends are. No idea if my parents or brother are even still alive. Having a useless degree is pretty low on my list of things to be in a bad mood about. And I don't have to worry about repaying student loans anymore."

"You're in a bad mood?" asked Madison.

"Not so much at the moment. Still feeling pretty damn relieved that I got away from those guys."

Harper shuddered at the idea of being stuck half naked with her hands tied for hours while trying to run away from men. She clutched the shotgun like a security blanket and edged a little closer to Cliff.

"How'd that happen?" asked Cliff. "If you don't mind saying."

"Nah. You've already seen all my secrets. Not a big deal."

He chuckled.

"I had a little apartment on the north side of my building, so it avoided the worst of the blast. Spent a couple weeks raiding other apartments and nearby houses for stuff to eat. Didn't really have much of a plan where to go or what to do. Saw some soldiers rounding people up, but something about them didn't feel right."

"Soldiers?" Cliff glanced at her.

"I saw them, too." Harper explained watching three people being 'arrested.' "I didn't think they were real soldiers. Just guys in camo."

"That's a possibility." Cliff turned his attention forward. "You see them grab anyone, Summer?"

"Yeah. But they didn't like arrest them. Looked more like forced evacuation."

"Doesn't make sense. Evacuate to where?" Harper gazed up. "Hey, is the smoke clearing?"

"A bit." Cliff nodded. "We're out of the city now. Should keep getting better the farther we go. And if they're genuine military, probably trying to get people away from irradiated areas."

"How much is destroyed?" asked Summer.

"No idea. We're in a dead spot here. EMP knocked everything out. The entire country could be like this, or just big metro areas. Hard to tell." Cliff pulled his facemask down to spit.

"So, anyway... I fell asleep on this couch. Woke up with those guys grabbing me. It's kind of a blur really. As soon as they ripped my pants off, I freaked out. Pretty sure I kicked one guy where it hurt, mashed my head into the face of the dude holding me down, and ran like hell."

Cliff nodded, emitting a grunt of approval.

"Why do the bad people wanna steal pants?" asked Madison.

Harper's brain seized up, stuck between not wanting to break her sister's innocence and thinking she deserved to be afraid of those guys.

"Because they're *bad*. It's winter. It's really mean to steal someone's pants when it's cold out." Cliff looked back, wagged his eyebrows, and resumed scanning the area ahead of them.

"Yeah, it is." Madison nodded. "911 still isn't answering. I don't think they're going to."

Harper looked back at the haze, unable to see any sign of Lakewood, only grey nothingness. The only home she'd ever known lay miles behind her, overrun with likely harmful smoke and even more dangerous people. Some of the blue gang were women, which baffled her. She didn't bother trying to figure out how some women joined the gang while others became prey.

Crazy didn't follow rules. Maybe they liked violence, being able to kill without fear of going to jail. It didn't fall on Harper to make sense of a world gone mad.

She only had to survive it.

13

FULL STEAM AHEAD

They stopped on the dirt median for a quick lunch of granola bars and canned peaches.

Two smallish bottles of water made the rounds. Cliff hadn't brought all that much water, due to weight. Of course, Evergreen wouldn't take *too* long to reach. Twelve bottles should be plenty. Madison huddled close to her while eating, though didn't appear outwardly upset or frightened.

I-70 lay strewn with cars, many of them askew or crashed. The smoky haze remained, though not as dense as nearer the city. Visibility lengthened to about fifty yards, give or take drifting clouds.

A dead electronic traffic sign came into view up ahead, a short distance in front of an overpass covering a brief swath of ash-free road. Another two overpasses followed close together. Beyond them, the highway stretched straight ahead as far as the smoke let her see, running along the top of a narrow manmade ridge. On either side of the road, the land sloped down at perilous angles, making a climb down an unwelcome prospect.

After another hour or so, a large rocky wall rose up on the right side. They soon passed a sign—or at least what remained of it—indicating exit 259 up ahead for Morrison. A tractor-trailer had mowed it down, coming to a halt on its side at the start of the off ramp.

Cliff decided to investigate the trailer, hoping for useful stuff, but after battling the lock for some time, they discovered the rig carried appliances. He kicked the trailer door in protest and resumed walking.

"It's getting dark," said Madison, a short while later.

Harper looked up. Sure enough, the sky appeared to be dimming. "Already? It hasn't been that long, has it?"

"Could be bad weather coming in." Cliff waved for everyone to get moving. "Let's look for a place to find some cover."

Not long after, a huge, curved wall on the right with numerous tall light posts beyond it suggested some kind of complex up ahead. The brick wall eventually reached the road right beside them, without any obvious way up. Cliff veered to the right, hiking up a hill of sparse grass. This area didn't have much of any ash on the ground, which she thought might be a good sign. They passed a few boulders on the way up the hill, eventually reaching level ground: a huge parking lot. Cliff kept going toward a red awning on the far side of the lot.

Harper glanced at a sign reading 'Wooly Mammoth Lot,' unable to help but giggle at the oddity of it. The red awning turned out to belong to a Conoco station. The right half of the building, darker beige than the rest, had a sign reading 'Full Steam Ahead' coffee. Both the gas station convenience store and the coffee shop doors had been broken open already.

Cliff pulled his handgun and approached the coffee shop. Harper hung back a few steps with the kids and Summer huddling behind her. It felt a bit strange to have a twenty-two-year-old woman looking to her for protection, but she *did* have a giant shotgun. Harper paused, realizing she hadn't reloaded since the attack by the Hyundai dealership.

"Sec," whispered Harper.

Two steps from the door, Cliff looked back at her.

Harper reached into her purse and grabbed shells, stuffing them into the shotgun one after the next until it wouldn't hold any more. She dropped the extra two back into her bag, and grasped the weapon in both hands.

Cliff entered the coffee shop with his gun up. It didn't take him long to reappear and wave everyone inside. "Empty."

"Cool." Harper put her back to the wall next to the door, waiting for the kids and Summer to go in before following them. She did her best to close the battered door, wedging a chair under it.

"Not bad." Cliff pulled his facemask down and grinned. "Where'd you learn that?"

"Bad movies." She shrugged.

A thin layer of dust coated all the tables, the floor, even the counter, though the air didn't smell like burnt everything in here. Harper pulled off her facemask and tucked it into her coat pocket. Everyone unburdened themselves of backpacks or bags, arranging them behind the sales counter out of sight. The case still had an assortment of giant pre-packaged cupcakes the size of baseballs. Cliff opened a cooler cabinet, yelped in alarm, and slammed the lid.

"The power of Christ compels you!" He half-shouted, waving his hand in a funny gesture.

"Say what?" asked Harper.

He pointed at the case. "Don't open that. I've seen some nasty shit overseas, but that"—he wagged his pointing finger—"almost made *me* throw up."

She laughed, certain he overacted for their amusement.

The cupcakes, being the only food in the place even close to edible, made for a sweet but stale dinner. Neither Madison nor Jonathan objected. Summer eyed the cupcake with a grimace that said 'oh, this is so totally off my diet'.

"You're kidding, right?" Harper stared at her.

"Eating healthy was just such an ingrained habit. I stopped even realizing what stuff tasted like, just saw calorie numbers." Summer picked up the huge cupcake and bit it. "Now I don't care what stuff tastes like as long as it exists. Still, this thing is so rich I couldn't help but flinch."

"Heh, yeah." Harper smiled, then took a big bite. The overwhelming flavor of dark chocolate surprised her. She adored it for only a moment before thinking she may well be eating the last cupcake on Earth. Who in their right mind would bother making cake now? For that matter, didn't chocolate come from overseas? No one grew cocoa beans in the US. She stared at the confection in her hands, seeing this thing that had always been such a non-thought feeling like an exotic, foreign treat.

"What's wrong?" Summer bumped her knee under the table. "Did they go bad? You look like you're either going to throw up all over me or you're about to burst into tears."

"Umm..." Harper sighed. "I was just thinking about how this is probably the last time I'll ever have a cupcake, or chocolate."

"Oh, wow." Summer eyed her 'meal.' "I guess we should eat it slow and enjoy it then."

"No point wasting it," said Cliff past a full mouth. "They're already stale. Another week or two and you could hammer nails with them."

Jonathan inhaled his cupcake and ran into the back. A moment later, he shouted, "Hey! This toilet has water!"

Hearing a ten-year-old as happy over finding water in a toilet as a kid should be getting a new PlayStation threw Harper into a pit of sadness. The idle thought that she and Madison might've been better off had they died instantly during the blast dug the pit deeper. Not even an overindulgence of chocolate helped.

She still had three-quarters of a cupcake by the time everyone finished eating. Everyone else made a visit to the bathroom. The kids took over the middle of the seating area to work on dance stretches and some short routines. Harper concealed her frown behind the cupcake while staring at them. *That's stupid. What's the point of dancing anymore? That won't keep her alive. They're only wasting time.*

"Hey." Summer sat beside her. "You okay? Not lookin' too great."

"This stupid cupcake. Why is a stupid cupcake making me want to cry?"

"I don't think it's really the literal cupcake. More what it represents: civilization. A world in which beans from like 8,000 miles away are brought all the way here and turned into chocolate and no one thinks that's amazing. Chocolate cupcakes are everywhere, at every corner store, every supermarket. No one used to think twice about how they got there or what went into making them."

"Yeah. That's exactly what I'm thinking about. Are you trying to cheer me up or push me over the edge?" Harper wiped a tear as she chuckled.

Madison ran out of steam, tired from walking for hours, and crawled into a sleeping bag that Cliff had arranged on one of the cushioned booth seats at the back of the room.

"I'm trying to tell you that you're not crying over a silly dessert. I'd say not having cupcakes isn't the end of the world, but…"

Harper groaned.

"Okay, that was awful." Cliff tossed another sleeping bag into a booth. "Harper, eat your dinner."

"Yes, *Dad*," she said, playfully sarcastic.

He snickered.

She finished the cupcake in small bites, trying to make it last as long as possible. After, she availed herself of the bathroom. Jonathan kept his clothes on—except for sneakers—to sleep. By the time it became too dark to see outside, only Harper, Summer, and Cliff remained awake.

Cliff rummaged the counter, gathering a collection of bagged coffee beans.

"Coffee?" asked Harper. "Really?"

"Damn right. How you felt about that cupcake? That's me with the coffee. Won't be much of this stuff left. Can't you tell I'm all broke up about it?"

"Oh, totally." Harper yawned. "Pass the Zoloft."

He laughed. "Okay, we're not in a known-safe location, so we should work out a watch rotation."

Harper glanced at Summer, not entirely sure the woman wouldn't grab their guns and take off in the middle of the night. All the people she'd run into after the blast, and only Cliff so far hadn't tried to kill or kidnap her. Jonathan didn't count since he was only ten. She wouldn't expect a kid that young to be a threat. Though... movies always had the little pickpocket characters. Still, considering the situation they'd found her in, she might be afraid to be alone. Harper considered being in her shoes—or lack thereof. If she'd run over to people who cut her free and didn't attack her, she'd probably trust them.

"How will we know when to wake the next person up?" asked Harper. "And Summer's unarmed."

Cliff set the Glock down on the counter in front of her, the same gun Madison had winged the thug with. "Here. She can have this one. Got it from one of those blue idiots. Only twelve bullets left and I don't have any more nine-mil. Save 'em for important moments."

"Okay." Summer gingerly picked up the weapon. "I've never shot a gun before."

"It's not too hard. Guns are the original point and click interface." Cliff winked. "That's a Glock, so be careful on the trigger. The little lever at the bottom is a 'trigger safety.' It'll fire with only a little pressure."

"Got it. So, three shifts? How long?" asked Summer.

"Figure since we're not in any great rush, we take three hours on watch. That'll make for a nine-hour camp, six hours of rest each. You a night owl?"

Summer nodded.

"Me too. I'll take first watch, you second, Harper third?"

"Sure." Harper stretched. "I wouldn't mind sleeping sooner rather than later."

"How do I 'watch?'" asked Summer.

"Pretty easy really. Find a spot to sit where you can see the front door. If anyone breaks in, point the gun at them and make a bunch of noise to wake everyone up. If a whole lot of people show up outside, wake us up quiet."

Summer gave a thumbs-up. "Got it."

Harper took off her sneakers and winter coat, then crawled into the sleeping bag on the opposite bench from Madison. Much to her surprise, she didn't stare at the ceiling for long before slipping off to sleep.

14

GOING AWAY

Harper awoke to a dimly lit room, Summer gently shaking her by the shoulder.

She sat up and looked around blearily. Cliff lay out on a bench seat across the aisle, apparently sleeping, once again wearing his jacket.

Summer had on a different coat with a furry collar.

"Where'd you get that?" She yawned again.

"Closet in back. Someone left it here."

"Gimme a sec to pee and I'll take over watch."

"Knock yourself out." Summer sat on the end of the booth by Madison's feet.

Harper unzipped the sleeping bag, cringing at the chilly air while pulling her sneakers on. She wished Cliff had made a fire or something, but he probably didn't want to burn the building down. Still shivering, she hurried to the bathroom. Expecting an icy toilet seat, she bit her arm before sitting to muffle the shriek. Once that torture ended, she returned to the booth where she'd slept and put her coat on. Summer crawled into a sleeping bag.

With only the ticking of Cliff's wind-up clock to break the silence, Harper paced. The clock didn't matter that much since she had third watch. After three hours, she wouldn't wake anyone else to take over—

they'd be leaving. She expected to pass out if she sat down, but maybe given the cold, she wouldn't.

She spent some time wandering, then remembered Cliff's suggestion she stay away from the windows so no one outside would notice activity here. Once standing behind the counter daydreaming about working there got boring, she grabbed a paper cup and filled it with water from the sink. Thoughts of radiation swirled in her mind as she drank, but the water neither smelled or tasted odd.

Soft murmuring drew her over to where Jonathan slept.

"I miss you guys. Yeah, he's taking care of me. I got two sisters now. Yeah, I like them a lot."

Harper choked up at being called 'sister.'

He muttered a few non-words, having a conversation in his dream that sometimes leaked out of his mouth. "Wish Maddie wasn't so sad all the time." Again, he made noises that didn't quite form speech. "My other sister's super brave."

His comment about Madison had made the lump in Harper's throat so big, she couldn't quite bark out a 'Hah' at being called brave. She set the shotgun on the table and tucked his stray arm back into the sleeping bag, then patted him on the head.

Jonathan babbled, snuggled into the red fabric, and smiled in his sleep.

The next few hours dragged by. Harper did her best to stay awake, but the approach of daylight snuck up on her. She stretched, clinging to the idea that if she had passed out, it had only been for a few minutes, not deep enough into sleep that she wouldn't have heard anyone trying to break in. Still, she abandoned the bench seat and stood to prevent another blackout.

Not long after, Cliff woke up and dragged himself to the bathroom. When he returned, he fixed himself a cup of water, chugged it in one long gulp, and refilled it. Eyes still half-closed, he ambled around behind the counter and opened one of the bags of coffee beans. Harper blinked in shocked awe as he stuffed a handful in his mouth and ate them.

Still crunching, he gave her a 'what?' look.

"You're eating coffee beans?"

"Old Army trick. I'd rather drink the coffee, but we're a little short on electricity or hot water." He poured more beans into his hand and offered them. "Here, try it."

Harper slung the shotgun on its strap over her shoulder and cupped her hands to receive the beans.

He chuckled at the unsure look on her face. "You ever eat chocolate covered espresso beans?"

"Yeah."

"It's just like that, only without the chocolate." He munched for a second. "Never did understand that about people. They complain when there's grinds in the cup, but they'll eat the beans."

She laughed. "Speaking of chocolate..." Harper grabbed another stale cupcake from the display case. Tossing a coffee bean or two in with each mouthful of cake made it more tolerable than eating the beans straight. She'd never been big on black coffee, and the bitterness of the beans lessened the overwhelming sweetness of the cupcake.

Summer woke next, hit the bathroom, and also ate two handfuls of coffee beans. The kids stirred at the same time. They appeared to get into a race for the bathroom, which Madison won due to the zipper on Jonathan's sleeping bag not opening. As soon as the girl disappeared into the bathroom, he unzipped it without a problem.

Harper smiled at him.

The kids split a cupcake and had a granola bar each for breakfast. Cliff and Summer ate the last two, leaving the display case empty of everything but crumbs. After repacking all their gear, Cliff loaded up two big plastic bags with coffee, which he asked Summer to carry since she had no other burdens.

They headed out, crossing the huge park-and-ride lot back to I-70 and continuing west past abandoned cars and trucks. A few had melt damage, almost all had been left with the doors open. Every time they encountered a vehicle, Cliff stopped to search it for anything useful. While he rummaged, Harper stood guard, keeping her attention on the world around them for threats. At this distance from the city, the smoky haze had further thinned, allowing about a quarter mile of visibility. Her shotgun wouldn't be much good at long range, but Cliff still had the AR-15 he'd taken from the one thug. He carried it over his shoulder instead of in a ready position, saying something about not wasting those bullets at pistol ranges. That made sense in the city when they could only see like thirty feet.

Searching cars slowed their progress, but he scored a couple sets of road flares, a gas can, and a cardboard box with ten MREs in it, which Summer also carried.

Harper walked along, eyeing the hills on both sides of the road. "This feels dangerous."

"What does?" asked Summer.

"Being at the bottom like this. Someone on the high ground could pick us off."

Cliff squinted, glancing up to the right. "I don't think most people would randomly open fire on a small group without a word... but keep your eyes open."

By mid-day, the smoky haze had all but vanished. Jonathan asked if they still needed the face masks. Cliff pulled his down, sniffed the air, then shrugged. Harper took hers off and stuffed it in her jacket pocket, then collected Madison's, keeping it in her other jacket pocket just in case the haze returned.

They walked—searching cars along the way—for a few hours, surrounded by rolling hills dotted with pines. Most of the trees here had survived, likely shielded by the taller hills between here and Colorado Springs. Harper figured that meant the bomb had gone off closer to ground level.

A sign over the road announced Exit 252 to Evergreen Parkway, Route 74 coming up on the right. Seeing the word 'Evergreen' in print stirred a mixture of joy, worry, and grief inside Harper. It wouldn't be long before she learned if what that man told her father was true. However, if this place *did* turn out to be a safe haven, then her parents would have died for stupidity.

We should've left with those people... not waited another three weeks.

If Evergreen turned out to be empty—or worse, dangerous—she worried what would happen to them. The blue gang had to have started in center city Denver or someplace like that. While these mountain towns up here didn't come anywhere near that in size, smallness didn't necessarily guarantee a lack of bad people. If the promise of safety didn't hold up, where would she go?

Harper glanced at Cliff, grateful to have an adult around to help make decisions. She eyed Summer as well.

She looks as scared as I feel. Can't say I blame her after what happened. At the thought the woman would probably run away instead of shoot someone, a sense of awkwardness came over her. Despite being five years younger, she felt more like 'the mom' while she expected Summer would act like the frightened teen. Then again, she had fought her way free from three men. Harper started to wonder if she'd have the guts to do the same if she ever wound up in a similar situation, but the mere idea of being that helpless freaked her out too much.

Cliff veered to the right, heading for Exit 252. A four-ish story tall rocky hill abutted the road on the right. Harper kept her eyes trained on the top, in case danger lurked among the sparse trees. The hill flattened before the road curved to the left. They passed a weird white building with a round roof that made it look like a gargantuan can of soup cut in half lengthwise. Not far past that, they crossed along the top of an overpass. Naturally, Jonathan had to lean over the concrete barrier and spit.

They continued along the path of Route 74. *Not* seeing ash everywhere felt strange.

Cliff paused to search an SUV.

"That looks like Dad's new Explorer," said Madison. She pulled the iPhone out of her pocket and hit the button a couple times. "They haven't called."

Harper patted her on the head. "Their phones are probably out of battery power."

"Yeah." Madison frowned at her phone. "They would've called us if they could. I hope they're not too worried about where we are. Mom's gotta be losing her mind. We've been away for like weeks."

Summer looked over at her, but didn't say anything.

"I…" Harper considered saying something about their parents would try to get to Evergreen, but bit it back. She couldn't set up such a cruel false hope. Of course, she also couldn't bring herself to say they'd died. Madison had to know that, at least on some level. Saying it, however, would make it too real—for both of them. "Umm."

"Their phones don't work." Jonathan hurried over and put an arm around Madison's shoulders. "The bomb made all the electronic stuff stop working."

"Oh." Madison stared into the blank void on her iPhone's screen. "I feel bad. Mom's gonna still have to pay for dance class even if I miss it. I wanna go, but we're lost out here."

"We're not lost," said Cliff from the SUV.

"They're gonna call as soon as they find new phones." Madison hugged her iPhone.

Harper let a long, slow breath out her nose. That bubble would have to pop eventually, but she couldn't stick a pin in it at the moment. Maybe once she stopped worrying about finding a safe place, she could deal with her little sister having an emotional breakdown. No ten-year-old child should react to everything that had happened with such eerie calm. Some manner of freak-out would eventually occur.

Maddie can't hold it all in forever. Maybe I should break her wall down sooner so it won't be as bad when it does crumble.

"Damn." Cliff slid down from the SUV, chuckling. "Smells like gun oil in the compartment. Nerve of those people taking their weapons with them."

"Yeah, how rude." Summer fake rolled her eyes.

They resumed walking, passing a Comfort Suites hotel on the right a few minutes past the SUV. It sat a fair distance down a hill of pine trees. Motion caught Harper's eye, and she dropped into a squat.

At her sudden reaction, both kids hit the ground flat on their chests. Cliff eased himself down on one knee, turning his head to look at her. Summer stood there, conspicuously confused.

"People down there." Harper pointed with the shotgun.

Cliff rose back to his feet, approached the guardrail, and spent a moment observing the distant hotel. "Looks like a small group. Doubt they're dangerous, but this ain't Evergreen. We should probably keep going. If those people down there think we're after their shit, they might not be happy to see us. They could be completely friendly, but no sense risking it."

Harper nodded.

The kids got back up.

"Is everyone mean now?" asked Madison.

"I wouldn't say everyone is 'mean,' but most people are going to be on guard." Cliff backed away from the guardrail and resumed following the road.

"What's the world gonna be like now?" Harper migrated to the left to reduce the chances of someone down at the hotel seeing her.

Cliff shrugged. "I'd say a mess, but it was pretty much a mess before. A lot of things will be different. No electricity, no cars. No jets. Won't be much intercontinental travel for a while. Even the boats relied too much on electronics. Might be a handful left that work if they'd been out to sea when the shit hit the fan, but the diesel fuel won't last long at all. The world just got a whole lot bigger."

"Huh?" Jonathan looked up at him. "The nukes made the Earth fat?"

Harper laughed.

"Nah." Cliff ruffled the boy's hair. "Most people are stuck walking or riding horses again. Takes longer to go anywhere, and traveling across the ocean is likely impossible now. Someone's going to need to reinvent sailing ships. When you can get from New York City to Los Angeles in a couple hours, the world feels smaller than if that same trip took months."

"Oh." Jonathan nodded.

"I missed dance class again. Mom's gonna be mad at me." Madison trudged onward, staring down at the road. "I hope the plugs work where we're going so I can charge my phone."

"We have our own dance class." Jonathan grinned at her. "We can practice whenever you want."

Madison looked up. She didn't smile, but she'd gone from glum to blank.

"I suppose one good thing came out of this war." Cliff paused again to pop the trunk on a Cadillac.

Summer gasped. "What could possibly be *good* about this?"

Cliff chuckled. "Won't be any stupid people becoming famous only because they're famous for a long damn time."

"Seriously?" Summer stared at him. "Like millions of people died and you're making a celebrity joke?"

"Gotta laugh at stuff or it'll drive you nuts." Cliff stared into the trunk for a moment, then slammed it with a disappointed sigh.

"Won't be anyone complaining about what's on coffee cups at Christmas," said Harper.

"Or going crazy on Black Friday." Jonathan punched at the air.

"Or 24-7 media blitzes whenever someone famous dies." Cliff shut the Caddy's door while walking past it and continuing along the road.

Summer sighed. "Or Hollywood constantly remaking the same movies over and over."

"They won't make new ones, either," added Madison a little over a whisper.

"Or books." Harper sighed. "People have a lot more important things to worry about than movies, TV, or telling stories."

"I dunno." Summer kicked at a small rock, sending it skittering off the side of the highway. "Even like Native Americans told stories. They didn't write them down, but I think stories are important. People need them."

Cliff started laughing.

"What about that is funny?" asked Summer.

"I used to work at a mall. Linda and Jeff at the bookstore argued all the time about e-books and physical books, which one's better." He snickered. "Guess that question finally got answered. Paper doesn't care about EMP."

"Did the whole country go dark?" Harper glanced off to the left at a Walmart building. The front doors hung open. *Ugh. Probably looted already.* "Is everything shot?"

"A lot of military-grade stuff is shielded. Wouldn't be surprised if there's still stuff on bases here and there. Older devices without solid-state electronics and some appliances like washing machines are probably okay, but the power grid's toast—so it's irrelevant. Maybe some stuff in basements survived, too. Being turned on makes something more susceptible, but all it takes is one diode burning out in something like a cell phone to kill it. Might be able to get something going small scale with a generator, but fuel's an issue. Not sure if those things will run on ethanol, but I don't have a still."

"Cars?" asked Summer.

Harper glanced up and left at a self-storage place atop a hill near the road. She wondered if it would be worth checking out, but they didn't exactly have the means to carry much more stuff.

"Older cars without electronic ignition or computer control would probably still work. If they rely on digital technology or electronic fuel injection, fair bet they're useless. 'Course, even if we found a working car, gasoline would run out fast. Stuff rots in a couple months."

"What about food? That's more important than cars." Harper slung the shotgun over her shoulder to give her arms a break. "Not like anyone's gotta commute to the day job."

Cliff and Summer laughed.

"Canned goods for now. But we'll need to either farm, hunt, or take extreme measures." Cliff flashed a scary-eyed smile.

"Not sure I want to know what you mean by that," said Harper, her voice quivering.

"Heh. Not talking about cannibalism. I meant survivalist stuff. Eating worms, bugs, certain mushrooms, weeds, that sort of thing."

"Eww!" said Madison.

Jonathan gagged.

Summer looked about ready to faint.

"If you get hungry enough, even a bug will look tasty." Cliff winked.

Harper shuddered. "I'd have to be *very* damn hungry to go that far."

"Well, let's hope what you heard about this place is true. I'm not too keen on that idea either. Grubs are kinda nasty. If you ever do have to eat one, make sure you close your mouth or the guts will burst out and go everywhere. Best to fire-roast them so they're not still squirming when you try to eat them."

Harper grabbed her mouth to hold back the urge to throw up.

Everyone more or less lost the urge to talk at the same time. The road led past rocky hills on the left dotted with trees. A ten-foot beige fence ran along the right side, separating the road from a sharp downhill grade. Tree-covered hills continued as far as Harper could see. The scenery would've been beautiful if not for the dread of surviving nuclear war hanging on her shoulders.

"It's getting dark." Jonathan pointed up.

"I thought you said this was only gonna take like six hours to walk." Harper sighed at the dimming sky behind them.

"We haven't exactly been hurrying." Cliff tilted his head at her. "Late for an appointment?"

She managed a nervous smile. "No, just tired of worrying if I've made Evergreen out to be this oasis of hope and it's going to be abandoned."

"Better abandoned than full of bastards," muttered Summer.

Jonathan flapped his arms. "At least there's no smoke here."

Cliff slowed when something to the left caught his attention. He moved to the side of the road, taking a few steps onto dirt. "Hey. Let's check that out. We should get in out of the cold before it gets too dark."

Harper moved up to stand beside him. Maybe 200 feet from the road, a large brown building stood at the far end of a field at the bottom of a hill. The lack of windows kinda made it look like a prison. A nearby basketball court—and the lack of barb-wire fencing around the place—suggested school instead. Either way, it appeared empty and the sky would be dark fairly soon.

"Okay." Harper waved Madison and Jonathan over. "Might as well. Looks quiet."

15

VULNERABLE

C liff led the way down the hill. He took a tool from his belt to snip a hole in a wire fence about halfway between the road and the building. A set of green double doors refused to open, so he headed left and went around toward the basketball court.

Apparently, they'd approached from the back of the building. The main entrance on the opposite side indicated they'd reached Bergen Valley Elementary.

Madison wailed, "Oh, no!"

"What?" Harper jumped, scrambling to get the shotgun off her shoulder and bring it into a ready grip.

"They didn't blow up the schools!" Madison's eyes widened.

Jonathan laughed. "Is that bad?"

"Yeah! That means we're gonna get in trouble for not going," whispered Madison.

"It's still closed." Cliff tested the doors, seeming surprised when they opened. "Hello? Anyone here?"

Everyone kept quiet until the echo of his shout faded to silence.

"We're friendly," yelled Cliff.

Again, his voice echoed into silence.

With a shrug, he entered.

Harper followed, a little sick to her stomach at the idea of walking in here with a loaded shotgun after all the active shooter drills she'd been through at her old school. Despite there having been a nuclear war, she felt like she did something *super* wrong.

Cliff grumbled, "Glad they hit the button so damn early in the day."

"Why?" asked Madison. "So we got a day off of school?"

He bowed his head and sighed. "Yeah, basically. Families were together."

At least on the West Coast. Harper bit her lip, not wanting to say it and hating herself for thinking it. Somehow, she doubted the people responsible for sending nukes at the US cared at all if children would be with their families, on the road to school, or at school when the weapons detonated. If they cared at all about children, they wouldn't have hit the button. The silence inside this place made her dwell on horribly sad thoughts about what might've happened to all the kids who should've been here—or in any school in the world. Little kids didn't deserve to wonder if they would live to see another day, be able to eat at all—or cling to a dead iPhone hoping to receive a call from their dead parents.

Overcome, Harper sank down to one knee, grabbed Madison, and cried. Upon noticing Jonathan standing nearby watching them, she grabbed him into the hug as well.

"My dad worked nights." Jonathan stared off into nowhere, his voice low but calm. "I haven't seen him since the bombs went off. He's probably dead because he worked in Colorado Springs."

Cliff winced.

Harper squeezed him tighter. Jonathan clung to her, sniffling.

"Yeah," whispered Summer. "Nothing's sadder than an abandoned school after a big-ass war."

Cliff kept quiet, allowing everyone a minute or two to recover.

Eventually, she forced the tears back and swung the shotgun over her shoulder on its strap, then took the kids by the hand. "We're not going to be able to see anything in a little while. Let's find a spot to sleep and maybe food."

They walked by empty classrooms, making their way to the cafeteria. Dead freezers and refrigerators held a horror of mold and spoiled food. After an inglorious feast of dry cereal and chocolate pudding from a giant can, they made camp in a classroom that had padded mats at one side for a nap area. Judging by the tiny size of the chairs, they'd found the kindergarten.

Harper recognized a device hanging on the wall by the door as a thing to barricade it from the inside. Though it had been intended to stop a school shooter, it would also work on people who went insane after nuclear war. She braced the door with it, and let out a sigh of relief at feeling somewhat safe.

"I gotta go to the bathroom." Madison approached, clutching a roll of toilet paper.

"Ugh." Harper pulled the lock off the door. "Okay. Not a bad idea."

Cliff and Summer also decided to hit the bathrooms. It had become dark enough that she needed to feel her way along the wall. Harper didn't mind the small toilets or tiny stalls, since they worked. Upon returning to the classroom, she replaced the door lock and spent the next few minutes fumbling around in the moonlight to help Cliff set up the sleeping bags.

"You had third watch last night. You want first this time?" asked Cliff.

Harper pointed at the door. "No need. That door isn't opening without high explosives. They had one of those emergency brace things for school shootings."

Cliff rubbed his beard. "Hmm." He got up and went over to the door, examined it for a moment, and gave an impressed grunt. "Okay. Seems solid. No one's getting through that without waking us up."

Though Harper felt funky spending a couple days in the same clothes, she didn't feel safe enough to take off more than her sneakers. Jonathan stripped down to his briefs and crawled into his sleeping bag. Madison took only her sneakers off as well, then dragged her sleeping bag close to Harper and burritoed herself in it.

A cozy sleeping bag on top of a soft mat with a winter coat for a pillow made for a surprisingly comfortable bed.

HARPER STRUGGLED TO GET AWAY FROM THE TWO MEN HOLDING HER BY THE arms.

Plastic ties bound her wrists behind her back, she had no idea where her pants or shoes had gone, and worst of all—Madison screamed for help from somewhere off in the haze where a group of shadowy figures dragged a smaller figure away.

The man on the left slapped Harper on her bare butt, laughing. "Come on, Red. Time to have some fun."

"Help!" shouted Madison, sounding too far away.

"No!" roared Harper.

She twisted to the left and rammed her knee into one man's groin. He doubled over, groaning. The other man grabbed her hair, but she kicked at him in a furious barrage until he lost his grip. Lost to panic, Harper ran as fast as she could down the street. Inches-thick ash made the ground feel like clouds, and muted any noise her bare feet might have made on the pavement.

A few shots rang out behind her, but none hit her. Barely able to resist screaming, she ran heedless of fear she'd fall and break her face open with her hands tied behind her back.

Buildings from downtown Lakewood blurred by on both sides, simultaneously alien and familiar. Shouting men pursued her, driving her up to a blind sprint. Her hair fell over her eyes, but she couldn't reach up to grab it. Again and again, she took random turns down alleys or cross streets, trying to put as many buildings between her and the thugs as possible.

Her legs protested after a few minutes, slowing her to a belabored loping walk. The shouts of the men chasing her had stopped who knows how long ago. Harper rounded a corner into a narrow passage between two stores, scurrying into a hiding place behind a dumpster.

Madison's desperate pleas echoed in her mind, bringing sobbing tears at her inability to do anything to protect her sister. She stared down at her pale legs, unable to remember who ripped her pants off. Grunting, she strained to snap the plastic around her wrists, spinning in search of anything she could use to cut herself free.

With each passing second, her terror grew. Lost somewhere in the city, unable to see more than fifteen feet due to the smoke, naked from the waist down, her hands bound behind her... Harper had no way to even *find* Madison much less get her away from the gang. If anyone caught her like this, she'd be in major trouble.

Part of her wanted to run and keep running, but she refused to abandon Madison. Despite her absolute need to protect her little sister, she couldn't shake the overwhelming sense of vulnerability gnawing at her. She walked down the alley, looking for a signpost or bit of glass or knife—anything she might use to get her hands free.

With each step in the soft ash, her sense of helplessness grew. Worse, she knew she'd be too late to stop them from doing awful things to Madison. Her sister would already have suffered permanent damage and would never be the same... even if she could find her.

But she couldn't.

Harper fell to her knees, bawling, thrashing at the cable ties, but they refused to snap.

Men emerged from the haze. She scooted back, though they kept walking toward her, faceless silhouettes laughing at her helplessness. The instant a hand closed on her ankle, Harper screamed—and snapped awake.

She found herself still wrapped up to the neck in a sleeping bag on the floor of a kindergarten classroom, breathing hard and covered in sweat. Harper stared up at the ceiling tiles, unable to tell if she'd screamed for real or only in her nightmare. Still zipped in the bag, she sat up, grabbing at her lower half to make sure she still had her jeans.

The padded mat creaked nearby.

Harper jumped and spun with a gasp.

Cliff took a knee beside her and whispered, "Hey… easy. You just had a dream."

She stared at him.

"Must've been a doozy. You okay?"

Harper shoved her arms out of the sleeping bag and clamped onto him, shaking like a terrified child while crying as quietly as she could manage. He shifted back to sit on the floor mat and put an arm around her. She clung to him, beyond grateful that she'd decided to trust him in the mall. He rubbed a hand up and down her back, letting her cry. When she'd seen Madison so engrossed in Cliff's story, she'd been momentarily angry with her as if she'd forgotten Dad. But he'd died. She couldn't be mad at Madison for liking Cliff, especially now. Having him there *did* make her feel safer, almost like her father was still there.

"You wanna talk about it?" whispered Cliff.

She took a few breaths, then relaxed her hug, leaning against him instead of clinging for dear life. "It's my fault."

"What's your fault? Having a nightmare?"

Harper shook her head. "My Dad died because I couldn't shoot a guy. Those guys with the blue sashes attacked us at home. I was supposed to watch the front door. Dad covered the patio door in the kitchen. A guy came in the front. He was gonna grab me, but when he saw the shotgun, he pointed his gun at me. I couldn't pull the trigger. I… just couldn't kill someone. Dad shot the guy, but when he turned toward me, another asshole shot him from behind. It's my fault." She buried her face in her hands and sniffled.

"Hey… enough of that." Cliff rubbed her back. "Two months ago, you were just a high school kid. The world changed out from under you. You're a lot tougher than you think."

Harper wiped her face on her sleeves. "I don't feel tough. A nightmare scared the crap out of me."

"You're protecting your little sister, your family. A nightmare's only in here." He tapped her on the head. "What matters is what you do out there. You didn't hesitate when it mattered. Those guys went after Maddie, you let 'em have it. There's no way your father would be upset with a seventeen-year-old kid for freezing up the first time they stared down the barrel of a gun. Hell, I've seen guys who went through boot camp, AIT, months out in a combat zone... some of them even lock up. It happens. You're a human being. But, you beat it already. You kept her safe."

"I got a li'l brother now, too." Harper took a deep breath, held it a few seconds, and let it out her nose. "Just a bad dream. Faceless men got Maddie, and I couldn't stop them." She stopped breathing, dreading that he'd ask why her face burned with blush.

Cliff nodded. "Just a dream."

"I felt so helpless." She wiped her nose. "I dunno how to fight at all. If I lose that shotgun or run out of ammo, I'm gonna be a defenseless kid."

He ruffled her hair. "I can show you some moves once we aren't walking all day. Picked up a few things in Ranger School. Now, go on back to sleep. Enjoy a night not needin' to have watch."

"Okay." She exhaled hard and lay back down. Even the few minutes she'd spent with her arms outside the sleeping bag made her cold. She snuggled back in, pulling the fabric up to her face.

Cliff knee-walked back into his sleeping bag, and flopped on it.

As best she could tell, neither kid nor Summer had stirred. At least for them, she could continue pretending to be brave.

Maybe if she faked it enough, she might convince herself.

16

A SEMBLANCE OF NORMAL

The next morning, everyone returned to the cafeteria to search for food in the daylight.

Other than the lone box of cereal they'd attacked last night and the mostly-empty can of pudding, the place appeared to have already been cleaned out—but it still had silverware. They tapped some of the canned goods they'd been carrying, making a breakfast of pears and baked beans.

"You'd think a school would have more supplies." Summer ate a spoonful of beans. "What happened to it all?"

"We're close to Evergreen." Cliff wagged a fork at her before stabbing a pear slice. "Could be there really are people there and they came here already."

"That's good, right?" asked Harper.

"Seems like it, yeah." He ate the pear slice whole.

Madison stared into her dead iPhone while eating. Her expression had changed from blank to tinged with sadness. Harper suspected she knew no one would ever call her on that phone, but still tried to deny the truth. As soon as they reached Evergreen—well, providing it turned out to be the safe haven she'd made it out to be in her mind—she'd tell Madison the truth and keep repeating it until she accepted it.

Though, that did seem needlessly cruel, like telling a kid Santa Claus didn't exist. What harm would it do to let her carry around a broken iPhone as a security blanket? Not like she had to be normal, finish school, get a job, and pretend to be a functioning member of society.

Ugh. I dunno what to do.

Harper licked her spoon clean of baked bean sauce and stuffed it in her pocket. May as well keep it for the next meal. Eager to finally put her insecurities about Evergreen to rest, she urged the kids to eat faster.

On the way out of the cafeteria, Madison stopped by an electrical outlet and plugged in her iPhone charger. She squatted there watching the screen, waiting for it to absorb enough power to show signs of life.

Harper crouched beside her, unable to bring herself to say anything.

After a moment of silent staring, Madison unplugged the cord and stuffed it back in her jacket pocket. She stood without a word and stared down at her sneakers. Harper took her hand and walked with her out into the corridor.

Cliff led the way out of the school. They went around the building to the back and again crossed the field before climbing the hill to Route 74. This section of road didn't have any cars to search, so they made good time. Harper wondered if there hadn't been any traffic out here at five-whatever in the morning when the nuclear strike happened or if this place had been far enough away that the EMP only knocked out the power grid and not every car.

They marched along the highway, passing fields of trees, a baseball field, and numerous large buildings that appeared to be commercial properties. The road became a bridge over a sloping valley to the right and a lake on the left. For a couple hours, the surroundings mostly consisted of fields full of trees with an occasional branching road leading away. Harper perked up with hope at the sight of something white up ahead.

Two city buses had been moved nose-to-nose, creating a fortification that mostly blocked off an intersection. Four men stood on something behind them that put them chest high to the roof of the buses. Two of the men aimed scoped hunting rifles in their general direction.

Harper lowered the shotgun, letting it hang, pointed at the street from her right hand. She raised her left, waving. Jonathan set his bags on the street and waved both arms. Madison kept staring at her phone.

Cliff raised one arm, waving it back and forth over his head. Two of the sentries climbed down out of sight. A black man in his mid-thirties and a somewhat older man with pale skin and light brown hair emerged from the gap between the buses and approached to about twenty feet away. Both carried bolt-action rifles, held sideways.

"Can we help you?" asked the white guy.

"Looking for Evergreen." Cliff gestured at Harper. "Got two kids, a teen, and a young woman. Heard this was a safe place."

"Oh? Now, where'd you hear that?" The other man smiled.

Sensing friendliness, Harper took a few steps closer. "Some people tried to get us to go with them here, but my dad didn't trust going outside so soon after the blast. We stayed in our house, but a gang attacked us. Killed my parents. I took my sister, Madison, and ran like hell. I had no idea what else to do, but I remembered that man saying Evergreen was a safe place."

"That's not your dad?" The white guy gestured at Cliff.

Harper smiled. "Not by biology. But he is now."

Madison emitted a faint squeak.

She glanced at her shotgun. "Is it okay if I sling this over my shoulder? I don't wanna be shot, and I don't think I'm gonna need to use it here."

The black guy nodded. "It's fine, kid. Yeah, you heard right. Got a bunch of people collected here, tryin' to get by. Gotta be careful who we bring in, but you seem like a bunch of normal people. You'll need to get the okay from Mayor Ned before you can stay, but it shouldn't be a problem. I'm Darnell. This here's Fred."

Fred raised a hand in greeting.

Harper gingerly shifted the shotgun onto her shoulder. Both men still behind the buses watched her through their scopes, but neither shot her. "Maddie, Jon, c'mere."

The kids walked up behind her.

"Hi. I'm Jonathan." He waved. "We just want a place to live."

Madison looked at the men for a moment, but said nothing.

"I'm Harper, that's Cliff and Summer."

Summer waved.

Cliff walked over and shook hands with the men. Once Darnell and Fred slung their rifles, the two men behind the buses relaxed.

They chatted for a few minutes about their trip here. Around the time Harper's story reached their arrival at the coffee shop, Darnell waved for everyone to follow him. She kept talking as he led them further down Route 74 before crossing a strip of grassy dirt, another small road, and a parking lot, heading toward a squarish brown five-story building that appeared to be some kind of medical center.

"Where are we going?" asked Summer.

"We have two doctors in town. They set up shop at the Evergreen Medical center. All new arrivals, not that we've got that many, have'ta be checked out. Shouldn't take long." Darnell headed for the door of the medical building.

"Oh, cool." Harper brightened at the idea of doctors—and normality. Perhaps the world hadn't completely fallen to pieces yet.

Darnell walked with them into a waiting room with soft grey-blue chairs, white walls, and a reception counter at which sat an auburn-haired woman roughly the same age as Mom. The sight of the place momentarily made Harper doubt the war had even happened. Of course, the TV didn't work, the ceiling remained dark, it didn't feel any warmer than outside, and an odd chemical twang stained the air.

"Hey, Ruby," said Darnell. "Got some stray cats looking for a home."

The woman looked up. She smiled at Cliff, nodded at Summer, went wide-eyed with 'aww' at the sight of Harper, and practically cried when she noticed Madison and Jonathan. "Oh, my! Of course. Go on and set your packs and such down, get comfortable. This shouldn't take too long." She stood, turned toward the hallway behind her room, and shouted, "Doc!"

Darnell took his rifle off his back and sat near Cliff, resting the weapon in the next chair. He didn't seem on edge or make any move to confiscate anyone's guns. While Cliff dropped the duffel of all their clothes and shrugged out of the backpack, the man mentioned he'd trekked up here from Littleton about two weeks ago.

"Ouch. That's closer to Springs. How bad is it down there?" asked Cliff.

"Lot of it's flat." Darnell sighed. "My ass got lucky. Not once in my wildest dreams did I think workin' for the sewer authority would save my life. I was underground when the blast happened."

Harper dropped her backpack and denim handbag in a chair, then flopped in the next seat. She kept the shotgun close like a security blanket, resting the stock on the floor by her foot. Madison perched in the chair to her left, still staring at the iPhone like it would come to life at any moment. Jonathan looked at the waiting area with an expression like he'd been brought onto an alien ship.

Ruby walked over. "Hi folks. Just for the record. Am I looking at a family here? You don't seem old enough to be 'Mom'"—she nodded to

Summer—"and he's not old enough to be your dad, so… please fill me in here."

"I'm just a mall security guard who found a couple kids who shouldn't be alone." Cliff put one arm around Jonathan. "But they seem to like me."

Tears fell on the iPhone screen. Madison kept staring down at it, but whispered, "It's okay if we're a family now."

Harper leaned over and gave her a squeeze, then looked up at Ruby. "Madison's my bio sister. Cliff's been like a Dad to us. Jon's my brother now. Might as well make it official."

"Yeah." Jonathan nodded.

Summer cringed. "They found me on the way here and saved my ass. I'm not related to any of them."

Ruby jotted some stuff down in a spiral notebook. "All right. So you four are a family unit, and the young lady's separate?"

Harper gave Summer a welcoming look. "Up to her."

"Yeah, that's fine." She smiled at everyone. "Bit young to shack up with Cliff, and you guys already have a family thing going."

"Hey." Cliff playfully scowled at her. "You callin' me old?"

She grinned at him, making him laugh.

"All right." Ruby lowered the notebook. "Thanks. Doctors should be out in a moment."

Not long after she returned to her seat and shouted "Doc" again, a man of Indian descent emerged from the door beside the counter, wearing jeans and a T-shirt under a doctor's coat. He looked a little older than Dad, probably in his fifties, and greeted everyone with a warm smile.

"Hello. I'm Doctor Khan. Welcome to Evergreen. Sorry for the delay, just some routine checks and questions. Before we start on that, is anyone injured?"

"Cliff was shot in the arm," said Harper.

The doctor's eyebrows went up.

Cliff smirked at her in a way that said he didn't think the injury a big enough deal to mention, but nodded. "Yeah… might be time for those stitches to come out."

"Why don't you come back first then?" Dr. Khan smiled.

"All right." Cliff left the AR-15 with Harper and followed the man down the hall.

She glanced back and forth between the Mossberg and the combat rifle, momentarily afraid of getting in trouble for having weapons in a doctor's office. A little part of her brain seized upon the normality of her present surroundings to reject the events of the past nine weeks, expecting a cop to show up and arrest her. People just didn't carry loaded rifles around all the time. She zoned out, daydreaming of the world she missed so damn much. How did she wind up here instead of hanging out with her friends after school?

"Miss?" asked a woman.

Harper jumped.

A thirtyish woman with blonde hair, blue eyes, and an apologetic smile stood a few feet away. She also wore a doctor's coat over a peach sweater and jeans. "Sorry for startling you. I'm Tegan. You can call me Dr. Hale if you want. Come on back."

Harper eyed the rifles. Leaving them unattended at her chair didn't seem like a good idea with two ten-year-olds plus two adults she didn't fully trust not to take them. Bringing them into the back with the doctor also didn't sound like a great plan.

"It's all right," said Darnell. "You can leave the hardware right there. I'm part of the Evergreen Militia, so basically the closest thing we have to cops."

She decided not to make a poor impression on day one, mostly since she didn't get a bad read on him. "Okay... Sorry. Rough couple months."

Darnell leaned back in his seat, nodding. "I hear that."

Madison looked up from the iPhone with an expression like a cat about to be abandoned at a shelter. Harper checked the safeties on both weapons, then remembered something Dad told her when he gave her the Mossberg three days after the nuclear strike: never let this out of your sight. Darnell raised an eyebrow when she picked the shotgun up and slung it over her shoulder.

"Sorry. No offense. Just promised my Dad I'd never leave it out of my sight."

He regarded her with an impressed look. "All right. No foul. Do what you gotta do."

Harper took two steps after the doctor before Madison jumped to her feet and ran after.

"It's okay, sweetie. I'll see you in a few minutes." Tegan smiled at her.

"No." Madison grabbed Harper's hand, squeezing it almost painfully tight.

Tegan crouched to eye level with Madison. "I need to ask her some questions that need to be private. She'll be right back."

"Please... it's..." Harper bit her lip, not wanting to talk about their dead parents in front of her just yet. "Been rough on her."

Tegan stood. "Well, if it's okay with you. Not like there's an AMA left to yank my license for bending the rules."

Harper followed her down a hall to a small exam room. "How, umm, invasive is this going to be?"

"Not very. I can check as much as you like if you have specific concerns." Tegan shut the door, then moved to the window to widen the curtains. "Normally, I'd have the curtains drawn, but the window's the only source of light we have at the moment. Do either of you have any allergies to medications?"

"No." Harper parked Madison in a chair below an illustration of kidneys, then hopped up on the exam table in the middle of the room, letting her feet dangle. She rested the shotgun beside her on the paper-covered cushion.

Tegan gave them each a plain white pill and a cup of water. "Potassium Iodide as a precautionary measure in case you've taken in any radiation from fallout. It'll help protect your thyroid."

Harper stared at the pill. The place seemed enough like a legit medical facility, and this woman enough like a legit doctor, that she pushed aside worry. As soon as she swallowed the pill, Madison took hers.

"Okay..." Tegan glanced at Madison. "Is there anything you need to tell me about the man you arrived with?"

She picked up on the vibe right away. "No... nothing like that. He's totally cool, like a dad."

Tegan smiled. "That's good. What about before you found him? Did you suffer any form of assault?"

"No. We stayed at home with our parents, hiding out in the basement for like two months. This gang found us and we had to run." Harper locked stares with the doctor and mouthed, "They killed our parents" without giving it voice.

Tegan cringed a little, then offered a sympathetic look. "All right. I'm a generalist, but Doctor Khan and I are all the town's got. If you ever need someone to check the plumbing, come see me."

"Okay." Harper stared down at her dangling feet. She'd always disliked going to the gynecologist, but wondering if the woman might've died still made her sad. "Think I'm good for now as far as that goes."

Over the next few minutes, the doctor performed a routine physical exam, jotting down notes the whole time. Harper gasped at the cold stethoscope sliding up her back under her shirt. It all seemed so damn normal—except for the shotgun next to her. The glaring reminder that everything was *not* all right with the world pushed her to the brink of tears, but she held them back. Fortunately, Tegan didn't ask her to say anything for a little while as emotion would've kept her voice from being cooperative.

"Okay, now for the embarrassing part. We need to check all new arrivals for injuries, parasites, and evidence of certain diseases. Would you mind taking your clothes off? You don't need to remove your underpants, but I'll need to take a cursory look under the hood so to speak. Any rashes, itching, or anything like that?"

"No."

"May I ask if you've been..." Tegan leaned close and whispered. "Sexually active?" She leaned back, again speaking at a normal volume. "You can tell me you don't want to answer as well."

Well. She is a doctor. "I've never... Before the blast, I was kinda shy."

Harper slid off the table and stripped down to her bra and panties, shivering in the room no warmer than outside. The doctor looked her over, touching her shoulder to maneuver her into the light from the window. She tugged the waistband of Harper's underpants open for a quick visual examination. Harper glanced off to the side, blushing until the doctor let the elastic snap back into place a moment later. The doctor turned her to face away, pulled her long curly hair off her back, ran a comb through it in a few places, then spun her around to face her again.

"All set. I don't see any ticks, insect bites, signs of parasites, or any lesions worth worrying about. Go on and get dressed. Does anything hurt or bother you?"

Harper hurried into her clothes. "Nope. Well, a lot bothers me, but not about my health."

"Yeah. I'm right there with you." She looked at the chair in the corner. "Madison, right?"

The girl looked up from the dead iPhone.

"C'mon over. You're up." Tegan smiled at Harper. "Since you're next of kin and she's a minor, I would've asked you to be in the room anyway during her exam."

Harper nodded. "C'mon, Maddie. It's okay."

She slipped out of her winter coat and walked over to the exam table. The doctor checked her throat, ears, pulse, flashed a penlight in her eyes, felt at her neck, and listened to her heartbeat and breathing.

"You're nice and healthy, Maddie." Tegan smiled. "Almost done. Just need to check you for infected cuts or scratches, or freeloaders."

"Are you a real doctor?" asked Madison.

"Yes. I'm an actual M.D. My degree's on a wall in Littleton. Though, I'm not even sure if my old office is still standing."

"Okay." Madison matter-of-factly stripped.

Harper blushed for her little sister who didn't at all seem to care that she stood there naked except for the iPhone in her hand in a maybe forty-degree room in front of a stranger. Tegan appeared to pick up on Harper's reaction to her sister's uncharacteristic lack of embarrassment and gave a 'we can talk later' nod. Having observed the examination of her older sister, Madison stepped into the patch of light from the window and allowed the doctor to check her over. A few passes with a lice comb came back clean.

"And that's everything." Tegan smiled. "You two are all set. Looks like you avoided the worst of it out there."

Madison got dressed.

"Yeah, I guess." Harper shrugged. "We were both covered in ash, but we cleaned it off."

"Did you breathe much in? Any coughing, dry throat?" asked Tegan.

"Little coughing but it's already stopped."

The doctor again asked her to breathe deep in and out for a minute or two while listening with a stethoscope, then repeated with Madison. "It doesn't sound like there's anything to worry about."

"Okay." Harper picked up the shotgun and slung it over her shoulder. She couldn't tell what bothered her more: carrying a weapon into a visit with a doctor—or that the woman didn't care.

Tegan walked them out to the waiting area, where summer and Darnell remained, no sign of Cliff or Jonathan. Harper figured the boy had gone in with Cliff the same way she and Madison went together.

"Miss?" asked Tegan, nodding at Summer.

Harper took a seat where she'd been before.

Madison climbed up into her lap. "How long do we have'ta stay here before we go home?"

A lead weight settled in Harper's stomach. "I think we're gonna be here a while. The bad people are still back there. They can't get us here, okay? We're gonna stay here because it's safe. The bad people can't get us here."

"Okay." Madison shifted sideways and rested her head on Harper's shoulder.

Darnell raised an eyebrow. "Bad people?"

She explained about the 'blue gang,' glossing over that their parents had been killed in a way that he'd hopefully pick up on but Madison could misinterpret. A few minutes later, Cliff and Jonathan walked out the door by the reception desk. He had a bandage on his arm over the gunshot, but otherwise looked the same.

"How'd it go?" asked Harper.

"Fine. You did a pretty good job sewing it. Scar's not gonna be too big." He winked. "Not even infected."

She smiled. "That's more the booze than anything I did."

"Maybe." He took the AR-15 as he went by, sat in the next chair, and glanced at Darnell. "So, now what?"

"Once you're all done here, I'll introduce you to Mayor Ned."

Cliff nodded. "All right."

They waited a little while for Summer to finish. Red ringed her eyes as though she'd been crying, and Tegan also appeared upset. Harper squeezed Madison at the sight. *Shit. Maybe she didn't get away from those bastards before they... of course, she wouldn't tell kids about that.* Summer broke down crying again when she caught Harper's 'I'm *so* damn sorry' expression.

The doctor locked stares with Harper.

She nodded, then whispered, "Can you stay with Cliff for a minute?"

Madison whined and clung to her for a moment, but eventually caved in and crawled into his lap.

"Thanks. I'll be right back." Harper got up and walked over to the doctor, then two steps into the hallway behind the door.

"Something bothered you before about your sister?" asked Tegan in a low voice.

"I'm worried about her. She... flung her pants off like no big deal. Maddie's always been a bit shy. Okay, more than a bit. Couple days ago, we had fallout dust all over us and she wanted a bath. Demanded I stay in the room with her. That's so unlike her. I think she saw our parents die, but I'm not a hundred percent sure if she looked or was hiding. She's carrying around her phone like Mom or Dad are going to call her at any minute, but the thing's dead as a brick. I've said the whole phone system is destroyed a couple times but she ignored it. I can't tell if she's just in denial or if she's like really delusional and thinks the phone's going to work."

Tegan let out a soft sigh. "Kids deal with traumatic events in their own way. From what you've told me, it's been less than a week since their death?"

Harper nodded.

"I'm not exactly a psychiatrist, but so soon afterward I wouldn't worry too much unless she starts acting out in ways that could be harmful to herself. Now, if she's still trying to get signal on that phone next year, it might be an issue."

"Okay."

Tegan put a hand on Harper's shoulder. "Are *you* okay?"

"I dunno. It doesn't feel real yet. Like I saw someone else's parents get shot. Like I'm gonna wake up tomorrow and the world's going to be back to what it was. I still haven't really processed that I've had to shoot people who tried to kidnap or kill us. Haven't really thought about much more than keeping Maddie safe."

"She's lucky to have such a determined older sister." Tegan handed her a slip of paper. "Give that to the mayor when you see him. Both you and your sister are healthy."

"For how long?" She took the paper and stuffed it in her pocket. "Are we gonna get cancer?"

"Well… Everyone within a good distance from here is at an elevated risk due to radiation. You said you stayed inside, underground pretty much for two months after the blast that hit Colorado Springs?"

"Yeah. At least a month. Like week five or so, Dad wanted to go back upstairs. He started going out to neighbor's houses to collect canned food and stuff. Almost everyone who lived near us disappeared. I have no idea where anyone went."

"There have been some efforts by what remains of the military to evacuate civilians, though I haven't seen any of them around here since about the second week after the war." Tegan scoffed. "Not sure I should even call it a war."

"Yeah…" Harper kicked at the floor.

"All right. Both of you seem to be handling things about as well as can be expected for anyone. I'm usually here in the daytime if you ever want to talk about anything."

Harper shook her hand. "Thanks. And wow, this place feels so… normal."

"We try. Be a lot more normal if Jeanette gets those solar panels working again."

"Solar panels?"

"Yeah. Town's number one project… collecting panels together so we can get something of a power grid back. Light, heat, hot water."

"Oh, sweet." Harper's eyes widened with anticipation. "Thanks."

"No problem. Welcome to Evergreen."

Harper headed back to the waiting room. *Wow. This place* does *seem safe. That guy was right. Dammit, Dad. Why did you make us stay home? We should've left with that group.*

Cliff stood, lifting Madison, and set her on her feet before approaching Harper. "Everything okay?"

She wiped a tear from her cheek. "Yeah. I think it's gonna be okay here."

MAYOR NED

Darnell walked with them down Route 74 from the medical clinic.

He veered left off the road by a sign next to a flagpole that read 'La Plaza Office Park,' heading for the rightmost of three white, square buildings. They appeared to be former offices which had evidently been repurposed to the town seat.

Once again, Harper found herself in a waiting room, though this one didn't have the same counter setup as the medical place, merely a nice room with chairs and two doors. A table on the right side held a coffee maker, paper cups, and a giant glass bowl with leaf patterns in it.

"Who's there?" called a woman from one of the doors.

"Hey, Anne-Marie. It's Darnell Buck. Got some new arrivals with me."

The door on the right next to the table swung open. A pale, black-haired woman in a somewhat frumpy grey skirt suit walked in. She seemed close in age to Cliff, early forties or so, and looked like she might've been a former model. The woman exuded an air of command and confidence, though also friendliness.

"Hello everyone." She smiled. "I'm Anne-Marie Kirby. Welcome to Evergreen. I'm basically the city manager, and you probably won't ever need to deal with me directly, but I'm happy to talk to anyone with a concern."

Cliff shook hands and introduced himself, as did Summer. Anne-Marie greeted Madison and Jonathan with a broad grin and the energy of someone meeting their grandchildren. The boy responded with an enthusiastic smile. Madison lifted her stare off the iPhone only long enough to emit a clipped, "Hi" without any emotion on her face. Since the girl made no move to accept the woman's handshake, Anne-Marie patted her on the head.

"And you are?"

"Harper Cody." She shook hands. "Sorry about Madison. We've had a rough month."

"Haven't we all." Anne-Marie twisted back to the door she came from and called, "Ned?" before turning back to the group. "Oh, do you have your slips from the medical check?"

Harper pulled hers out, as did Cliff and Summer.

Anne-Marie collected them, giving each one a skim, and grinned. "Good. All clear then."

A man walked in, rocking a white polo and khakis. He, too, looked around Cliff's age, though skinny, and kept his light brown hair short and neat as if civilization hadn't ended two months ago. "Hello, everyone! I'm Ned O'Neill, but most people just call me Ned or 'Mayor Ned.' Hear we got some new people lookin' for a place to live?"

"You heard right." Cliff nodded.

"Anyone have any special skills or training we should know about?" Ned smiled, mostly at Cliff. "We're trying to keep things as normal as possible. Obviously, we've had to become self-sufficient given the war. No more shipments comin' in from across the country, so we need to have people helping out where they can do the most good."

"Ex-Army."

"Excellent. What job?" asked Ned.

"Ranger."

Ned's eyes bulged. "My good man, I'd sincerely like you to consider a position with our militia."

Cliff chuckled. "Yeah, kinda figured that'd happen. No problem. About all I'm really good for."

"You make a pretty decent dad, too," said Harper.

Madison didn't react.

"Yeah." Jonathan grinned.

Ned approached Summer. "Hello, Miss. What about you?"

"Nothing useful really. Unless you need someone with a degree in business and a marketing minor." She shrugged. "Not a bad cook, and I can kinda draw okay."

"Oh, it's not completely useless." Anne-Marie chuckled. "Three months ago, I was a Senior Vice President at United Airlines. Could use someone with management skills here, helping keep the town organized."

Summer blinked. "Sure. Okay."

Ned eyed Harper. "Hmm. Are you eighteen?"

"Seventeen."

"Still in high school then. Not much in the way of job training. Got any particular skills?"

"She can make fart sounds with her hands," muttered Madison. "And get a spoon to hang off her nose without falling."

Harper laughed—as did everyone else. "That's not exactly what he's asking about. Umm. Not really. I'm pretty average."

"Were you a good student?"

"Decent. Mostly As, but I got Bs in trig and chemistry. But just high school level stuff. I didn't have AP classes."

"Might ask you to help out with Violet over at the school since being in school is so fresh in your mind." Mayor Ned snickered at his own joke. "Of course, you'll need to give over that cannon of yours to the militia who'll put it to use."

Harper clung to the strap. "Do I have to? It belonged to my Dad. I promised him I'd never lose it. I mean, I know I'm a kid and all, and like normally, people would take a gun away from a kid… but things aren't exactly normal anymore."

"You ever use that thing?" Ned leaned back to appraise her, clasping his elbow while rubbed a finger back and forth across his chin.

She looked down. "Yes. I didn't have a choice."

"How many?"

"Three maybe." She squirmed with guilt. "They were gonna kidnap and do horrible things to us. I had to."

"Well… it *does* take a certain kind of person to be able to protect others with necessary force. I suppose we could put you on the militia if you'd rather not give up that cannon."

She picked at the nylon strap, trying to figure out how she felt about the Mossberg. Part of her wanted never to see it again since it reminded her of her hesitation causing Dad's death. The bigger part of her brain regarded it as the only way she had to protect Madison. "If no one's going to *take* it away from me, I'd like to keep it."

"Got any training?"

"I've been going to the gun range since I was nine. Won four competitions at thirteen with shotguns, couple more after that. Clay pigeon stuff and multiple shooting station courses. Best time and accuracy in my age group that year. Madison's been to the range, too, but… she's only ten. And she didn't do competitions."

"I shot a bad guy," said Madison. "He was trying to hurt Jonathan, and he grabbed me, too."

Everyone got quiet. Anne-Marie emitted a soft, "Aww!"

Harper hurriedly explained that her little sister hadn't killed anyone, merely winged him.

"Okay then. If you're sure." Mayor Ned patted her on the arm. "Welcome to the militia."

"Umm." She lifted her head and made eye contact with him. "Can I change my mind later on or what happens when I run out of shells?"

Ned stuck his hands in his pants pockets. "Hopefully, you won't need to use them that often here that ya run out before someone figures out how to make more or we find some. 'Course, you're young yet, so I don't have any problem with you wanting to change your mind if being on the militia doesn't work out for you. But, we can cross that bridge if you ever reach it."

"What's involved? I'm not gonna like have to go to boot camp or something?"

Cliff snickered.

Ned shook his head. "Nah. No such thing anymore far as I know. Walt Holman's in charge of defending the town and keeping the peace. He'll bring you both up to speed. For the most part, it's a lot of standing around making everyone else feel safe. Guard duty, walking the streets on patrols, that sort of thing."

She swallowed saliva, and nodded. "Okay. I guess I'll give it a shot."

"You must really like that shotgun," said Darnell. "Though, it is a damn nice one."

"As for the children, they're too little for jobs. But"—Ned winked —"I'm sure you'll be thrilled to know we have a school."

Cliff raised both eyebrows. "Wow. Really?"

"Indeed." Ned gestured off to the side. "Violet Olsen's put together sort of an old fashioned 'one-room-schoolhouse' type thing in the middle school."

"What about Harper? She's only seventeen. Not done with school yet.

Still has a year left." Cliff tried to give her a 'just kidding' wink, but it had an undercurrent of concern.

"Oh, darn, you're right." Ned slapped himself in the forehead. "If she doesn't get her high school diploma, she won't be able to get into college."

Cliff let out a halfhearted chuckle. Harper fidgeted, not terribly happy with the reminder the world had changed so damn much. Anne-Marie gave her a pitying stare.

Ned exhaled. "Forgive my sarcasm. Things aren't exactly the same given the recent nuclear bombardment. As best we've been able to figure out, the national infrastructure is gone. Society may or may not remain intact beyond what we're aware of. Doesn't seem like there's much need to get kids ready for college and batter them with tests. We're focusing on basic education up until about fourteen years old, then on practical skills. Can worry about the fancy stuff once we're thriving."

"What about doctors?" asked Harper.

Ned whistled. "I'm afraid we don't have the resources for a proper medical school. Anyone interested in medicine would have to wind up in an apprentice type situation with Dr. Khan or Dr. Hale."

"We're registering Cliff, Harper, Jonathan, and Madison as a family unit, is that correct?" asked Anne-Marie. "And Summer as an individual."

Everyone murmured agreement.

Mayor Ned conferred with Anne-Marie for a few minutes by a large map on the wall. She tapped a spot, then a second one. Ned nodded and walked back over to the group.

"All right. Mr. Barton, since both you and your eldest daughter are in the militia, you can take a house on Hilltop Drive, fairly close to here. Evergreen does stretch quite a ways south, far enough that it's cumbersome to patrol the entire original town limit on foot. We're concentrated on the north end, since Route 74 represents the most likely point of entry for any group large enough to be threatening. Keeping the critical stuff reasonably close together helps out since most vehicles are useless or will run out of gasoline soon. It's possible we'll see some form of bio-diesel operational, but that'll also require the farm gets up to production capacity."

Cliff scratched at his beard. "All right. Eldest daughter, huh?"

Harper looked over at him. Though she missed Dad like crazy, she didn't think he'd mind her having someone to look out for her. When she managed a grateful smile, he dropped the fake awkwardness.

Ned approached Summer. "Miss Vasquez, since Anne-Marie thinks you'll be a good help to us here in the office, we're thinking you and her might room together for the time being."

"The house has four bedrooms." Anne-Marie smiled. "And it's kinda lonely."

"That's fine. I don't exactly have much stuff to move." Summer emitted a weak laugh. "And not being alone sounds good."

Mayor Ned backed up to address everyone. "We don't have quite the population we did before the shit hit the fan, but we're trying to keep things running as much like the society we're used to as possible. Food is communal. We've got a quartermaster set up across the street and up a ways in the big building next to the old dog place. Provisions are assigned out. We're still living off whatever canned and dry goods we can collect until the farm's up and running, but we hope to be self-sustaining by next summer."

"When you leave here, head back out onto 74 Frontage for a little ways. The next street's Hilltop. Go left and keep walking until you pass Butternut Lane. That one doesn't have a street sign. It's the one that's at like a forty-five degree angle. Your new house is the fourth one on the left." Anne-Marie pointed at the map. "It's not very far from here at all. Close to the quartermaster as well. Call it a militia perk. Normally, we place families with school-age kids closer to the school, but it's more critical that you two are more central for response purposes."

"All right. Easy enough," said Cliff.

"So, what do we do now?" asked Harper.

"Now? Go and get settled in, swing by the quartermaster and talk to Liz. She'll allocate you some food. You two are on the militia, so, just sit tight until Walt sends word about what to do. Might be a day or two to enjoy as a settling in period." Ned again shook hands with Harper, Summer, and Cliff. "Glad to have you here."

By the time they left the mayor's office, the sky looked ready to give up for the day.

The directions to their new house proved simple to follow since the building containing the mayor's office sat at the corner of Hilltop Drive and Route 74. Summer hugged everyone, repeatedly thanking them over and over for helping her get away from 'those bastards' and bringing her here. Anne-Marie's house also basically sat on Hilltop, but only like 200 feet from the mayor's office recessed a little bit on a side street. Despite the woman's emotional 'farewell for now,' it wasn't like they'd never see her again.

Harper headed down Hilltop Drive heading east, looking for the street going off at an angle.

A woman carrying an AK47 in a flannel shirt, jeans, and work boots coming the other way slowed to observe them. She appeared a little older than Summer but still probably in her twenties, with fluffy-curly brown hair.

"Hey." The woman waved once the group came close enough not to require shouting. "Guessing you're new since I haven't seen you before." She eyed the Mossberg. "Damn, that's a howitzer."

"Yeah. We just got here." She fought back the urge to shy away from a new person. *Introvert Prime is now a cop. Yeah. That's going to work.* Of course, the idea of standing in front of a whole class of students potentially as a teacher frightened her more than having to maybe shout at (or shoot) a small number of people. "I'm Harper. This is my sister, Madison, my brother, Jonathan, and our father, Cliff."

Jonathan beamed.

"Leigh Preston." The woman nodded in greeting.

Madison peered up at Harper with a confused expression.

"Getting a look around on your first day here?" asked Leigh.

"Actually, we're heading, uhh, home." Harper let a silent sigh leak out her nose. "Fourth house past Butternut."

"Oh, yeah, right over here. C'mon, I'll show you." Leigh pivoted and began walking. "Your dad on the militia?"

"Yeah. Me too." She patted the shotgun.

"Cool. You're a little young, but we could use all the help we can get."

Cliff glanced over. "That bad? You see a lot of trouble here?"

"We had a couple idiots since I got here. Usually, it's kinda quiet like in terms of people attacking us or causing problems. Other than that, we have the usual crap like this guy Tommy slapping his wife. Also, militia's responsible for going out and looking for supplies and useful stuff. Spreads us a little thin back in town. So, more people means the civilians stay safer whenever there's a scavenging run."

Harper suppressed a shiver. She hadn't signed up for *that.* Leaving Evergreen did *not* fit her plan. Weeks of daydreaming about going to the safe place had no room in it for being a dumbass and leaving said safe place on purpose. Shooting those idiots back in Lakewood happened because she had to in order to escape. Roaming around *looking* for trouble sounded like a horrible idea. Maybe they'd let the 'kid' stay back here for a few years. And… well, if things got too hairy, she could always give up the shotgun and 'go civilian.'

But… could she bring herself to surrender her fate to other people? As long as she had the shotgun, *she* could protect Madison. And, she had Jonathan depending on her now, too. They all had Cliff, but one man couldn't protect everyone—as her real Dad had so aptly proven. Harper squeezed the shotgun strap. No… she couldn't hesitate, not ever again.

Leigh stopped in front of a nice, but small, square house painted in light blue. The front had a tiny concrete porch in front of a central door, one window to the left, two to the right, one small—probably the bathroom. "Here it is. Fourth one from Butternut."

"What happened to whoever lived here?" asked Cliff. "They gonna come back and want their house?"

Leigh shrugged. "I suppose that's possible. Anne-Marie assigns people to houses that have been abandoned. Heard the Army came through here rounding people up for evacuation like a week after the blast. Not sure where they took them."

"Rounded them up?" asked Harper. "Like forced?"

"I don't think so, but I wasn't here then so I can't really answer that." Leigh wandered over to the door. "Anyway, it's intact and in good shape. There's no keys, and Gage removed the locks already. Got a deadbolt still, so if you're inside, you can lock it."

"All right…" Cliff looked the place over.

Jonathan dashed inside.

"Oh, one more thing, in case no one told you this yet." Leigh glanced back and forth between Cliff and Harper. "Until further notice, whenever it rains, everyone's required to stay inside. Mayor Ned's concerned there might be radiation in the rain due to airborne fallout. He said it might take like five years for that to stop being a worry." She put on a bizarrely cheerful smile after such a statement. "Welcome home! Go on and get settled in. Holler if you need anything."

"Yeah, uhh… thanks." Cliff chuckled and headed inside.

Harper gazed up at the sky. *Radioactive rain? Ugh. Talk about nightmare fuel.* She smiled at Leigh and approached the door. *At least this place isn't covered in smoke and ash.*

18

HILLTOP DRIVE

The house on Hilltop Drive had two bedrooms and a smaller room with a computer desk. Its modest living room and dining room merged without much of a division between them. A cup still lay on the floor by the coffee table, perhaps dropped by the former resident when they saw a news report of the nuclear attack and ran straight out.

Evidently, the presence of a fireplace had been one of the criteria for assignable houses. For the next hour or so, they explored their new home. The two bedroom closets held an assortment of linens and comforters. A hall closet had bath towels, a broom, vacuum, and other cleaning supplies. A bit of empty plastic hinted that there may once have been toilet paper there, but someone had taken it.

Harper and Madison got the second bedroom with Cliff taking the master. Jonathan claimed the little computer room for himself. Since they had no way to tell if the computer still worked (due to a lack of electrical power) he gently relocated it to the dining room. If ever power returned, they could try it out. A back door led from the kitchen to a modest yard with a few trees, separated from the property behind them by a wooden fence.

It felt awkward just walking in and taking over a house. How would the town handle it if a prior resident returned and found their home occupied by strangers? Would they just give them some other random house? The person could get violent, but that idea made her doubly glad to have kept the shotgun, even if it did make her think about Dad's death. Being in this place had a surreal quality like she'd started off having a nightmare that ceased being scary and took a turn for the weird.

Though on the small side, the bathroom was clean and functional in all ways except hot water. The sight of it made Harper crave a steamy shower, but, alas. Cliff found some candles in a kitchen drawer and set them out in preparation for later when it became too dark to see. With the survey of the house and bedroom assignments worked out, the girls gathered the packs of canned goods they'd carried with them—as well as their coffee stash—into the kitchen. Cliff tested the sink, which also worked.

"Well, that's something. No idea how much longer that'll last."

She grimaced. "It's gonna stop?"

"Depends on where it's coming from. Some of the more remote houses around here feed off their own wells. Without electricity to work the pumps, they're SOL. This might be coming from a water tower, but I don't remember seeing one. So, umm. Try not to run it too much. We should prepare for the eventuality that we'll wind up having to live rough. Bringing in water from elsewhere by bucket."

She nodded. "Like in a movie about a long time ago."

"Yeah. Something like that." He scratched at his beard. "Hell, who knows. It might stay working. This place has doctors, so it might still have a plumber."

She held up a hand, fingers crossed.

"Gonna go see about a bed for Jonathan." Cliff patted Harper on the shoulder, Madison and Jonathan on the head, then headed out the front door.

Harper searched the cabinets, finding them bare of food. They held plenty of glasses, plates, bowls, mugs, cookware, and cups. She figured the townspeople had gone around to all the abandoned homes after giving up on the residents coming back and took all the cans. Against her better judgement, she checked the fridge. At least whoever raided the house had cleaned it out. No science projects or mold demons waited to ambush her. Without electricity, it would serve primarily as another storage space.

Jonathan opened the door that led from the kitchen to the back yard, and went outside.

Madison opened the backpack and passed cans to Harper, with little emotion on her face. She put them away in the cabinet above the countertop, wondering if she'd have to deal with a meltdown at some point when her sister realized this place had become home and they'd never be going back to the house they grew up in. She tried not to think about how much she missed it, or she'd wind up bawling right there. If Madison ever did freak out over their old house, she'd break down right alongside her.

Jonathan walked in carrying an armload of firewood.

"Where'd you get that?" asked Harper.

"There's a big pile of it two houses over."

"I think you just stole someone's firewood."

He walked by into the living room, dropped the wood on a cradle next to the fireplace, then placed two logs inside it. "They share food here, right? Gotta share firewood, too." He crawled over to Cliff's backpack, rummaged a few things out of it, and returned to the fireplace.

"What are you doing?" called Harper.

"Getting a fire started."

"Don't play with fire. You're not old enough." She shoved the two cans she held into the cabinet and hurried over to him.

Jonathan arranged a small pile of wood shavings on top of one of the logs. "It's okay. Cliff showed me how to do it. And I'm not 'playing with fire.' I'm trying not to freeze. It's cold in here."

Never in her life had she thought fireplaces did anything but look pretty. The idea of heating a house with one didn't even seem possible. The boy picked up a combat knife and an eight-inch metal rod about as thick around as her finger. She started to relax at the lack of matches, but jumped back with a startled yelp when sparks flew. Each time Jonathan scraped the knife down the rod, a shower of bright orange sprayed forth.

She stared in awe, too confused at the sight of a plain metal rod doing that to say anything. Eventually, the wood shavings smoldered. He leaned in and blew on them until a fire sprang to life. Cliff had obviously showed him how to start a fire, so maybe she didn't need to hover over him.

"Ferrocerium rod," said Jonathan, throwing another shower of sparks on the shavings for good measure.

"Umm..."

"The metal. It's called ferrocerium. It's prophylactic."

Harper burst into laughter.

Jonathan paused scraping to look up at her. "What's funny?"

"Did Cliff tell you it was *prophylactic*?"

He bit his lip. "Umm. Maybe not exactly that."

It didn't seem completely smart to leave a ten-year-old alone with an active fireplace, but nothing about the past two months had been normal.

"Be careful with it, okay? You need to stay here and watch it until someone else is in the room. We can't leave it burning with no one here."

He looked up at her. "I will."

Harper dragged the duffel bag down the short hallway to the bedroom she'd be sharing with Madison. Her little sister followed close behind, perching on the bed with her iPhone in both hands.

The room already contained a small dresser, which had been emptied of all contents. Most likely, whoever raided all the canned goods had taken the clothes as well. Harper unzipped the duffel and rummaged out the clothing they'd taken from the mall for themselves, leaving Cliff's and Jonathan's stuff in the bag.

She opened four packets of underwear for Madison, packing them on one side of the top drawer and threw the other packets, presently too big for her, into the closet. The assortment of shirts, dresses, leggings, jeans, and socks amounted to barely a sixth of the stuff they had back home, but it beat having only one outfit.

The front door opened with a clatter. Harper froze, listening. After ten seconds and Jonathan not shouting, she relaxed. A moment later, Cliff's laughter bellowed from the living room. He came down the hallway carrying a twin mattress and leaned into the girls' room long enough to say "pyrophoric" before dragging it into Jonathan's bedroom.

"Huh?" asked Harper.

"Not prophylactic," shouted Cliff.

Harper giggled.

A young Chinese man she hadn't seen before went by carrying a box spring. On the way back out, he paused at the door.

"Hey, Harper?"

She looked over at him. "Yeah."

"Ken Zhang. Welcome to Evergreen. I'm on the militia as well. Good to have you."

"Hey." She waved.

"Hi," said Madison barely over a whisper.

Cliff appeared in the doorway.

"Need a hand with the frame?" asked Ken.

"Sure. That'll speed things up." Cliff glanced at Harper. "Be back in a few minutes."

"Okay." Harper proceeded to pack her clothes in the third drawer.

Madison flopped on the bed and emitted a groan.

"What's wrong?"

"Tired from all the walking."

"Yeah. Me too." Harper stuffed a sweater into the drawer. Tonight, she'd be in a strange bed in a strange house, but she doubted she'd have *any* trouble falling asleep.

"How long do we have to stay here before we can go home?" asked Madison in a toneless voice.

Harper's breath caught in her throat. She froze, leaning on the drawer, a pair of jeans under her hand. A barrage of memories from her old life ran by in her thoughts, birthdays, holidays, funny moments, sad moments... more than the house, she missed her parents. The house could rot in Hell for all she cared if she could have Mom and Dad back. All the grief she'd been holding in at their deaths threatened to come crashing down over the wall she'd built to contain it. The sense of security offered by the mundanity of a doctor visit and a new home far removed from roving bands of criminals offered a reprieve from the hypervigilance she'd been running on.

"Harp?"

She pushed herself up and went over to sit on the edge of the bed. As much as she tried to look brave and tough for her sister's benefit, tears still rolled down her cheeks. "Hey, Termite. You remember how that big explosion happened?"

Madison swiped her finger around the black iPhone screen. "I'm ten, not five. I know we had nuclear war."

"Yeah. There's no more police or anything. It's not safe back home. It might not be safe there for a very long time. All the good people left, trying to find places like this, up in the mountains where no bombs came down." She paused long enough to get her quivering voice under control. "This house we're in is gonna be our home now."

"I don't like it here," said Madison, her voice still emotionless. "This is someone else's house."

"It's what we have." Harper sniffled, hating herself for 'giving up' on the place she spent her entire life, less the past two weeks. "I want to go back there, too. But we can't. It's too dangerous. I won't let you get hurt, you know that."

Madison dropped the iPhone in her lap, sat up, and leaned against her. "I know. You shot people."

Harper hugged her tight. "Yeah. I hated it, but I didn't have a choice."

"How are Mom and Dad gonna find us here?" Madison swiped her hand at the phone. "Or my friends? I miss them. Are they okay? Did the bad people kidnap them?"

She might've tried to tell her that their parents had died—if she could've made her voice work.

"Mom would've called if her phone had charge."

The dam broke; Harper lapsed into sobs. Her sister remaining blank-faced made her weep harder. *She's broken... and I don't know how to fix her.* "I'm sorry." She sniffled. "I'm sorry." She held Madison like a giant teddy bear, rocking her side to side, no longer able to contain her grief. Both of her parents had died right in front of her, but only Dad had been her fault. Panic had kept her from feeling much of anything at all about losing them—until that moment.

Madison rambled about her friends, Becca, Melissa, and Eva, coming up with ideas about where they might be and why they hadn't called her yet. Fortunately, her guesses didn't include death or kidnapping by the 'blue gang.' Harper clung to her, muttering random incoherent attempts at saying "sorry," though even she couldn't tell if she apologized for failing Dad, for not being able to tell Madison the truth, or for not being able to fix whatever had gone wrong with her mind.

She missed her parents so damn much it hurt, and couldn't do anything but curl up on the bed and cry. Madison cuddled close, continually running a hand through Harper's thick, red hair. It eventually struck her as backward for the little sister to be comforting the big sister. That thought helped her calm from bawling to staring into space.

At the clamor of Cliff and Ken coming in the front door, Harper hastily gathered her composure. She sat up and faced away from the door so neither man could see how red her face had likely become. They dragged something heavy down the hallway to Jonathan's room. Madison grabbed her phone and poked its button.

"Siri, call Mom."

Harper brushed her sister's hair out of her eyes. "Maddie... Mom and Dad are, umm..."

"Trying to call?"

Harper bowed her head. "They can't call us. They—"

"Have no phones?"

"It's—"

Heavy knocking shook the front door.

"Harper, can you see who that is please?" yelled Cliff between grunts.

Argh! She wiped at her eyes, grabbed the shotgun, and trudged down the hall to the living room, which already seemed a little bit warmer—though still remained too cold to take off her coat. Madison followed, staring at her phone. Jonathan, seated on the floor near the fire, had taken his coat off.

At seeing a smiling thirtysomething woman with strawberry blonde hair in the small window, Harper slung the Mossberg over her shoulder and pulled the door open. Their visitor carried a cardboard box of plastic containers. Her blue ski vest, flannel shirt, jeans, and work boots seemed a bit too casual for the aftermath of Armageddon.

"Hi! I'm Carrie Rangel. I live right next door. Noticed I have new neighbors." She offered the box. "Here's some food to get you started. Figure you had enough work getting settled in, so I ran over to Liz and got you some stuff."

"Oh, thank you." Harper accepted the box. "That's really thoughtful."

"Are you okay, hon?"

Being caught with red-ringed eyes embarrassed her enough to make her look down. With Madison hovering right behind her, she couldn't talk about their parents—at least not until she'd broken that news in private first.

"Yeah. It just hit me hard that we're kinda safe here. Had a scary couple weeks. It feels so *normal* here I started thinking about all the stuff that's gone."

"Oh, yeah. That's gotta be rough. Especially on someone young like you."

"You're not old."

"Thanks, hon. Most kids your age think thirty-four is ancient." Carrie laughed.

"Guess you're on the militia, too, if you live on this street."

"Naw. I ain't cut out for that. I've lived here for the past eight years. Didn't leave with the others."

"Oh." Harper's eyes widened. "What happened to them? Did they run or did the Army force them out?"

Carrie shrugged. "I can't rightly say. My husband was in New York on a business trip. He called me a couple minutes to five in the morning when he saw a news report about a detonation in Washington DC. He said people in his hotel were already in a total panic. They didn't have any warning. The line went dead. Still don't know if he survived. I hid out in the root cellar for a couple days. By the time I risked poking my nose above ground, half the people around here'd already took off."

"Oh. I'm sorry about your husband."

"Thanks, dear." Carrie patted the box. "There's a woman, Elizabeth Trujillo, up the highway a little at the quartermaster place. They work out food allotments. Sometimes it feels like they're being a bit stingy, but they have to make it last until the farm's up and running."

"Yeah." Harper nodded. "Mayor Ned gave us the explanation already."

Ken emerged from the hallway. "Oh, hey Carrie."

"Hi, Ken. Stopped by to say hello; brought them some provisions."

"Nice." He nodded at Harper. "Great meeting you. Sorry to run so quick, but I need to get back out there."

"Umm." She looked over his unremarkable coat, jeans, and boots. "Is there like a militia uniform or something? If someone needs us, how do they tell who to look for?"

Ken smiled. "There ain't all that many of us yet that people can't remember. But generally, anyone walking around with a gun looking like they're not in any hurry to be anywhere is probably on the militia."

"Oh. What am I supposed to do?"

"If you just got here today, nothing really. Get settled in, rest from the trip. Walt will send one of us over to bring you to the HQ eventually."

"Okay. Yeah… rest sounds good. Feels like I've been walking for weeks."

Ken laughed, waved, and slipped past Carrie out the door.

Cliff trudged over, appearing somewhat winded. He paused by Jonathan long enough to tell him he now had a bed, then approached the door where he fell into an easy conversation with Carrie. Harper took the chance to check out the box. It contained mostly canned goods, but one of the plastic containers held fresh chicken.

Oh, that's not going to last. Guess we have that tonight. "Umm… how are we supposed to cook this?"

"Fireplace," said Cliff and Carrie at the same time.

"You'll need to rig a metal rack to hold a pan in the fire so you don't have to hold it. I'm using an oven shelf." Carrie walked over to the kitchen, opened the oven, and removed one of the wireframe shelves. "Our houses are pretty much identical. This will work."

Cliff appeared amused at the woman making herself at home in their house.

While Carrie worked the oven shelf into the fireplace, wedging it in the bricks, Harper carried the food to the kitchen counter. She decided to make use of two vegetable cans—one peas, one carrots—plus the chicken. Granted, as cold as the weather was, she could probably leave it outside and it would be as safe as being refrigerated, but no sense risking a critter making off with it.

Also, she hadn't eaten actual food in months.

She had no idea what time it was, but they'd been rattling around the house long enough that it had to be a few hours past lunch. Perhaps a little early for dinner, but no one had eaten anything since they woke up. A few scattered seasonings the former occupant had collected remained on a rack above the stove, evidently of no interest to whoever had raided the place. She picked up one bottle. It didn't look *too* old, and the chicken needed something. She doubted butter or oil in any form existed here anywhere.

"Looks I'm cooking on borrowed thyme," muttered Harper.

Cliff groaned. "Why don't you have dinner with us tonight?"

After washing her hands, she took the chicken out of the container, dropped it in a large pan, and dusted it with an assortment of seasonings. The peas and carrots went into two separate aluminum pots. Those could sit at the edge of the oven-shelf-turned-grill as they didn't need to cook so much as warm up.

Harper grabbed a pair of tongs from a drawer and headed into the living room.

"You ever cook over a fire before?" asked Cliff.

She gave him epic side eye.

"I'll take that as a no." He chuckled. "Okay, best thing to do is use glowing coals for food heat, not over the actual flames. Move the burning wood to one side."

"This fireplace isn't *that* big."

He grabbed the poker and jabbed it at the wood. "It's plenty big enough for this. Of course, we're trying to warm this place up as well as cook... don't do what I did as an idiot teenager."

Jonathan scooted back, grinning.

"What happened?" Harper slid the vegetables onto the oven shelf, as away from the open flame as possible.

"Friend of mine had this cabin up in the hills. Our dumb asses thought it would be an awesome idea to go hang there for a week in freakin' February. It was so damn cold and the place was, uhh... 'rustic.' No electricity or heat. We only had the fireplace for warmth. My cousin John lost his damn mind. Found a railroad tie or something abandoned in the woods behind the place and chopped it into bits with a maul."

"If there was a mall, why didn't you just buy firewood?" asked Harper.

Cliff glanced at her. "Please tell me you're joking."

She blinked. "Kinda. Pretty sure you don't mean mall, but I have no idea what you do mean."

"A maul is kinda like the bastard offspring of an axe and a sledgehammer, but dull."

"What the heck is the point of that?"

"Splitting wood." Cliff threw another log in. "So anyway, we were freezing our asses off. We burned so much wood so fast we got the temp up to ninety something inside the place. Guy next door came running over because we had literal flames coming out the top of the chimney."

"Wow."

"Yeah." Cliff laughed. "That was a fun week."

Harper set the chicken pan over the fire and knelt nearby. "Probably not as fun to be stuck living in a cabin out in the woods."

"This isn't exactly a 'cabin in the woods.'" Carrie smiled. "Evergreen's a real town. Just... without electricity for the time being."

Cliff prodded the fire. "We're a *ways* off before anyone's going to get a power plant online again."

"Maybe those solar panels will work out?" Harper shrugged.

"Maybe." Cliff pushed himself up to stand. "Gonna go pack out my room."

Carrie sat on the couch, making idle chitchat with Harper while the food cooked. Prior to the war, she'd worked from home, doing crafty stuff she sold online mostly for fun as her husband made enough for them to live on as a lawyer. Madison sat on the floor beside Harper, her attention absorbed on the dead iPhone as thoroughly as if it worked and she played a video game. The sight of her like that made Harper want to scream, to grab and shake her, do something, but guilt got in the way. What if Madison blamed her for not shooting the guy? Did she see it all happen? Her sister could've watched everything from under the table in the dining room—if she'd been looking.

Harper thought back to that moment when the bullet exploded out the front of Dad's chest. Her dying father emptied the rest of his magazine out the patio door to keep the thugs at bay. He'd survived only long enough to grab Madison and shove her at Harper while yelling, "Run!" The bloody handprint he'd left on that T-shirt all they had left of him.

Once he stopped firing, the men came rushing inside. It hadn't even occurred to her until hours later when the running stopped that pausing to grab Madison's flip-flops from the lawn might've gotten them both captured.

But, the bigger question remained: had Madison curled up with her face to the rug *because* she'd watched her mother stabbed to death and her father shot, or had she been like that the whole time?

Harper talked about her old life and friends with Carrie, sounding like a robot. Words came out of her with no more emotion than if she described a movie she'd watched, not reality she'd lived. She almost envied Madison in that her little sister probably didn't have such dark fears as to what may have befallen her friends. Some of them probably left with the large wave of evacuations within the first few days. But escaping Lakewood didn't guarantee bad things didn't happen to them elsewhere.

Eventually, the chicken looked and smelled done. She took it off the fire and carried it into the kitchen, set the pan on the stove (since that wouldn't burn) and cut each breast in half both to check it and to split the portions. Satisfied the meat had cooked through, she turned to grab the vegetables, but Carrie walked in with the peas, using her flannel sleeves as oven mitts. Harper dodged around her, grabbed actual oven mitts, and went for the carrots.

"Cliff, food," called Harper, while portioning out the four half-breasts on each of four plates, plus a pair of thighs on a fifth plate that amounted to a roughly equal portion of meat. To each plate, she added as even as distribution as possible of peas and carrots, then carried them all to the kitchen table.

He hurried out from the bedroom. Jonathan scrambled over to the table while Madison dragged her feet. Everyone dug in at once, except Madison, who just stared at her plate.

"C'mon, Termite." Harper prodded her. "It's actual food. Hot food. Eat."

"It's chicken."

"I know… it's what we have."

Madison looked down. "But it's an animal. It makes me sad that it died. You know I can't eat meat."

Cliff looked up with a 'you gotta be kidding me' expression.

"I know you don't eat meat, but things are different now. There isn't food like there used to be. We don't have a supermarket to go to and get veggies and tofu and whatever. We can't be picky."

Madison scowled. "It's not picky. It's wrong. The chicken *died*."

"So did the world," said Jonathan past a mouthful.

Madison's lip quivered.

Unbelievable. Everything that's happened and she's about to cry over a piece of damn chicken. Harper drew in a breath to scream, but couldn't bring herself to do it. Her little sister, the only family she had left, had become emotionally brittle. Shouting over chicken was both pointless and excessive. Instead, she wrapped her arms around Madison and hugged her in silence.

Forks clinked and scraped.

"We have to eat, Maddie. Some days, we might not even have food at all. The war destroyed civilization. There's no supermarkets. Even if no one bothered to nuke the big farms, there aren't any trucks to bring the food anywhere. These people are sharing their food with us. We can't waste it. It totally sucks that a chicken had to die, but I don't want *you* to die. Okay?"

Madison stared at the chicken for a little while before picking up her fork and stabbing it. She raised the half-breast to her mouth and nibbled on it while crying. She whispered an apology then took a bigger bite, crying harder as if she made a meal of a family pet.

Harper had to look away. "I'm sorry, Maddie. Please don't think I'm asking you to eat that just to be mean."

"I know," sniffled Madison. "I still feel bad."

Cliff looked like he wanted to ramble off about vegetarians, but he contented himself to chat with Carrie about the city. According to her, a little over two thousand people remained out of the ten thousand or so that had lived within the official limits of Evergreen prior to the nukes. The remaining citizens had only just started getting into anything like a routine. Someone she referred to as Earl wanted to reopen a bar, though they didn't have a lot of liquor around. With money being useless, he planned to ration it out like they did food until the farm got going and he could brew beer. Maybe people would wind up trading whiskey rations as a form of money.

Madison ate her chicken between sobs. Despite that the girl *needed* real food, Harper felt like a monster for twisting her arm into eating meat. Maybe once the farm got underway, she could arrange a vegetarian diet for her. Thanksgiving had always been a bit of a joke at home. Dad got into the habit of molding a tiny turkey out of tofu for Madison.

No one cares about Thanksgiving anymore. No one noticed Halloween.

Harper sighed, thinking about Christmas and the new laptop she'd been begging for (for school of course) and dropping hints that having her own car would be awesome even if she got an older one—but now, if Christmas still existed in any form, the only thing she'd want would be her mother and father alive and with her.

Harper barely held back the rising emotional storm long enough to finish off her plate, then stood without a word and ran down the hall to her new bedroom. She leapt onto the bed, face-first in the pillow, and sobbed for her parents, trying to keep as quiet as she could.

19

GONE

Harper opened her eyes to a dark room.

She couldn't remember at what point she'd fallen asleep while sobbing into the pillow, crushed by guilt and loss over her parents. The truth that they would forever be gone had been stalking her like a wraith ever since she'd dragged her little sister out of the house. It followed her all the way here, and finally sank its claws into her heart once she allowed herself to hope this place might be safe.

Madison lay beside her, still asleep. She clutched her iPhone the way normal kids slept with teddy bears or dolls. The girl hadn't at all been phone-obsessed before, and that worried Harper the most. Sure, she'd texted a lot with her friends, but this new fixation came not from the lack of a phone but out of some futile attempt to disbelieve reality in hopes their dead parents would call.

Someone had covered them both with the comforter they found at that other house and also taken Harper's shoes off. Crying so hard had left her tired despite having napped for a while. Her head swam with emotions: grief and guilt over her parents, anger at whoever launched the nukes, fear at what she'd gotten herself into by joining the militia, loss and worry over the future she wouldn't have. A little hope snuck in there somewhere, hope that perhaps Evergreen might offer something akin to civilization. So far, the people here had been friendly and helpful. She could've done without the strip search, which made her feel a bit too much like she'd been sent to prison. But, with only two doctors and limited medical facilities, it made sense to make sure no one brought anything nasty into the town. Even something as mundane as a bad flu could kill people now.

We're back in the Old West. Doctors making house calls with the little black bag or some crap like that.

Her guts felt like a wrung out dishtowel. Despite the crazy tangle of emotion and horrible sadness stabbing her in the heart, she'd cried herself out. Numb, she stared over the pillow at the wall, barely visible in the moonlight.

After a few minutes, the need to use the bathroom urged her into motion. She slipped out from under the comforter into an annoyingly chilly room. The fire had warmed the house somewhat, though it had undoubtedly been allowed to burn down before everyone went to bed. Harper hurried into her sneakers and crept down the hall to the bathroom, feeling her way along in the dim light. Sitting on a block of ice would've been warmer than the toilet.

She returned to the bedroom, stood there for a few seconds feeling like she didn't belong there, then grabbed her coat and went outside via the kitchen door. A constant, frigid breeze made the interior of the house feel heated by comparison. Her breath puffed in small clouds of moonlit fog that drifted off to the left. She shut the door and stared up at the stars, awestruck that the sky glimmered with such clarity.

Maybe that nuclear winter stuff won't happen. Or maybe the crap just hasn't spread out yet.

Harper stared into the infinity above her, trying to memorize what a starry sky looked like in case she spent the rest of her life under a permanent cloud. The silent tranquil beauty of it allowed a new emotion to break free of the pack and take over her thoughts: jealousy. She swung between anger and worry, overwhelmed by everything she'd lost and been through. How dare Dad die and leave her alone. She shouldn't be dealing with a mentally checked out ten-year-old who may or may not sincerely believe their dead parents would try to call her on a dead cell phone. How could she be expected to deal with that on top of everything else?

She rubbed her arms through the jacket, trying to warm up. "I'm seventeen. I'm not done being a kid yet. It's not fair I've become Maddie's mother. I should be worrying about not failing exams and getting into a reasonably decent college. I should be hanging out with Andrea,

Christina, and Renee doing goofy crap, not wondering if I'm going to need to shoot someone."

A long sigh leaked out.

"Dammit. Why did this happen? Why?" Harper stood there, gaze on the stars, arms at her sides, crying silent tears for her parents, friends, college, the life she'll never have... and a broken little sister she didn't know how to help. She resented that the universe had dropped all this on her. Maybe she could fail Dad for the second time and surrender the shotgun to Mayor Ned, hide in the house like the terrified child she still was inside.

Surrender...

No. I can't give up on Maddie, even if I have no idea what to do.

Again, she thought about the way her sister leaned back into her in the bathtub when she mentioned pretending to be her mother as a little kid. No way had Madison remembered that. She wouldn't have even been two years old at the time. Did her sister ask her to become 'Mom,' or had the moment of closeness simply been shared grief?

"What am I supposed to do?" whispered Harper. "I'm not ready for any of this."

"I'm sorry," said Madison, right behind her.

Harper jumped, clutching her chest. "W-what? Why are you apologizing? You didn't do anything."

"I'm sorry for existing." Madison looked down.

"No..." Harper melted into an emotional puddle and clamped onto her sister in a fierce hug, terrified the girl might be so shattered she'd hurt herself. "Don't listen to any of what I just said. I'm scared. I don't know what I'm doing and I'm freaking out that I'm gonna mess up and hurt you."

"You're doing okay."

Harper squeezed her tighter. "I can't lose you, okay? When I was eight, I used to pretend I was your mother. You were so damn little then. I'm not pretending anymore, Termite. Whatever I have to do to protect you, I'm gonna do. Sorry for that crap I said. I'm just scared and having trouble dealing with the whole world changing."

They held each other in silence for a while.

"Mom and dad aren't coming back, are they?" asked Madison.

Harper relaxed the hug and leaned back to make eye contact. "No. They're not. I'm sorry, Termite. They died. It's my fault. If I didn't hesitate..."

"I saw," said Madison in a brittle voice. She reached up and brushed a tear off Harper's face. "It's not your fault about Dad."

"I couldn't—"

"You never yell or got in any fights at school. Even bugs, you carry 'em outside instead of squishing 'em. It's not your fault you're too nice to like killing people. Daddy wouldn't be mad with you 'cause you didn't shoot that man."

"But, I did… I have shot people."

Madison clamped on in a tight hug. "I'm sorry for making you."

"You didn't."

"Yeah, I did." Madison sniffled. "If I didn't exist, you wouldn't need to shoot people to keep me safe."

"It's a different world now." Harper patted her sister's back. "I'll never like having to do that, but I promise I won't hesitate ever again."

"Like chicken."

"Huh? Yeah, I guess I was a chicken."

"No." Madison leaned back, wiping her nose. "I mean, me eating chicken. The world's different."

"Yeah. Hey. There's gonna be a farm here. If there's a choice, I won't make you eat meat, okay?"

Madison nodded. "Okay. Umm. What about my friends? Did they go away forever, too?"

"I really don't know."

"Am I bad?"

"No. Why would you think that?"

Madison bit her lip. "I shot that guy. Kids my age aren't supposed to touch guns except at the range with Dad. But, he was gonna hurt Jonathan."

"No, you're not in trouble for that. It's okay to protect yourself when someone's trying to hurt you bad."

Her little sister's eyes widened. "I heard what you said before. Please don't run away. I don't wanna be alone."

"I…" Harper barely held back guilt tears. "I'm not going to go away."

"Promise?"

"Yeah, Termite. I promise." Harper touched foreheads with her.

"Are you still gonna call me Termite when I'm older?"

"Probably." She sniffled. "Why, does it bother you?"

Madison smirked. "It used to. But now, whenever you call me that, it makes me wanna cry, 'cause I think about being mad at you an' how Mom and Dad are gone and our family's just us now."

"Okay, I'll stop using it."

"No." Madison squeezed her. "It's like saying we're still family. We lost everything else. You can keep calling me Termite." For a second, it seemed as though Madison might burst into tears, but she somehow remained calm.

"C'mon, Termite." Harper nudged her. "Let's go back inside before we freeze."

"'Kay."

Harper held her hand on the way to their bedroom. They shed their winter coats, shoes, and jeans, then crawled in under the covers, huddled together for warmth. She had no idea who slept in this bed before, but it beat a mattress of trash bags behind a dumpster. It also beat a sleeping bag on a booth seat in some restaurant where she only got a few hours of sleep due to having to keep watch. It took a few minutes, but eventually, the bed became cozy.

"Harp?" whispered Madison.

"Mmm?"

"I still miss home, but I don't hate it here."

Harper squeezed her sister's hand. "Yeah. That's exactly how I feel."

20

STARTING SLOW

Over the next two days, Harper settled into her new home. Madison had gone back to being quiet and a little withdrawn, still clinging to her iPhone. She stopped asking Siri to call Mom or Dad, though still acted as though she expected one of her friends to call. Cliff spent a couple hours each day teaching them all 'woodland survival' stuff, like how to use a ferrocerium rod, how to harvest fatwood from old logs, and even what plants or bugs could be eaten in an emergency.

They discovered the pile Jonathan had taken firewood from belonged to Carrie, a huge mound of it that her likely deceased husband had collected before the war. The quartermaster did allocate firewood as needed, though the town didn't prohibit anyone from going out to collect their own. Of course, with no working vehicles, people could go only so far. Carrie didn't mind sharing as she had a crapload—on the condition Cliff help her find and split more when the need arose.

A few cars *did* seem to be working somewhere in the area, since the sound of a running engine had become unusual enough to stand out. None came close enough to see, so she had no clue who drove what or why. Cliff said gasoline would last maybe six months before becoming useless, so perhaps people used the cars while they could to gather supplies from distances too great to walk.

No longer driving bothered her more than it should. She hadn't possessed a license for long at all, and felt cheated. This became guilt at the thought that millions had likely died across the globe, so being moody over such a 'first world problem' like not getting to drive anymore made her feel shallow.

Sometimes Cliff cooked, sometimes Harper did. Most of what they ate still came out of cans, but at least they heated it up. Jonathan appointed himself 'fire marshal,' and made it his mission to keep the house warm. By the third day, no one needed coats or shoes inside the house. He and Madison amused themselves with practicing dance routines or playing with some toys they'd found while exploring unoccupied houses.

Cliff had gone looking for the militia commander on the second day, and over dinner that night, said it seemed 'reasonably well put together for a bunch of townies.' The conversation that followed about people roaming the city with rifles and Coleman lanterns at night made Harper feel like she'd truly gone back in time to like the 1850s Old West.

A dark-skinned woman with straight black hair knocked four days after their arrival in Evergreen.

Harper pulled the door open and smiled. "Hi. Umm…" She eyed the AR-15 over the woman's shoulder. "Guess you're militia?"

"Hello. Yes. I'm Annapurna. You must be Harper." She offered a hand.

After shaking, Harper nodded. "Yep."

"Oh, wow. You're so young." Annapurna shook her head. "Crazy world we're in now, huh? Anyway, Walter wants you to head over to the north HQ and meet him."

"Okay. Uhh, 'north HQ'?"

The woman smiled. "Yeah. Since cars aren't exactly reliable anymore, the militia is split over two command centers. One's on the other side of the dog place from the quartermaster building. Used to be an office or something. Two-tone with stone on the bottom and wood on top. Little castle tower type thing at one end. Pretty hard to miss. Basically, head outta here onto Hilltop, go all the way back to Route 74, turn right and it's the third building on the left. Just look for that little stone tower deal at the one end."

"All right. Let me get my coat and shoes. C'mon in a sec."

Harper jogged to her bedroom, put her shoes on, then grabbed her coat and shotgun. Madison ambushed her in the hall when she emerged, diving into a clinging hug.

"What?"

"Don't go away," whispered Madison.

"I'm not 'going away.' This is like going to work or something. I think I'm meeting the boss today, so I shouldn't be gone *that* long."

"I wanna go with you."

Harper cringed inside. Being on the militia probably didn't amount to the safest choice of job in a post-nuclear-war society, but that whole 'post nuclear war' thing made *any* job dangerous. She didn't think people like the 'blue gang' would care if someone called themselves militia, a teacher, a doctor, or whatever. They'd attack anyone. Much better for her if she still had her father's shotgun. The girl who couldn't even kill bugs had taken at least three human lives in the past two weeks. Reality wouldn't care about her being seventeen, or a girl, or that her junior class had voted her 'sweetest person.' *Gawd that had been so embarrassing.* No, reality would throw everything it had at whoever it could crush, and she didn't want Madison being run over.

"I have no idea what I'm going to have to do. You don't really want to wind up walking back and forth all over town if they make me do a patrol. I need you to stay warm and safe here, okay? I promise I'll be home as soon as I can."

Madison again almost seemed about to cry, but held it in. "But, Cliff's 'at work,' too. What if something happens here? A spark could fly outta the fire and burn the house."

"I'm not gonna torch the house," said Jonathan from the end of the hall.

"If you need someone, go to Carrie's next door. You two are both ten, and I trust you to keep yourselves out of trouble for a couple hours, okay?" Again, she winced internally. Mom would never have left Madison alone at home this young. She might've trusted Harper home alone at thirteen, but not with a six-year-old sister. Home alone without parents hadn't happened until two years ago.

Madison bowed her head, trudged to the couch, and sat.

"I don't like having to leave you alone. You know that." Harper walked over and patted her on the head. "I love you, Termite. I'll be back as soon as I can."

"'Kay."

Jonathan looked up at her.

She thought back to him talking about having two sisters in his dream, and hugged him. "Love you too, kiddo."

He grinned. "Go kick some ass."

"Heh. Thanks."

Harper stepped outside with Annapurna, pulled the door shut behind her, and sighed. *What the hell am I doing?*

They walked to the end of Hilltop Drive and kept going across a grassy swath to the highway, hung a right, and followed the road for a couple hundred feet. Annapurna went off the left side, climbed a short metal fence, and led her over another road to a curvy driveway next to a small, fancy office building. The end facing the road had a rectangular tower of stacked stone with a pyramid roof above a strip of windows.

"This is the HQ. That"—Annapurna pointed at the next building to the right, all wood with kind of a barn-ish look. "That's the dog place. Used to be a boarding kennel, but now it's more like a shelter. Anyway, this is the northern HQ. The other building's down in the old sheriff's office, south of Evergreen Lake. Bit of a hike."

"Right..." Harper looked around, then followed the woman up a paved path to the back. A telephone pole on the right had blackened near the top. Only a few metal scraps remained of a transformer can that had exploded. Loose wires lay in a bundle near the base, where someone had gathered them off the road. Annapurna headed around to the end of the building and up a stone path to a blue-framed glass door.

The interior still looked like an office, though portable camping lanterns hung from recently-added hooks. Nothing electronic appeared to be functional. She wondered if the devices had fried, or merely the power grid. An improvised gun rack holding a handful of bolt-action hunting rifles stood next to a shelf laden with giant coffee cans labeled in various bullet sizes. That, too, she figured hadn't been here before the war.

"Ahh, Harper," called a fiftyish man with white hair from a doorway. He had the look of a recently-retired cop about him, giving off a friendly air that verged on paternal. "I'm Walter Holman. Please, come on in."

"Hi." She accepted his handshake and went into a former conference room. Huge maps covered a twelve-person table as well as the walls. An ordinary desk sat in the corner, probably Walter's. Except for the lack of a computer, it looked like something she'd have seen at her Dad's former workplace.

Ugh. It's take your daughter to work day—with guns.

"Okay, so, first thing. Welcome to the militia." Walter smiled.

"Thanks."

"Guess you've heard I'm in charge of it for the time being. Used to be with the Jefferson County Sheriff's office. Couple of us are left, but since I had the highest rank, Ned asked me to manage this lot."

She nodded.

"All right." He gestured at the maps. "This is Evergreen. Before everything went to hell, the town covered a fair bit of land. We're down to about two thousand people at this point, so to keep things in the realm of doable, we've mostly collected at the north end, where we are now." He tapped at Hilltop Drive. "Farthest north we really have settled at the moment is Evergreen Middle School. Violet's up there, teaching the kids. She lives in the building as well." He traced his finger around the map to the south of the school. "Bunch of families in this area here."

"Oh, wow. On the way in, we spent the night at a school. I think it was that one." She pointed at a building along Route 74 farther northeast.

"Bergen Valley Elementary." Walter nodded. "We're not using that for anything. Kinda remote. Though we did grab all the useful stuff we could out of it, and the grocery stores west of it."

"Yeah. Thanks for leaving us a can of pudding." She laughed.

Grinning, Walter jabbed his finger at the map by the Mayor's office. "The area south from here to Stagecoach Boulevard is pretty much filled in. Also, east and north of Hilltop. We're putting single people with no kids in the apartment building on Wallace Road for now. When that's full —if it fills—we're likely to start placing them in the old assisted living complex. Ain't a lot of difference between an apartment and a hospital when all the cookin' happens outside over a fire."

Harper nodded. "Okay."

"There's a couple of families still living in their original homes here." Walter tapped the map to the east of a big building marked 'Safeway,' then dragged his finger down along one of the roads, tapping again about six inches past a lake. "This is our southern HQ. Janice Holt's in charge down there. She's my second in command. The area north of Evergreen High School is still fairly populated. Bunch of people there decided to hole up and not evacuate. Still spread a bit too thin for my liking, but if people want to stay in their homes, I ain't goin' to force them out. Hopefully, we don't have any 'situations,' but it's on them if we can't get out there in time."

"Situations?" asked Harper, eyebrows rising.

"Well, you know. All them movies about nuclear war have bandits running around. Seems a little farfetched to me, but I suppose there are people out there who'd do whatever they think they can get away with."

"Yeah. Lakewood's got a gang problem." She sat on the edge of the big table and explained about the people wearing blue.

Walter listened, rubbing his chin and nodding. "Damn, girl. Sorry about your folks."

"Thank you." She looked down.

He set a small can on the table beside her, about the size of a Red Bull, with a red plastic horn on one end. "This is your radio."

"Umm." Harper picked it up and looked it over.

"It's the best we've got for now. One short pip is basically an acknowledgement tone. Two short blasts is 'need help over here, but no one's about to die.' One long blast is the 911 call. Three long blasts is a fire alarm."

"Is this for me because I'm a kid?"

He chuckled. "Nah. Everyone on the militia carries one. Not sure what we're going to do yet when these run out, but for now…"

"Okay." She stuffed it in her jacket pocket. "One pip is okay, two short is need help, one long is holy crap get over here now, and three long is something's on fire."

"Right." He regarded her for a long moment, then put a hand on her shoulder. "Are you sure you're ready for this?"

"Is anyone? I mean… yeah, I've never had any experience fighting before. Won some competitions with a shotgun, but like karate? No idea. I used to be the girl who just sat there and hoped to avoid conflict at all costs. Basically, I'm just a normal high school kid… or I was right up until like two months ago when the world went to hell."

"Well, a shotgun's a great equalizer, and anyone can be taught enough to manage a fight. See, the thing about cops, well… militia now. We're not usually alone."

"I really hate shooting at people. But, my sister needs me to protect her. My new brother does, too."

"Are you sure you want to do this, Harper? I understand Mayor Ned told you that you can change your mind if it doesn't work out. Don't feel pressured. I'm glad to have you with us, but you shouldn't worry about 'disappointing me' or some macho BS like that. You're seventeen, right? You've been through some bad stuff. No one will think less of you if you want to do something else."

Temptation needled at her. *What am I doing? I have no idea how to fight. I hate fighting. I hate even getting loud with people.* She fidgeted at the nylon strap over her shoulder. That shotgun was her best chance to keep

Madison safe. Jonathan, too, but he had Cliff. Well, technically, they *all* had Cliff. If she wanted to feel like a child again, she could admit to being weak and crawl back home, in need of protection like the 'kid' she thought of herself as.

The kid who used to trap spiders and bugs alive instead of stepping on them.

The kid who shot a dude in the face to keep him from abducting Madison.

I can't fail Dad again. She clenched her fist around the shotgun's strap. Giving it up so the mayor could hand it to someone else felt like a stupid thing to do. The militia didn't have cars. They didn't even have horses. If some random lunatic made it into Evergreen, no one would get there in time to protect her or Madison or Jonathan. They'd show up in time to go hunt down their killers.

"Yeah. I'm sure." Harper swallowed the saliva that had built up in her mouth and sat up tall. "I have to keep my family, and I guess the town now, safe."

"All right." Walter offered a warm smile and a look that said if she changed her mind later on, it would be okay. "I'd like for you to spend the first couple days exploring and patrolling the area to make yourself familiar with it. Might want to head up to the middle school and work your way south. For now, stay north of Hilltop drive, establish a working familiarity with that area. Spend a couple hours every day this week coming up walking the streets, learning the lay of the roads and such."

"Okay. I can do that."

"Obviously, you're not going to know people right off the bat, so part of this is so you can get used to seeing who should be there. That way, you'll be able to recognize anyone who *shouldn't* be."

She nodded.

"If you have any questions, worries, concerns, whatever, ask anyone in the militia or come back here and find me."

"What do we do with like criminals now? Is there a jail?"

"There is one down at the south HQ. The old sheriff's office, but we have better use for resources than keeping prisoners alive."

Harper's eyes widened.

"Oh, no." He held up a hand, chuckling. "I don't mean that like we just shoot everyone who breaks the rules. Depends on what they did. Trivial things, we might slap them around a bit and tell them to knock it off. Issues like stealing, serious fighting, grabbing on women, and so on, we'll usually kick them out of town. If there's a dispute, we'll incarcerate them until we can hold a trial. Murder, rape, and the real bad stuff… well… no sense turning a problem like that loose only to have it sneak back up on you."

"Right. So is there like a badge or uniform or something?"

"Not yet. Been tryin' this place to order uniforms, but they're not answering the phone."

She laughed.

"Word gets around here pretty quick. Militia already knows you're on board. Ain't that many girls your age with red hair and a shotgun here."

Harper looked at the map. *Yay. I've got an air horn and a shotgun. This is so messed up.*

"We have a smaller group assigned to patrol at night. It's a rotating thing, so no one gets stuck on it for too long. We'll talk about adding you to the rotation once you've gotten comfortable. Town's unfamiliar enough to you in the day. Won't do anyone any good having you out there blind in the dark."

"Thanks."

"All right then." He offered a handshake. "Welcome to the militia, Harper. It's been pretty quiet here so far, but I'm not so naïve as to think our little bit of paradise is going to stay perfect. Some people are gonna have trouble adjusting from the old nine-to-five grind to having to fend for themselves. Don't really expect much problem from people here losin' it. More likely, any trouble would come from outsiders, like those fools you mentioned. For the next couple weeks, your job's going to be getting to know the town and the people in it. But keep your eyes open, and use the horn if you see something you don't like."

"Right. Just one more question." She slid off the table to stand. "Should I call you 'sir,' Mr. Holman, or something else?"

"You might be seventeen, but the complete collapse of civilization has a way of making people grow up fast. You're on the militia, willing to put yourself in harm's way for other people, even if 'other people' is mostly your kid sister." He grinned. "Walter or Walt is fine. But if you're uncomfortable with that, Mr. Holman works, too."

"It does feel kinda weird." She managed a feeble smile. "Like calling a teacher by their first name."

"Fair bet you've never got into a gunfight standing shoulder to shoulder with your chemistry teacher."

"No, that's never happened."

Walter patted her shoulder. "If it hits the fan, call me Walt for brevity. When it's quiet, use Mr. Holman if you want... but that will make me feel like an old fart."

She nodded.

"If you've got no other questions, may as well get started."

"Okay, Mr. Holman. What time do I go home? My sister's kinda... brittle. She wasn't always like this, but I think she saw our parents die."

"Ouch." Walter sighed past clenched teeth. "I'm sorry. Give it a couple hours today. Ease into it slow then, give her a chance to get used to things."

Harper exhaled. "What if she wants to go with me? I should probably stop home and grab some more shells. Didn't bring any."

"Given the time of day, you should probably get her over to the school to meet Violet. I think with the little ones to watch, it's fine if you do your patrol shift from first light 'til the kids get outta school. Can't rightly leave them home alone that little, and you're young yet so no one will mind."

"Oh. Duh. Ugh. No one's going to be at the house. It'll get cold."

"Another reason to head to the school. Jeanette's got that building online with solar, so there's heat. We're working on expanding that, but we need to grab a whole bunch more panels, and all the poles in town blew up. In the event of a brutal cold snap, we've got an evacuation plan to move people susceptible to cold there. Elders, pregnant women, small children, so on."

"Got it. Okay..."

"This probably goes without saying, but you should avoid shooting people unless they are a direct and immediate threat to your life, or the life of someone else. This ain't the Wild West where people shoot each other over a bad hand of poker. We are trying to maintain civilization."

"That's my plan." She looked down. *I have enough trouble shooting people who* are *a direct threat.*

HARPER RETURNED HOME LONG ENOUGH TO COLLECT A DOZEN EXTRA shells, plus both kids.

Jonathan didn't want to abandon the fire, but they couldn't leave it burning in an empty house. Hopefully, the mesh cover would contain the embers. Of all the things Harper ever daydreamed about wanting in her life, simply having electricity for heat hadn't even come close to making the list. Power had just always been there, barely an afterthought—barring a few outages during storms. In that moment, she'd have given almost anything for it.

"I'm going to be patrolling for a couple hours every day," said Harper. "They want me to get familiar with the town."

Madison stared at her with a wide-eyed expression of sorrow, as if she'd been abandoned at the doors of an orphanage.

"You two are coming with me." Harper play-punched her shoulder. "Go get your coat and shoes."

The kids ran off down the hall, returning in a few minutes dressed to go outside.

Harper led them down Hilltop Drive to Route 74, and followed it north. A few people out and about waved at them and/or shouted greetings, though no one came close enough to start a conversation. They passed the bus barricade at Lewis Ridge Road, spent a few minutes talking to Darnell, Sadie, Fred, and Cameron, the four militia staffing the barrier. Upon closer inspection, she noticed a small solar panel hooked up to one of the buses, powering a space heater. Though the interior didn't exactly qualify as 'warm,' compared to the outside, it did.

Madison kept quiet and hovered at Harper's side, offering polite smiles whenever one of the other militia people tried to talk to her. Jonathan climbed all over the bus and pestered the sentries about their rifles and scopes. He thought it fascinating that this location allowed them to cover a long stretch of Route 74. Darnell explained that pulling duty at the 'buses' required passing a rifle marksmanship test, so it wound up being something of a prestigious position.

After about twenty minutes, she mentioned her 'assignment' of learning the area and how she needed to go up to the school. The militia sent her on her way with back pats and words of encouragement. From what she recalled of the map, she had to follow Route 74 north and then turn right. The fastest way there involved going across the grass and what (at least on the map) looked like a running track. Alternatively, if she overshot the school, she'd be at the animal hospital. So, she'd have to backtrack and take a right turn there, and then another right turn, hopefully not getting lost in the meandering suburban streets.

Of course, she didn't exactly have a deadline. The entire point of doing this was to learn her way around. So... getting lost could only help.

"Ugh. Why doesn't real life have a minimap?"

"I know, right?" Jonathan laughed.

Harper pulled the paper out of her pocket where Walter had sketched a rough approximation of the roads in the neighborhood near the school. He'd labeled the right turn she should take as 'Bergen Parkway.' That would only help if a street sign existed. She couldn't remember seeing one with that on it on the way in, of course, she'd been exhausted and emotional... and four days had passed.

A few minutes north of the buses, she encountered a Hispanic guy sitting on the side of the road in a long dark Brooks Brothers type coat over a nice pale grey suit that he'd probably been wearing for a few weeks. He glanced up at them.

She froze in her tracks at the sight of a gun in his right hand, regretting that she carried the shotgun over her shoulder. If that guy meant to hurt someone, he'd definitely shoot if she tried to bring it to bear. *Maybe I should be carrying it like a soldier.* "Umm. Hi."

He looked her over, glanced briefly at the kids, and resumed staring down at the road.

"Is something wrong?" She peeled Madison's hands off her arm, gave her a 'wait here' look, and took two steps closer to the man.

The guy lifted his head to stare at her. "Are you serious?"

"Yeah."

"Is something wrong, she says." He barked a sarcastic laugh. "Yeah, something's wrong. *Everything* is wrong."

"Do you want to talk?"

"Not really." He again stared down at the street. "What's the point, anyway?"

"The point is, we survived. I know how you feel. I lost my parents. Don't give up."

He started to give her a confused look, but seemed to realize he held a gun and put it in his coat pocket. "Oh. That. No, I'm not gonna do anything."

"I'm Harper, just joined the militia."

"Arturo, and I'm useless."

"Aww, you're not useless." She took another step closer. "You're alive."

"Easy for you to say, kid. Did you even make it out of high school yet?"

"Nope. Seventeen."

"Damn. I wasted so many years going to law school. What the hell does the world need with me now?"

Oh. Heh. "Well, yeah. There's not much need for lawyers anymore. But hey, at least you're not a politician. No one's going to actively try to shoot you."

Arturo chuckled.

"We're, umm, trying to keep civilization going. Lawyers will probably come back. They had them in medieval times, right? And you're still kinda young. There's going to be something you can do."

"I didn't put myself two hundred grand in debt to get a law degree so I can wind up picking goddamned vegetables like my grandfather did. Dammit! I'm a citizen!"

"Umm. Arturo?"

He looked at her.

"I'm not sure 'citizen' means anything anymore. We just got hit by nuclear weapons. Working on a farm is different when you're growing food you're going to eat. And who says you have to work on the farm? You made it through law school. That means you're smart, and you're not afraid of people. Why don't you teach? Or go to the clinic and learn like nursing or something? Or go talk to Mayor Ned about doing manager stuff. A woman I came here with had a degree in business. How useless is *that* now?"

He let out a long sigh. "Yeah... I guess."

"You're not really sad about being a lawyer." She took another two steps, stopping right beside him. "You're sad for the same reason I am. We had hopes and dreams for a world that's been taken away from us. I wanted to go to college, be with my friends and stuff. You wanted to do the lawyer thing and be all successful."

"Yeah."

She squatted, lowering her voice to hopefully keep the kids from hearing. "I'm only seventeen. My father was shot dead right in front of me because I couldn't bring myself to kill a creep breaking into our house. I spent a week hiding out with my little sister, not knowing if we were gonna wake up the next morning. We found this guy at the mall who's kinda become our new dad, and we walked here. I've had to kill people. Somehow, I'm still holding it together. No, not somehow. I'm holding it together for them." She nodded toward the kids. "You're not useless."

"Okay, okay. Easy kid. I ain't gonna shoot myself. Just bummed out."

She stood. "And hey, look at the bright side. You're not in debt anymore."

Arturo blinked at her. A second later, he burst into laughter. He muttered something in Spanish, grinning and shaking his head. "Wow. I must've been zoned out. Never even thought of that."

"Have you gone into town yet?"

"Nah. Just been wandering along this road for what feels like days."

Harper pointed back down Route 74. "Keep going that way. There's a couple of buses set up like a wall. Talk to the guys there if you want to like move in. We need smart people."

"All right." Arturo stood with a grunt and dusted his coat off. "See ya around, kid."

She waved. "Yeah. I'll be around… walking around a lot."

He smiled and headed off down the road.

Madison and Jonathan scurried over.

Harper swung the shotgun off her shoulder and carried it, just in case she ran into another strange situation. She kept going, glancing to the right every so often in hopes of seeing the school, but only caught glimpses of the occasional house past the trees lining the road. Eventually, she spotted a huge field with a big oval track, though a tall chain link fence blocked it off from the road.

"Not like we're gonna get tickets…"

She helped the kids over the fence, then climbed it. A short strip of forest gave way to a grassy hill overlooking a running track with a soccer field inside it. They walked down, followed a bit of the track, then took a paved path past a baseball diamond on the left, and some tennis courts on the right. The sidewalk led to the rear of the middle school building, though she circled to the front instead of trying the doors there.

The sound of children came from inside, a din that reminded her of the cafeteria in the morning, only not quite as loud.

"Ugh, we have to go to school?" asked Madison.

"I thought you liked school."

"There's a subtle difference between 'not hating' something and liking it. Seriously, what kind of kid *likes* having to go to school?"

Harper shrugged, flashing a sarcastic smile. "The ones who wind up not serving French fries."

Jonathan laughed.

"That doesn't matter anymore." Madison pouted. "We're like primitive now."

"Even back in like the Wild West, kids still had to go to school. You have to learn basic stuff." Harper ushered them around the building to the front door. "Sounds like there's kids here your age, too. You can make some friends."

"I don't want new friends. I have friends already... just don't know where they are."

Harper paused at the front door and hung the shotgun over her shoulder again. It *still* felt too weird carrying a weapon into a school at all, much less holding it like she meant to use it. She squeezed Madison's hand.

Her sister huffed and hung her head, but offered no further protest as they went inside. The dramatic change from 'holy crap it's cold' to relative warmth shocked her. Functioning heat reminded her that Walter said something about solar panels and gave her a little hope that someday, she might not need to rely on a fireplace not to freeze at home.

She followed the din of students to a large classroom packed wall to wall with at least fifty kids. The youngest looked about six years old, the oldest maybe fifteen. They sat with their desks clustered by age, each group working on different subjects.

A late-twenties black woman in a lavender T-shirt and jeans paused in her attempt to explain multiplication to the nine-to-eleven year old group, and looked over at her. The expression on her face would've been perfect for a normal teacher in a normal not-just-nuked world having a student bring a shotgun to class. For an instant, a chill ran down Harper's back, settling into a ball of nausea at the pit of her stomach. The brief jolt of dread that she'd go to jail and her entire life had just been ruined faded after a breath or two.

"Can I help you?" asked the woman, a hint of nervousness in her voice.

"Hi. I'm Harper Cody. My family and I just arrived in town a couple days ago. This is my first day on the militia. These are my siblings, Madison and Jonathan."

"I think he's adopted," yelled a girl of about twelve.

A quiet wave of laughter swept over the kids. Neither the comment nor the laughter struck her as mocking, more like most of them here had recently been adopted and they welcomed another kid to the club. One girl didn't laugh, nor did she even seem mildly amused. She appeared a little younger than Madison, likely eight or nine, with jet-black hair, sapphire blue eyes, and a black dress that made her pale skin seem as white as paper. That kid stared at Harper with such intensity she expected the child to float up out of her seat and say something like 'you're gonna die in that house'—and then rotate her head all the way around.

Whoa. Okay, maybe Maddie's not that broken. Poor kid.

The woman approached, offering a handshake. "Oh, hello. I'm Violet Olsen. The only teacher who didn't run for the hills."

"Aren't we technically in the hills?" Harper smiled.

"Hah. Yeah, true. So… Madison and Jonathan." She smiled at the kids. "School here's going to be a little different from what you're used to."

"Well, yeah," deadpanned Madison. "There's only one teacher and you've got all the kids in the same room."

Violet nodded. "You're right. It's a bit overwhelming at times. I'm hoping they send someone over here soon to help out. It would be nice to at least split this menagerie in half so we have some more room. Don't really need a legit degree in education to handle the basic stuff for the little ones."

"Yeah." Harper looked at all the kids watching her. The oldest boy stared at her with a dumb grin while the younger kids mostly gave off curiosity. Creepy Girl kept giving her a look between 'I want to drink your soul' and 'are you going to shoot us all?'

Having so many sets of eyes focused on her pricked at her shyness. Her alter ego, Introvert Prime, shorted out and collapsed into a twitching heap of cartoon robotics. Though, compared to having guys wearing blue sashes trying to kidnap her—and killing like three of them—being the center of attention in a room full of children didn't bother her anywhere near as much as it should have. Working here in the school would definitely be safer than playing militia girl. Public speaking terrified her, but not as much as being shot at or abducted.

Harper imagined Introvert Prime ceasing her convulsions and smiling the cheesy smile of someone caught playing the drama queen.

Okay, this isn't so bad. Should I try to do this instead?

"Let's see…" Violet looked around for a few seconds before grabbing two desks from the side of the room and adding them to the cluster of nine- to eleven-year-olds. "Madison and Jonathan, you can sit here. Specific desks aren't assigned, but this is your cluster."

Jonathan ran over to a desk. Madison stayed put until Harper walked with her.

"As you can imagine, we're a little short on textbooks and stuff. So"— Violet flashed a big smile at Madison—"there isn't any homework. Once you leave for the day, you're done."

"Whoa." Jonathan blinked. "That's awesome."

Even Madison appeared pleased.

"Okay, everyone. Please go back to what you were reviewing. If you have any questions, hang on to them for a minute."

Most of the kids chorused, "Yes, Miss Olsen."

Violet pulled Harper off to the side by the teacher's desk. "Not much at your age range I'm afraid. Not enough kids in town at the high school grades to make an issue of it. And they're all being given jobs."

"Yeah I know. I've got one, too. Militia."

"Wow. Didn't think they took them that young. You're kind of a skinny thing."

Harper chuckled. "Yeah, well... Mayor Ned saw Dad's Mossberg and asked me to join."

"I'm not exactly thrilled with having that thing in a classroom."

"Heh, yeah. I know what you mean. It feels weird bringing it in here. I keep waiting for the SRO to fly out of nowhere and tackle me." She lowered her voice to an almost whisper. "Really, I don't even like it. I'm only keeping it because it belonged to my dad and... Every time I see this damn gun, it reminds me of his death."

Violet's expression softened. "Oh, no... do you want to talk about it?"

"I couldn't talk about it at all for a while. Now it seems like I'm just telling everyone." She raked her hair off her face, offering a wan smile. After a deep breath, she told the story of the gang attacking her home, killing her parents, and forcing her to run away with her sister. "I have to protect Maddie. I don't trust anyone else to do that."

"Harper..." Violet took her hand. "You're a scared seventeen-year-old kid. No one would've expected you to be able to kill a guy like that. Your father wouldn't be upset with you for hesitating."

"I guess." She sighed. "So, you're an actual teacher?"

"Yep. Wasted all sorts of money on that piece of paper that used to mean something. I suppose I can't really complain too much. Before the war, I worked at a private school in Broomfield. At least the pay here's better."

Harper tilted her head. "Pay? There's no money anymore. The town just gives us a ration of food, firewood, and a house."

"Like I said, the pay here's better." Violet wagged her eyebrows.

"Ouch."

"Yeah, ouch is right. So, militia, huh?"

"Apparently." Harper shrugged.

She explained how she needed to roam the town and 'get to know' people and streets. Violet moved among the tables while they talked, helping the kids of various grade levels with whatever project she'd set them to task on. The youngest kids took the most attention as they needed more active teaching, less able to be given stuff to read or problems to work on. Sometimes, Violet would address the entire group at once, most recently to discuss the war that happened.

A little blond boy of about seven, Jax Davis, asked Harper for help with a terrifyingly complicated math problem (11 − 3). As soon as she helped him work it out, a timid brown-haired girl the same age named Robin Wheatley asked her a question. Before she knew it, she sat with the youngest group and pretended to be a teacher. She wound up putting the Mossberg on a high shelf a short distance away, since having it on her while interacting with kids exceeded her threshold for feeling like she did something extremely wrong/dangerous.

Madison kept glancing over at her, seeming not at all to mind school as long as she remained in the same room. Violet directed her attention mostly at the older two groups for the next hour or so, leaving the little ones in Harper's care.

Schoolwork bounced back and forth with chatting, the kids asking her questions or offering bits of their stories. A frighteningly thin girl who appeared around five with platinum blonde hair, Lorelei Frost, told her she'd been orphaned and spent days wandering alone before a man found her. The child's soulful blue eyes nearly made Harper scoop her up and take her home like a stray kitten.

"I was so hungry I didn't wanna wake outta bed, but he made me." Lorelei tucked her hair behind her ear and smiled. "I think I almost died. I'm glad he didn't let me stay in bed."

Two other kids also had been wandering alone for days, but all three had found new parents here. She suspected a few of the quiet ones had seen horrible things before arriving in Evergreen. Roughly half of them had lost at least one parent. One boy told her his family tried to leave home in their car, but a big piece of junk fell on it, crushing his mother. All had friends they hadn't seen since the blast. An eight year old named Emmy said she expected the 'sky fire' to come back at any minute.

I don't think Walter wanted me to spend all day in the school... but, hey. I'm getting to know people, even if they are kids.

A boy in Madison's age group named Christopher waved her over with a question while Violet appeared busy with the oldest students. He had a question about Civil War history, which Madison didn't remember —though she found the answer in one of the three books the group shared.

"Been a while since I was in fourth grade." She winked.

"Yeah. You're like old." He grinned.

Creepy Girl, sitting two desks to his right, kept staring at Harper in the same eerie 'you're about to die' way she'd been doing the whole time.

"Hi," said Harper. "What's your name?"

The girl continued staring.

"That's Mila Cline," said Christopher. "She doesn't talk much."

She nodded. "Hi Mila. I'm Harper. It's okay if you don't want to talk."

"The shadow man is coming for me," said Mila in a half-whisper. "But I think he's going to get you first."

Whoa. Harper forced a smile. "Shadow man? Who's that? Did someone try to hurt you? My job is to protect people now. If you tell me who it is, I'll make sure he doesn't hurt you."

Mila looked down at her handmade worksheet and filled in a few answer blanks.

Given the girl's obvious mental situation, Harper didn't feel *too* insulted at being ignored.

"He tried to get me, but I'm good at hiding." Mila looked up at her. "You're too big to hide."

Harper blinked, unable to come up with anything to say.

"Okay, everyone." Violet drew all attention with a sharp clap of her hands. "It's time. See you all tomorrow."

The predictable scramble of cheering kids ran for the door. Twelve remained, including almost all the six-to-eight year olds.

Harper grabbed the shotgun and slung it over her shoulder in preparation to head out and do what she should've been doing, wander the streets, but gave the lingering children a confused eyebrow lift.

"School doubles as a daycare. Parents ought'a be here in another hour or two once they finish whatever they're doing for the day. Or, some want them to stay here a little longer due to the working heat."

"Yeah, that's nice." Harper let out an *oof* when Madison hugged her at ramming speed. "I should get going. Nice meeting you."

"Thank you so much for the help. It's overwhelming at times trying to keep up with fifty-two of them. Err. Fifty four." Violet smiled at Madison and Jonathan.

"It was... kinda cool." Harper waved and headed out.

Mila Cline stood a few feet outside the main entrance at the end of a faded hopscotch grid, arms at her sides, staring off into space.

Harper slowed, glancing over at her. "Mila? Are you all right?"

The little black-haired girl blinked as if snapping out of a trance. She peered up at Harper with an expression of pitying sorrow. "The shadow man's coming. He'll be here soon."

Before Harper could get a word out, the girl dashed off down the little approach road in front of the school toward the street.

Damn. That kid's got issues.

Madison took out her iPhone and sighed at it in disappointment before stuffing it back in her pocket.

Speaking of issues. Walter had said she could go home once school let out, but she'd spent the whole day there, which felt like she did something wrong.

"C'mon guys. I gotta do this patrol thing. Do you wanna go with me or go home?"

Madison squeezed her hand.

"Whatever." Jonathan flapped his arms.

"Okay. Let's stay together then."

Harper walked down the school's driveway to the street, hooked a right, and made her way into the residential neighborhood.

Ugh. It's going to take me forever to remember where everything is.

She couldn't help but look back over her shoulder every so often. Whether or not Mila had seen some creepy person she called the shadow man who possibly tried to grab her, Harper didn't believe in that paranormal stuff. Even if some physical creep existed, the girl saying he would be going after Harper soon had to be pure fantasy.

There's no such thing as psychics. She's just a disturbed little kid who maybe loves being creepy and weird.

Despite how silly she considered it, she found herself unable to shake the worry that this 'shadow man' might actually exist—and might be watching her.

FRONTIER LIVING

Once the sky felt darker, Harper ceased wandering and made her way home.

The part of her that remained a bit of a child dragged her to the militia HQ so she could check with Walter to make sure it was okay to 'quit' for the day. He talked briefly about how her day went. She admitted to spending much of it at the school, which he surprisingly didn't mind. He did reiterate that she should patrol while the kids sat in school, and go home with them when it let out.

Upon returning to their new house, the kids got into a brief argument over who got to use the bathroom first. Jonathan gave up without much of a fight and announced his intention to 'just go water a tree' because 'boys can do that.'

Harper stood there for a moment debating if she needed to keep the shotgun in arms' reach at all times, or if she could put it in her room. She decided that home felt safe enough, so she stashed it in her bedroom before flopping on the sofa and staring at the dead TV.

"Wow." Jonathan ran inside and raced to the fireplace. "It's cold out."

"You just noticed?"

He emitted a non-word and proceeded to get a fire going.

Madison returned with the Uno deck in one hand, iPhone in the other.

By the time Cliff returned, the living room had at least warmed up to the point no one needed coats on. He brought a treat: a fresh loaf of handmade bread from a wood-burning oven. Harper warmed up soup to go along with it, a mix of chicken, minestrone, and vegetable from cans. Of course, she gave the vegetable soup to Madison.

"Tomorrow, the kids will need to check in at the school," said Cliff between bites of bread.

"Already did." Harper smiled and explained how her day had gone.

"Ahh. Nice. Was wondering what you did with them while on patrol."

"Since I'm just walking around to learn the layout of the place, I figured it was okay for them to come along today. I know they won't be able to keep doing that."

Madison stared over her spoon at her.

"I was talkin' to Jim this afternoon. He's the guy managing the farm project." Cliff dipped a hunk of bread in his soup. "Once spring hits, they're gonna start bringing the kids over to the farm for a two-hour session after school twice a week."

Harper blinked. "What for? Are they going to make children work?"

Cliff stifled laughter while chewing. "Nah." He coughed. "Basic farm education, like what they used to do back in the forties or so. They'll be learning about planting, taking care of animals, that sorta thing."

"I don't wanna," said Madison. "Farming is cruel to animals."

"Hon, not to sound too harsh here, but you know grocery stores stopped working." Cliff set his bread down and reached across the table to take her hand. "Those big factory farms that used to exist *were* cruel to animals. I agree with you completely. The farm they're building here is not like that. Think 1930s. Mostly hand tools. No cages for the chickens. You don't want to starve, do you?"

"No." Madison looked down. "Harper said I can just eat vegetables if there's enough."

"Yeah, that's fine. And learning farming is also learning how to grow vegetables. Besides." He picked up the bread again. "You're not being told you have to spend the rest of your life working on the farm, just learning some basics."

Madison smirked. "What else would I do when I grow up? Go to law school?"

Cliff snickered.

"How long do you think it'll be before they have electricity back? I really want a hot bath." Harper ate a spoonful of chicken soup.

"For the time being, it's a question of heating water over a fire out back. Spent a few hours building a thing today outta cinderblocks. Couple metal pails of boiling water added to the tub should make for a warm bath. Old West style." He chuckled. "I'll be cutting wood soon enough, but we can't blow through it too fast. Probably once a week for the bath thing, maybe once every two."

"Eww." Madison scrunched up her nose. "Every two weeks?"

"Yep. If wood's low, you might wind up having to share a bath, too." He grinned. "Or you could just keep stinking."

She stuck her tongue out at him.

After dinner, the kids stretched and did dance stuff in the living room while Cliff took the AR-15 apart on the table to clean it. Harper rinsed off the dishes and put them away, then sat at the table watching Cliff work and chatting about gun maintenance.

Once it became difficult to see inside due to lack of light, Cliff lit a candle. "One thing I don't understand—"

"Just one?" Harper smiled.

"Hah. You're a funny kid." He poked her in the arm. "What the hell did people do back in the 1800s when it got dark? I do kinda miss the PlayStation."

Harper shrugged. "Guess they went to bed. Woke up at the butt crack of dawn. Not much to do in the dark except read by candle light or, well… back then people had tons of kids."

Cliff coughed. "I've already got three. That's plenty."

"Are you sure? Carrie seems to like you."

He stuck his tongue out like Madison had earlier.

Harper giggled. "Anyway… I think I'm going to sleep. My legs hurt from all that walking."

"Heh. All that walking. I've got some Army stories for you about walking."

"C'mon you guys." Harper collected the kids and ushered them to bed.

She grabbed one of the toothpaste tubes Madison grabbed from that house and had the kids brush, rationing out the paste to last as long as possible by giving them only pea-sized blots. The closet only had two toothbrushes, so Harper used her finger. Madison offered to share a brush with her, but she couldn't quite go that far.

Once in the bedroom, Harper undressed and put on a man's T-shirt as a nightgown. It felt wonderful to be able to sleep in a real bed without having to stay dressed. Spending almost two weeks wearing the same underwear all day and sleeping in it hadn't registered at the time, but looking back on it, the idea made her skin crawl. Madison also changed into a T-shirt nightgown and crawled into bed.

A sheet, three blankets, a comforter, and an afghan made for a cozy nest, even without the fire burning all night long. Madison snuggled against her side, offering a physical demonstration of why old-timey families often shared beds: warmth.

Harper barely had time to think much about her day before sleep snuck up on her.

FOR BREAKFAST, EVERYONE MUNCHED ON BOWLS OF DRY LUCKY CHARMS and shared a can of peaches.

Harper didn't so much mind the food, as she'd resigned herself to the truth of having something to eat at all made for a good day. She did, however, hate that she couldn't be normal and start each day with a nice hot shower the way she'd done since she'd been old enough for showers instead of baths. She missed nice shampoo, scented soap, bath bombs, and so on.

At the thought she'd likely never use nice shampoo again, she choked up.

Only Madison noticed her at the verge of tears and stopped eating to give her a 'what's wrong?' look.

Ugh. Why am I tweaking out about shampoo? I still have Madison. And Jonathan doesn't even have any bio family left. I should be tweaking out that we might run out of food, or firewood, or bullets, or some crazy idiot showing up. She sighed.

"Harp?" whispered Madison.

"I'm okay. Just worrying."

"What about?" asked Cliff.

"Is 'yes' a valid answer?" She managed a weak smile.

He nodded. "Considering the circumstances, yeah."

After breakfast, everyone left the house at the same time. Cliff headed straight south ignoring the road, while Harper took the kids to school via the same route she went the previous day. She didn't stop too long at the bus barrier, only enough to exchange good mornings with the sentries.

A little ways past it up Route 74, she decided to start the argument. "I can't stay at the classroom all day again today. I'm supposed to be doing the militia thing, so I gotta do that or I'll get in trouble."

"Okay," said Jonathan.

Madison squeezed her hand tighter. "Tell them to let you guard the school."

"I'll ask about that, but I've still got to learn my way around here."

Her sister emitted a grunt-whine and stared at the road.

Clattering from up ahead drew Harper's attention to an athletic woman pushing a large cart down the highway. It looked like one of those things people used at Home Depot to buy lumber and held a stack of silver-edged tiles the size of house windows as well as a big toolbox. The woman slowed to a stop when they got close.

"Hey. You must be new here." She eyed the shotgun. "Militia?"

"Yeah. Harper Cody." She offered a handshake.

"Jeanette Ortiz."

"Oh, the electrician? Those are solar panels, right?"

"Yep." Jeanette patted the stack. "Collecting them from wherever I can find them. Idea is to make an array for the town, though we're way short on the number of panels it'll take for that. First priority is to get some juice to the medical center."

"Umm… you gave the school power before the doctors?" asked Harper.

"School already had panels on the roof. That didn't take much work to fix. EMP flash just killed a couple breakers and the voltage controller. Basically anything with chips or transistors."

"Panels?"

"Nah. They're fine. Might be a tiny bit of performance degradation, but they still work."

"Cool. Hey, can I make a suggestion?"

"Shoot."

Harper grinned. "If it's going to be too difficult to give power to the whole town, can you set up like a bath house or something so we don't need to use firewood for heating bathwater and stuff?"

"Hmm. That's not altogether a bad idea. I'll run it by the mayor."

"You do electric stuff?" asked Madison.

"That's right." Jeanette smiled at her.

"Can you fix my phone? It won't turn on."

"Oh, I don't work on those kinds of electronics. I fix power lines and circuit breakers, hot water heaters, lights, that stuff."

Madison sighed, nodded, and stared at the ground.

"Anyway. I need to get this back to the storage room." Jeanette shook hands again. "Nice meeting you."

"Same."

Harper continued on toward the school, again cutting across the field. Upon rounding the corner of the building to the front, she stopped short at the sight of a young man with unruly brown hair in a long coat standing near the main doors. He reminded her of the weird kid at her school who everyone thought would 'do something' one day. She squeezed the pistol grip on the shotgun, but kept her finger away from the trigger.

Come on, Harp. You can do this. You're supposed to be a cop now, remember.

She silently cleared her throat and approached him.

He glanced over at a scuff from her sneaker. "Hey."

"Hey. What's up?"

"Not much. You?" She glanced from him to the school and back. "Kinda odd to just be standing here like that."

"Kinda odd to see a kid with a shotgun."

"Yeah, well, it's an odd world these days." She widened her stance, but kept the gun in a relaxed grip.

"Guess they put you on the militia, huh?"

"Is that the shadow man?" asked Madison, a little above a whisper.

Harper froze with a sudden spike of panic. *Wait. No. That's just some kid being mental.*

He chuckled. "Shadow man? You've been talking to Mila?"

"You know Mila?" asked Harper.

"Not personally. I've seen her a few times while dropping off this kid I'm looking after."

"You have a kid?" Harper blinked.

"Not the usual way. I'm only nineteen." He smiled. "Was out there wandering. Found this half-starved little girl all alone in a gas station, asleep on the sofa in the waiting room by the mechanic shop. Brought her here 'cause I heard about this place being safe. Wound up turning into dad."

"Lorelei?"

He nodded at her. "Yeah. The doctor thinks she'll be okay, but it's hard getting her to eat. Can't have too much at once since she had so little for so long. I'm Tyler, by the way."

"Harper."

"Pretty name. Unusual. Totally works for you."

Something about this guy didn't quite sit right with her, but he seemed nice, didn't have any obvious weapons, and if he saved Lorelei, he couldn't be bad. *Stupid jerks.* She frowned mentally at the kids at her old school who used to tease that kid... Elijah or Ethan something. He'd had the same kind of off-center vibe as Tyler, though as far as she knew, he never spoke to anyone except teachers who asked him direct questions. At least this kid... well, nineteen-year-old, spoke to her.

Then again, she did have a shotgun.

"Sec," said Harper. "Be right back."

She slung the Mossberg on its strap over her shoulder and walked the kids to the classroom. Jonathan ran over to his group and jumped into a seat at an empty desk, getting into the conversation without hesitation. Madison whisper-begged her to stay. After a few minutes of going in verbal circles, Harper got her to calm down by saying the sooner she could find her way around town, the sooner they might let her stay at the school as a 'guard.' Madison sniffled, hugged her tight, then trudged over to the desks.

Harper had a quick chat with Violet about wanting to spend the day here, but couldn't because she had an assignment from the militia. Though Violet clearly wanted help, she understood. Harper waved at Madison. Despite feeling like a complete monster for leaving, she forced herself to. When she left the building, she found Tyler standing where he'd been before. She walked over to him.

"Bad?" he asked. "You look like someone died."

"My sister's been real clingy since we had to leave home. I can't keep bringing her on patrol."

"Patrol?"

"You know, militia."

Tyler grinned. "Seriously? Are you even eighteen yet?"

"Like seven months away from it."

He whistled a few bars of a song she didn't recognize. At her clueless expression, he feigned shock. "Come on, Winger? Seventeen?"

"Huh?"

"Oh, you poor deprived child."

Harper folded her arms. "What are you talking about?"

"How can you not know of one of the greatest Eighties bands ever?"

"Probably because I'm A: normal, and B: the Eighties happened forever ago."

He fake scoffed. "Poor kid. Bet your parents know it."

She stormed past him. "My parents are dead, asshole."

"Hey, wait." Tyler ran up alongside her, jogging to keep pace. "I'm sorry. I didn't know."

Harper slowed to a normal walk. "Okay, so you didn't know. It's still... well... whatever."

"Sorry. Sometimes I forget there's been a war. I guess I shouldn't just assume everyone's parents are still around like that."

She glanced over at him. He didn't seem to be trying to hit on her, or maybe he did and her frazzled emotions couldn't tell. The boy *did* look genuinely apologetic. "Are yours?"

"Not sure."

"Sorry."

He shrugged. "Don't be."

"Harper?" called a distant woman.

She stopped and looked ahead down the road.

A dark-haired woman wearing a camo jacket over jeans jogged up the street toward her. A compound bow, also camouflage, over her shoulder wobbled with her stride and a quiver of arrows hanging from her belt rattled. She also carried a smallish handgun in a holster on her right hip.

"Gotta take this call," muttered Harper. "I think it's work."

Tyler snickered.

Harper headed toward the woman. "Yeah. That's me."

"Marcie Chapman." She shook hands. "Walt figured you'd be at the school."

"I know. I wasn't gonna spend the day here, just dropping my siblings off."

"Oh, that's fine for now at least. That's not why he sent me to find you. We're putting together a scavenging trip and you've been tapped for it."

"No!" shouted Madison. She bolted out of the bushes in front of the school and sprinted down the road, crashing into a hug. "Don't go!"

Harper shot a helpless look at Marcie while cradling the back of Madison's head. "It's only—"

"Please don't go away and leave me here!" Madison burst into tears. "Please!"

The girl had barely sniffled about their parents' deaths. Seeing her explode in a fit of scream crying slapped rational thought out of Harper's brain.

Tyler slipped away and wandered off down the road.

"Well, it's only the briefing." Marcie pointed over her shoulder with her thumb. "Might as well bring her along for now."

Harper watched Tyler stroll away. So far, she hadn't seen anyone else in town that close to her age. Well, the fifteen-year-old was also two years apart, but he still looked like a *boy*. Tyler didn't. As odd as he seemed, at least having a friend in her age group would be cool.

Madison kept screaming 'please don't go' every so often while tugging at her.

"C'mon, Termite. It's just a briefing." She took her sister's hand, which appeared to placate her for the moment.

Together, they followed Marcie back down Route 74. Violet didn't come out chasing Madison, a fact that worried Harper. It also felt wrong to arbitrarily drag her away from school. But then again, normal society had gone off on break for a while. Maybe by the time Madison had a kid, they'd get in trouble for missing school again.

Or maybe something would go drastically wrong; Violet would die and humanity would devolve into primitive tribespeople who'd sooner eat a textbook than try to read it. A group like that might speak fondly of 'the ancients' who once ruled the Earth, worshipping old computers or phones like magical artifacts. She straddled both worlds, having grown up (as much as seventeen years constituted growing up) surrounded by modern things, and now stepped foot into an unknown world of primitivism. Would society slip back to the 1900s, the 1800s? Worse?

She didn't want the modern world to end, but she had no say in what had already been done.

And the men who 'hit the button' certainly wouldn't care what one teenage girl thought.

Maybe she had a point when joking with that lawyer.

People these days might just shoot politicians on sight.

22

GROWING UP

Walter Holman raised a hand in greeting when Harper entered a large conference room at the militia HQ.

Five other people stood at the table. She recognized Ken Zhang, Darnell Buck, and Fred Mitchell, but not the thirtysomething blond man with striking blue eyes. A somewhat grungy Hispanic man stood beside him, smelling of industrial chemicals and looking like someone used him as a rag to clean up an oil spill.

Everyone glanced at Madison, who still clung to Harper's side, sniveling.

"Harper," said Walter by way of greeting. "Okay. Now that everyone's here, I'll get started. Rafael's gotten one of the rigs working, so we're going to hit the Walmart in Littleton. We have no real information about what the situation is like there, since we're a little short on helicopter recon."

Chuckles went around the room. Harper forced a smile and faked laughing.

"The good news is, Rafael managed to work his magic. You're going in with an operational tractor-trailer. The only walking you'll have to do is in and out of the store. Primarily, your objective is to recover canned foodstuffs and bottled water, anything that's still edible. Second priority is clothing. Considering the size of the store, I'm thinking you'll be making several trips if things go well. We want to grab as much useful stuff as we can get our hands on before anyone else lays claim to it. We're not going to forcibly take it if there's already someone there. By all means defend yourselves, but we're not going in there to strong-arm anyone."

Harper exhaled with relief.

"Also," said Walter, "if the area is too dangerous, back off. We're not at the verge of starvation… yet. So, there's no reason to take foolish risks."

Everyone nodded.

Madison squeezed her tighter and started crying again.

"Colorado Springs took a direct hit," said Marcie. "Ain't nothing there worth a darn. Couple new arrivals showed up last night with good news about Littleton. Walt's right. We gotta hit it fast before someone else does."

"I wanna go too," yelled Madison. "If you're gonna make Harp go, I wanna go too. Please don't make her leave me."

Walter walked over and crouched to eye level with her. "Maybe in a few years, hon. We can't send you out there. It's too dangerous."

"Harper shouldn't go either then. She's only seventeen. Not even old enough to drink."

Ugh. What am I doing? Harper bit her lip, doubting herself. She didn't belong 'playing soldier' like this. If she went out there and something happened to her, Madison would be completely alone—and ruined. She squeezed the strap, starting to tug it off her shoulder. *Just give the shotgun to Walter and say I can't do this. Maddie needs me more than I need this gun. I'm a chicken. I save beetles from bathtubs.* A brief flash of screaming filled her head—her and Maddie home alone here in Evergreen, some faceless man kicking in the door. *Being a chicken killed Dad.*

Harper stopped pulling the strap. *I'm not a kid anymore. Maddie can't afford me to be.*

The men laughed.

"No such thing as a drinking age anymore," said the blond man.

"Yeah, even you can drink now." Ken swatted him on the arm.

"Eat it, Zhang. You're younger than I am."

"You're both babies." Marcie shook her head at them. "You hit twenty yet, Ryan?"

"Thirty." He smirked.

"Your sister is going with a whole team." Walter patted Madison on the shoulder, stood, and gestured at the assembled people. "And a working big rig. They'll be as safe out there as we are here."

Madison buried her face in Harper's shirt and wept.

"Hey, Termite." She rocked her side to side. "It's just like going shopping. I'll be back before it's even dark out."

"What if you get shot?"

"We're not going to start a fight. You heard Walter. If it's too dangerous, we back off."

"If it's not dangerous, then bring me with you."

Harper brushed her sister's hair off her face. "It's not perfectly safe. I need you to stay here where it is. Part of looking out for you is making sure you've got food. I gotta do this, Termite. For you, for both of us."

Madison clung tighter and cried. "Don't go away."

Ugh. "It'll be fine. We walked all the way here from Lakewood. That place is full of bad people and we made it okay. If I know you're here and safe, it'll be easy for me to stay alert. I'll be back before dark. Promise."

Madison whimpered something inaudible.

"She should really stay with Violet," said Marcie. "Can ask Leigh to walk her back up there."

"No." Harper shook her head. "I'll bring her back to school."

Walter gave her a quick nod. "All right. Hurry back so you can get underway then. Faster you get out there, faster you're back."

"Right."

Harper took Madison by the hand and headed out. She spent the whole time walking to the middle school saying comforting things, promising to be super careful, and apologizing. Madison kept her head down and didn't say a word.

When they reached the field by the school, Harper stopped, grasped her sister's face in both hands, and kissed her on the forehead. "I don't really want to be on the militia, but I have to."

"Why?"

"Do you remember what Mayor Ned told me? If I didn't join the militia, I'd have to let someone else have Dad's shotgun."

Madison kept quiet, wearing a pathetic stare.

"Most of me wants to do exactly that, let someone else have it, go back to being a kid again, let other people protect us both… but, I don't trust them."

"You don't?"

"Not like that. I mean… I believe they would want to protect us and do everything they could, but they can't be everywhere at once. Dad gave me this gun so I could protect our family. I messed up bad back home. I chickened out and it got Dad killed. I'm terrified if I chicken out again, you could be hurt."

"But what if *you* get shot? Then I'll have no one."

"I'm going to say something creepy, okay? You're probably too little for this, but the world's broken."

Madison wiped her nose.

"I'm a young woman. Most people out there who would be dangerous... *killing* me isn't the first thing they'd want to do. I'm more likely to be kidnapped than shot."

"That's bad, too."

"Yeah. Maybe worse than being shot." She shivered. "But... I can escape being kidnapped. And, we're not going to start a war. If there are too many bad guys there, we're just going to leave. This shotgun might be powerful, but it's still a shotgun. It's meant for close range. I'll probably spend more time keeping my head down than anything."

Madison managed a weak smile.

"Come on. You gotta learn stuff."

Staring at the ground, Madison followed her across the field to the school.

23

DEEP DISCOUNT

Harper trotted across the field to Route 74.

Madison had lapsed into sobs the instant she let go, curling up in her desk like she had no intention of talking to anyone or paying attention to anything going on around her. Seeing that started a war inside Harper's head. Would Madison hate her for making her stay here while she ran off? If she ran right back to the school, she could repair the rift between them. If she went to Littleton, her little sister might never speak to her again. The girl hadn't cried at all over their parents, so watching her melt down over being apart from each other for only a few hours hurt.

Am I being selfish or realistic? She can't cling to me like a tumor for the rest of her life. But, she's still hurting from losing Mom and Dad. Maybe I shouldn't run off so soon. When we get back, I'll ask Walter if I can like have an exception for a year or so because my sister's got mental problems. Can't be alone. Private Ryan type stuff. She lost her whole family but me. Maybe I should ask him right now.

A low rumble coming up the road stalled her thought train.

She hopped the fence and walked out onto the highway, looking up in awe at a white long-nose Peterbilt pulling a huge box trailer. Had they intended to go without her, or did they come out here to pick her up?

The truck rolled to a stop nearby. Rafael waved from behind the wheel. Fred, in the passenger seat, gestured for her to get in on that side.

Damn. In an ironic twist, she chickened out of chickening out, unable to bear the shame of saying no and walking away from the militia in the truck to go whine at Walter. Like an obedient kid, she trotted past the front end and climbed up into the cab. Ken, Darnell, Marcie, and Ryan sat in the sleeper cabin. Harper plopped down in the middle of the mattress, the only open spot. She felt like the only girl at a college frat party, though her nerves didn't come from the guys around her.

Being in an operational motor vehicle, even a big rig, reassured her that modern society might not completely be lost. Of course, one functional semi didn't a technological reawakening make. Rafael might've gotten lucky getting it to work. She didn't understand exactly how EMP destroyed cars, only that it ruined the electronics inside them and her father had once complained that modern vehicles were more computer than car. Maybe trucks like this had simpler systems or this truck in particular got lucky.

Though, the world didn't have an unlimited supply of gas—or diesel. It seemed pretty likely that nuclear war would've destroyed the majority of refineries. If not outright targets for warheads, they'd have complicated computer systems and automation, all of which would be fried by EMP. People would be too busy trying to survive in a world largely without electricity or modern conveniences to worry about keeping up the supply of gasoline, or medicines, or anything really. Maybe it would come back in a few decades, but for now, people wanted to simply continue living.

She jostled back and forth as the truck rumbled on, daydreaming about where the world would be headed and feeling like a complete bitch for abandoning Madison. Hopefully, being extra clingy with her tonight would be a suitable apology. That and promising that she'd ask not to be sent out of town again. Walter seemed like a nice guy, and they'd all witnessed her sister's freak out. They wouldn't think she lied out of cowardice.

Going to a Walmart to grab supplies didn't sound that scary. Evading the 'blue gang' on the streets of Lakewood had been much scarier. If not for what it did to her sister, Harper wouldn't have had any problem going on this trip. Though, if Madison had been killed along with her parents, she probably would've wound up like that lawyer guy… not really caring if she lived or died.

Marcie and the guys started discussing their plan for the Walmart mission, but wound up going off on random tangents. Harper didn't pay too much attention to them until they started asking her questions, the sort of crap people asked when they tried to get to know someone else.

Introvert Prime screamed, but Harper sat there with a stoic expression, voicing answers without much enthusiasm.

"You don't need to be that scared," said Marcie. "This isn't going to be bad."

"I'm not really that scared. It's my sister. Our parents died right in front of us like two weeks ago. She's terrified I'm going to die, too, and I think she's going to hate me for going on this trip. I'm really not sure it's good for her mental health for me to be away from her."

"Poor kid." Darnell sighed. "Yeah, you got a point there. When we get back, if you wanna talk to Walt, I'll go with ya."

"If it gets shitty in there, keep your head down, okay?" Marcie clapped a hand on her shoulder. "You're new, and you're still a kid. No one here's going to give you a hard time if you lay low."

"Okay. I'll be careful. But I won't choke. And I don't wanna hide in the truck the whole time. I'm not that much of a chicken… anymore."

They all laughed.

A little over a half hour later, Rafael said, "We're almost there."

Fred whistled. "Ugh, what happened here?"

Everyone scrambled forward to peer out the windshield. Harper squeezed between Ryan and Darnell, her cheek mushed into the side of Fred's seat. A few bodies littered the road up ahead in the haze. Mounds of ash in the shapes of abandoned cars forced Rafael to slalom the rig among them. Once or twice, proceeding required that he choose between ramming a vehicle out of the way or running over a dead person. He opted for the softer corpse.

Harper cursed herself for not mentioning the breathing masks, though if everything went well, they'd be inside the Walmart for most of the time and wouldn't be out in the crap. She cringed when the truck bounced over another body. Silhouettes of damaged buildings drifted by on both sides, a few with gaping holes from flying debris. The remains of the city reminded her of everything that would no longer be: her intact family, school, college, a job, holidays, meaningless random trips to Starbucks or pizza places.

A sudden, intense craving for pizza almost made her cry upon realizing she'd likely never taste it again. At least, until Rafael ran over another dead guy and the *squish* filled the cabin. That totally destroyed any thoughts about food.

How twisted is this? We're running people over on purpose. They're already dead. It's more twisted that I've killed people. She shrank away from the windshield, retreating into the sleeper cab to get away from the gruesome sight outside.

Harper sat on the mattress with the shotgun draped across her lap. A shotgun she'd probably fired thousands of shells out of at the range, trying to nail clay pigeons or paper targets. She would never claim to be as into guns as her father had been, but sport shooting *was* fun. She used to win trophies for her times and accuracy on a competition course, running from station to station. Dad thought she could become a 'professional shooter' someday, but she didn't have that much interest in it.

Putting buckshot into a clay disk had been one thing, but she'd used the shotgun on people. She'd done something she could never take back no matter how much she wanted to. Even thinking of those men as nameless enemies in a video game only helped so much. Ten weeks ago, they'd been relatively normal people going about whatever lives they'd had, until the breakdown of society allowed them to release their inner creeps. *They could've gone nuts. Maybe someone they loved died, and they said screw it I don't care.* Of course, they could've been criminals, too. Prisons had to have emptied by now. She smirked. Men started noticing her at like twelve, and thinking back on it, she probably had a brush with a real creep when she'd been nine. Some random dude had walked up and started talking to her in Kohl's when her mother had been distracted reading tags. At that age, she hadn't thought much of how fast he ran off when Mom came back over. In hindsight, she shivered. Maybe that explained why Dad started teaching her how to shoot. No way he looked at his daughter and thought 'I'm going to make a professional shooter out of you.' That she took so well to tagging clay pigeons with buckshot had been a surprise.

But, she'd killed.

Harper brushed her hand over the Mossberg. It no longer felt like 'sports,' and not at all fun. The emotion she read from it wound up part way between guilt and 'this keeps me alive.' She could quit the militia and become a teacher like Violet. Sure she didn't have a degree in education or even a high school diploma, but who cared about that anymore? She got along with the kids and, while she'd been no valedictorian, she'd gotten good grades. The militia could protect Maddie.

Dad appeared in her mind, handing her the Mossberg with a grim-faced expression. Every other time he'd loaded it and passed it over, he'd been grinning ear to ear since someone had been about to gawk at a 'little girl' getting phenomenal scores at the range. That last time in the house, he knew he handed her a killing machine. Maybe he knew she'd freeze up and not be able to kill a man.

I can't give up. I won't. She clutched the shotgun. *I'll protect Maddie. I'm sorry, Dad. I won't mess up again.* She rummaged her pockets, counting eighteen shells plus the nine in the weapon. *Crap. I should've brought more.* She let a long breath out her nostrils. *Please don't let me need more.*

The truck slowed and took a long sweeping left turn that made her slide to the right. They stopped. Spanish cursing came from Rafael along with some grinding noises. The truck reversed, a slow, steady beeping coming from somewhere outside. After a moment of barely moving, a startlingly loud *thump* emanated from behind her.

"Whoa," muttered Fred.

"It's okay. Trailer's empty, so it's loud." Rafael patted the wheel.

"Let's do this," said Darnell.

"No one in sight… of course visibility is shitty." Marcie sighed.

"Good thing we brought two snipers then." Darnell wagged his eyebrows. "Rock paper scissors for sentry?"

Fred raised a fist. "You want sentry detail or you prefer lugging crap around?"

"I'd rather relax on top of the truck." Darnell grinned.

"Go for it then." Fred slung his hunting rifle over his shoulder. "Just don't fall asleep. And oh, the sniper's the first one they shoot at."

Darnell brushed some dust off his sleeve. "Being dead don't make me tired. Lugging crap back and forth makes me tired."

Marcie, Ryan, and Ken chuckled.

Harper couldn't tell if he really intended to be lazy or if he had a giant pair of balls, volunteering for the most dangerous role. She followed everyone outside, sliding down from the passenger side door. The truck had backed up to a loading dock, which made things much easier. It took Ryan and Ken a few minutes to get past a steel door all the way on the left and head inside. Marcie counted her way down the garage doors until she reached the one by their truck, and proceeded to work the manual pull chain to raise it.

Everyone else spread out to search the dock area. They scored early, finding three pallets of canned ravioli that had been dropped off the day of the nuclear strike. No one had made it in to work that day to unpack it.

Fred and Rafael grabbed pallet jacks and got started transferring them to the trailer. Ryan went out to the store, a 9mm pistol in a two-handed cop grip. Marcie followed with her compound bow at the ready. Ken, a larger handgun out, went next with Harper at the back.

She looked out at the Walmart the way she did at the competition ranges, walking in a cautious left-leading stance as if expecting pop up targets to spring at her from anywhere. Hopefully, no innocent person would decide to jump out and startle anyone.

On the off chance some orphan like Lorelei, Brian, or Kim got in here and decided to hide out, she kept the safety on. A two-second delay could kill her, but she'd rather risk that than blow the head off a child out of reflex.

"Hey," said a deep male voice on the left. "Welcome to Walmart."

Harper jumped and swiveled, training the shotgun on a tall, muscular black man in a bright orange jumpsuit. He didn't have a firearm, though he did have an axe... and a frightening amount of blood spattered on his chest. Her heart nearly stopped at the sight of him as her brain tried to work out if his smile came off as friendly or psychotic.

Ryan jumped back with a yelp, pointing his handgun at the guy. Perhaps due to the man being twenty or so feet away, Ken reacted more calmly. He pivoted toward the guy, his weapon held ready but not aimed directly at him. Marcie kept her eyes on their surroundings, on guard in case the man showed himself as a distraction for an ambush.

"We're not here to cause trouble," said Ken. "Just looking for food."

Harper continued to stare platter-eyed at the bloody convict.

"Same here," said the big guy. "Figured I'd check out the deals in the gun section, too."

Ryan used his gun to point at the man's chest. "What's with the blood? Don't mind us if we're a bit on edge, but your outfit's a bit... distinctive."

"Yeah, yeah." The man nodded. "I was in the joint. Bank robbery. Night job, hit it when no one was there. I ain't no threat to ordinary people. Only one I ever had a problem with was 'the man,' and he dead. Them sons of bitches left us locked in after the blast."

"Aww, damn." Marcie sighed. "That ain't right."

Harper exhaled, and lowered the shotgun.

The big guy laughed. "Some of them mother—" He glanced at Harper. "Some of them dudes deserved it."

"So, what's the blood from?" Ken relaxed.

"Kid-toucher."

Ryan blinked. "What?"

"Ran into this skeevy son of a bitch from the joint. I ain't gonna horrify you all tellin' what I heard 'bout what he did beyond sayin' they knew about sixty victims. That kid you got with you would'a been way too old for him. Everyone knew what the guy did, so they kept him in isolation. I ain't never killed no one before that."

Harper fidgeted. *I've killed more people than a convict.*

Ken spat to the side. "You still haven't killed a person."

The big guy chuckled.

"You got anywhere to stay?" Marcie nudged Harper with an elbow. "What do you think?"

Ryan looked at her. "You're inviting him to join us?"

"Damn right."

Harper looked up from the floor and studied him. Though he stood to an imposing height with broad shoulders, wore a prison jumpsuit, and had blood all over him, in the absence of the initial shock of his appearance, he didn't frighten her *too* much. Something in his eyes struck her as reassuring. This guy didn't fit within the normal structure of society, hence the bank robbery and prison thing, but she didn't get any sense of threat from him. In fact, she felt inclined to hover close to him for protection. Harper smiled. "Yeah, he's cool."

Ryan glanced at her, surprised.

"Sure, why not." Ken nodded. "Hell, someone with the skills to break into a bank could be kinda handy. And, he removed a malignant tumor from the gene pool."

"Right on." The man walked closer, offering a hand to Ryan. "Name's Deacon Owens."

He shook hands with everyone in turn introducing themselves. Deacon gave Harper a 'you gotta be kidding' face.

"Might wanna swing by menswear and change." Marcie winked at him.

Deacon pulled at his jumpsuit. "Too avant garde for the apocalypse?"

"Just a bit." Ryan laughed.

They headed toward the food section, with Deacon making a quick stop for normal clothes. Once sure the store held no danger, everyone jogged to the front to grab shopping carts. Harper slung the shotgun over her shoulder and ran around gathering 'substantive' canned goods, going for things like pasta or hearty soups rather than vegetable sides, sauces, and such. She laughed in her head at 'combat shopping.' Shoving a cart down the aisles of a store with a weapon on her back felt simultaneously normal and bizarre. Random memories of past trips to the grocery store with Mom got her misty eyed, but she didn't feel safe enough here to surrender to grief.

Again and again, she filled the wagon and jogged it back to the loading dock. Box pasta would come in handy as it lasted for a long damn time. Rafael and Fred stayed in the back, transferring everything the others dumped on the floor into the giant fifty-three foot trailer. After they got all the good cans, Ken headed for the pharmacy section while everyone else went to the clothing area. On the way, Harper stopped near sporting goods and pointed out a case of compound bows.

"Those won't run out of ammo… unless the arrows break."

"Not a bad idea." Ryan nodded at her. "You know how to use one?"

"Nah. Never touched one. My dad was a gun nut, not a bow hunter." She caught sight of shotguns in another case. "Ooh."

While Ryan smashed cases and loaded his cart with bows and arrows, Harper raided the gun cabinets, grabbing pump shotguns and hunting rifles. Marcie swooped in beside her and collected all the ammunition in the case, overloading her cart.

"I can't believe all this stuff is still here. No one else took it already." Harper grabbed the last two rifles and stuffed them in her wagon.

"Ryan had to pick the lock on the door. People probably would have taken this stuff if they could've gotten in." Marcie grunted, her sneakers sliding on the floor as she tried to push the ammo.

Deacon ran over and helped. Harper followed them, shaking her head at the twenty or so rifles and shotguns in her cart. *Christmas shopping for the apocalypse. I hope it doesn't mean I've gone crazy that I wanna laugh at this.*

Fred and Rafael cheered at the haul of ammo and weapons. No one wanted to dump the ammo cart for fear of having to gather up scattered loose bullets, so they just pushed the entire cart into the trailer.

Harper, Deacon, and Ryan headed to the clothing area. She grabbed mostly stuff in Madison's size, taking whole rows off the display rack at a time. The guys took an assortment of adult clothes. Marcie rushed over after a few minutes with a new wagon and headed for the socks and underwear.

A squeak came from an aisle where no one should be. Harper threw a bundle of tween-sized leggings in her wagon and yanked the shotgun off her shoulder. A filthy twentysomething guy with wild brown hair—and a scrap of blue cloth around his neck—leaned past an endcap display of bras, raising a handgun at Deacon from behind.

Harper aimed and fired, thinking of the man's head like a pie-plate target.

Boom.

The thug fell out of sight in a spray of gore.

Deacon threw several pairs of jeans into the air while bellowing a surprised shout. Ryan screamed like the ditzy cheerleader from a horror movie. Marcie barked a few nasty words and swiveled to glare at Harper for startling her.

Another guy popped up over the top of a shelf. Harper pivoted and fired at him, launching an explosion of fragments from the boxes along the top. She couldn't tell if she hit the guy or he dropped down a split second before kissing buckshot.

"Incoming," shouted Marcie.

"Cover," barked Ryan.

Harper darted away from her wagon and hunkered down behind a steel shelf full of shirts sized for six-year-olds. The twang of a compound bow launching an arrow came from somewhere in front of her on the other side. Deacon roared. Men grunted. Banging and clattering came from everywhere. A rifle went off somewhere outside with a sharp *crack*.

At a *crunch* to her right, Harper swiveled and aimed. Another guy with a blue sash peered around the other end of her shelf, maybe thirty feet away. He locked stares with the end of her shotgun, offered a weak smile, and backed out of sight.

She swallowed, unsure if she should regret not shooting him, or be happy she didn't since all he'd done was look at her. Loud zombie-like moaning from behind startled an *eep* out of her. She spun the other way, gawking in horror at another gang punk, his skull split open almost at the middle of his forehead. Blood gushed down his face. His left eye pointed askew while the right one focused on her. Harper stared for two seconds at exposed brain before Deacon's axe came down again into the back of the guy's head. A revolver fell from the standing dead man's grip, and he collapsed over sideways.

The shelf in front of Harper's face shook with a hard impact from the other side. Marcie grunted, gasped, and gurgled.

Harper popped up to her feet, aiming over the shelf at a wild-eyed woman in the middle of strangling Marcie with a bright orange extension cord. The tip of the shotgun barrel hovered a mere two feet away from her head. "Get off her!"

No sooner did the crazy woman lock stares with her, than someone grabbed Harper from behind. Startled, she pulled the trigger and screamed. The woman strangling Marcie vanished in a bloody flash. Harper struggled, kicking and squirming as much as she could, fighting the man dragging her backward down the aisle in a bear-hug.

"Easy, girlie. You ain't gonna be hurt. Course, first time usually hurts a little." He licked her left ear.

"Gah!" Harper tried to wriggle away in disgust. Her thoughts filled with the accusatory, pleading look Madison gave her when she left the school. The need to get back home to her sister set off an explosion of fury and determination inside her. She roared, "No!" and rammed her head back, mashing her skull into his teeth.

He staggered, but didn't loosen his grip on her.

A short, fat guy with a blue sash rushed into the aisle in front of her, hurrying over to help contain her. Harper squirmed in an effort to aim with her arms pinned to her sides. The guy holding her swung her to the left the same instant she pulled the trigger. Buckshot tore up the pudgy man's hip; he collapsed to the floor, screaming.

The man squeezed the air out of her lungs and bashed her into the shelving repeatedly. "Drop the damn gun and maybe you won't need to be punished."

Gunfire went off in sporadic blasts somewhere beyond the shelves. Deacon grunted in exertion and a man's scream went by as if he'd been thrown. A subsequent *crash* confirmed it.

"Ngh," groaned the pudgy guy, dragging himself closer. "Gonna beat that bitch. She *shot* me."

Nothing mattered but getting back to Madison. Harper tried the head-butt again, but only hit the guy in the upper chest. He swung her the other way at empty steel shelving. She got a leg up, bracing a foot against the shelf, and shoved back. The man stumbled, keeping his balance.

Marcie yelled, "Son of a bitch!" and a few rapid pistol shots came from the same direction as her voice.

Harper stomped her heel into the man's foot. His grip faltered enough that her thrashing allowed her to slip loose. She whirled toward him and mashed the butt of the shotgun into the mouth that slobbered all over her ear. The guy grabbed his face, staggering into the shelving. She locked stares with the same guy who'd peeked at her before.

"Son of a bitch," muttered Harper—and shot him point blank. An explosion of red dots decorated his chest around a much larger central wound. He gurgled, and slumped to the floor.

A soft *click* from behind made her spin.

The fat guy pulled a handgun from his thigh pocket. Harper dove to the floor, sliding on the polished tiles as the man fired several shots over her. A bullet struck the shelf inches from her head with a loud *clank*. She scrambled up to all fours and speed crawled onto the carpet, hiding among round rack stands full of little girl dresses. Ten feet in front of her, a late-thirties guy with a blue sash lay dead, a metal arrow jutting up from his chest.

Harper spun side to side, shaking from adrenaline, a hair's breadth from shooting anything that moved.

A loud wet *crunch* came from the aisle where she'd been, along with the pudgy man's gurgled scream. Seconds later, a man stepped into view past the end cap. Harper swiveled to aim at—Deacon. She flicked her finger off the trigger and stopped pointing the gun at him.

"You okay?"

She shook her head. "Yeah."

He laughed and walked over to her. "I know that feeling. You hurt?"

"Just bruises." She stared at the pudgy guy's gun in the waist of Deacon's pants.

"Thanks for savin' my ass." He offered her a hand.

"Thanks for saving *my* ass." She accepted, allowing him to pull her upright. "I hate these guys."

"Seen 'em before?"

Harper nodded. "Yeah. They're like a gang or something. They killed my parents and tried to grab me and my little sister."

"The world's gone crazy." He patted her on the back. "Not bad with that thing."

"For a girl, right?" She smiled. "Been hearing that since I was thirteen." Her smile died. "Never thought I'd ever be shooting it at people."

Deacon sighed. "Yeah. Like I said, the world, she gone crazy."

"Clear!" yelled Ryan.

Ken ran into view, aiming around like a character in a bad action movie. "Don't see any more."

Harper hovered close to Deacon, walking with him back to where she'd left her cart of children's clothes. She tried not to look at any of the dead guys as she took shells from her jacket pocket and stuffed them into the Mossberg.

Marcie, her face spattered with blood, ran over and hugged her. "Holy crap! Thanks for saving my ass. That crazy bitch... I was *this* close to blacking out."

"I didn't mean to shoot so close to your face... that guy grabbed me and I... the gun went off." Harper cringed. "I'm really sorry."

"No. No sorry." Marcie squeezed her again. "I'm good. Just got covered in gore. This isn't my blood."

Harper looked away. "I didn't wanna kill that woman."

"Not your fault." Marcie tore the shirt off a dead guy and wiped her face. "I really owe you one, Harper."

Mute, she managed a weak nod. Too rattled to put the shotgun over her shoulder, Harper one-armed it, gathering more clothes with her left hand until she couldn't add anything else to the mound in the shopping cart without it falling.

Marcie gathered any useful items from the dead thugs—including a few of her arrows—while everyone else pushed the wagon train of clothes back to the trailer. Ken and Ryan had been wounded, from knives as well as bullets, though their injuries appeared relatively mild. Other than a red line around her neck from the extension cord, Marcie didn't appear hurt. Harper shivered at the understanding of why she and Marcie hadn't been shot or stabbed. Despite being utterly disgusted at the idea of men regarding her as a thing to be taken, she couldn't help but feel somewhat relieved their first thought hadn't been killing her.

She learned from Fred that Darnell had shot three or four men outside, protecting the dock. Since no one knew if any of the thugs who attacked them had survived to bring help, they packed the trailer as densely as possible, crawling in on top of cans to jam softer items like clothes, blankets, and such straight to the ceiling.

Fred and Ken discussed hurrying back to Evergreen, unloading, and coming back as fast as possible before more bad guys showed up to loot the place. Harper dreaded the idea of having to return, especially considering there'd probably be thugs waiting for them. She hadn't really looked at any of them, and wondered if the man who'd killed her father might've died to his shotgun after all. There couldn't be *that* many of them, and Littleton wasn't too far away from Lakewood. Unfortunately, she hadn't really seen the face of the guy who killed her father. He'd been outside on the deck, firing in through the patio door. She'd never know if that guy ever paid for what he did. Vowing to kill everyone in that gang she saw came off as a touch melodramatic, and totally unlike her.

Ryan re-locked the Walmart door once the trailer could hold no more stuff. Everyone piled back into the truck cab, all carrying plastic shopping bags of what Fred called 'looter's privilege,' a few items each person got to keep without turning in to the quartermaster. Harper claimed two pairs of sweat pants for herself and two pairs each for her sister and brother. She also snagged a couple nightgowns and a plush rabbit that looked like one Madison had on her bed back in their old house.

The growl of the engine starting right up set off a series of relieved sighs and cheers. Harper curled up in the back corner of the sleeper cab, face against her knees, trying to stop seeing the blurry figures of the men she'd killed. She wiped her ear on her sleeve, inches from throwing up.

Marcie checked over the guys' injuries, tending to them with a couple first aid kits they'd grabbed on the way out. Everyone had *way* too much energy from the lingering adrenaline. Harper's hands wouldn't stop shaking. She wanted to cling to someone and react like a normal teenage girl who'd just been forced to shoot people, but she couldn't. At least she couldn't cling to anyone here. Maybe she'd trust Cliff to see her that vulnerable in the privacy of home, maybe not. She had to think of those men as monsters, bad guys from a virtual reality video game with amazing graphics. They hadn't been people. *People* didn't grab young women and girls. Those same blue-bandana wearing sons of bitches had tried to take Madison, too. Maybe that's why she trusted Deacon so fast. He'd killed a kid-toucher. So had she. What else could she call a grown man trying to grab her little sister? Harper clenched her fists, shaking as much from anger as excess adrenaline. Those guys didn't even have names, merely 'creatures' in a sandbox environment she couldn't stop playing no matter how much she wanted to log out.

More than any sense of guilt over taking life—after all, those people had attacked them—or fear that something would go wrong on the way back to Evergreen, Harper dreaded one thing:

Madison would hate her for leaving her alone.

24

ALONE

A few minutes short of an hour later, Rafael backed the rig up to a small receiving area on the side of the quartermaster's building. Liz Trujillo and the people working with her would allocate all the stuff they'd taken from the Walmart as needed. Harper climbed down from the rig and started to jog toward the school, but stopped herself, torn between wanting to find Madison and fear of getting in trouble for leaving too early. Of course, the militia couldn't 'fire' her. Worst they'd do is kick her off and confiscate the shotgun… and it represented most of her ability to protect her family. Even if Madison hated her, she wouldn't let anything hurt her. As much as the Mossberg called her a failure every time she looked at it, she refused to let anyone take it.

Liz and her staff came out of the building and helped unload the truck. Harper halfheartedly joined in, preoccupied with worry. After a few minutes, Walter arrived. It didn't take him long to chase Ken and Ryan off to the medical center. Marcie spent a moment muttering with him. As soon as he nodded, they both approached Harper.

She paused on her way to the door with an armload of clothing.

"Hey. Heard it got a little rough out there," said Walter.

"Uhh. Yeah."

"You okay?" Walter tilted his head, a look of concern on his face.

"I'm not hurt. Just worried about Madison. She kinda freaked out when I left her at the school."

Walter patted her on the shoulder. "Go on, check on your sister if you want."

Harper blinked at him.

"Yes, really." Marcie reached for the bundle. "You're practically shaking."

"Okay. If she's not too messed up, I'll bring her back here and help."

Marcie smiled and shooed her away from the truck. "Go. Check on her."

Harper jogged down the road from the quartermaster's building to Route 74 and hurried north. She practically leapt the fence by the track and dashed across the soccer field to the front of the school. At the sound of kids still inside, she relaxed. The trip hadn't taken as much time as it felt like. Hopefully, Madison would see her back in one piece and forget all about how upset she'd been earlier that morning.

She barged into the classroom with a big, hopeful smile on her face... and froze at not seeing Madison anywhere. Harper scanned the desks of kids, who'd all paused in whatever they'd been doing to stare at her. Mila, aka Creepy Girl, stood out due to her black hair, the same color as Madison's, but her little sister wasn't in the room. Violet sat at the littlest kids' group going over vocabulary words.

"Violet?" Harper walked over to her. "Where's Madison?"

The woman started to point at the cluster of nine- to eleven-year-olds, but froze, looking around the room. "Umm."

"How can you just lose her?" blurted Harper, nearly shouting.

Violet winced, but hardened her stare. "There's fifty-four kids in here." Her glower softened with an apologetic sigh. "If one of them wants to sneak off, there's only so much I can do. I'm sorry... I've been asking Ned to give me at least one more person to help out here, but no one wants to put up with this many kids all day every day. Only two expressed interest. One guy couldn't read, and the woman had too short a fuse."

"Argh." Harper grabbed her hair and paced, then shouted, "Madison!?"

"The shadow man took her," said Mila in an emotionless voice.

Everyone fell quiet.

"Mila's weird," said Christopher. "She just says stuff like that to be scary."

"The shadow man took my mom, too." Mila stared into Harper's eyes.

"Mom's not coming back. When the shadow man takes someone, they never come back."

Violet pursed her lips, looking at Mila, and whispered, "I got this. Don't panic."

Harper's hands resumed shaking. No way in hell did she seriously believe some supernatural shadow entity had taken her sister. Perhaps a living, breathing threat followed Mila here from wherever he'd attacked her mother, but no one could have plucked Madison out of the classroom without being noticed, but if she'd run off... what might Mila have seen out the window?

"Madison?" shouted Harper, flying into a panic.

She ran out of the room, going up and down the school hallways, calling for her sister over and over. Upon finding no trace of her in the building, she raced outside, running blindly in random directions while shouting her sister's name. Tears streamed out her eyes, blurring the trees and houses into a meaningless smear of color. People emerged from doors, watching as she zoomed by. Her brain re-engaged with the idea that Madison probably ran home, so Harper headed as straight south as she could, cutting across a stretch of golf course before jumping fences into another residential area. Giant houses with lots of space between them probably meant the people who used to live here had been well off.

In the fifth yard she crossed, an athletic man wearing sunglasses, a pink bathrobe, and sweat pants observed her from an elevated deck beside a pool. A tumbler glass in his left hand held about an inch of brown liquid. He looked a little rough around the edges, but would clean up into a pretty boy if he shaved. Something about him seemed kinda familiar.

"Hey," said Harper. "Have you seen my sister? She's ten, black hair, skinny."

"What are you doing in my yard?"

She pointed the shotgun at him. "Missing child. Have you seen my sister?"

"Whoa there, hot pants. Take it easy. This is my house. Don't you know who I am?"

Harper scoffed. "No. Didn't anyone ever tell you people who say 'don't you know who I am' are usually assholes. I have no idea who you are, but you do kinda look like I've seen you somewhere."

He bowed his head, sighed, and raked a hand over his dark, thick hair. "Well, that didn't take long at all. Lucas Garza?"

"Nope. Sorry. I really don't care who you are right now while my sister's missing." She shivered at the sight of him. "You realize you have no shirt on and it's like forty degrees, right?"

"Yeah." He toasted her with the glass. "This stuff keeps me warm."

She approached the deck. "Hey, I get it. You're upset. Everyone's messed up now. I need to find my little sister before she gets hurt."

"*Pirates of Whitebone Cove?*" He struck a swashbuckler's pose. "*The Night Sword* series?"

"Nope, sorry. I think I might've seen you on TV or something. You an actor?"

"Was. Used to be famous, wealthy, girls throwing themselves at me. All that money… it's gone. Maybe it wasn't ever real, just numbers in computers."

Harper couldn't quite feel too sorry for a rich guy who lost it all when the banking network melted. Money didn't matter anymore. "Yeah. That really sucks. Sorry. I gotta go."

Lucas toasted her again and took a sip from his drink.

She ran across the yard, scaling fence after fence before running through trees, down a hill to a road crossing her path. A solid reddish fence with stone posts every twenty feet or so blocked further progress directly south. The roof of a large building with a narrow strip of windows barely peeked over it, suggesting the other side had quite a drop. She turned right, heading for Route 74. The red fence gave way to pickets, then trees overlooking a series of fluffy white inflatable buildings. The ground still looked too far down to risk climbing, so she kept going west until she hit the intersection with Route 74, and veered south.

She contemplated blaring the horn to call for help, but wasn't sure Madison cutting school deserved a 911 blast, especially if she'd only gone home. However, if she didn't find her at home, Harper would use up that whole air horn until they found her.

Leigh Preston jogged up to her when she passed by the medical clinic. "Hey, Harper."

"Leigh!" She darted over and grabbed the woman's arm. "Maddie's missing! She ran away from school."

"Oh, no." Leigh looked around for a few seconds before she blinked like an idea hit her in the head like a rock. "Oh! Sadie said she saw a kid crossing the highway an hour or two ago, heading west."

"Why didn't she stop her?" shouted Harper.

"Hey. Calm down." Leigh squeezed her arms. "No need to yell at me."

"Sorry."

"Sadie's at the buses. She spotted the kid a couple hundred yards away."

Harper whined out her nose. "Crap! Was she alone?"

"I think so. C'mon, let's go check."

Leigh jogged down the road to the bus barrier, where Sadie, Cameron, and Annapurna stood sentry.

"You saw Madison?" asked Harper.

Sadie shrugged. "I saw a kid. Too far away to recognize. Long black hair, blue coat."

Harper's stomach churned with worry. "That sounds like her. Where'd she go? Was she alone?"

"Yep. Headed west off the road, little south of the farm."

"Where? Show me. Please." Harper bounced on her toes.

"Can't leave this post unless there's a serious emergency... Tell ya what. Head up the road, and I'll give a pip when you're at the spot." Sadie pulled out her air horn can. "Soon as I chirp the horn, you'll want to go to your left off the road."

"Okay. Thanks." Harper hurried back up Route 74.

Leigh ran to catch up, her AK47 clattering in her grip. "We'll find her."

"It's so stupid. This other kid at the school keeps talking about a shadow man taking people. I'm terrified something might really be out there."

"Ehh. Some of those kids saw some nasty shit on their way here."

Harper glanced over at her. "I'm one of those kids. Though... I guess the nasty I saw was my fault."

"Don't blame yourself."

"No, I mean I shot a guy right in the face from like four feet. His head exploded."

Leigh coughed.

"He was trying to kidnap Maddie."

"Sick bastards out there."

"Yeah. I hate it. What idiot thought launching nukes was a good idea?" Harper fumed. "I don't even remember what pizza tastes like!"

Leigh stared at her.

She lapsed into sobs for a few seconds, but composed herself. "Sorry. I don't know what the hell's wrong with me. Maddie's missing and I'm bitching about pizza."

"Hey, it's normal. You're upset. The brain does weird things."

A distant *meep* came from an air horn.

Harper stopped and turned to look back toward town. At that distance, the buses appeared as little more than a whitish line across the road. Sadie only looked about as tall as tall as a grain of rice.

"Here, tracks." Leigh squatted and pointed at the dirt. "Looks like a kid."

"Madison!" shouted Harper. "Where are you?"

Her voice echoed over the tree-dotted field. A hundred or so people to the right paused in their effort to construct a farm, looking her way. Various incomplete buildings, pens for animals, storage barns, and so on, stood in different degrees of completion. A few dozen chickens roamed about a fenced area beside the only intact structure, a large shack. Harper disregarded them and walked out into the grass, going in the same direction the tracks indicated.

They walked past trees, dirt trails, and hills. Here and there, Leigh paused to look at the ground, but didn't find any more tracks. A fair distance ahead to the left, Harper spotted a tall mound of rock. It looked like a reasonable spot to climb for a better view of the area, so she jogged for it.

Soft crying coming from the other side stopped as she drew near.

"Maddie?" yelled Harper, breaking into a run.

She scrambled to the hill, grabbing trees for balance on the shifting dirt as she climbed to the other side. Madison sat on the ground in the shadow of a huge boulder, her back to the rock, staring at the dead iPhone in her hands. She looked as though she'd been crying hard for hours, but other than having blue lips, didn't appear hurt.

"Maddie!" Harper ran over, skidding to a stop beside her. She dropped the shotgun and grabbed her sister in both arms. "Please don't hate me."

"Why did you leave? You told me you wouldn't go away." Despite the girl's surly tone, she embraced her.

"I'm sorry. They said it was safe and wouldn't take long. We found a Walmart and got a whole bunch of good stuff. Food, clothes, shoes... even some medicine."

Madison sniffled.

"You scared the hell out of me."

"You scared the hell out of *me!*" cry-shouted Madison.

Leigh exhaled in relief.

Harper jumped at an air horn going off behind her with three short pips. She looked back and up at Leigh. "What's that signal mean?"

"All clear. Sadie should understand that as 'we found her okay.'"

"Oh." She squeezed Madison so hard the girl gurgled. "I'm sorry."

"I'm not mad at you." Madison clung.

Harper's heart all but melted as her second worst fear dissolved. She knelt there holding her sister for a few minutes, unable to talk. Finally, she found a voice. "Why'd you run off?"

"I wanted to be alone. The school was too peopley."

Leigh stifled a snicker.

"I hate it here. I wanna go home," said Madison. "Mom and Dad are gonna be mad at us for being gone for days without calling."

Harper burst into tears. *No... I thought she understood...* She shifted from kneeling to sitting and pulled her sister into her lap. "Mom and Dad are..."

"No." Madison's face scrunched up with grief, and she, too, burst into sobs.

Leigh sat on a nearby rock, hand over her mouth, eyes wet.

A minute or six later, Harper gathered herself and exhaled slow. "Maddie, Mom and Dad aren't going to be angry. They're gone."

"I know," said Madison, her voice warped by grief. "But if I keep talking about them like they're alive, I don't have to believe it. It hurts too much." She coughed, and lapsed back into sobs.

Harper held her until she quieted. "I know you don't like it here. Please give it a chance, okay? It's the safest place for us."

"I don't really hate it here. I hate that we can't go home. I hate that the world broke. I hate that I lost my friends. I hate that Mom and Dad died."

"I do, too, Termite." Harper rocked her back and forth. "I do, too."

Madison sniffled. "Sorry for being a butthead."

"It's okay. Just don't run off again?"

"'Kay."

"C'mon." Harper patted her on the leg. "Your lips are blue. You've been out in the cold too long. We should go back to the house."

Madison stood, bowed her head, and sighed. "You can call it home if you want."

"Are you sure?" Harper got up and took her sister's hand.

"Yeah. We live here now. I have scary dreams about our old house. It's not home anymore. Mom and Dad died there when those people broke in. It's a grave. A grave of memories."

Harper felt as though a knife hit her in the heart. She couldn't find the will to take even one step, her mind awash with scenes from her old house: holidays, friends over, even boring days or arguments with the parents.

"You okay?" asked Leigh.

"I'll get back to you on that."

Madison tugged on her arm. "C'mon, Harp. Let's go home. I don't wanna be alone anymore."

25

A WHOLE LOT OF USED TO

Leigh walked with them back to the bus barrier.

Sadie and Annapurna both hugged Madison and asked her not to run off again. She begrudgingly apologized and promised not to. Harper hugged Sadie, tearfully thanking her for spotting Madison going across the road.

"Walt stopped by." Annapurna nodded toward the militia HQ. "We told him about Madison. He wanted us to tell you to go on home for the rest of the day. Stay with her tomorrow, too if you need. Given what happened at the Walmart, you're off the hook for a bit. Another group's gonna be heading back there in a few minutes."

"What happened at the Walmart?" Madison looked up.

"Umm. We ran into a couple bad guys."

Madison's eyes tripled in size.

"I... didn't mess up again." Harper looked down.

"Hey..." Annapurna crouched and rested a hand on Madison's shoulder. "They're not sending her back there. It'll be okay."

Madison sniffled.

"Thanks." Harper smiled at the women, and led her sister down the road toward Hilltop Drive. She crossed the dirt strip to the smaller highway paralleling Route 74, and followed it past the medical clinic. Deacon emerged from the building in mid conversation with Fred. Both men appeared in good spirits and waved at her. Harper figured Deacon passed his medical check and headed over to have his talk with Mayor Ned.

Up ahead, a shadow moved behind a large wooden sign reading 'Elk Meadow Center.' Someone appeared to be trying to hide from her. Harper shifted Madison to the right, putting herself between the sign and her sister. She started to raise the shotgun, but froze when Tyler stepped out with his hands up.

"What the heck are you doing?" asked Harper.

"Sorry. Just... I dunno." He scratched his head. "Was on my way to the school to pick Lorelei up and kinda got sidetracked."

She narrowed her eyes. *Is he stalking me?* "Sidetracked by what?"

"The hills." He gestured off to the west. "It's so quiet here. Doesn't really look like anything happened. I guess I zoned out on a daydream. Kept thinking about walking off into those hills and just keeping on going."

"Oh." Harper relaxed, but thought it odd he refused to look directly at her. That 'weird kid' vibe hit her again, but he wouldn't be the first boy who got a bad case of the awkwards while talking to her. "You look worried about something. Is Lorelei doing okay?"

"Yeah, she's hanging in there. Maybe I shouldn't have taken her in though."

"Why?"

Madison leaned against her.

"I'm... I dunno. What do I know about raising a kid? She gave me this look and I just kinda agreed right away without thinking about it. I'm only nineteen. Didn't exactly have the best example of parents. Lori would be better off with someone else." Tyler stuffed his hands in his coat pocket and gazed out over the hills. "Evergreen's probably not right for me."

"What do you mean? This place is pretty nice." She looked down at Madison. Blue lips, shivering, but a content expression. "I should probably get home. Maddie's been out in the cold."

A distant squealing cheer broke the silence. Harper twisted to look behind her at a fast-approaching streak of white. Lorelei, in a winter coat a little too big for her, sprinted down the road, emitting a joyful non-word. The six-year-old crashed into Tyler, beaming. "Hi!"

Harper opened her mouth to comment about him letting a girl that small run home alone, but Tyler didn't seem at all concerned about it. Her non-confrontational nature got into a brawl with her role on the militia.

Only her doubt as to whether or not what remained of society would still consider it wrong for a six-year-old to be alone outside kept her quiet.

"Hey, kiddo." Tyler patted her on the head. "How was school?"

"I had fun!" Lorelei bounced on her toes, little lights in her sneakers flashing. She proceeded to ramble about what they'd learned—mostly writing, reading, and basic math.

Harper sighed at them. In all likelihood, by the time that girl was old enough to have a child, kids would be thrilled to have shoes at all, and couldn't care less if they lit up, wouldn't even imagine such a thing as shoes-with-lights could exist. They warped into a metaphor for a society that had gone *way* off the rails and had nothing better to do with its resources than put blinking lights in kids' sneakers.

"We need to get inside," said Harper. "Before Maddie freezes."

Tyler nodded and started to wander off, but hesitated when Lorelei started chatting with Madison. The little platinum blonde sprite was about as opposite as possible to her: energetic to glum, nearly white hair to black, thrilled to bits with life to a burden of grief too heavy for a ten-year-old. Before the war, the two of them would've been quite alike.

"Might as well walk together." Tyler fidgeted again, not looking at her.

"Sure." Harper stared down and resumed walking.

Dad always made jokes about having a pretty daughter and shooting boys who didn't bring her home on time. This kid Gerald she'd dated sophomore year made a remark that she was 'epically cute' more than hot. Of course, Introvert Prime had a universal reaction to any sort of compliment: blushing.

Madison and Lorelei—mostly Lorelei—chatted the whole way back to the house. Tyler walked beside Harper. For the most part, he looked at houses or trees, sometimes sighing. He seemed worried, but not in a guilty way. She didn't think he'd done something and feared being caught. Perhaps he'd survived violence and hadn't quite accepted his demons wouldn't find him here.

The sight of smoke coming out of the chimney at the house worried Harper up to a run. She dashed the last forty feet to the door and barged in to a somewhat-warmer-than-outside room saturated with the fragrance of wood smoke.

Jonathan smiled up at her from where he knelt in front of the fireplace. "Hey."

Cliff didn't appear to be anywhere nearby. She opened her mouth to yell at him for starting a fire while home alone... or being home alone at ten, but stalled. *Did people in the 1800s lose their minds having a kid his age alone?* She decided to skip the pointless argument. Admittedly, Jonathan *was* far more responsible with fire than any boy his age had a right to be. *Probably not. We all have to grow up fast.*

Madison rushed in and hopped on the couch. Lorelei invited herself along, scampering up beside her. When her sister smiled, Harper had to turn away so they didn't catch her getting teary-eyed.

"What's wrong?" asked Tyler, stepping inside.

She nodded toward the kitchen and shut the front door. "Should probably figure out what we're eating tonight."

Tyler followed, leaning on the dead fridge while she rummaged cabinets, sorting among canned goods.

"My sister doesn't make friends too easy. It just hit me in the feels that she's getting along with Lorelei so quick." She sighed at a giant can of lima beans and put it back in the cabinet. *No, we're not that desperate yet. Oh, who am I kidding? We are, but not tonight.*

He smiled. "Yeah. They look happy." Awkwardness fell over them for a moment. "Uhh, sorry. Never was really good at random conversation."

"So, how was your day at work? Not too bad. Killed a couple of guys trying to kidnap me, had some creep lick my ear. We looted a Walmart. Now I'm just gonna cook dinner."

"Ouch. Yeah, Lori's real outgoing. You'd never think the poor kid almost starved to death. Still hasn't said anything about her parents or how she wound up alone out there. At least she seems happy here."

"You aren't?"

"Are you?"

Harper shrugged one shoulder and selected three identical cans of mini-potatoes. "I'd rather be at the house I grew up in with my parents still alive, but, I can't, and they're not, so yeah. This place is okay." She grabbed the pan she'd used yesterday off the stove and set it down on the counter a little too hard.

"Sorry."

"What for?"

"Upsetting you."

"I'm not upset." She peered back at him, throwing red curls over her shoulder with a sharp head motion. "I just killed a couple of dudes today who tried to kidnap and rape me. Came home, found my sister missing. I'm pretty damn calm, all things considered."

"Maybe I should go. I'm upsetting you more. Maybe I should just keep going."

Harper leaned on the counter, head down, and sighed. "Sorry. Not your fault. I *hate* that I had to do that. It doesn't feel real sometimes, yanno? I used to be the kid who'd catch bugs and carry them outside and get upset if my father stepped on one. And, you should stay here. It's safe here. Out there, it's like chaos."

"It can't be that bad everywhere. I'd like to explore places, check out all the stuff I could never see or do before. Like rich people's houses. Big boats, fancy cars. Go into all the places at like airports where they never let people go. See what's inside a hospital's operating room or a secret government base."

She attacked the potato cans with an opener. "Heh. You know most cars don't work anymore, right?"

"Depends on how electronic they are and if EMP got them. I saw a few working ones on my way here. Older cars aren't affected. Like classics with carburetors and stuff."

Harper dumped a bunch of egg-sized potatoes into the pot along with the cloudy water they'd been packed in. "Gonna run out of gasoline at some point."

"You're not tempted to do stuff you'd have gotten in trouble for doing before? I want to go to a big city and check out the corporate offices, the big computer rooms. Mansions, that stuff. Drive on the wrong side of the road. Talk in a library!" He laughed.

"Nah. Not me. All I want to do is keep Maddie and Jonathan safe."

"What about keeping you safe?"

She smiled. "That's implied. I can't protect them if I'm not alive. And it sounds like you're just restless. It's much safer here."

"Safer..." He stared off into space.

"Yeah. Safer." Harper dumped the second can into the pot. "Fallout, crazies, bad stuff going on out there."

He crossed the kitchen to stand beside her. "You don't sound like a badass militia soldier."

"Hah." She added the last can to the pot. "Probably because I'm not." She set the empty can down and stared at it for a few seconds, lost in thought. "I haven't told anyone this yet, but I've been thinking I don't really belong on the militia. I'm still a kid. I don't know how to fight, just have a shotgun."

"Not many kids know their way around shotguns."

"My dad got me into competition shooting when I was like eleven. By thirteen, I'd won a couple trophies. Even kinda got YouTube famous among the gun crowd. You know, check out this bad ass little girl on the timed course. She's only twelve but she's scoring better than men three times her age. That sorta BS."

"Nice."

"*Nice* is shooting clay pigeons or water jugs. People, not so much." She looked into the cabinet for something to have with the potatoes and wound up staring in horrified awe at 'canned meatloaf.' "Ugh. Seriously? Who thought that was a good idea?"

"Speaking of shooting things..."

She laughed until tears ran down her face. What he'd said hadn't been that funny at all, but she couldn't stop. Maybe the tension finally snapped. Or the premise of meatloaf in a can had been one last scrap of wrongness on top of 'the world is broken' that her brain couldn't process it.

"I didn't think it was that funny."

"It's not." She wiped her eyes. "I don't know why I'm laughing. But, maybe the idea of me being on the militia is just that ridiculous. As ridiculous as meatloaf in a damn can."

Tyler leaned on the counter. "Stuff's different. We gotta grow up now."

"Yeah. Grow up..." She glanced sideways at him, wondering if he'd try to put an arm around her—and not sure if she'd mind. "I used to get mad when Starbucks ran out of the skinny Mocha stuff."

"Totally!" shouted Madison from the living room. "She used to whine for hours whenever they ran out."

Harper blushed. *How much did she hear?*

"Heh. I used to hate it when some news story cut into my favorite show." Tyler grinned. "Totally freaked me out. Broke my routine and stuff."

"Might want to stand back. I'm gonna open this atrocity." She attached the can opener to the meatloaf. "I used to love getting pizza on Fridays."

"Used to get angry at the way I'd get caught at every damn red light on the way home from work." Tyler made the sign of the cross at the can.

The smell that emerged when she punctured the lid worried her because it approached appetizing. Canned meatloaf should be the exact opposite of appealing. "I used to hate homework."

"I *still* hate homework," said Madison from the doorway.

"You don't have homework now." Harper smiled back at her.

"What's homework?" chirped Lorelei beside her. She'd taken her shoes off, and had removed her puffy winter coat. The girl looked too damn thin to be a real person. Deep grooves outlined her collarbones where her pink dress didn't cover. Still, she grinned at everyone.

"It's school stuff you do at home." Madison muttered 'duh' and rolled her eyes.

"Oh." Lorelei giggled.

Harper upended the canned meatloaf over a pot. A perfectly cylindrical slug of 'meat like substance' emerged with a long slurp and fell with a plop. She repeated the process with a second can. "You can probably eat this, Maddie. I don't think it counts as meat."

"Bleh." Madison stuck her tongue out. "It's probably all the scraps they can't use for anything else and a bunch of chemicals to make it taste like beef."

"There are probably enough preservatives in that to add five years to our lives." Tyler grinned.

"Fireplaces used to be decorative." Harper picked up both pans and carried them into the living room. She set them on the oven rack over the fire, then backed off to remove her winter coat, which she tossed on the recliner before kneeling to worry at the embers with the poker.

Madison and Jonathan decided to show Lorelei some dance moves.

Tyler took a seat on the sofa. He fidgeted, right leg bouncing while looking around. His unsettled energy made him seem like he desperately waited for the right moment where he could leap up and run away without being noticed.

"I used to take dance classes," said Madison.

"I used to complain about having to drive you there." Harper sighed. "I'm sorry."

"I used to have parents," said Lorelei in an entirely wrong, happy tone.

Everyone stared at her.

Madison let go of her foot, which had almost been touching the back of her head, and lowered it gradually to the floor. "Yeah. Ours died too."

Lorelei attempted to mimic lifting her foot up behind her head, and fell over. She bounced on her butt, landed flat on her back, and burst into giggles.

The front door opened. Harper jumped, grabbing for the shotgun on the floor beside her. Cliff walked in before she could pick it up. She melted into a puddle of nerves, freaked out that a simple door opening had scared the crap out of her so bad. Cliff stopped two steps into the living room and locked stares with Tyler.

"Hey," rasped Harper. "What's up?"

Cliff walked over to her, holding up a bundle wrapped in paper. "Got some venison."

She stood. "Okay."

"I can get it. You've had a heck of a day so I hear."

Her lip quivered. "Yeah. Bit."

"C'mere." He held his arms out.

She leaned into a much-needed hug, surprising herself by not crying. Merely holding onto him comforted her in a way that reminded her of Dad. Over the next hour or so, she quietly told him about the Walmart raid while he cooked the venison. Going over it in a safe place brought on some twinges of nausea and anger. He thought she did right by not shooting that one guy who only looked at her, even if he did wind up grabbing her later.

Soon, everyone crowded around the dining room table for a feast of fresh grilled venison, canned potatoes, and questionable meat from a can. Cliff continued to discuss the Walmart raid, suggesting he start teaching Harper some hand-to-hand techniques. In the back of her mind, she resisted the idea, still half tempted to give up the shotgun and maybe help Violet out at the school. If it didn't feel so much like failing Dad all over again, she would've done it already. Unable to make a firm decision, she nodded at him and kept eating.

Lorelei ate daintily, as befitting her appearance. Despite taking tiny bites, she seemed intent on finishing her entire portion.

A moment of tension settled over the table when everyone stopped speaking at once. Cliff stared at Tyler with an odd note of hostility or distrust hanging between them. Harper glanced from one to the other, the kids oblivious to the bad energy. The last time she'd seen *that* look on Cliff, he'd been staring at her while she sat handcuffed to a chair in the mall and tried to lie her way out. Fortunately, she'd been so terrified she cracked in under a minute and wound up sobbing.

Oh, he's doing the dad thing. Thinks Tyler's trying to get in my pants.

"Never had venison before," said Harper, a little bit too cheery. "It's good."

"You're eating Bambi." Madison frowned. She'd tolerated some of the canned gunk but had no interest in the fresh meat.

"Bambi tastes good," chirped Lorelei.

Cliff wiped a hand down his face, laughing. "Okay, that's wrong."

"Yeah, this is really good." Tyler nodded.

"So, what's your story?" asked Cliff, again staring challenge at him.

"Not much to say really," replied Tyler, gaze locked on his plate. "I lived with a couple roommates. Didn't get along with my parents at all. No idea if any of my family's left. Can't say I really care to find out."

"Bad blood?"

"You can say that, yeah."

"Gay?" Cliff ate a whole mini-potato in one bite. "Nothing wrong with that, just curious."

Harper stared at him, trying to say *'really?'* with her eyes.

Tyler sputtered. "Umm, no."

"You work?"

Harper blushed and looked down. *He's totally doing the dad thing. Crap. We're not dating.*

"No. I mean, I kinda lost my job when the nukes fell." Tyler let off a feeble laugh. "Before, yeah. Worked at Walmart."

Madison ate a little more of the canned meatloaf, but made a horrible face at it.

Cliff watched Tyler like a gunslinger about to throw down. Any minute now, he'd either shoot the kid, throw him out, or do something embarrassing.

I'm not even thinking of... She glanced sideways at Tyler. Okay, he was kinda cute in the 'weird outcast' sort of way. And he had a soft spot for kids, taking Lorelei in. He sounded reasonably smart. Not like Evergreen had much of a teen population. From what she'd seen so far, just her and Tyler. The oldest kids at the school all looked around fifteen or so. Not that Harper felt any need to have a boyfriend, but if it happened, she'd prefer someone close in age rather than being assigned to an adult man. But, she had far too much on her mind to even contemplate romance. Dead parents, broken little sister, people shooting at her for going shopping at Walmart, worry over her inadequacy as a soldier. Yeah, kissing boys had fallen quite far down her list of stuff to do.

Technically, nineteen is an adult. She smirked to herself. *Speaking of used-tos. I used to be jail bait.*

This, of course, brought on the mortifying thought that things like birth control, condoms, tampons, pads, and such would be damn hard to find fairly soon if not already. Her cheeks burned hot with blush. Maybe she *would* volunteer to go on another scavenging trip for looter's privilege. Her little stash of razors wouldn't last long before shaving her legs with steak knives would seem like a less painful idea.

Naturally, Cliff misinterpreted the blush wrong based on the scowl he shot at Tyler. No way could Harper admit to freaking out about feminine products going extinct in front of everyone. Hell, she probably couldn't tell Cliff that even in private. No slight on him, though. That conversation she couldn't have had with her actual father either. Maybe she'd visit Carrie later and ask her for advice.

Cliff sliced off a strip of his venison and transferred it to Madison's plate. "I agree. That brown goop is nasty. And I've eaten bugs."

She made a sour face at it, a worse face at the canned meatloaf, then tentatively cut off a piece. "I used to be a vegetarian."

Jonathan laughed. Cliff smiled. Harper stared apologies at her sister. Lorelei made silly faces at everyone. Tyler kept his attention on his plate, but snuck a feeble smile at Harper. She couldn't tell if Madison's quip amused him or he tried to send her a message. Though she wanted to crawl under the table and hide, she didn't.

I used to be socially awkward. Nope, wait. Still am.

26

RAIN

A strange sound intruded upon Harper's dream, pulling her away from a slumber party at Christina's to her stolen house in Evergreen.

She and Madison clung to each other under the heavy layers of blankets and comforters, both in the new nightgowns she'd grabbed at Walmart. Given the infrequency—or potential impossibility—of washing laundry, it couldn't be smart to sleep in her clothes. On some days, she used to go through three complete outfits. Having only a sheer nightgown on while sharing a bed embarrassed her at first, but Madison didn't seem to care at all. Better a little blushing than either of them contracting an infection that doctors might not be able to treat.

There had to be *some* way to wash clothes. Laundry detergent and washing machines hadn't been around for the entirety of human history after all. A mental image of cavemen pouring detergent into a cap and running a machine made her snicker. Madison grunted and snuggled closer, rolling on her side with one knee across Harper's legs. The inflexible presence of a nonworking iPhone pressed into her side, compressed between them.

Her little sister had cried over the plush rabbit, even if its newness had given it away as not *her* bunny. She'd fallen asleep hugging it (and the iPhone) to her chest like a girl half her age.

This bed is going to get kinda cozy when she's older. Harper yawned and spent a while wondering how her sister would handle it if ever she did the boyfriend thing and moved in with someone. At that moment, she didn't have much of an urge to. She could be happy staying here with the only family she had left. Who cared if people thought it bizarre for a pair of grown women to sleep in the same bed? They were sisters. Not like anything icky would happen. Some people might think Madison's degree of clinginess to be a bit creepy ten years down the road, but maybe she'd grow out of it. Not much time had passed since she witnessed her parents' death. And if they grew older and turned into the creepy, 'sisters on the hill' from some bizarre redneck horror movie, so be it.

I just need to be here for her. Make things feel as normal as I can.

She looked up at the wall behind the bed, gazing at droplets of rain running down the window. The sight made her want to stay right there in the cozy nest, spend the whole day comfortable. Not like she had to be at school. Harper closed her eyes and let her head loll to the left, against Madison's.

Her eyes snapped open. *Shit! Rain!*

Leigh had told them their first day in Evergreen that people had to stay inside when it rained, something about the rain collecting radioactive fallout from high up and bringing it down. Being so close to a window didn't seem like an awesome idea, but really... if 'glowing' rain fell on the house, moving a few feet inward wouldn't make much difference.

Madison woke up, stretched, and rolled flat on her back. "It's raining."

"Yeah. We have to stay inside, remember. No school."

"Okay."

"Heh. I figured you'd be totally upset."

"Totes." Madison swished her feet back and forth.

Harper rolled on her side, facing her sister. "It's not that bad, is it?"

"Too peopley." She stuck her iPhone out from under the thick layer of blankets and pressed the button, but nothing happened. "But I'll go back. I was just scared you'd get hurt."

"I know. I'm worried about you the same way. I can't let anything happen to you, and that includes running out of food or freezing to death."

"I gotta pee."

"Yeah. Me too."

Neither one of them moved, not wanting to leave the cozy warmth of bed to brave the frigid air in thin nightgowns.

Madison poked at the phone, gazing into the black screen. "Since we gotta boil water on a fire to take baths now, it's okay if you want to share a tub. But I don't want to share the bathroom to pee."

Harper laughed. "Go on. I can hold it a little more."

"It's cold. I don't wanna get out of bed."

"Umm. It's not actually as cold as it should be." Harper stuck her hand out from under the covers. "It's chilly, but not freezing."

"So, go check the bathroom. If you scream like a girl in a horror movie, I'll wait."

"Hah. The toilet's going to be freezing no matter what. It's winter in the mountains."

Madison traced her finger around the screen, hopefully *pretending* the phone worked and not hallucinating it. Harper eventually surrendered to urgency and slid out of bed. Once the shock of cold air passed, she padded out into the hall and went to the bathroom. Someone had left the door shut, which unfortunately caused the bathroom to retain the frigidity of outside.

A few highly uncomfortable minutes later, she hurried back to the bedroom. While Madison ran off to the bathroom, Harper changed from her nightgown into a T-shirt, sweater, and a set of sweat pants, plus socks, then made her way to the living room.

Jonathan had a nice fire going, which had already warmed the place up to cozy. Seeing him there in only his briefs made Harper shiver. Cliff sat at the table, cleaning the parts of his disassembled AR-15. Inspired, Harper ran back to get her shotgun. She sat across from him, carefully unloaded the weapon, and proceeded to clean it as best she could with the tools available.

Madison wandered into the room, still in her nightgown. She took the seat next to Harper and resumed staring at her phone.

"So, raining. We're all stuck inside today." Cliff held up a gun part to examine it in the light.

"What if the town gets attacked?" Harper picked up a brush and attacked the shotgun's chamber. "Or are they hoping bad guys are afraid of the rain, too?"

"Battles are miserable affairs to begin with. They suck three times as much in the rain. Trust me. The only reason soldiers fight in the rain is the goddamned generals." Cliff chuckled. "Generals who give orders from nice warm bunkers."

She laughed.

"A pack of idiots probably won't be motivated enough to do anything in bad weather. But I think they've got at least one person in the buses on lookout. I doubt the radiation risk from rain is going to persist for five years, but it *is* a risk."

"If the rain is radioactive, the house isn't going to protect us much more than being out in it." Harper puffed air at the chamber and moved on to the bolt.

"More than you think. Being inside is much better than having particles get on your skin, into your pores, in your eyes, and so on. Be better if we had a basement here. Still, some distance is better than literally bathing in rads."

"Hey Dad?" asked Jonathan.

Cliff looked up.

"What did kids do before video games? Like when you were my age."

"Hah. When I was your age, I had video games. Ever hear of Pong? Atari 2600?"

Jonathan shook his head. "What's that?"

"Old ass video games." He grinned.

"Is 'ass' a bad word?" asked Madison without looking away from her phone.

"Yeah. You're not allowed to say it." Cliff patted her on the head.

"Because I'm a girl?"

"Because you're ten. You can say ass when you're twelve. Everything else waits for sixteen, except the f-bomb. That's twenty-one, like beer."

Madison shrugged.

"So, what *did* kids do before they made video games?" Jonathan leaned back with his hands on the rug behind him, swishing his feet side to side.

"Aren't you cold?" asked Harper.

"No. I'm right in front of the fire."

Cliff rubbed his beard. "Went outside and ran around, went swimming, or did chores, or played with stuff like jacks, jumping rope, or stuff."

"We can't go outside," said Madison. "It's raining and cold."

"Board games?" Harper sighed at the bolt. The last time she'd cleaned the Mossberg, she hadn't used it on people. That thought had changed the way she looked at the gun. Revulsion and desperation dueled. She needed it to keep herself and her family safe, but it horrified her to think about what she'd done.

Self-defense. I had no choice. They were not people anymore.

"Board games are lame. That's why they're called *bored* games." Madison clicked the side button on the phone. "But I guess if it's all we have."

Once she finished putting the Mossberg back together, she reloaded it but didn't chamber a shell right away. It still felt like a bad idea having a loaded weapon out and about with two children in the room. Dad had been *way* cautious about that, but it had been a totally different world. Still, she stashed it in the bedroom against the wall by the headboard. The house had a deadbolt on the front door, so if someone bad did show up, she'd have time to go get it.

For breakfast, they munched on dry cereal and a few pieces of Halloween candy.

A search of the house didn't turn up anything remotely entertaining until she investigated the hatch up to the attic. She climbed into the freezing space only long enough to grab the first item of promise: a cardboard box of books. A brief glance around didn't reveal anything like board games or toys, so she hurried back down the folding steps into the warm house and shut the trap door.

Cliff settled in the recliner with a fat book that looked boring. Harper grabbed *The Secret Garden*. Madison and Jonathan flopped on the floor in front of the couch playing Uno. Amid the constant backdrop of rain, the soft flutter of pages or sounds of cards pervaded the silence.

It had been quite a while since Harper sat down and read a book. Honestly, if given the chance, she'd have preferred a video game, but some idiot in a government chair somewhere decided to ruin everything. She read a few pages before she found herself staring at the letters, a meaningless blur. Reading on a rainy day made her think of being fourteen, home sick from school and wrapped in blankets. Mom had checked in on her a couple times an hour, keeping her stocked with almond cookies and hot tea.

Harper pictured her mother's face peering at her over a mug of tea. They'd looked quite a bit alike with the same red hair and pale skin. In her imagination, Mom leaned over and kissed her on the head, checked her temperature, and left a cup of tea next to her. Rain pattered against the window just like it did that day. The smell of honeyed tea came out of nowhere.

A crippling spike of loss rammed itself into her heart. Harper went straight from blah to being too sad to cry. Tea led to other memories, Mom smiling for this or that, surprising her with little gifts or surprise trips out for coffee to unwind. She also remembered arguments: cell phone bills, laundry all over the floor, staying out too late, not wanting to drive Madison to dance class so Mom didn't have to do it. All of it felt so inconsequential in hindsight. At least they'd had a final two months together after the war, ironically, the closest the family had ever been with each other.

She closed her eyes and wished hard to hear her mother's voice even one more time, but only the patter of rain beating against the roof reached her ears.

Jonathan hopped up and ran down the hall.

Neither Cliff nor Madison noticed Harper's mood. It felt like she'd been doing nothing but crying for two weeks. How long did it take to 'deal with' watching her parents murdered right in front of her? How long did it take a person to cope with the destruction of society? Would anything ever feel normal again?

Madison pushed herself up to kneel and peered at Harper for a moment. Like a cat sensing its human in distress, she crawled up onto the couch and cuddled up beside her. Harper put an arm around her and closed her eyes. Madison squeezed her hand.

"The toilet's broken," called Jonathan from the hallway.

Cliff got up with a grunt and headed to the bathroom.

Madison raised her head, staring worriedly up at her.

"I miss Mom," whispered Harper. "Dad, too."

"Yeah. It's okay if you gotta go shoot more bad guys. Maybe you'll get the ones who killed them."

She brushed her hand over her sister's hair. "Mom got the guy who stabbed her."

"Oh. What about Dad?" Madison rested her head again on Harper's shoulder.

"Didn't really see the guy who shot him. He was outside."

Madison scowled. "I hope he gets a bullet right in the face."

"People like that usually wind up getting shot in the face eventually."

Cliff trudged by, went to the kitchen, and returned after a moment, falling into the recliner. "Welp. If anyone's gotta go, use a bucket for now."

"That bad?" Harper looked over at him. "Please tell me the water isn't gone."

"Not yet. I think the pipe feeding the toilet froze. Kitchen sink still works."

"If the pipe is frozen, why is it raining and not snowing?" asked Harper.

"Colder underground? Maybe it froze overnight?" Cliff shrugged. "Maybe a piece of ice somewhere else in the pipe moved and blocked it."

Madison clicked the button on the iPhone. "When are my friends gonna call?"

"Umm…" Harper cringed at the 'is she okay?' glance from Cliff. "As soon as it's possible for them to."

"Okay." Madison held the phone to her chest, smiled, and leaned against her once more.

THE WILD WEST

Harper walked west along Hilltop Drive, Jonathan on her left, Madison on her right.

By some miracle, the weather had stayed warm enough that the rain yesterday hadn't turned to snow. She figured it a good sign, since unseasonal warmth even if only by a few degrees hinted that nuclear winter might not happen. However, snow would eventually fall—sooner rather than later. All three of them only had sneakers. She remembered seeing winter boots in their Walmart haul, so she decided to head over to the quartermaster's after dropping the kids off at the school.

She hooked a right where Hilltop met the frontage road paralleling Route 74 and followed it for a little while before meandering across the dirt to the main highway. As they reached the area by the Militia HQ, three younger men appeared in the distance, sprinting past the dog boarding place. One spun and fired a handgun back toward the quartermaster's a few times. Return fire thundered from someone too far away to see.

A bullet zinged off the road with a spark, only a few feet from Jonathan.

He screamed.

Madison lifted her stare off her phone and looked around.

"Down!" Harper grabbed the kids and dragged them forward and left to the nearest abandoned vehicle, a white pickup.

More gunshots rang out along with shouting and cursing.

Harper huddled low to the ground clutching her siblings tight, painfully aware she'd left the shotgun back home in her bedroom. It hadn't even occurred to her to grab it merely to walk the kids to school. Madison squatted beside her, calm as anything. Jonathan, trembling, got stuck on repeat muttering, "Oh no" over and over again.

A sharp *click* and zing like a movie laser came from the road nearby. The ricochet startled another scream out of Jonathan. Madison sat on the road, calmly staring at her iPhone, even as another bullet hit the truck they all hid behind. Glass fragments fell on them from the shattered window overhead. Harper pulled her as close as possible and held on.

Someone ran by the other side of the truck. A dull *thump* accompanied a male voice barking *oof*, then a second after, a distant gunshot. She shivered at the thud of a dead guy landing on the road, her arms aching from how tight she clung to Madison and Jonathan. A distant woman shouted, "Clear on the right."

Cautious footsteps came around the end of the truck to the left. Harper lifted her head, peering past a curtain of red curls at Ryan Herman, the blond militia guy she might've thought cute if he hadn't been in his early thirties. It surprised her to see her hands didn't shake—all the trembling came from Jonathan.

"You okay?" asked Ryan.

"Yeah... I think." She checked the kids over and started breathing again once she didn't find any blood.

"Where's the cannon?"

She looked up at him. "Uhh. At home. Didn't think I'd need it taking these two to school."

Ryan stuffed his handgun in a belt holster and squatted next to her. "Except for that one dude who ran by, a shotgun wouldn't have helped much at long range... but you should always have it with you in town."

"Sorry." She looked down. "Guess I just woke up feeling too normal today."

He stood and offered her a hand. "It's cool."

"What are we gonna do when the bullets run out?" She grabbed his hand and let him pull her to her feet. "No one's making more."

Jonathan kept clinging to her side while Madison remained seated on the road, fixated on the phone as though it revealed the deepest secrets of the universe.

Ryan shrugged. "I dunno. Probably use swords or something. We got a bunch of compound bows from the Walmart run. Shouldn't be *too* hard to jury-rig some arrows when all the ones we took are broken. Second run got the rest of the clothes and some tools. Marcie's trying to talk them into another trip to grab bicycles and toys. Maybe crap like paper towels, razors, that sorta thing."

"Well, the bikes could be useful for us... militia, too."

"Hey, good idea. I'll suggest that." He grinned. "Ehh, go on, get 'em to school. Don't look back on the road there. Darnell got him in the head."

She cringed. "What happened anyway? Who are those guys?"

"Just a couple of morons wandering into town. They gave Liz a hard time, tried to raid our food stores. Bandits basically." Ryan shook his head. "Dunno why anyone would bother. We'd have given them food if they decided to live here."

"If people always did what made sense, there wouldn't have been a nuclear bombardment." Harper sighed.

"Yeah." Ryan patted her shoulder. "Okay, I gotta help clean this up."

Harper nodded at him, grabbed Madison's hand, and tugged until she stood. They walked onward along Route 74 for a minute or two before she couldn't keep quiet anymore.

"Maddie?"

"Yeah?" She didn't look up.

"If anything like that ever happens again, you need to make yourself as small as possible. Try to stay behind something solid, okay?"

"Okay."

"You're too calm. What's wrong?"

"Nothing."

Harper stopped, crouched, and forced eye contact. "Please, Maddie. Talk."

"Nothing's wrong." Madison shrugged. "I'm just not scared. I don't care if I get shot. Then I can be with Mom and Dad."

"No, Maddie... no..." Harper clamped on and hugged her. Only the adrenaline from a few-minutes-ago shootout kept her from breaking down in sobs. "What if that stuff isn't true and dead is dead? I need you to stay with me, okay? We're still family."

Madison fidgeted.

Harper put an arm around Jonathan and pulled him in, squeezing him and Madison together. "You, too, Jon. You're my brother now, okay. Both of you. I need you to stay."

Madison's calm fractured. Her lip quivered and a bit of red appeared at her eyes. "Okay. I'm sorry."

"You didn't do anything to be sorry for, Termite." Harper rested her forehead against her sister's shoulder and let out a long, relieved sigh. "Just don't be like that. I need you to want to stay safe."

"In case ghosts aren't real?" asked Madison in a shaky voice.

"Even if they are. You know how sad you are about Mom and Dad? That's how sad I'm gonna be if anything happened to you."

Madison nodded, finally hugged her back, and sniffled quietly. "Are those guys gonna get arrested for shooting guns in town?"

"Umm," said Harper. "I think those guys are a little past being arrested."

"There's no more cops." Jonathan covered his mouth in both hands, breathing hard, still obviously terrified.

"There kinda is." Madison pointed at Harper. "Militia."

He cringed. "But they don't arrest anyone."

Harper stood, took them by the hands again, and resumed walking toward school. "We do, but those guys started shooting first. The militia doesn't simply shoot everyone for everything. Enough people have already died."

Jonathan looked down. "Yeah. Too many. Thanks for chasing me."

"What?"

"If you didn't chase me, you wouldn't have found Cliff and we wouldn't be a family now. Is it wrong that I'm happy about that?"

"You can be happy about that and still miss your parents." She smiled at him. "Love isn't pie. There's enough for everyone."

"I miss pie," said Madison.

"Yeah, Termite. Me too."

FIRST DATE

Seeing Madison settle in at school without protest offered Harper hope that her sister might eventually heal and stop being this broken shell of her former self.

Mila stared eerily at her the whole few minutes she stood in the classroom to have a brief chat with Violet. The other kids either waved or ignored her, except Lorelei who ran over for a hug and yelled "Hi!"

Harper headed straight home to get the shotgun, checked in at the HQ, and swung by the quartermaster's place to see about winter boots. The building had become a scene of controlled chaos between two tractor-trailer loads of stuff and an attack. She spotted Liz Trujillo, the person in charge of resource distribution, standing by a huge pile of clothes with a clipboard. The woman had to be in her later thirties with high cheekbones, darkish brown skin, and long, straight black hair. She gave off an air of friendliness, but also authority… which might've come from her personality, or the giant silver revolver hanging from her belt.

"Hi." Harper walked up to her and tried not to smile when the woman turned out to be shorter than her. "Miss Trujillo?"

"Bah. Don't call me that. Makes me feel old. Liz is fine. You're the new girl, right?"

"Yeah. Are you on the militia, too?"

"Nope. I manage this place, make sure people who need stuff get stuff and we don't run out."

Harper gestured at the pistol. "But you've got a… is that a .44?"

"Yep." Liz smiled. "Big rats around here sometimes. And the militia doesn't collect *all* weapons, just major hardware."

"Oh. Yeah. Does that happen often?"

"First time. Usually, everything's inside, so this place doesn't look any different than an office building… but big pile of stuff out here at the moment."

Harper nodded. "Speaking of stuff… It's gonna snow soon. Got anything better than sneakers? I used to have boots, but we kinda got chased out of our old house."

"Aww. What happened?"

She gave Liz a brief version of the day her parents died. "We ran out the door with only what we had on."

"Well, you're gonna need boots with the militia. Kids can stay inside if it's too snowy, but no sense leaving stuff sitting here. Bring the little ones by later today or tomorrow and we'll see if anything fits. There's gotta be boots in this mess. Still working on sorting it."

"Okay. Thanks."

She shook hands and left Liz to her duties. For the remainder of the day, Harper walked around northern Evergreen, exploring and trying to memorize the lay of the land between Hilltop Drive and the middle school. The whole area west of Route 74 would become farm soon, though work on that project didn't exactly progress too fast in November.

Later in the afternoon, she spotted a handful of kids wandering along, among them Madison, Jonathan, and Lorelei. Most of the people not originally from Evergreen with children had been assigned to houses in the streets she'd been patrolling all day. Given the lack of cars, Anne-Marie had decided to keep them close to the school building to make life easier. Their house on Hilltop Drive made for a long walk. Only a handful of kids had to go that far.

Walter told her to go 'off shift' when the kids got out of school. It kinda irked her in a way that he expected her to watch the kids while Cliff stayed with the militia all day, but her sister needed not to be alone. It didn't seem right to leave ten-year-olds home without someone to watch them, especially with an active fireplace. More so with Lorelei along. Harper fell in step with them and walked home.

Lorelei wanted to come over and play and Tyler hadn't been at the school to pick her up, so Madison invited her over. Harper worried about him on the way back to the house. He'd seemed preoccupied with leaving

Evergreen. Being bothered by that idea caught her off guard, and not entirely because it meant he'd be abandoning Lorelei. *That* made her angry with him, but she found herself feeling sad at not seeing him again.

This, of course, pinked her cheeks with blush and got her scolding herself for being foolish the rest of the way to the house. Once home, Jonathan went straight to the fireplace. Everyone kept their coats on for the better part of the next hour until the house warmed up. The kids had eaten lunch at the school, though Harper hadn't. She nibbled on stale pretzels while pretending to be a mother. Fortunately, the kids didn't go too wild and spent the afternoon either doing dance routines, playing Uno, or running around the yard.

A knock came from the door about an hour after the fire warmed the house enough that they no longer needed their coats on inside.

Harper got up from the couch and hurried to the window, peering out at Tyler. He stood with his hands stuffed in his pockets, half turned away from the house like he almost regretted knocking and contemplated running.

She pulled the door open. "Hi."

"Hey." He looked up at her, but shied away, taking a step back. "I should probably go. Just wanted to check up on Lori."

"She followed Maddie and Jon. You didn't pick her up at school. She's a bit small to be on her own."

He scratched at his hair. "Sorry. I got lost. Went out for a walk and couldn't figure out which way to go to get back to town."

"Oh."

"I'm not still lost."

She folded her arms. "Obviously. You're here." Something about him triggered her need to take care of people. "C'mon in before you freeze. It's a little warmer in here."

Tyler hesitated.

"Heat's escaping. Come on."

He stepped inside. "Where are the kids?"

She shut the door. "Backyard."

They sat together on the couch.

"Guessing your dad doesn't like me that much."

"Probably thinks he has to protect me from all the boys or something."

Tyler chuckled.

"I mean, not like there's tons of boys here."

"Yeah."

They sat in awkward silence except for the joyful shouts and squeals of the kids outside.

Harper thought about her handful of past boyfriends. None had progressed much beyond making out. Most lasted only a few weeks since they hadn't been into *her* as much as fascinated by 'the redhead.' Of the two she stayed with for a couple months, one she broke up with after a fight because he wanted to go all the way and she didn't. The other skipped arguing over her desire to wait and got what he wanted from another girl on the sly. Not that Harper had any old fashioned need to 'save herself for marriage' or anything like that. She just wanted it to 'feel right' before taking things that far. For most of her high school days, she'd fantasized about an idealistic romantic moment when she finally agreed to give up her virginity to the storybook-perfect boyfriend in a storybook-perfect moment.

She fidgeted at her jeans. That fairy tale moment would never come, at least not without a dusting of nuclear ashes. Someone changed the genre of her life story from cute romance movie to wasteland survival. At least they left out the zombies. She still felt no great urgency to hook up with a boy, especially considering an unexpected pregnancy had far worse potential complications now than simply screwing up college or causing her to become socially ostracized. She doubted anyone in Evergreen would look down their noses at a pregnant seventeen-year-old. In fact, reproduction had become super important. No, the problem lay in knowing they'd metaphorically gone back in time. Pregnancy could kill her.

However, she couldn't help but feel something about Tyler. Exactly what, however, eluded her. Worry for him, worry that he might not be equipped to handle Lorelei, pity for the boy who didn't get along with his parents, a bit of attraction to his disheveled, shy demeanor, and the way his broken smile stirred a sensation deep in her stomach all mashed together into a giant ball of confusion.

Perhaps Cliff's reaction to him had come from noticing *her* reaction to him. Had she been giving off signs of interest without even knowing? *Gah. I don't even know him. It's not like me to go after the first boy I see in a new town.* She smirked to herself. *It's not like me to shoot people either. How messed up is it that I'm more afraid of speaking in public than shooting a bad guy now? Crap. I'm as broken as Maddie.*

"So, umm… what happened with your parents that you guys don't get along?"

Tyler shrugged. "We, uhh, didn't get along. I got tired of hearing how much of a failure I was going to be, so I left."

"Oh. I'm sorry. A friend of mine had demanding parents like that, too. They used to scream at her if she got Bs. To hear them go off on her, you'd think she got caught doing cocaine and cutting school."

"That sucks."

They talked for a while about life before the war. She spoke of missing her friends and how she still hadn't really come to terms with losing her parents. Hearing him be so blasé about his parents possibly being dead bothered her, but she likened it to how she felt about Mr. Cartwright, the mean-spirited chemistry teacher she'd had sophomore year. No one at her old school liked him, especially girls who he always graded more harshly. Rumor said he didn't believe women belonged in science, so he tried to make the experience so awful they wouldn't pursue it. If that man died during the bombing, she wouldn't really care.

Tyler told her of how he'd lived with a couple guys his age in an apartment after he'd stormed out of his childhood home. For a little over a year, he shared a place with two potheads, a yoga instructor, and this guy Carl, a computer geek who totally didn't fit in with the others. Still, the nerd had the best job and probably could've made rent on his own, so he wound up being the 'adult in the room.' Tyler had no idea what happened to any of them. He'd been at work when the blast happened. By the time he got back to his apartment, they'd all left.

"Stayed there for a while in the basement, raiding other apartments for food. Finally decided to go check out the world. Grabbed most of my stuff and headed out. Couple days later, I heard what I thought was a cat stuck in a sewer. Turned out to be Lori talking in her sleep."

"That was so sweet of you to help her." Harper leaned against him.

"What else could I do? She looked so pathetic. She'd been alone ever since the blast. Couldn't just leave her there to die, yanno?"

"Yeah." She stared into his eyes, wondering if her presence put him on edge and made him sit in such a rigid posture.

He swallowed. "So, umm… you're happy here?"

"I guess. I'd rather the war didn't happen, but since it did…" She caught herself leaning closer to him, not understanding why.

Tyler sat as still as a deer paralyzed by the headlights of an approaching big rig, staring at her as their lips drew closer. Seconds after their lips made contact, the doorknob rattled. Harper jumped back, certain her cheeks had become as red as her hair.

Cliff walked in, not looking at either of them on his way to the kitchen. "Hey. Got more venison."

"Cool." Harper squeezed Tyler's hand and whispered, "Relax. Please don't go. It's fine."

He nodded.

She got up and hurried after Cliff. "Need help?"

"Harper..." He set a bundle of meat on the counter next to a giant can and turned to face her. "It's not my place to tell you who you can or can't get involved with. I just want you to be careful, okay? I realize there aren't really any other kids here your age, but don't think you've gotta do anything with him because he's here."

"I don't." Harper glanced away, certain he'd rattled the knob on purpose to give her warning. "And thank you for being protective. It's sweet."

He smiled for a few seconds, then shot a serious look at the living room.

"You don't like him," whispered Harper.

"Ehh. Might just be too much time as a mall guard. He's the kinda kid I'd have kept my eye on. Something about him I can't put my finger on. Just be careful and don't get hurt, okay?"

Harper nodded. "Okay."

The giant can looked like something from a school cafeteria, big enough for a severed head to fit inside. Peas. This hunk of venison almost doubled the size of the other one he'd brought, so it would be plenty to feed everyone. Tyler excused himself and left with a 'be back in a bit.' Perhaps twenty minutes later, he returned with a loaf of sliced bread, some kind of heavy grain-and-nut health food creation they'd brought back from Walmart because it hadn't looked bad even after sitting for two months.

It did have a little mold, though Cliff sliced the fuzzy parts off and declared the rest safe. Harper practically gagged at the idea of eating bread that had been moldy, even in a small spot. Mom would've fainted in disgust. Still, the desire not to starve proved more powerful than a non-broken society's definition of edible.

The kids came inside while the food cooked and occupied themselves with Uno. Cliff tended the pots while Harper ran around the house tidying up and cleaning as best she could with the supplies on hand.

Over dinner, Cliff mentioned he'd arrived home a bit later than normal due to having to deal with a deceased guy found in one of the houses to the southeast. He kept the details kid safe, but it sounded like natural causes. They'd found old insulin injectors in the kitchen trash, so as best anyone could figure, the man had been diabetic and ran out of medical supplies.

The story seemed to rattle Tyler. He fell silent, head down, refusing to look at anyone. Harper prodded him with a few inquiring glances, but he didn't make eye contact. He fidgeted and kept looking at the front door. Given his unkempt longish hair and frumpy clothes, she thought of him a bit like Jack Dawson having dinner with the high society crowd where he totally didn't belong. Only, Tyler didn't fake it anywhere near as well.

Madison again cried the whole time she ate, but finished her portion of venison. Dad had teased her when the whole vegetarian thing started a few years ago. Madison stumbled across a video of someone keeping a chicken as a pet, and it appeared to show affection for its owner the way any cat or dog might. Ever since, her little sister couldn't bear the thought of eating animals. Dad thought it silly at first and teased her about hugging trees and such. Despite him not being mean about it, a few too many jokes eventually set off an explosion of tears. Ever since, he'd let the little vegetarian have her meatless existence in peace.

After dinner, Harper sat with Tyler on the sofa, Cliff in the recliner off to their right. He'd moved the chair from the other side so it didn't put his back to the door. They talked about high school and the sorts of crappy jobs teenagers worked as though everything remained normal. He seemed to relax, and no longer looked ready to run screaming out the door the second no one watched him.

With Cliff right there, Harper couldn't bring herself to even think about kissing him, or even going for his hand. That she wanted to confused her.

Eventually, it started to get dark. Between the danger of candles and lack of electricity, 'bedtime' coincided with the end of daylight. Not being able to see a darn thing tended to get in the way of doing stuff, so the kids didn't protest going to sleep way earlier than they would have normally. Of course, they also woke up at sunrise, so it balanced out.

All three kids scrambled into the living room and stood in a cluster, eyeing Cliff and Harper.

"Can Lorelei sleep over?" asked Madison.

"Pleeeeease?" chirped the six-year-old.

"Sure," said Tyler without any hesitation.

Cliff shot him a look, then made a 'what do you think' expression at Harper.

She scrunched her eyebrows. *Why are you asking me? Am I big sis or Mom?* "Umm. Okay."

Harper set up a sleeping bag on top of a sleeping bag (for extra padding) in her and Madison's room. She left the kids to get ready for bed and headed back to the living room. Cliff sat alone in the recliner, reading by candlelight.

Did he leave? She looked at the front windows, the kitchen, and back down the hall—the open bathroom door said he hadn't gone in there.

"Where's Tyler?"

Cliff pointed at the kitchen. "Went out the back door."

"Excuse me?" asked a tiny voice.

She turned to find a rather naked Lorelei standing there holding one of Harper's T-shirts. Madison and Jonathan peered around the doorjamb of the girls' bedroom, snickering.

"Is it okay if I wear this to sleep?" asked Lorelei.

Harper laughed. "Yeah. It's fine."

"Thank you!" Lorelei pulled the shirt on and ran back to the bedroom.

"That one's going to be a handful." Cliff chuckled. "Fearless and full of energy."

"So happy, too," whispered Harper. "Even after everything she's been through."

"Kids are resilient." Cliff turned a page and glanced over at her with a 'that goes for you, too' wink.

"Some more than others." The relatively happy sounding chatter coming from the bedroom eased her worry about Madison. She crossed the kitchen to the back door and pulled the curtain away from the window.

Tyler stood a short distance into the yard, staring up at the sky. She ran to the dining room to grab her coat from the back of a chair, then slipped outside. The blast of chill shocked her; she hadn't realized how warm a simple fireplace could make a house.

At the creak of the door, he glanced back, his expression a weird mix of worry and smile. "Hey."

She walked over to stand beside him. "Hey."

"*Groundhog Day.* Didn't we do the 'hey' thing already?"

"Yeah."

"So this is the world." He again peered up at the stars.

"Such as it is."

"Doesn't feel too different, does it?" He looked over at her. "I mean, except for not having electricity."

Harper shrugged. "It's not that easy to let go of my parents and friends."

"Oh. Yeah. Sorry. Sometimes I forget that most people don't hate their parents."

"My dad used to say it's messed up that people need a license to drive but anyone can have kids."

"You can't legislate life like that." Tyler quirked an eyebrow.

"No. He wasn't serious. Just saying like so many people who shouldn't be parents have kids. Something that important, being a parent, and anyone can do it. It's like someone's whole life in your hands. Messing up as a parent could totally change who they grow up to be. Lot of responsibility."

"Yeah." He looked down. "Lorelei likes you."

She took his hand. "She likes you, too."

Tyler shrugged. "She pretty much likes everyone who isn't mean to her. Hey, you know things are kinda crazy and random now. If... anything ever happened, will you take care of her?"

"Nothing's going to happen to you." She squeezed his hand, surprised by her sudden sense of possessiveness toward him. "You're not going anywhere, okay?" *Crap. I don't even know this guy. Why am I feeling like this?*

"Just trying to be realistic. Anything could happen to anyone now. Look at that guy your father had to deal with today. Ran out of insulin and gone. Heard gunshots earlier, too. Stray bullets don't care who they hit."

"Yeah." She looked down and explained about the attempted robbery of the quartermaster. "You're right. We could die at any moment."

"I didn't mean that in a romantic way."

She leaned over and kissed him. "I know."

Tyler stiffly grasped her shoulder and kissed her like he'd never done so before in his life. She grinned, finding it cute. Any of them could be killed five minutes from now. Why keep waiting for the storybook-perfect moment that might never come. Uncharacteristic spontaneity pushed her into a tighter embrace, kissing him deeper, and not much caring if she wound up back at Tyler's house for more.

"What are you doing?" rasped Tyler.

"Kissing you." She crossed her wrists behind his neck and went in for more.

He got into it for a little while, no longer seeming like he'd never touched a girl before. After a few minutes, he abruptly pulled back. "Wait. This wouldn't be right."

"Why? What's wrong?"

"It's not you." Tyler looked off to the side. "You're way too beautiful for me and so nice. You probably already have a boyfriend."

"Yeah." She squeezed his hand. "Micah hasn't called me in a while."

Tyler laughed.

"He could be dead. I don't know. We could be dead tomorrow."

"We could." He brushed a hand over her cheek, a spark of something in his eyes. "I never thought a girl like you would even look at me."

"A 'girl like me?'"

"You had to have been a cheerleader. Popular. Probably rich."

"Zero for three." She poked him in the side. "I mean, we weren't poor but no one could accuse us of being rich. Never did the cheerleader thing. I'm way too shy. And, I'm for sure not—wasn't—with the popular crowd."

"What crowd were you in?"

"None really. Somewhere between the hippies, the introverts who sit under trees all day reading, and the nerds. But none of them. Didn't read much. I'm a gamer. And my grades were too good to be one of the popular girls."

"Band geek?"

She puffed, blowing hair off her face. "Introvert, remember? No way could I handle being in front of an audience."

"Nathan, one of my pothead roommates, thinks cops are all bullies who never grew out of wanting to feel better than everyone else. How's a shy girl wind up on the militia?"

Harper leaned against him, hugging his arm. "I'm still trying to figure that out. Mostly, I didn't want to let them take Dad's shotgun away. I don't trust anyone else to protect Maddie. Now I've got Jonathan to watch out for, too."

"They would've taken the gun?"

"Yeah. I think they let people keep handguns. Ugh. It's *so* messed up." She buried her face against his shoulder. "I can't believe the stuff I've done. Shooting people, sleeping in alleys." Harper looked up at him. "Kissing a boy I barely know."

He managed a weak smile.

She stretched up and kissed him again, craving that sense of being with someone she could talk to. Someone at her level, not a parent, not a child. Maybe they wouldn't wind up having sex at all. She still couldn't explain why she felt drawn to him, but being the only two teens in an entire town—or what remained of it—had to be a large part of it.

Tyler backed off again. "No... it isn't right."

"Nothing's right anymore." Frustrated, she let go of his arm and took a step, raking her hands through her hair. "The whole world is gone. We're going to run out of canned food eventually. What if the farm doesn't work? No one's making any medicine anymore. We all might've sucked up enough radiation to kill us already. No one even knows how bad a dose we got."

Tyler stepped closer and brushed a hand through her hair. "You're not losing any. If you got a bad dose, it would already be falling out."

His touch sent an electric tingle down her back. She blushed and bit her lip. The conflict in his eyes frustrated her. He simultaneously seemed to want to be with her as much as he wanted to run off alone into the ruins.

"I dunno if I'm going to stay on the militia. Especially if I run out of shells. I can't fight at all." She held her arms out to the sides. "Look at me. I'm scrawny. Once we run out of bullets, I can't be on the militia. And what the hell is wrong with me? Why am I worrying about *bullets*? I shouldn't care about having 'enough ammo.' I'm seventeen!"

"You're not scrawny."

"No? What would you call me then?"

"Kinda hard to see with that fluffy coat on, but you're, I dunno. Normal."

"Normal." She folded her arms.

"Yeah. Normal. Okay, a bit on the thin side, but you probably do yoga and eat lots of granola."

She laughed. "One for two."

"Went to yoga with your mother, right?"

"Ugh." Harper rolled her eyes. "Am I that much of a cliché?"

"Nah. Well. Did you go to Starbucks after yoga?"

"Butt." She stuck her tongue out at him.

He laughed. "Don't worry too much. You've got it pretty good here. Not like the world went total Mad Max."

"You didn't see Lakewood." She folded her arms.

"No, I wasn't there."

She leaned against him again, shivering at the chilly air. "It was bad." A bit over a whisper, she explained the blue gang, meeting Cliff in the mall, having that guy try to grab Madison straight out of the street, and finding Summer running for her life with no pants and her hands tied behind her back.

"Wow." Tyler blinked. "That's messed up. I think most people are decent... except for the ones who aren't."

An unexpected chuckle slipped out from under her gloom. She moved in close again. "It's cold out here."

"Yeah, well. That kinda happens in winter."

She blinked. *Is he really that oblivious?*

"Your dad's gonna shoot me any second."

"No..." She let her head fall against his shoulder. "He's being protective. And I love that he's willing to look out for me, become my second dad. Heh, you know the first time he saw me, he put a gun to my head?"

"Really?" Tyler blinked.

"Yeah. Well. Okay, it wasn't the first time. He busted me for shoplifting when I was fourteen. But I mean since the world blew up. Maddie and I went into the mall to look for some clothes, and I saw Jonathan. He ran away from me, so I chased him around a corner thinking he might be alone—and Cliff was there." She made a finger gun and poked him in the forehead.

"That's wild."

"Yeah. Wild. I nearly pissed myself." Harper leaned back and gazed up into the stars. "My real dad died 'cause I couldn't kill someone."

"I'm sorry you lost your parents. I didn't like mine at all. They tried to kill me a couple times. Poison. I ran away at seventeen."

Harper gasped. "Holy shit! I'm so sorry." She reached for his hand, but he backed up.

"Sorry. I... gotta go." He took another step back, hesitation and conflict clear on his face. "You're a really awesome person, Harper. I just... Sorry."

She stood there staring into the dark as the rapid scuffing of his shoes on the dirt grew distant. Momentarily embarrassed at being so forward, she blushed, but Tyler had a point... either one of them *could* die any day. That had been technically true before the war. People could get hit by cars, or suffer accidents, unforeseen health problems... whatever. But everything had changed. Any day now, some random person could try to rob Liz again and start shooting.

He kinda seemed to like her, but having a boy act like he couldn't wait to get away was new. Maybe she scared him by kissing him so fast. And true, that had felt a bit weird. Tyler didn't give off closeted vibes, so she didn't think he lacked any interest in girls. Though, something like that could be a reason why parents would try to poison him.

"What's his deal, anyway?" Harper bit her lip. *Duh. His parents tried to kill him. He's probably got issues.*

29

TOO QUIET

Harper roamed the streets the next day after dropping the kids off at school.

Her thoughts orbited Tyler, trying to make sense of the conflicting signals he'd given off. One minute, he'd been totally into kissing her. The next, afraid of her. She analyzed everything she did or said yesterday in an attempt to figure out where she screwed up. It stood out in her mind that he'd had such a strong reaction to Cliff telling them about the man who died after running out of insulin. Could Tyler be a diabetic, too?

She gasped. *Of course! That's it!*

"He asked me to take Lorelei if anything happened to him. Oh, shit. Maybe he's on insulin, too and he knows he's gonna die soon."

Harper stopped in the street, shivering from emotion. No wonder he acted that way. He didn't want her getting close to him only to drop dead and break her heart. She started crying at the tragic, romantic, noble idea of it... but collected herself after only a minute or so.

"I'm getting all wound up over guessing. Should I ask him or—"

A loud *crash* came from a few houses ahead on the left along with a woman's angry scream. The bellowing shouts of a man followed, then a series of loud slams and the same woman shrieking in fear. Harper swung the shotgun off her shoulder into a two-handed grip and ran toward the commotion, coming to a stop about six paces from the door.

Am I supposed to like kick it in or shout at them to knock it off?

The man roared something about stupid and lazy. His wife or whatever started to shout over him, but her voice stopped along with a meaty *smack*, and a thud.

Harper pulled her air horn can out, raised it high, and sounded one long blast.

A woman's crying apology filled in the silence in the wake of the horn.

Grr. Harper widened her stance, aimed at the door, and shouted "Hey! Get away from her."

"Mind your business, bitch," shouted a man.

A series of quick air horn pips came from the distance, mostly to the south.

"Militia!" shouted Harper. "Get the hell away from her, now!"

Two footsteps thudded inside the house, then a quick shriek, and a heavy slam.

"Where do you think you're going? I didn't tell you to go anywhere," yelled the man.

The woman screamed.

Harper rushed forward. Certain the door would laugh at her if she tried to ram it down, she grabbed the knob first and pulled. Amazingly, it opened easily. She ran inside toward the commotion of a brawl knocking furniture and cans around in the kitchen. A dark-haired woman in her thirties wearing only an oversized T-shirt crawled back and forth under the table trying to avoid a man about the same age dressed in flannel and jeans. Neither wore shoes. Cans littered the floor and counter from where they spilled.

"Hey!" shouted Harper.

Both people turned to stare at her. The woman had a giant bruise on her face. A crescent-shaped cut along her forehead looked an awful lot like the aftereffect of a hurled soup can. Blood streamed from her nose.

"Don't shoot him," whispered the woman. "Please."

"Screw off, kid," snarled the man. "Your daddy know you have his gun?"

She shivered with rage. "Does yours know your dick is so small you have to hit your wife?"

He glared at her. "Why, you little…"

"Out the back door." Harper gestured at it with the shotgun. "Make a move toward her or take one step toward me, this is gonna be over real fast."

"Don't shoot Tommy, please." The woman crawled toward Harper. "We've got a son."

"Does he hit your boy, too?"

The guy leaned at her. "Oh, a mouthy thing." He took a step toward her.

Harper pointed the Mossberg at his face and narrowed her eyes, fully intending to fire if he moved even another inch closer. "Don't."

His anger shifted gears from raging to simmering. Perhaps he saw something in her stare, a certain glint that said she'd already killed and wouldn't hesitate. He leaned away, raising his hands. The woman kept crawling toward her, likely to grab her around the middle any second. Though she felt sorry for her, if that woman knocked her off balance, that guy would be on her in a hot second—and probably beat her to death.

Harper sidestepped left. "Ma'am, please stay back. If you grab me, I can't trust what Tommy's going to do."

She continued crawling after her.

"That means if you grab me, I have to shoot him."

The woman stopped. "No. Please don't kill him. My Tommy."

"Is an asshole."

A tentative air horn bleep went off somewhere nearby.

"In here!" shouted Harper. She waited a few seconds, then gingerly released her left hand from the front end of the shotgun, keeping it trained on Tommy one-armed.

He stared at the tip of the barrel, only a few feet away from his nose. She asked him not to move with her eyes while reaching into her pocket for her air horn. Fortunately, both he and the woman remained still as she pulled it out and sounded a long, painfully loud 911 bleep.

"Jesus..." Tommy cringed back, hands clamped over his ears.

The woman cringed back, also covering her ears.

Annapurna tromped through the house to the kitchen, her AR-15 not quite pointed at anyone. Ken and Marcie followed soon after.

"You sounded an alert?" asked Annapurna.

"Yeah." Harper pointed at the woman kneeling on the floor. "Heard them screaming. Think he mashed her in the face with a can." She explained what she heard and saw, and that Tommy nearly came after her.

Ken holstered his handgun and walked up on Tommy. "Again? Really, Tom? You know you can't keep doing this shit. And I wouldn't test Harper. She might look sweet and innocent, but your head wouldn't be the first one she filled with buckshot."

"Oh, she *is* sweet. Just not so innocent now." Marcie sighed. "None of us are."

"It's my fault," said the woman. "I miscounted. I thought we had more than we did. We ran out of corn. Tommy loves corn, you know. I told him we had some, but we don't."

"Rachel..." Marcie holstered her Beretta and helped the woman up. "Come on. We need to talk. And I need to get you over to see Doc Hale."

Rachel looked down at her bare feet. "I'm not dressed to go outside."

"Well go get dressed. C'mon." Marcie walked her out of the kitchen and down the hall.

Harper lowered the shotgun, finally breathing again. She stood there like a fifth wheel while Ken and Annapurna grilled Tommy about hitting his wife, evidently for the fifth time that month.

"One more time like this, and Ned's gonna kick you out of town," said Ken.

"Let him. My wife and kid will go where I go." Tommy folded his arms. "Ain't none of Ned's business what happens under my roof."

"Actually, it is." Annapurna shot him a glare. "We're not savages here in Evergreen. You want that, you're free to wander off into wherever."

He glared at them.

Rachel, dressed in jeans, sneakers, and a winter coat, emerged from the back and went with Marcie out the front door, refusing to look toward Tommy. Ken and Annapurna held an uncomfortably silent staring match with him for about five minutes before Ken nodded toward the hallway out and started walking.

Harper followed, keeping a cautious eye on Tommy. Annapurna brought up the rear. No one said a word until the three of them collected on the street outside the house.

"So, what happens now?" asked Harper.

"We're going to have Rachel stay either at HQ or the medical center for a little while. The boy, too. Keep them both away from Tommy." Ken shook his head. "This guy might be a threat to them out of spite."

"What about me?" Harper eyed the house. "He's gonna come after me now, too, isn't he?"

Annapurna sighed. "It is possible, but unlikely. I think he understands you wouldn't hesitate."

A lifeless chuckle slipped out of Harper's mouth. *Ironic.* "I hate that it feels like the best answer to problems anymore is to shoot someone." She sighed. "Well, not the best. I mean the easiest."

The other two both nodded.

"You handled that well." Annapurna patted her shoulder.

"I watched a lot of cop shows." Harper smirked. "I thought that crazy battered wife attacking the police who are trying to help her thing was made up for TV. What's wrong with people?"

"We could debate the answer to that question for years." Ken smiled. "Keep your eyes open, but again, nice job."

"Thanks."

Harper stood there for a little while after the other two walked off. No sound came from Tommy's house, though she couldn't help but feel eyes on her. More than the idea of speaking in front of people, having someone who might really want to hurt her personally brought a new level of discomfort she didn't at all like.

She resumed walking, no longer sure if she merely tried to memorize the area or had become a 'real' part of the militia and patrolled now. The suburbs south of the school hung in peaceful silence, the crunch of her sneakers on pavement as loud as a herd of horses. Every so often, someone near a window waved at her. A couple guys and a woman or three came out of their houses to chat, having seen her several times over the past few days. She explained she was new in town and had joined the militia. A few thought her too young, but liked to see they had finally sent someone to patrol this area. One twenty-something guy who still managed to find cologne tried to ask her out, and an older woman radiated a vibe like she would've given her an apple pie to take home if she'd had one to spare.

For a while, it felt as though she wandered an ordinary neighborhood that hadn't been ninety some odd miles away from a nuclear strike. Although, an as-the-crow-flies line up from Colorado Springs mostly went through mountains, so this place had to have been shielded from the worst of it. Airborne fallout notwithstanding.

After an hour or so, the silence became oppressive. It occurred to her that she couldn't hear anything at all other than whatever noise she made. No cars, no music playing anywhere, no horns, distant airplanes, no central air units whirring or daytime television leaking out a window. The bizarre silence unsettled her, a stark reminder that the world she'd known for seventeen years had been forever changed.

And stopping to pee outside behind some trees also bothered her. Mostly because it didn't feel like she did something socially inappropriate anymore.

She couldn't pry her thoughts away from the glare Tommy had given her. Having Ken and Annapurna tell her she did a great job didn't assuage her fears. If that guy grabbed her from behind, she'd be in trouble. If he could beat the hell out of his wife—who he theoretically loved—what could he do to someone he didn't even like?

The shotgun became a leaden weight in her hands that made her feel like an impostor. Who was she to pretend to be a soldier? *What the hell am I doing? I'm still a kid.* She bit her lip, wondering where she would wind up if she quit the militia. Honestly, she had no business fighting. The only thing that stood between her and being a defenseless, ordinary girl started with Moss and ended with Berg. After the Walmart raid, she had eighty-six shells at home, twenty in her pocket, nine in the gun. Once those ran out, she'd be carrying a glorified club. Industry had collapsed. No one would be manufacturing bullets anymore.

If I quit, I could help Violet out at the school. I'd rather wrangle kids than shoot people. That poor woman's stuck trying to watch fifty-four of them. I could handle teaching the small ones.

Giving up felt like, well, giving up. If only she'd had the same determination she showed when staring down Tommy when the thug kicked in her door back home. While it might give her the illusion of safety, quitting brought on a wave of guilt the same as when she'd caused Dad's death.

Harper roamed the streets, thinking about what to do with herself as well as trying to figure out how she felt about Tyler. Well, she knew how she felt about Tyler even if it made no sense for her to be into him. Not two days ago, she decided she had no interest in anything romantic, too worried about Madison, too messed up about her parents, too freaked out about everything she knew being taken away from her. But for reasons she couldn't explain, all of a sudden a strong sense of attraction toward him came out of nowhere. Perhaps he looked like a lost puppy in need of someone to take care of them. They had that in common at least.

His notion of going out and exploring places normal people couldn't go before the breakdown of society did have a romantic sort of notion to it. Getting to see rich people's houses, climbing on their boats, going in all the 'employee only' doors she could find just to see what lurked back there—breaking secrets. In a way, she understood the temptation.

But, no way would she actually do any of that. The exploring part didn't bother her—the men with blue sashes (or worse) did. The week and change she and Madison had been on their own had been a nightmare of fear, worry, and hypervigilance. She hadn't realized how tightly wound she'd become until arriving in Evergreen.

Harper adored that sense of security, enough to where she'd carry a gun to protect it.

Of course, she'd much prefer not having to keep looking over her shoulder for Tommy.

A few hours later, an explosion of children's gleeful shouts rang out. She whirled about and fast walked toward the school. Madison and Jonathan emerged from a curve at the end of the street ahead after a few minutes, so she stopped to wait.

Upon seeing her, Madison broke into a sprint, shouting "Harp! Harp! Harp!"

Her sister's happy tone kept her from panicking.

Madison crashed into her with a pounce hug. "Harp!"

"What?" she asked, chuckling.

"Becca's here! She's alive!" Madison bounced, tears of joy streaming down her cheeks.

Harper pictured a blonde a year younger than Madison, but couldn't remember much more than what she looked like. "Is she the princess or the smart one?"

"Becca's the smart one. Eva's the princess."

"That's awesome!" Harper picked Madison up and spun her around a few times before setting her down.

"Yeah!" She beamed. "I'm not even jealous that her parents aren't dead."

The breath caught in Harper's throat. She stood there, teetering at the verge of tears while her sister bounced in glee. Jonathan, though much more reserved, also appeared quite happy. Memories of Mom and Dad started a slideshow in her head that threatened to throw her into sobs. Somehow, Harper held it in, but she couldn't move or speak under the weight of grief.

"Can we go home?" asked Madison. "Harp? You okay?"

She took a deep breath and rasped, "Yeah. Fine."

Madison waited a few paces away, grinning.

"We need to stop by and see Liz. Going to get some food and see if they've got any boots for us."

"Ooh, shopping!" cheered Madison.

Harper blinked at her sister, struggling to process the giddiness radiating from this girl who had been so broken for months. She decided not to question it and forced a smile. "Yeah. Shopping. I heard the truck go out again. They might even have toys."

"Yay!" Madison clapped. "Uno's getting kinda boring. I'd like at least one other thing to play."

Jonathan thrust his fists in the air. "Cool!"

"Don't get too excited. I'm just guessing. C'mon."

Harper headed off down the street, with Jonathan... and someone doing an awfully good impersonation of pre-war Madison behind her.

30

FAMILY

Children's shouts and cheers came from the backyard, along with the occasional thump of a foot hitting a ball or a louder *thud* of the ball striking the house.

Harper sat on the couch working on her book, *The Secret Garden*, a page or two at a time before worries about Tommy broke her focus. The essence of cheap beef gurgled in the back of her throat despite having eaten dinner over an hour ago. Carrie from next door had joined them for dinner since she had a huge five-gallon commercial can of beef stew she couldn't possibly eat all herself before it went bad. Conversation over their meal had mostly been about how people in ancient times living in villages would often share meals. Cliff suggested things might start becoming more and more primitive as consumables left over from society got used up. Conservation of firewood made a strong case for town meals.

He summed their future up as "Medieval times, but with plastic."

The soccer ball thudded off the wall again. In the back of Harper's mind, her mother shouted at the kids, worried they'd break a window. She couldn't bring herself to yell at them, even though if they broke a window, there'd be no way to replace it. Her scrambled brain burned far too much time trying to figure out what people did 'way back when' to make windows. Obviously, houses in antiquity had glass windows… certainly not double pane folding ones, but they somehow made glass.

There had to be some people left who knew how, or would humanity wind up becoming fully tribal until people re-invented all the stuff she used to take for granted.

"Heard about the situation," said Cliff.

Harper jumped at the sudden end to silence. "Oh. You mean that asshole? There's been nuclear war and he's still hitting his wife?"

"Probably worse for it. Guys like that hate feeling powerless."

"Think he's going to come after me?"

Cliff turned a page in his book. "Not if he knows what's good for him, he won't. Word is you handled the situation well. Kinda surprised you ran in there and did that."

"What else would I have done? Run to get help like a kid?"

He smiled. "Or a trainee."

"Trainee implies training. This is like the first day I worked retail. Manager just had me walk around learning where everything was."

"Yeah, well… it's much harder to defend land you aren't familiar with. Back when people got into fights with Native Americans, or hell, even in Vietnam. Foreign soldiers had a hell of a time dealing with locals who knew the land well despite vast differences in weapons and technology."

"Wow. Feels like I'm in school." She raked her hair off her face and smiled at him.

Cliff made a silly face at her and resumed reading.

A kid outside emitted a happy squeal. Harper leaned back and stared up at the ceiling, wondering how the heck she managed to survive. So many what-ifs circled her head that she had to push them aside or go nuts.

"Hey… Thanks for being there. In the mall. I don't know where I'd be if we didn't run into you."

"Ehh, you're tough. You'd have found your way here. I should be giving you the back pat for mentioning Evergreen, or I'd still be in that damn mall with Jonathan trading bullets with those idiots."

"Cliff?"

He looked up from the book.

"Do you think it's a bad idea for me to be on the militia? I'm not totally cool with killing people. I shot those guys to protect myself, to protect Maddie and Jon, but… maybe I shouldn't be running around looking for violent situations."

"Heh. Same here."

"What?"

"I spent eleven damn years as a soldier, the last eight as an Army Ranger. We didn't *look* for violence, but we were prepared for it if it happened. None of us enjoyed killing—okay, maybe Wilbert was a special case there—but most of us didn't. Yeah, it's not quite the same thing comparing a group of soldiers going in to take on enemy troops to a kid with a shotgun drilling a guy trying to kidnap her, but, you know what I mean."

"Do I?"

He waved dismissively. "Soldiers, cops... most of us, violence is something that *can* happen, but we aren't trying to create it. Only the damaged bastards *try* to get into combat situations when they don't need to. Way I look at it is, something changes when you kill a person. You don't have to like it. Hell, it might horrify you. But, you've already crossed that threshold. And you're more trained than you give yourself credit for. How many other people in this place won trophies for shooting at thirteen? Hell, I never touched a gun until after I joined the Army. And, you've got something that's really damn hard to train into people—you don't *want* to use lethal force."

"But that's all I have, a gun. If Tommy got past it and grabbed me, I'd have been dead. He's huge."

He nodded. "If going civvie is what you wanna do, you do it. If stepping up to protect people is what you wanna do, do it. The world's changed, Harper. Question you should be asking yourself is do you really want to be helpless? Do you really trust other people to protect you, or Maddie? No one's saying you need to enjoy having to shoot someone."

"I don't."

"Good." He chuckled. "I'd be seriously creeped out if you did."

"And I trust *you*, but that's about it. If something happened, no one will get here in time." Harper debated staying on the militia vs. quitting. Even resigning wouldn't give her back the life she *really* wanted—being a normal high school student on her way to college in a year. The more she thought about it, the more she questioned if she really feared being on the militia as much as she refused to accept the world that had been thrust upon her. "I guess I'm just being whiny. I want to go back to just being a kid, going to school, hanging out with my friends, not having to worry if I'm gonna die at any minute or get kidnapped and... well, you know." She blushed.

Cliff set his book on a small table next to the recliner, got up, and moved to sit beside her on the couch, an arm around her shoulders. "It's your choice. Whatever you decide, I'll support it."

She leaned against him. "Can you show me how to fight without a gun?"

"Yeah, I think we can work on that sometime."

A soft but rapid knock came from the front door. Fred's face appeared in the window. He nodded and waved.

Cliff patted her shoulder. "Gotta do a night patrol. I'll probably be back a little before sunrise. Upside is, I'm off tomorrow. Maybe we can work on some techniques after you're home."

"Okay."

He threw on his coat, grabbed the AR-15, and headed out with Fred. Harper went over to the door and secured the deadbolt, thinking of Tommy. She eyed the fireplace, well on its way to going out, and decided to leave it be since everyone would be in bed within twenty minutes. Tomorrow, she'd also pester Cliff about a bath since it had been over a week… and over two months since she'd had a warm one. Even if she had to share a tub with Madison to conserve water and wood, a bath would definitely happen soon.

Harper crossed to the back door, pulled it open, and beckoned. Jonathan and Madison had a rapid goodbye with a blonde girl a little shorter than her sister. The poor kid looked like she'd crawled through a warzone or a refugee from one of those 'feed the orphans' commercials. Under the grime and wild hair, Harper almost recognized Madison's friend Becca. After their farewell, Becca ran over to Cliff and Fred, who'd cut through the yard heading north, asking them for help finding her house.

Madison and Jonathan rushed inside, scrambling down the hall to their rooms.

Too worried to sleep, Harper lit a candle at the dining room table, planning to read for a little while longer. Tommy may or may not know where she lived, but she figured if he did, and planned to do anything, he'd probably show up soon after dark rather than waiting for the wee hours.

The kids used the bathroom, sorta-brushed their teeth, and hurried to bed.

Couple months from now, there won't be any more toothpaste left in the world. We don't have a dentist either. She lowered her head, bonking it on her crossed forearms. *Nuclear war sucks.*

"Harp?" Madison's voice floated down the hall.

She got up and walked down the hall to their room. Madison lay in bed, covered to the nose under the four-inch-thick layer of blankets.

"You gonna sleep?"

Harper smiled. "Yeah. In a bit. Thinking about a lot of stuff."

"Like what?"

"Everything I'm afraid of. Like running out of toothpaste."

Madison scrunched up her nose. "That's not scary."

"It is when there's no more dentists."

"Dentists are scary."

She laughed. "They're not scary if you get cavities."

Small arms encircled Harper from behind. She almost fainted in shock, but managed not to react outwardly.

"Night, Harp," said Jonathan, hugging her.

She twisted around and squeezed him back. "Night, kiddo."

Madison giggled. "He scared you. Your eyes almost popped out."

"Yeah." Harper sat on the edge of the bed.

"I don't wanna sleep alone."

"Okay. Bear with me a few minutes to let my head stop spinning?"

Madison sat up. "Can you stop your head spinning in here?"

"Yeah."

"You don't have to worry about Christmas."

Harper blinked. "Where'd that come from?"

"When you gave us candy for dessert. It had a pumpkin face on it. Halloween didn't happen this year."

"No... it didn't."

"It would've been bad anyway. Nobody was home to give any candy out."

Harper pictured kids in costume wandering the ash-covered streets of Lakewood, knocking on empty houses. *What's wrong with me? I gotta stop thinking such sad thoughts or I'm going to make myself into a basket case.* "Yeah. We can do Halloween here next year. There's people."

"Yeah." Madison nodded, smiling. "You don't gotta worry about Christmas either. I know it was really Mom and Dad, not Santa."

Harper scooted closer and hugged her. "We can still do something. Just to remember them, okay?"

"Okay." Madison took in a big breath and let it out. "I know the war made the world stop. There's not really gonna be Christmases anymore, 'cause all the stores and stuff are gone. You don't gotta ever get me anything again if you give me one thing for the last Christmas we'll have." She looked into Harper's eyes, tears streaking her face. "The only thing I want for all the Christmases ever is not to lose you, too." Her voice fell to a raspy whisper. "Please don't die."

Speechless, Harper pulled her sister into a desperate hug. A minute after, she burst into tears and couldn't stop. Her mind went in circles. Did Madison ask her to quit the militia or tell her not to give away the shotgun and become a defenseless civilian? 'Please don't die' could mean stay home as easily as it meant don't hesitate and shoot the bad guys first. Her little sister's trembling little body clamped around her kicked Introvert Prime in the head. She couldn't be passive anymore. Harper couldn't hope to go unnoticed and avoid conflict. Mom and Dad weren't there anymore to watch out for Madison. The job fell on her.

And she decided to own that bitch.

"I promise."

Madison mumbled a teary thank you.

Harper shifted to get up.

"Don't go. It's too dark."

"There's a candle lit out in the front room. I have to put it out."

"Oh. Okay." Madison flopped back.

And the shotgun's out there.

She got up and hurried down the hall. Her book, the still-lit candle, and the shotgun sat on the dining room table where she'd left them. It struck her as weird that she felt somehow naked without the shotgun being nearby. Even here on the table when she'd been in her bedroom tweaked at her nerves like she'd done something stupid.

Will home ever stop feeling like a war zone? Heh. Maybe if six months pass without anyone firing a shot in town.

The book mocked her for barely making it thirty pages in, though she didn't want to read it as much as she'd wanted to do something other than go to sleep. Madison had a point: comfortable under covers in total darkness with her sister safe at her side would be even better for relaxing than squinting to read by candlelight. She picked up the shotgun and puffed out the candle.

Her sister's Christmas wish hit her over the head with guilt. Mom and Dad would never hide presents in the attic again, or wear stupid sweaters, or make them drink at least one cup of egg nog. She wondered if anyone left alive after the nukes came down would even care about holidays. How many years would it take before people felt like celebrating anything?

She wiped her eyes of tears. "Dammit. I really need to stop thinking such depressing thoughts."

Harper stood there in silence, trying to clear her mind of everything. Mom once said things she had no power to change weren't worth stressing out over.

"Focus on things I *can* change."

The war had happened. No one could undo that. The life she expected to live had been taken away from her. She couldn't get it back. She could, however, make the best of what she had control over. Her little sister remained alive and healthy, largely because of her. She had a new brother, and even a sorta-father.

Okay. This isn't too bad.

Madison let off a shrill scream and a *thud* shook the floor.

THE BRAIN BUG

Harper sprinted for the bedroom; she whirled around the doorjamb, shotgun high, committed to blowing Tommy's head off.

She wound up aiming at an empty bed. Freezing air blew in the open window.

Enraged, Harper started for it, but stopped when her foot hit something soft.

A child's moan came from the floor.

Her heart stopped, but she forced herself to look down. Jonathan lay curled on his side in his briefs, clutching his face, blood seeping between his fingers.

"Tommy, you son of a bitch. You're a dead man." She took a knee, pulling the boy's hands aside so she could examine his injury.

"T-abah," said Jonathan, blood oozing out of his nostrils.

"I know." She held him up into the moonlight, relaxing slightly upon noticing he seemed only to have suffered a punch to the nose.

"No! It's Tyler!"

Harper blinked, rage shifting to confusion in an instant. "What?"

"He was on the bed trying to stick Maddie with a knife. He said something about saving her from a bug. I tried to pull him off but he hit me."

Madison's shriek came from outside.

Harper grabbed his shoulders. "Listen to me. Go to my coat. Get the horn. One long blast. Got it?"

He nodded.

Madison screamed again.

Harper leapt to her feet and scrambled out the window, landing in a mostly controlled half stumble. As soon as she got her feet under her, she ran, fast and heedless of obstacles, chasing the sound of her little sister shrieking. Her foot caught something hard, tripping her into a somersault, but she rolled straight to her feet again and kept going. A long, clear air horn blast went off behind her.

She fixated on a scrap of brightness up ahead, moonlight glowing from Madison's nightgown, and forced her legs to go even faster. Another rock nearly took her down again, but she kept her balance. Seconds later, she hurdled a fence, crossed a swath of grass, and reached a loop in Butternut Lane. The maybe hundred feet of paving let her gain some ground. She spotted Tyler out of the gloom ahead. He carried Madison under his left arm, her noodle legs flailing as she tried to kick and struggle free.

Tyler ran past a house beyond the curve in the road, veering to the right and into a copse of trees. Once out the other side, he nearly fell trying to make it over a fence while carrying a terrified ten-year-old, though the frigid weather on her sheer nightgown took much of the fight out of her.

Harper slowed to a stop and raised the gun, considering shooting at his legs, but didn't want to risk a pellet striking Madison. It hit her that she recognized the area, and got an idea. She veered to the right, sprinting over a clear swath of grass and a dirt path to Sun Creek, then following the road's zig-zaggy path. Assuming he didn't stop in a yard or turn, going that way should put her in front of him.

She reached the intersection, but didn't see him anywhere.

Please let me be ahead!

Shouting for Madison would give her away and ruin any ambush, so she forced herself to stand there and listen.

Madison screamed from the west.

Shit! He turned.

She bolted down the road past darkened houses, following the sound of her sister's voice. Amid a thick group of trees, she found Tyler on one knee, struggling to pin Madison to the ground. She had one foot up, kicking at his face. He clasped her wrists together in his left hand, his right held a large knife.

"Sit still," rasped Tyler. "Gotta get it out of you. You'll be fine. I gotta make them stop."

"Tyler!" shouted Harper, rushing up to a few feet away from him, the Mossberg leveled off at his back. "If you don't get off her right now…"

He stopped trying to bring the knife down, but didn't let go of her. "You don't understand."

"I understand how buckshot works. Get off my sister. What the hell is wrong with you?" She stared over the gunsights at his head… gasping at a trickle of blood running down his forearm from a two-inch cut midway between wrist and elbow that looked deep.

"I can't." He looked back at her, his eyes wild with terror. A spritz of blood covered his face. "The CIA did it all. There's no war. They only dropped one nuke here as a social experiment. They wanted to see how people react. We all have bugs inside us, listening, watching. Everything we do. Whatever we say, even what we *think*. They know."

"Tyler," said Harper in a stern voice. "That doesn't make any sense. Listen to yourself. The news reported global nuclear war."

He laughed. "Of course they would. Don't you see? The CIA controls the media."

Madison gurgled.

"Easy, Maddie," whispered Tyler. "This won't take long. It's for your own good."

"Tyler…" Harper took a step closer. "We can talk, but I'm going to give you two more seconds to let go of my sister or I'm going to remove the bug from your skull with a goddamned shotgun."

He peered back over his shoulder at her. For an instant, he looked stunned, as if he'd done something horrible and only now realized it. Madison pushed at his throat with her foot, struggling to get her pinned hands out of his grip.

"One…" Harper aimed high, going for the back of his head.

Tyler leapt to his feet, yanking Madison up in front of himself as a shield. "They put it in the little kids first. I gotta save her before the bug kills her. We need to cut it out, but it's in her head."

"Please, Tyler. You sound like one of those idiots on late night radio talking about children working in sweat shops on Mars. This isn't an experiment." She hesitated, thinking back to the soldiers she'd seen arresting people. He had a point. The government *could* control the media, fake a news report, make it seem like the entire world had been incinerated. But... why would they? No way in hell could they use a real nuke on their own people as an experiment. There'd be a global outcry. And... they'd never do it to Colorado Springs. Not right in front of Cheyenne Mountain. They'd hit some nowhere spot in like Kansas. Still, a tiny bit of doubt set her hands shaking.

"You don't understand. It's all them. It's *always* them." Tyler backed up a step.

Madison shivered so bad she couldn't even speak coherent words.

"It's not *them*, Tyler. You're talking crazy."

A loud air horn *blart* from about twenty feet behind almost killed Tyler by making Harper jump.

She clenched her jaw and moved her finger off the trigger. "I'm serious. You're talking crazy. This isn't a messed-up social experiment. This really happened."

"Put it in little kids. They don't deserve it. Gotta cut it out of her brain."

"No, Tyler. You need to put her down. This is crazy."

He burst into laughter. "Yeah. Crazy." His snickering faded to a serious stare. "I am."

"You are?"

"Crazy." His grim expression became sad. "My parents thought so, too. That's why they kept giving me poison. They're part of the plan. The CIA has things in their heads, too. They kept giving me the little poison pills. Even tricked me into taking it myself for a while after I ran away. But now, there's no more poison."

"Poison?" Harper blinked. *Holy crap. He's legit psychotic.* "Are you talking about meds?"

"Meds... that's what *they* call the poison to fool people. No one makes it anymore. All gone. Tyler's gone, too. He was just a mask, the boy everyone expected to see. But I don't have to pretend anymore. There's no more poison. I'm free of it. I can see all their lies. They can't control me."

"Shit. That's why that insulin guy got you so bad. You knew you'd..." She cringed at a tiny stab of heartbreak as whatever dreams she might've had with him died.

"Freak out?" He nodded. "Yeah."

"You kept talking about leaving Evergreen. You knew you'd run out of pills and lose it. No wonder you kept telling me about exploring places. That was you trying to push me away."

Tyler started to laugh, but choked, then sighed. "Yeah. I'm not right. I've never been right. I'm dangerous. I shouldn't be around people when I'm off meds. I'm going to hurt you. Not like cheating hurt you. Like"—he made stabbing motions at the air with the knife—"seriously hurt you."

Harper swallowed hard. "Lorelei…"

"She's fine. I couldn't… she's got a bug, too. But she's so damn skinny. Starved. She wouldn't survive the removal procedure. You're gonna have to do it for her later. They put it in the brain near the pineal gland. It's really damn hard to remove without killing someone."

Madison tried to scream.

"There are no bugs, Tyler." She stepped closer. "Please put her down. That person you are on meds? That's the real you. That's my friend. I'm not sure who you are right now, but there's gotta be some part of you still in there somewhere. Please don't hurt Maddie."

"They're making you kill me because I know."

Harper shook her head. "No, Tyler. There is no *they*. You have a mental illness that you've been taking pills to manage. *Think*. You tried to warn me. You knew what would happen when your medicine ran out. You knew you needed to leave and not be a risk to people without your medicine. I'm sorry for talking you into staying. Please let her go and I promise I won't hurt you."

Rustling fabric announced Jonathan walking into view off to the left, still in only the briefs he'd worn to bed—plus her coat, which he hadn't zipped.

Tyler stared at her. His expression shifted between the way he looked at her when they kissed and panicky terror.

"You saved Lorelei from starving to death. You're a good guy, Tyler. There's something wrong in your head, but inside, the *real* you, is a good guy. Good guys don't hurt children."

A few shouts rang out in the distance, more militia closing in.

He sighed and let Madison slip down to her feet. She scrambled over and clamped onto Harper, shaking, teeth chattering.

Tyler smirked at the shotgun still pointing at him. "I'm dangerous, Harper. I really shouldn't be around people. They're going to lock me up or shoot me. Every now and then, the fog lifts and I can think right, but I'm gonna lose it again. It's taking a lot of work for me to keep my thoughts straight right now."

"They're not going to shoot you. Everyone's okay."

Tyler grimaced. "No… I tried to cut a bug out of the boy in the house next to mine."

Her stomach gurgled, near to throwing up. "D-did you kill him?"

"No. I don't think so. He woke up when I started. Little bastard's pretty strong for his size. Nailed me in the nose and ran off. He's bleeding pretty bad though."

Harper nudged Madison. "Go share the coat with Jon before you freeze. You've only got a nightie on and it's as thin as a damn tissue."

Madison whimpered, squeezing tighter. "It's not a tissue."

"Maddie. Now," said Harper in 'mom voice.' "We can hug once we're home in a warm bed."

She reluctantly let go and trudged over to Jonathan, clamping onto him under the coat.

"Gah! You're freezing." Jonathan squealed while closing the zipper.

Harper eyed Tyler. "The boy's alive?"

"Far as I know."

She wagged the shotgun to the left. "You need to leave town. Go. Before the rest of the militia gets here."

"You're gonna let him go?" Jonathan gasped. "Seriously?"

"I'm half his size. If he wants to run away, I can't stop him. And I can't murder an unarmed person."

Jonathan reached out a hand. "I can. Lemme have the shotgun."

"He's got a knife," said Madison in a weak voice. "He's not unarmed."

Tyler glanced down at the knife and slid it back into a sheath on his belt.

"Just go before they catch you." Harper lowered the shotgun. "If I see you here again, I'll have to…"

He stepped back. "I understand. It was nice meeting you, Harper Cody. I'm sorry it couldn't have been different. Damn nuclear war."

The scuffs and crunching of people drawing close came from the woods behind them.

Tyler's eyes flared manic for only a second before he took on the posture of a roguish highwayman, bowed with a flourish, and ran off.

"Yeah." She sighed. "Damn nuclear war."

DANGEROUS MERCY

C liff, Fred, a fortyish guy with long, curly black hair she hadn't seen before, and a muscular bald guy she also didn't recognize tromped out of the woods. The bald guy had a body armor vest on as well as a utility belt that made him look like an actual cop. Fred and the long-haired guy carried Coleman lanterns.

"Harper!" yelled Cliff, running up to her. "What's going on?"

"You were right about Tyler." Harper bowed her head.

The other three men jogged over.

"What?" Cliff grasped her shoulders.

"You always kept looking at him weird. I thought you were just like 'dad vibing' on him and being overprotective of me, but you knew something was wrong with him."

He smirked. "Something was off about that kid, yeah."

"*Real* off." Jonathan shook his head.

"What happened? Why are Maddie and Jon out here in basically nothing?" He took a step toward the kids. "Christ, what happened? He's covered in blood."

"Tyler punched me in the nose." Jonathan sniffed.

"He kidnapped Madison and tried to cut her open to get rid of a CIA listening device. He seriously believes the nuke that hit Springs was some kind of messed up social experiment. He's crazy. Legit crazy. Was on meds but he ran out."

Cliff muttered a string of swear words.

"He said he attacked a boy in the house next to his. Cut him bad, but didn't kill him. I don't know which house is his. Never saw Tyler around here."

"Search? He can't have gotten far," asked the guy with long hair, his voice way deeper than she expected from his appearance.

"Yeah, Dennis." Fred looked at Harper. "Where did he go?"

I gave him a head start at least. I can't lie to these guys. She pointed. "That way. I told him to get lost. I couldn't just murder him."

The bald man smiled. "Not easy to talk a guy like that down."

"Why'd you let him run off?" asked Fred.

"That's what I wanna know." Jonathan grumbled.

"Uhh." Harper fidgeted. "I guess you're right. I had Maddie and Jon right here, and Tyler's bigger than me. But, I could've kept the gun on him. Maybe I kinda liked him or something and I felt too sorry for him."

"You *liked* him?" The bald guy blinked.

"I…" She blushed. "Dunno. The world got really weird. He was cute."

"Eww," said Madison.

"He tried to hurt my sister and he hit my brother. I don't like him anymore."

"It's admirable of you to take pity on a kid with mental problems, but he could wind up hurting someone else if he's not detained." The bald guy took two steps in the direction she pointed. "Damn, that kid's moving. Probably not gonna catch him before he's past the town limit, but we should check anyway in case he tries to break in somewhere. And, he's got no provisions. Better for him if we find him."

"Holy crap. Those kids are out here barefoot." Dennis gestured at them. "We need to get 'em inside before they lose toes."

Fred gestured off at the woods. "Roy, you and Cliff go after Tyler. Dennis, try to find that kid he stabbed. I'll head back and check with Anne-Marie, figure out which house he was in so we at least know where to start looking for the boy. Sound a three-blast if you locate the kid."

Dennis nodded.

Fred looked at Harper. "You go on and take the kids inside before they get frostbite."

"And be more particular about boyfriends." Roy, the bald cop, patted her on the arm. "Whole busload of teens came in last night. Hockey team or some such thing… and their cheerleaders. They got stranded on a class trip when the nukes went off. Plenty of boys around your age now."

Harper rolled her eyes, but also breathed a mental sigh of relief at not being in trouble for letting him go. "I'm not desperate for a boyfriend. I dunno why I even thought that way about Tyler. I'm way too messed up emotionally to even think about dating anyone right now."

"Broken rabbit," muttered Madison between chattering teeth. "You always wanna fix the hurt animals. You knew he was hurt."

Cliff and Roy hurried off in the direction Tyler had gone. Dennis ran south, hunting for the boy Tyler supposedly stabbed. Fred grabbed Jonathan and Madison by a fistful of jacket and pushed them into Harper.

"Your family is freezing. Get them inside. And get yourself inside. You've only got a T-shirt on."

Harper slung the shotgun over her shoulder. "Okay."

The cold finally hit her. She grabbed at Jonathan's hand, but the kids hugging chest-to-chest inside her coat made it almost impossible to walk anywhere. She struggled to pick them up, but couldn't—not both at once.

Fred slung his hunting rifle. "I got 'em."

He scooped both kids up in his arms and carried them with Harper leading the way back home. Fred set them down near the house and jogged off down Hilltop Drive on his way to the mayor's building to wake Anne-Marie up.

Compared to the outside, the house still felt warm despite the fire having died down.

"We're all too cold. C'mon." Harper shut the back door. "We gotta huddle together under blankets, quick."

The kids shed the coat and tossed it over a chair in the dining room. Harper headed to her room, gasping at the chill from the window still being open. Gritting her teeth, she walked into the frigid breeze and closed the window.

Not at all caring that Jonathan stood nearby, she changed into her nightdress as fast as she could, then gathered her two siblings in bed, cuddling them close and shivering. The kids' legs against hers felt like rubbery icicles.

"Can you feel your toes?" whispered Harper.

"Yeah, but they're cold." Madison huddled close on her left.

Jonathan rested his head on her shoulder. "I still think you should'a at least hit him."

Harper chuckled. *Yeah. No way am I sleeping tonight.*

Cold gradually warmed to cozy as they shared body heat under multiple layers of covers. Madison fell asleep first. Jonathan passed out soon after.

Harper kept staring at the darkness since she couldn't see the ceiling. Losing Tyler still somehow hurt, and she hated the world all over again for taking that away from her on top of everything else. She snuggled tighter with her siblings, begging the universe to leave them alone at least until they grew up.

The back door creaked open a while later. Harper threaded her arm out from under the covers and grasped the shotgun leaning against the wall. Slow footsteps came down the wall, hovering outside her door. If Tommy's head appeared, she'd blow it straight off.

"If you're awake," whispered Cliff. "It's just me."

She relaxed and eased the shotgun down, hastily yanking her arm back into the warm world under the covers. "Yeah. What happened?"

Cliff peered around the doorjamb into the room, barely a silhouette she could perceive. "That boy's quick. We didn't catch him. If he comes back, we'll give him a nice room at the sheriff's old office."

"What about the boy?" whispered Harper.

"Found him. Slice above the ear, lot of blood but not much of a threat."

She exhaled hard. "Nice."

"Oh, one more thing." Cliff walked up beside the bed, evidently carrying something sizable.

"What?" Harper strained to see what he had in his arms.

"Someone wanted a sleep over." He pivoted into the moonlight, revealing a sleeping Lorelei. So thin and frail, she looked like a large doll.

"Aww…"

Cliff pulled the covers up and set the girl down on top of Harper. "Gonna need to get a second bed in here."

"She's staying?" whispered Harper, pulling the girl onto her chest.

"Yeah. Can't exactly leave her alone, can we? And the little bugger kinda likes you. Now, go to sleep, young lady."

Harper stuck out her tongue.

"I saw that."

She pulled it back in and stifled a giggle.

EPILOGUE

Home

Harper sat on the tiny concrete slab porch in front of her home, gazing off into a clear December sky. The shotgun across her lap didn't even feel strange anymore.

Something like two weeks had gone by since she'd told Tyler to run. The militia hadn't seen him since, but at least the boy he attacked would be okay. Stitches and antiseptic, which the medical center still had, did the trick. Lorelei had gained a little weight, but still remained thinner than what Harper considered normal. Still, she improved. The girl settled in as a member of the family with eager smiles. She'd been sad over Tyler for a few days, but as far as she'd been told, he'd become too sick to take care of her. Thinking of 'medicated Tyler,' Harper explained that he loved her and hated having to leave, but he had a dangerous sickness that could hurt other people.

Sharing a bed with a ten- and six-year-old (even an undersized one) redefined cozy. That room could accommodate two twin beds, but there wouldn't be much space for anything else. Not like they needed a spot for a computer desk or TV. Much like the 1800s, they only went into the bedroom to sleep. For now, she didn't mind the sharing. The same way Madison had become a sort of living teddy bear for her to cling to at night, her little sister had adopted Lorelei. Without the need to chase away frostbite, Jonathan happily returned to his own room, but he'd started asking Cliff when he'd be old enough to carry a handgun to protect his sisters.

The militia went back to the Littleton Walmart twice more. Harper volunteered for the first trip, amazingly without a ton of protest from Madison beyond a 'please be careful.' She'd used her 'looter's privilege' to fill two shopping bags with toothpaste and hygiene products, also grabbing some toys for the kids.

Tommy *had* gone off the deep end, but his wrath didn't focus on Harper. He'd stormed the militia HQ, demanding to know where they'd put his wife. Summer and Anne-Marie had evidently broken through to her and convinced her to leave him. Rachel refused to be anywhere near him, and in the ensuing meltdown, he'd pulled a gun. Walter took a bullet in the shoulder, which Doctor Khan removed. No one bothered extracting any bullets from Tommy's corpse.

That busload of teens Roy mentioned had been in Denver from Colorado Springs for a high school hockey game. The nuke went off not quite two hours before they would've left the hotel to go home. Their coach randomly got the idea to head into the mountains thinking it safer from radiation, and they'd stumbled across Evergreen. A whole hockey team plus cheerleaders, two coaches, and two parent chaperones with nowhere else to go, decided to stay. At least Violet had some help now. One of the parents had been a math teacher, one coach a gym teacher, the other taught at the attached elementary. They might even split the kids into multiple classrooms. The students, a mix of juniors and seniors, wouldn't be going to school anymore, except for one kid who might wind up apprenticing with the doctors.

Christmas would come next Tuesday, but it still didn't seem like anyone had any intention of noticing. For too many, it would remind them of family lost. Too soon for happy thoughts to intrude on the somberness of mourning. Harper sighed. Thinking of her parents hanging ornaments from years past didn't make her cry. Their death had gone from intensely painful to a subdued but heavy sorrow she'd likely carry for the rest of her life.

Crunching footsteps approached down Hilltop Drive.

She looked up at Fred Mitchell lugging a bundle of pine branches stuffed in a coffee can to approximate the shape of a Christmas tree, decorated with blue and red smushed soda cans. He smiled and waved on the way by.

A laugh started, but emerged as a wistful sigh. She returned his wave and smile, and resumed staring off into the clouds, reconsidering her opinion that no one would care about holidays anymore. Perhaps the gloominess came from her, not the world.

"Hey... Dad, Mom?" whispered Harper. "I'm not sure if you're out there in any sort of way, maybe watching us. You guys never believed in that stuff." She let out a long sigh. "It's so messed up. Months ago, I never would've imagined even punching someone. I've killed people. I'm so, so sorry I froze up and got you killed, Dad."

She sat there for a while, listening for an answer that wouldn't come. The Dad she knew would forgive her for that, happy she'd kept herself and Madison alive.

"I guess the world's changed. It's not coming back any time soon. I've changed, too. Mom, you always said 'you can't un-break eggs' right? This is my world now. Our world. Me and Maddie's... and Jon and Lorelei." Harper brushed her hand over the shotgun. *This is Dad's legacy. All I've got left of him.* "You're still here, Dad. Still keeping us safe. I won't give up without a fight, and I'm not gonna let anyone hurt us. I'm gonna give Maddie her Christmas present. I'm not gonna die."

Harper bowed her head and wiped a tear.

"I'm not gonna die, Dad. I wish you were still here. Yeah, I know I'm still a kid. Ammo won't last forever, but Cliff's teaching me how to defend myself. He's a Ranger, and I guess they're kinda like badasses or something. And, honestly, this world isn't *all* bad. The people here are pretty decent, even Mr. Rosales. He's still whining about being useless since no one needs lawyers anymore. Even that celebrity guy Lucas is pretty cool. He finally got over losing all that money. You know he was a plumber before he became famous?"

She leaned back, letting the breeze push her hair off her face. Having a day off felt strange. Nowhere to be, no school, no work, no worries—well no worries beyond watching over three kids. It had been months since she'd heard—or even thought about—music, but for no particular reason, she hummed *Fight Song*. With each note, an upwelling of confidence grew stronger. Harper squeezed the shotgun and smiled, firm in her decision to stay with the militia.

Guess I'm not a mouse anymore. Heh. She hummed a few more notes from the song. *No idea where it came from, but I've got a lot of fight left in me.*

"So, yeah, Mom... Dad... if you're out there somewhere, I want you to know I'm okay. It's primitive and weird, and sure the future's kinda scary, but Evergreen is home."

Brett Cooper and his sister Nicole, the people who lived three houses away on the opposite side of the street, went by lugging a sad excuse for a decorated tree. Before everything went to pieces, Harper would've laughed at it, but now… it gave her a sense of hope.

Her butt had gone numb from sitting on concrete.

She stood, brushed off the seat of her pants, and turned to go inside.

The front door opened fast. Madison, Jonathan, Lorelei, Becca, Christopher, and Mila ran outside, everyone—except Mila—waving at her as they rushed by to play in the front yard with a Frisbee. Mila had dialed back the eeriness and greeted her with an 'oh hi there' glance. Harper smiled and started to walk into the house, but froze halfway in the door at the sight of Madison's iPhone on the coffee table.

"Maddie?"

Her sister looked over with a 'hmm?' expression.

"You forgot your phone."

"Oh. It's broken." Madison shrugged. "No one has phones anymore. I don't need it."

Harper covered her mouth and leaned against the doorjamb, speechless, watching Madison running after the Frisbee and laughing with her friends. She'd carried that stupid dead iPhone everywhere as if it were a precious infant for months. Perhaps Madison hadn't been as broken as Harper feared. She glanced back at the abandoned phone. Part of her wanted to break down in tears again, but she didn't.

Hope, something she'd almost left behind in Lakewood, held them at bay.

She stepped inside, pulled the storm door closed to keep the heat in, and gazed out the window past laughing children scattered around the front yard at the early afternoon sky.

Maybe the future won't totally suck after all.

fin

ACKNOWLEDGMENTS

Thank you for reading *Evergreen!*

Harper's story will continue soon in *The World That Remains.*
Additional thanks to Lee Hargrove for editing.
Thanks to Alexandria Thompson for the cover design.

MORE POST-APOCALYPTIC STORIES

The Forest Beyond the Earth

What's worse than being a child in a world shattered by nuclear war?
Being alone.
After Wisp's father vanishes, she ventures out into the Endless Forest,
desperate to find him.

The Summer the World Ended

Fourteen-year-old Riley hoped for the best summer ever.
She never expected she'd spend it far from home hiding underground from nuclear bombs.
After fourteen days without sun, Riley must overcome the sorrow of losing everything to save the only family she still has left.

Citadel: the Concordant Sequence

Earth has become a toxic wasteland.
People barely cling to survival as scattered tribes. Almost every trace of the world that came before is gone.
Humanity's fate rests with an unlikely savior: an eleven-year-old who only wants a home.

The Roadhouse Chronicles

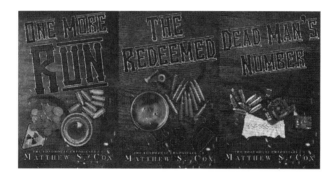

Civilization came to an abrupt and fiery end in August of 2021.
Humanity crawled from the ashes decades later. Men like Kevin earn a living driving other people's crap from settlement to settlement.
He had a dream. He wants a Roadhouse of his own, and doesn't care about anything else, until he finds a conscience.
A conscience with blue eyes and snow white hair.

ABOUT THE AUTHOR

Originally from South Amboy NJ, Matthew has been creating science fiction and fantasy worlds for most of his reasoning life. Since 1996, he has developed the "Divergent Fates" world, in which *Division Zero, Virtual Immortality, The Awakened Series, The Harmony Paradox, and the Daughter of Mars series* take place. Along with editing for Curiosity Quills press, he has worked in IT and technical support.

Matthew is an avid gamer, a recovered WoW addict, developer of two custom RPG systems (paper & dice), and a fan of anime, British humour, and intellectual science fiction that questions the nature of reality, life, and what happens after it.

He is also fond of cats, presently living with two: Loki and Dorian.

Visit me online at:
Facebook: https://www.facebook.com/MatthewSCoxAuthor
Pinterest: https://www.pinterest.com/matthewcox10420/
Goodreads: https://www.goodreads.com/author/show/7712730.Matthew_S_Cox
Twitter: https://twitter.com/mscox_fiction
Instagram: https://www.instagram.com/mscox.author/
Email: mcox2112@gmail.com

- One More Run
- The Redeemed
- Dead Man's Number

Faded Skies series

- Heir Ascendant
- Ascendant Unrest
- Ascendant Revolution

Temporal Armistice Series

- Nascent Shadow
- The Shadow Collector
- The Gate to Oblivion

Vampire Innocent series

- A Nighttime of Forever
- A Beginner's Guide to Fangs
- The Artist of Ruin
- The Last Family Road Trip

Standalones

- Wayfarer: AV494
- Axillon99
- Chiaroscuro: The Mouse and the Candle
- The Far Side of Promise anthology
- Operation: Chimera (with Tony Healey)
- The Dysfunctional Conspiracy (with Christopher Veltmann)

Winter Solstice series (with J.R. Rain)

- Convergence
- Containment
- Catalyst

Alexis Silver series (with J.R. Rain)

- Silver Light
- Deep Silver

Young Adult Novels

- Caller 107
- The Summer the World Ended
- Nine Candles of Deepest Black
- The Eldritch Heart
- The Forest Beyond the Earth
- Out of Sight
- Evergreen

Middle Grade Novels

Tales of Widowswood series

- Emma and the Banderwigh
- Emma and the Silk Thieves
- Emma and the Silverbell Faeries
- Emma and the Elixir of Madness

- Emma and the Weeping Spirit

Standalones

- Citadel: The Concordant Sequence
- The Cursed Codex
- The Menagerie of Jenkins Bailey
- Sophie's Light

Printed in Great Britain
by Amazon